GAUNTLET

Terry L. Vinson

GAUNTLET

DOUBLE DRAGON

Prologue: The Pre-Competition (Final) Media Interview

He glances about, obviously avoiding the camera eye with each turn of the head or shift of the eyes. Outside the cordoned-off, well-guarded lobby sways a raucous crowd of perhaps two-hundred fans of the rabid variety. Another six to seven-hundred cheer and clap outside the thick glass walls, the sub-freezing temperatures doing little to damper their wild enthusiasm.

Eventually, as the gleaming, silver-tipped microphone is thrust just inches from his chin, he focuses on the unseen individual at the device's other end. His smile is painfully forced; more grimace than grin. He inhales deeply as the initial query is tossed his way.

"So, man from Lexington, how are we feeling less than sixteen hours from day one of the ultimate gauntlet?" spouts the interviewer in a tone that reeks of faux dramatics in true pay-per-view, second-rate pro wrestling style.

"Ready as I'll ever be," he responds with a playful wink towards the camera, though his lips appear to have freeze-dried—severely chapped—in a matter of seconds, "it's a great relief to finally have all the preparatory jazz out of the way. "

"Final physical exam a success? I didn't notice any undue limping…"

"Fit as the proverbial fiddle, or so the staff sawbones said. I guess if he's lyin', I'll be dyin'. "

Standing before a fluorescent green backdrop of the hotel lobby's far wall, the man's red and white striped, sleeveless tee appears practically blood-spattered.

"Clever! I like it. On a more serious note, I would imagine the pressure of representing one of the lowest ranked states in terms of overall economics is enormous. Does the recent unemployment numbers released just yesterday by the State Department add a layer of apprehension in what your Kentucky brethren might expect from you?"

His response is without hesitation, spewing forth with a sudden surge of confidence fueled by what he rates purely a soft-toss question when a blazing heater had been expected.

"Not at all, since the same exact stats weren't much better a month ago. Sad fact is, we've been scraping the bottom for the past several years. Rest assured I'd be in there swinging with all I've got even if we were on the other end of the spectrum. "

"Fine then, understood," the interviewer replies while shifting the microphone away from the interviewee's squared chin. Pursing his lips as to drop the frozen grin, *Kentucky* steps back, places both hands on his hips and peers at the shiny waxed floors below. Once his audio-video sparring partner resumes, it is with a tone so dramatically altered, so darkly shifted, it is as if another personality entirely has gained possession of the mike.

"So I take it getting your rear-end waxed by the representative of say…New Hampshire or New York State, two of the more fortunate republics, would bother you no more than say, the rep from Arkansas, Tennessee, or poor old Mississippi passing you by? Come on now, you old log-splitter, talk to me…no deep-seeded grudge from an old *southern* boy towards the rich yanks sharing the trail? Better yet, how about this scenario to smoke your down-home sausage? Let's say the rep from the recently added state of *Puerto Rico* whizzes by wearing a big ol' sarcastic grin?"

Unable to completely disguise his comic dismay, *Kentucky* reaches up and runs curled fingers through his graying coif. Though his words are relayed calmly enough, there is no denying the tensing of his upper body and the gleam shining from both ocean-blue eyes, each birthed from an underlying layer of barely-submerged anger.

"Log-split…? Brother, I'd as soon kick the ass of an Alabama corn farmer than that of a New York cabbie. Once the game starts, all fifty are my enemy, just a mass of bodies in the way of my claiming the prize. I didn't come here to lose, geography be damned. I'm sure my esteemed opposition feels the exact same way. Otherwise, they're fools. In other words, check your cliques at the door. The only loyalty one has to him or herself is to the state they were so proudly chosen to rep. Besides, if you don't mind my saying, your questionnaire guru desperately needs some updated material. The *North versus South* thing was played out…oh…about a dozen or more decades back. Pretty much the whole of the nation is sharing the same leaky boat these days and damned if any of 'em can locate the crack to properly seal it up. "

The interviewer pauses yet again, clearing his throat in the background while possibly scrambling to reset his bearings. In the interim, *Kentucky* crosses his arms, blows out a labored breath and grins, only this time with unmistakable sincerity.

"Point well taken, *Kentucky*," his interrogator politely retorts with the cheery tone of personality one securely back in tow, "and I have to say, I did feel a bit foolish attempting to bait a southerner who possesses nary a twinge of the resolute accent.

Now, bear with me as we cover the mandatory personals. You're listed as forty-seven years of age; recently divorced; six-feet-one, one-hundred and eighty pounds, and appear quite fit. In the six months since being chosen state rep, how did you prepare both physically and mentally for what's to come?"

Seemingly deep in reflection, *Kentucky* appears to stare over the camera, squinting mightily as if focusing on a faraway object.

"Well, first off, I took a slew of long, contemplative walks. "

Following a brief respite, and once it was apparent the man behind the mike wasn't the least bit amused, all further attempts at levity halted.

"Actually, the physical aspect was less daunting. In retrospect, the job I'd held for twenty-plus years was a godsend. In the aftermath, I tried to stay in shape via daily workouts, more so when I hit the big four-oh and the gut began to expand a bit. Once the word came down on the gauntlet, I increased said workouts two-fold. Added three-times-a-week jogging sessions to the list and dropped my body fat by an extra six percent. "

The interviewer could be heard frantically flipping papers.

"You were...let's see. . . my oh my...a mailman in your former life...daily snail-mail route delivery, no less. Wore out many a sneaker, I'd venture..."

"Easy bet. Probably covered five, six miles a day, five days a week, that is until paper delivery went the way of home telephones and wired cable; museum pieces...relics to be gawked at and snickered over by the generations to come. "

"And the mental preparation?"

Staring unblinking into the camera he'd so readily avoided just moments earlier, *Kentucky* juts out his jaw and frowns.

"Pardon the clichés to follow, but the way I look at it, you can't measure heart or determination, meaning there's no way to obtain either if you don't already possess 'em. Mental toughness can be developed to a degree, but in the end it's all about one's personal experiences. Besides, there really is no mental prep for the colossal challenge the fifty-one of us have coming. I figure all of us qualified for this competition with a butt-load of grit intact. Thing is, which one will prove to possess that little bit extra that it's gonna take to come out on top?"

"Butt-load of grit? Hey, I like it...now there's a little nugget you can only hear below the Mason-Dixon line, I'll wager. And, speaking of which...Vegas odds currently list you at twenty-two to one, Kentucky, a middle-of-the packer, one might say. Does this boost or hinder your confidence?"

"Neither. Nada. Means nothing. The odds-makers don't know me or what I've got in here," he says, lightly pounding a clenched fist against his chest, "in the end, it's all gonna come down to will power... *Iron-Will* power, pardon the play on words; the host with the most, you might say. No matter what we've went through as individuals throughout our lives, none of the fifty-one really know the limits of our inner competitor. "

"You truly believe you have what it takes to be last man. . . um, *person* standing, *Kentucky*?"

Again, the grin, this time stretched ever-wider, even boyish despite the grayish stubble lining his cheeks, "Well, by god, it seems we'll know soon enough now won't we?"

"Indeed we shall. Good luck, man from Lexington. Rest assured all residents of the blue grass state, be they of human or equestrian variety, are tucked securely in your corner. "

With that, *Kentucky* steps back as the interviewer practically leaps in front of the camera, flashing teeth so hideously white they threaten temporary snow-blindness.

"Next up after this short pause to pay the bills, we'll rap with the woman chosen to rep the Lone Star State. Remember gang, the one and only *Iron-Will Gauntlet* will be available in all its live streaming glory at gauntlet-thon. com. For the poor remaining souls on the planet, all eighteen of ya, still on a desert isle *without* internet access, there is the archaic yet still available pay-per-view option. Contact your local cable carrier. Back in moments with the beauteous belle that all of *Texas* will be hootin' and hollerin' for come tomorrow morning. Cue promo!"

Leaning against a nearby podium that has, strangely enough, gone unused in what the sponsors billed 'media day', *Kentucky* peers across the massive lobby to a nearby flat-screen dominating a far wall as one of many Gauntlet-eve promos flash flamboyantly to life.

The comically overdone, borderline gaudy, production leaves Kentucky feeling less amused than woefully bemused. A nation on the verge of utter financial ruin forced to bank the foreseeable future on an event that, less than a decade previous, likely would never have made the cut in an endless sea of mostly pathetic reality-based TV programs.

As the promo kicks into full gear amid a jarring hip-hop beat and blinding flashes of pyrotechnics, he glances over to his left while being joined by a tall, lanky brunette wearing a white-tee adorned in yellow roses. Keeping her focus pointed directly at the screen, she skips over wearing a wry grin, never actually making eye contact.

"What marketing genius birthed this overcooked slice of ham, ya think?" she asks in a drawl so thick it sounds a tad manufactured.

"You got me, but somebody at the top had to green-light it," he replies with a solemn shake of the head.

"True enough, Sugar. Sad, sad, sad..." she concludes with a scowl, her overly thick eyelashes batting at warp speed and thus resembling a pair of fluttering moths attempting to take flight.

The promo concludes before inexplicably

replaying in all its horrid tawdriness. *Kentucky* gives the swarming masses—standing both inside and outside the hotel lobby—a parting glance and begins to turn toward a nearby elevator, but soon enough finds himself hypnotized yet again by the spot's campy yet undeniably stout draw, the luridness of which he can only compare to a live auto crash.

"*This isn't your mom and dad's Iron-Will Gauntlet, no sir!*" shrieks the MC as a covey of lithe, scantily-dressed fem fatales dance a wild jig over what appears to be a faux nature-trail setting, the background of which appears a garish hybrid of CGI and ancient 'jungle-movie' footage from the mid-twentieth century.

"*Fifty-one brave, life-tested, determined souls, one chosen from each state in our great nation, will challenge the limits of human will in order to bring home the federal bacon to those they so proudly represent. Unlike the previous Gauntlet, which was solely a test of endurance, this new and improved competition will provide potentially fatal dangers at every twist and turn; an obstacle course filled with chills and spills, with the biggest dangers being cooked up and served by none other than that sometimes ruthless, sometimes cunning, sometimes unforgiving goddess of the elements, Mother Nature herself!*"

As the dancers continue to jiggle and gyrate in unrestrained glee, the background images shift and contort to showcase various calamities of nature to include raging floodwaters, multiple funnel clouds, black skies littered with lighting strikes, and ferocious snowstorms, all cheaply executed as to amuse rather than strike fear.

"It may take days, it may take weeks, but in the end, when the smoke clears and the fat lady has belted out that final, lingering note, only one will emerge victorious; victorious to bring home the spoils to those so badly in need in whatever state they so gloriously represent, while simultaneously cementing their place as a treasured icon for all times! A tried and true champion who's Iron-Will prevailed over not only fifty other similarly brave souls, but the considerable wrath of the four season's harshest elements as well!"

Just as a fresh hip-hop riff thumps forth, the screen temporarily fades to black only to flash back to life to display a gleaming gold trophy in the form of a man poised on his knees and reaching skyward with outstretched hands; the design and theme of which obviously falling under the heading of 'winner triumphs over insurmountable odds'. With that, *Kentucky* hears the interior crowd practically swoon in awestruck wonder, as if viewing the trophy for the first time, though its garish likeness has been showcased on both TV ads and the internet for several weeks as part of the public-appetite-wetting process.

"Make no mistake, America...the man or woman with the mental and physical stoutness to carry this solid-gold beauty home will have, no ifs, ands or buts, mother-(bleeped for content) earned it!"

Wearing a wry smile and with a final, bone-weary shake of the head, *Kentucky* whirls about and

13

heads for the elevator. Keeping his back turned to the lobby even after entering the boxed space, he hears the crowd erupt yet again as no doubt the Lady with the butterfly lashes steps forward for a live grilling from Mister Ivory-Choppers with the silver mike. Allowing his shoulders to slump and his chin to rest atop his chest, the overwhelming sense of relief he feels while riding smoothly upwards towards his fourth-floor suite isn't merely palpable, but a full-blown cloak; a soothing message for a soul battered not merely by obvious outside pressures, but an inner self-expectation whose confidence grows weaker with every tick of the clock.

So clearly he recalls the very moment he was chosen to represent; the inhalation of pride that ensued, soon followed by a triple-dose of self-important cockiness that seemed so easily justified upon beating out an estimated fourteen-thousand fellow state applicants, at least a few thousand of which he figured were equally qualified, if not more so.

Fast-forward, seemingly at the speed of light, six months later to the very eve of the competition. The aforementioned pride had long-since dissipated, just as all signs of brash arrogance had gradually metamorphosed into mind-crippling, gut-curdling fear. In retrospect, perhaps he should've heeded the governor's advice and taken on a trainer, while also allowing an entourage of loyal followers to bow to his every want and wish, to pamper his ego and continually recharge his sense of self-worth. As it was, he stuck stubbornly to the belief that going the lone-wolf route was for the best. It would allow for freer thought for the necessary meditation. Unfortunately, it had also allowed for creeping pessimism, not just as to why he'd volunteered for this lengthy torture session, but also for the sad, pathetic answer to said query. Simply put, he'd had nothing to lose and everything to prove. Surely not his sanity, the bulk of which he'd misplaced roughly a year to the day that he'd applied for the Gauntlet. As it was, the man earmarked to don Kentucky blue in less than fifteen hours in front of an estimated paying crowd of one-hundred forty million nationwide was just as apt to openly self-destruct as he was to emerge victorious in a manic free-for-all involving fifty other similarly deranged maniacs.

Hours later, as he rolled recklessly between tangled sheets and the much-anticipated dawn grew ever-nearer, the man from Lexington could only vaguely recall the life he'd previously known while giving great effort to embrace the one soon to be embarked upon as destiny fulfilled.

He would awaken safely cocooned in a state of emotional numbness, seemingly free of all apprehension and fear—an empty vessel with a cleanly wiped slate. Today, all baseless speculation from a vast army of media talking heads ceased. Starting today, the past, with all its weighty baggage, was just that. Starting today, the focus was crystal clear. Starting *now*, the future lay straight ahead.

The time to show that certain someone just how blatantly mistaken they were about him had finally arrived. The time for *talk* was finally over. The time to *walk* was here.

Prologue II: The Pre-Competition Briefing

Time: Oh-five-fifteen   hours,   day   of competition
Place: Dome Auditorium

"Okay folks, listen up. I could use this time to spout the usual cliché-rich garbage about this being the *moment of truth* when the lot of you *dig down deep* to find the *inner warrior*, but for decency's sake I'll spare both you and me such drivel. You've all been briefed ad nauseam about the strict qualifications that landed you here, along with the stakes, rewards and potential dangers, so I won't bore you with further repeats of same. "

The tall, thin man paces the auditorium stage like a perturbed bandy rooster, keeping his rail-thin arms pinned at the pit of his back as if bound at the wrists. Sporting a pointy gray goatee but little hair atop his shiny dome, he speaks with a faint Brit accent and dons reading glasses that sit precariously from the edge of his bulbous nose as if artificially attached.

"Ah, but I *jest*, you see. Afraid to inform I've been paid quite handsomely to do just that, to repeat ad nauseam. That being so the lot of you may relax a bit as I cover the high points yet again, though not to shut me out, you understand, as I will assume no blame if a lack of *understanding* on your part comes to fruition at competition's end. "

Spaced with an empty seat on either side in an arena with a seating capacity of well over five-hundred, the fifty-one appear to sigh as one as their fast-talking, faster walking host resumes seemingly without the need to pause for breath.

"The qualifications were, as noted, fairly simple; each contestant chosen was to be over forty years of age. Unlike the previous Gauntlets, which allowed any qualifier over the age of twenty-one, it was decided that personal life experiences might well go a long way in dictating a victor in such a decidedly different contest as the Iron-Will. Thus, you were evaluated on such experiences that most below the age of forty could not possibly claim. Secondly, there were to be no former professional athletes of any ilk chosen, as this might provide a definite edge in the physicality aspect. High school and college participation was allowed, but no blue-chip type backgrounds. Along the same lines, no marathon lifers made the cut. Thirdly, the interview process-twelve per contestant and presided over by special panels consisting of high-ranking military and civil-servant personnel, were to be graded for the highest overall tally. These included numerous psych examinations, a few of which utilized hands-on scenarios to test the very limits of mental toughness under extreme duress, as well as an extensive polygraph that weeded out literally thousands of non-qualifiers.

Lastly, there were the two separate physical exams, one conducted before the barrage of interviews and the last after; extensive and extreme, these were used to ensure levels of endurance and perhaps highlight any red flags prior to the competition.

As for the stakes, simplicity in itself, folks; the winner bags a quite sizeable check for his or her home state. A check duly endorsed by Uncle Sam that will, at the least, double the federal aid currently earmarked for said stomping grounds. Needless to say, this fact alone is apt to make the champ quite a popular pin-up at the statehouse. The rewards that follow suit, though not guaranteed by any means, are quite ample.

Some of these will likely include numerous national endorsement deals; screen and internet exposure on both a local and national level, cable television offers for reality-based programming and of course the usual book-publishing deals.

A quick reminder on the cap-cams, remember your training, and also remember this; those golf-ball sized viewfinders may not mean beans to you once the trail gets treacherous, but to the paying masses they serve as a personal spy in the sky. We have techies monitoring all fifty one of those bad boys every second of the competition.

As for the dangers, well…you might say this new, updated version of the Gauntlet has seen a major upping of the ante. The first two competitions were merely endurance tests, plain and simple. As harsh and unrelenting as they appeared, they were merely marathons of a more perilous type. The Iron-Will Gauntlet, ladies and gentlemen, is a twenty-first century *obstacle course* that can and will claim your life in the blink of an eye. You all signed off that such risks were duly noted and understood. We stand now…"

He pauses briefly to check his wristwatch even as the insistent pacing continues unabated from one side of the wax-slick wooden stage to the other.

"…a mere forty-five minutes from the starting gun. Meaning, and I say this only once, that the time to default your participation is in the next fifteen minutes. After that, there will be no backing out. I repeat, no…backing… out. Once we reach a half-hour before show-time at the entry point of the *Harlan Harrison monster dome*, the time for cold feet will have ended. There will be no excuses, people. A migraine headache, no matter the level of discomfort, will be endured. A skin rash that threatens to cocoon your entire frame will be scratched, be treated and dealt with. Explosive diarrhea at the starting gate will not serve to delay. You will simply compete with foul-smelling, soiled under-shorts. "

There are a few muffled giggles, though accompanied by a tangible undercurrent of apprehension. Undeterred, the host temporarily halts in mid-stride and turns towards the audience with a raised forefinger.

"Fifteen minutes from now, folks, and then the window of opportunity slams tight and is subsequently double-padlocked. This will barely give us time to roll in your state's runner-up as a last-second replacement.

In closing…" he continues, clearing his throat and pacing yet again with arms pinned at the pit of his back, "…I am hereby required by my terms of employment to state the following: make no mistake, your government cheers each of you on with equal favoritism. Each of you was chosen following a grueling selection process, and your participation alone in this unprecedented test of wills marks you all as winners no matter the eventual outcome. Make no mistake, win or lose, both your home state and this great nation beam with pride at your bravery and selfless, can-do attitudes. At this perilous time for this great land, with unemployment at nearly forty percent, poverty levels at all-time highs and the potential for the next *war to end all wars* rumored almost daily, the populace needs heroes, roll models, such as you. Good luck to all and God speed..."

Turning his back to the masses, he first bows his head and then slowly shakes it from side to side.

"Now that the mandatory *horse-hockey* is out of the way, allow me a moment of truth, soldiers of the gauntlet..."

Wearing a wide, malicious grin, he whirls about in a wild frenzy, a skinny middle-aged man who suddenly resembles the stereotypical mad scientist with gleaming, bug eyes and ringing hands.

"...There is but one true victor sitting in this room. It may take weeks to properly crown this individual...it may take merely a matter of days. Obviously, the duration of said event is all up to you folks. There are no moral victories for finishing third or second runner up, as a woeful lack of notoriety and commercial endorsements will attest. There will be no Olympic-style bronze or silver medals awarded for coming in second or third best. Simply put, folks, there is one winner and fifty *losers*. The order of finish isn't the least bit relevant. No apologies to be found. Simply the world we presently reside in. "

Pausing to scan the motionless masses a final time, the man frowns deeply while crossing his arms across his narrow chest. Bowing his head, he squints over the black-rimmed glasses sitting at the outer edge of his nose as if staring into glaring sunlight.

"One of you will, very soon, be regarded as an immortal of sorts. The rest will return to their home state a failure. That is the uniqueness of this event that separates it from all others. It isn't merely about regional pride, folks. It's about your individual responsibilities to the states you represent, and if many of them will be furnished a better way of life because of what you accomplished. Many will eat meals they would have never been afforded otherwise. Many more will be given a place to live—a roof over their heads-a warm place to sleep. No doubt millions upon millions are laying down what little money they have to root for you; money they can ill afford to waste. Money better spent on food; clothing; unpaid bills. You see, people, it isn't about fame or individual riches as much as it's about sharing the wealth with those in desperate need. You folks, the fifty-one, are serving as guardians to the needy masses. You alone stand as their potential bread winners. Sadly, there is only one prize to give away, and the winner takes the entire loaf, leaving behind nary a crumb to the rest of the field and their many loyal constituents. So, I say all that to say this…"

Snapping to attention with no less than a Gestapo-like clicking of the heels, the skinny man with the wishbone build and grumpy-old professor demeanor extends his right arm and clenched fist in a comically stiff salute that is executed with the utmost of sincerity.

". . . You walk this gauntlet cloaked with the very souls of those depending on you. You will be tested like none before. You will face dangers like none before. You will experience fatigue like none before. One of you...will experience a level of ambrosia like none before. Good luck to one and all, and to that special *one* who is to be granted immortality, I will greet you at the finish with the many spoils in hand. "

The fifty-one applaud as he exits stage right in a jog, first politely and a bit subdued and then a bit more raucous, to include a spattering of whistles and assorted verbal volleys.

While being herded from the auditorium to a side door, where a warming bus awaits their arrival, the man from Lexington overhears the random whispers of several of his worthy opposition.

"You're sure? I thought the dude was just some inspirational speaker for hire," the first, a male, says with a slight drawl, perhaps of Midwestern origin.

"Not quite. Man is notorious for keeping the lowest of profiles," chimes in the second, a female possessing a distinctive northeast accent, "Harlan Harrison, architect to the stars and designer of the dome. I hear the dude has a net worth of six, seven billion. Speaker for hire my ass. "

"But...what's Mister Green Jeans doing here

giving us the Knute Rockne routine?" Midwestern drawl responds sarcastically. Northeast's reply comes off as rudely indifferent, as if she were holding the conversation exclusively with herself.

"The one and *only* reason; he's running the whole shebang for the feds. Who better than the man with the Midas touch? I'd always heard HH was hands on. Built his empire from the ground up with very limited assistance. "

Midwestern grunts, his final words barely audible over the roar of the bus engine that grew louder with every step.

"No fooling. Dude appeared a few bricks shy of a load, ya ask me. Then again, the filthy rich usually are. "

Stepping outside as light flurries buzz about like swarming bees, a cool, stiff breeze slaps his exposed flesh like a wet glove. With a slight shiver, the man from Lexington ponders his peer's words with a heavy layer of skepticism. He'd heard similar speculation during the interview and exam phases, with literally dozens of the world's power brokers mentioned as the proverbial 'man behind the silk curtain' spearheading the government's prize project.

Peering out from the darkly tinted window of his assigned seat on the double-decker Pullman, the man from Lexington spots a sleek, pitch-black limo turn a nearby corner and speed from sight. A concerto of groans and grunts accompany similar sightings, no doubt fueled by the license plate so easily read from beneath the limo's glimmering chrome bumper: *"$HH INC$"* laid out in bright gold lettering. Well, so much for speculation, he mused. Not that it mattered a single iota in the grand scheme. Collusion and conspiracy angles aside, the ultimate race was soon afoot.

Sector A: *Slow Burn*

Part One: Separate but Equal

Time: Day one, thirteen minutes, forty-eight seconds into the Iron-Will Gauntlet

Place: Sector A (*Southeastern U. S. summer climes*)

Narrator*:* Codename '*Kentucky'*

"And aaaawwwwaaaayyy we go, huh Blue-Grass?" the big-boned, strawberry-blonde woman blurted with a strained huff while blowing by me in a fast-walk, her deep, down-home drawl making it less than a challenge to determine which state the 'M' pasted on her shirt stood for. Surely not *Michigan, Minnesota* or *Maine*, but a ways further down the atlas.

"I'd say yeah. Better pace yourself there, Ole Miss. Remember the tortoise and the hare," I bantered back good-naturedly, surprised at how relieved the simple act of speaking made me feel.

"You do it your way, Blue Grass, I'll do it mine," she spat, her chubby, fish-belly white legs pumping like fleshy pistons, "gotta use the home-field advantage while we have it, right? See ya up the road, my brother. "

In the half-hour or so since gear handout (short-sleeve tees, parachute shorts, jogging/running sneakers and a small backpack containing poncho-style raingear, an I-Pod-mini loaded with music of

26

choice, water canteen and assorted protein bars), those were the first words I'd uttered aloud since the previous night's interview. Though I'm sure a small portion of my 'mum's the word' act was simply taking heed of the advice given by my self-appointed Gauntlet consultant: making an acquaintance, much less a friend of a fellow competitor was a potentially fatal mistake. Still, a larger portion could be chalked up to my overall nature. I'd never been known as much of a conversationalist. As a postman, a kind of inner isolation merely came with the territory. Not to say I'd ever been labeled a hermit or social misfit. Then again, I'd never be called the life of the party either. I was normally just one who spoke when spoken too. Both the selection panel and my aforementioned advisor had seen this as a rather large advantage on my part. The talkers, or *instinctual communicators* as they referred to such personalities, were apt to burn out at a faster clip as both miles and hours piled up along the long, winding trail. Energy conservation by *whatever* means would be a definite plus, all had agreed, leaving the lock-jaw types such as myself in the driver's seat in terms of fighting off a Gauntlet competitors more formidable enemy: fatigue. All that said, I'd got a surprising amount of pleasure out of that initial exchange with a fellow traveler, advice to the contrary be damned.

The dome itself was every bit the futuristic Sci-Fi marvel I'd expected, and more. Truly, no glossy slideshow or interactive internet tour did it justice. We'd read all the accolades upon its completion and been bombarded, like everyone else in the free world, with amazing tales of its construction, almost four full years in the making and involving fourteen separate construction companies and a multi-million-dollar team of scientists and architects. There had been problems, as with any project of such colossal proportions, and rumors of mass firings in the aftermath. It'd been said Harlan Harrison had little patience for human error. There had been rumors that, mid-way through its construction, a government shutdown order was a mere presidential signature away, only to be averted as a major technical issue had been solved by an outside source.

While in the planning stages, estimates of a potential cost had been attwo or three billion dollars. Not exactly chump change, for certain, though the final unofficial tally four long years later stood at over twice that. Once scuttlebutt reached public and media ears concerning such an unfathomable amount, it's safe to say the news went over like the proverbial lead balloon. One particular talk-show pundit had referred to the dome as a one-hundred eighty-six square mile 'walking trail' that had cost the already financially strapped taxpayers more than if they'd footed the bill for fifty-one separate sports arenas, or basically one for each state represented in the competition the dome was built to house. In the aftermath of the news, there'd been the expected demonstrations, many birthed within the fast-swelling ranks of the many anti-government groups so prevalent these days.

Regardless, I cannot stand here and honestly

say I can't see where all that money went, and this is just the first of four twenty-plus mile sectors. Every copper penny accounted for thus far, yes sir, and then some. I mean, to not be amazed at this indoor wonder is to either be universally jaded or monumentally dense. Case in point, we were bused from the hotel to the surrounding mountains in a light snow with temperatures surely no toastier than the high teens. We dismounted the double-decker taxicab as ice pellets struck my cheeks and I had to strain mightily to avoid allowing my kneecaps to smack together. Well, here I stand…stroll actually, less than an hour later atop a hard-dirt trail surrounded by what appears strikingly similar to the heavily forested regions of my home state. Tall oaks, pines and elm trees engulf on all sides; a slight breeze does little to relieve the building humidity as mid-morning is fast changing to afternoon and a fresh coating of sweat fills my every pore. Astonishing on so many levels it's hard to fathom; from the bone-chilling landscape of a Wyoming mountain range to a summer day in the Southeast, all seemingly created with the simple flick of a switch. Well, perhaps not so simple, but for such a thing to even be possible, certainly makes me wonder— well, perhaps *fear* is a better word—what lies ahead. Mysteries abound within the great dome, but one in particular can't help but weigh heavy on a naturally curious mind such as my own. Just how far can one travel off the beaten path without running into a glass wall or perhaps even a metallic one? To the naked eye, it appears the surrounding forest and countryside goes on indefinitely, as in the real world. Logically, since the outer fringes of the pathway serve no purpose, one would assume that perhaps even the trees and shrubbery blanketing the shoulders might themselves be nothing more than a CGI based illusion. I would wager one, if not many, will test those limits long before reaching Sector D. In all honestly, that certain someone might just turn out to be cloaked in bright Kentucky blue. So many unknowns, the answers to which we may never be privy too. One thing for stone-cold certain, however, is the realization that the majority of the field would...*will* crack long before that final sector is ever stepped foot into. Some would surely collapse from pure fatigue, drawn to the hard ground as if visualizing a sleep-number bed coated in feathers. Others, the majority by far, would crack from the neck up; reduced to lumbering zombie-like husks of their former selves residing in a wholly hallucinatory state, a bleary, unearthly existence where not only would the purpose of the competition become meaningless, but also their very reason for being. . . period.

"They're going to put you through the grinder, KY," my advisor had warned, a rather heavyset, middle-aged brunette named Kay whose comically frozen expressions had hinted at a rather obvious fondness for Botox, "I won't sugarcoat. It's going to be tough and get increasingly tougher before the real challenges even begin. KY—" she'd continued in an obviously rehearsed speech I'd found almost as irritating as her habit of referring to me as a water-based lubricant, "you're going to be forced to discover an inner-strength you never knew existed.

You truly won't know the person you are to become. It will be a transformation for the ages that will serve to propel you to ever greater heights in life once this competition is long completed. "Spoken like a true sports agent, which I later discovered had once been the lady's occupation. Thus, mystery solved in terms of her constant barrage of clichés meant to both inspire and motivate. Maintaining a straight face had been quite the challenge in light of the more syrupy offerings, particularly the 'old self transforms into butterfly' spiel. The thing was, Kay wasn't blowing smoke rings up my rear merely for giggles. Turns out the Gauntlet's hand-picked advisor was apt to collect one whopper of a government bonus, not to mention a potential book deal of their very own. I figure they probably pocket a decent payday win or lose, much like *all* those involved with the glaring exception of the fifty poor souls destined to finish no better than second in the race itself. No matter. I know damn well what I signed up for. Accepted the terms without hesitation or question, as I'm fairly certain the majority clogging up this faux clay-packed trail did likewise. We made our collective beds, one and all. Nothing to do now but put up or shut down and fly home with the life-loser label stamped permanently across the forehead for all to see. Yeah, that thought alone ought to be enough to keep the feet pumping and the mind focused solely on the prize. As far as the state of Kentucky goes? Honestly I couldn't care less what the population as a whole thinks of me in the aftermath. Nope, only opinion I give beans about is that of a former resident. That *particular* opinion provides all the motivation this here boy will ever need.

"Beep-beep! Such detached daydreaming is libel to find you flat on your stomach with multiple sneaker marks trailing up your back," a husky voice boomed from close behind and to my immediate left as I centered the relatively narrow trail, which at widest appeared no more than a dozen feet across.

A flash of *silver and blue* whizzed by, the baggy tee showcasing the initials 'NV' between the wearer's considerably wide shoulder blades. The large, pot-bellied man tucked within said shirt was in full fast-walk mode, with elbows swaying like twin pendulums and feet practically slapping together as they crossed in mid-strike. It was to be a popular mode of travel, though one I'd personally pass on due to the probability of shin splints becoming problematic further on down the trail.

"Slower traffic, keep to the right. That means you, *Kentucky.* "

"My bad, Vegas," I responded with a bit more sarcasm that I'd really intended.

"Just call me the Gambler. That is, if you're ever able to catch up with me again," he concluded, briefly raising his right hand in greeting but never bothering to turn about.

My next response was delivered with a purposely upbeat tone to make up for the temporarily surliness.

"Oh, we'll jaw again, poker-face. You count on it. "

Nevada quickly strode out of sight around a sharp curve, vanishing behind a protruding patch of shrubbery that lined the right side of the trail like a leafy guardrail.

Pulling the backpack from between my shoulders, I rummaged through the darkened interior for the I-Pod, eager to avoid any further dialogue from whoever passed me next. I'd was in the process of setting the earpiece when still another figure approached from the left, this one purposely pausing as to apparently garner my full attention.

"I'm with you, Kentucky. It's all about energy conservation. *Utah* and a few of the rest that took off like bats straight outta hades are fools. We'll be passing 'em up in no time, eh?"

Even without the state name plastered across his *yellow, green* and *gold* tee, the pronounced accent left little doubt of the man from *North Dakota*'s region of residency. I might've incorrectly guessed Minnesota or perhaps even Iowa, but the boy was definitely not from my neck of the woods.

We locked eyes for a split-second only, but long enough for me to feel strangely comfortable in the stranger's presence. Perhaps in his mid-fifties with a bushy gray mustache and matching eye brows, the man was rail-thin but not at all gaunt; what some might refer to as 'wiry'. He also possessed perhaps the palest set of legs I'd ever seen. The kind of chalky whiteness that was almost blinding upon initial viewing, as if he might've dipped them in flour or slapped on a coat of ivory paint before commencing.

"Well, here's hoping you're right. "

"Got to say, though, this damned southern heat and humidity isn't exactly my cup of tea. Haven't been hoofing it but a half-hour and I'm about ready to suck the canteen dry, you know?"

"You get used to it," I lied as the man reached up wipe away the building sweat from his brow.

"Oh, but your fibbing now, *Kentucky*," he beamed, smiling wide to reveal a set of yellow-stained choppers not nearly as white as his legs.

"I'm melting into my joggers, and the oven hasn't even preheated yet. Thanks for the effort though, eh? See ya up the road. "

"Not too fast though, right Dakota?" I replied with a wink as he picked up the pace just enough to put some space between us.

"Right as freezing rain, Kentuck. Adios. . . "

With my I-Pod tune of choice set and my ears filled with the soothing sounds of Bach, Beethoven and Strauss, three others soon passed me by at various speeds. A short, pudgy man displaying the *blue, green* and *cranberry* colors of *Delaware* came first, staring down at his own feet as he sauntered quietly by.

Next to stroll by was *Oregon*'s contestant of choice; a stoutly build, muscular gentleman in a *navy blue* and *gold* tee that appeared at least two sizes too small, the bill of his cap-cam facing the rear and thereby filming those on his heels. I couldn't help but ponder both the media and audience reaction to this rather bizarre strategy, if that's what it was. As far as I'd heard, there'd been no set rule against such a technique, though for the life of me I couldn't fathom a credible reason to do so.

The state colors of *California* came next, its

wearer a tall, well-built brunette whose shapely rear end I couldn't help but ogle as it's jiggling beauty moved so gracefully into my line of site. She had scooted by in a half-dance, half-jog, her lips moving to the lyrics of whatever tune spewed forth from the I-Pod plugged into her left ear, never bothering to acknowledge my presence while boogieing past in a gyrating blur.

"Consider yourself fortunate," I heard a faint female voice say, breaking the trance-like state Miss *California*'s flawless posterior had so magically created.

"I...who...what's that?" I babbled, blinking madly while gently reaching up to pull my earplug free and thus so rudely interrupt Bach's *The Art of Fugue*.

"Just said you aren't missing much in terms of quality of conversation with that one. Might just be the dimmest bulb on the trail. "

A thin, rather attractive blonde, the latter deduced from the select locks hanging loose from beneath her cap-cam, it wasn't until she casually twisted about to better reveal the front of her bright-colored tee that I was officially introduced to *Arizona*'s chosen rep.

"Just saying. Chick's been talking my head off since in-processing. Former failed actress, singer, the whole bit. Told me to call her *Hollywood*. Over forty and counting on the gauntlet to rejuvenate a career she hasn't even had yet. Ah well, it takes all kinds, right?"

"Obviously," I responded with a nod, at once shocked and revolted at how much, from a side view anyway, she favored a *certain* person, "a thousand stories in the naked city type thing."

"The naked ci- . . . damn, *Kentucky* . . . you *are* old," she said smiling, her eyes hidden in the shade beneath the cap's bill.

"No springs chickens in this outfit, *Arizona*, or hadn't you noticed?"

Her grin widened as her face turned about and up just enough for me to garner a full impression. At least, I instantly deduced with no small amount of relief, the eyes in question were bright hazel and *not* a piercing shade of blue.

"Speak for yourself, mister. Personally, my feathers may be lighting up a shade, but that's all."

"Where's the fire?" I blurted, gesturing with a raised hand to the line of fast-walkers and half-joggers blazing the trail ahead, while doing my best to prevent her from rambling away too quickly. Much like with *North Dakota*, I felt weirdly at ease, the banter between us as natural as that between two old friends. Plus, there was the amble supply of charisma she brought to the table, and while she would never be considered gorgeous by the mainstream, the term 'easy on the eyes' seemed perfectly fitting.

She huffed, forced to pick up pace to keep up with my longer strides. In turn, I slowed up just a hint.

"Bull-headed, swim-up-streamers. Going completely against all the expert advice about pacing ourselves for the long haul, and most of 'em doing it for precisely for that reason."

"Guess they'd rather burn out than fade away."

"Now a *Neil Young* reference, no less? You some kind of historic pop-culture freak, *Kentucky*? Thought you folks were only into secret recipe fried chicken, horse-racing and homemade sour mash. "

"You left out share-cropping and in-breeding," I replied purposely stone-faced, "besides, look who's talking. You sure identified that lyric in a hurry, *Sagebrush*. And, while we're on the subject of stereotypical, decades-old clichés, what exactly are you doing off the ranch? Ain't there some doggies to rope or cattle to brand back in your neck of the woods?"

"Touché, point taken," she said, briefly lifting her arms in surrender, "nothing personal. Have to confess that my lone personal experience with southerners goes no further than what I've seen in movies, the net or the boob tube. Just my way of sizing up the opposition, especially those inclined to show some basic, common horse sense, pardon the expression, concerning the rules of the game. "

"Better watch fraternizin' with that one, K-Man," a new voice exclaimed in a thick, deliberate drawl that by comparison made Mississippi's representative sound like a lifelong native of Yonkers.

"Her kind ain't to be trusted by the likes of us, brother. Ya ought to know better. "

Coming up on my right until the three of us were perfectly aligned, *Alabama*'s person of choice flashed a toothy grin before glancing past me to shoot *Arizona* a worrisome glance. An average-sized man of perhaps fifty with a barrel chest and taunt, muscular arms that showcased several fading tattoos, my neighbor from the south appeared bald beneath the cap-cam and was otherwise clean-shaven save a dark brown, pencil-thin mustache that curled at the edges in true homage to silent-movie villainy.

"Well, if it isn't Foghorn Leghorn. There goes the neighborhood," *Arizona* grumbled with wholly manufactured malice. My next query surely sounded more sincere than it actually was, though there was a faint curiosity there.

"I take it you two have been formally introduced already?"

"Oh yeah, me and *Fast Drawl* over there were back to back on the pre-comp interview circuit last night. Hey Johnny Reb, anybody remaining behind us that hails from *above* the Mason-Dixon line?"

Before I could estimate a guess, *Alabama* whirled about and walked backward, though easily staying in step due to our less than rapid pace.

"A few stragglers, though it seems the majority have opted to play roadrunner. *Alaska* is a few dozen yards back…poor guy's complexion is carrot red. *Wisconsin, Ohio* and…looks like *Maryland* are all shoulder to shoulder and seem to be havin' a similar jawin' session as our own. So much for the unwritten rule of stayin' tight-lipped and stone-faced. "

"We were just discussing said strategy," I interjected with a nod his way once he'd turned back around, "as being quite idiotic, especially with all the lectures on endurance. "

"Right with ya, partner," he said, lightly slapping my right shoulder with a flat palm, "what the hell good does getting ten, twenty miles ahead of the pack do when exhaustion kicks in and ya watch 'em all pass ya right back? Nobody can keep up the jackrabbit pace those pea-brains have set. That is, let's hope not. Still, the farther they get ahead, the more jittery I'm feelin'. "

"Not to worry, 'Bama," I reassured, though suddenly feeling a bit shaky myself in the realization that three-fourths of the field had already passed us by, "we middle-aged southern boys recognize bonehead stupidity when we see it, right?"

"Most assuredly, my good man," he blurted in easily the worst attempt at a Brit accent I'd ever bore witness too, "yes indeed, the south will rise yet again, and I for one will be proud to be her withered old flag-bearer!"

"Lord love a duck," *Arizona* spewed between giggles, finally covering her mouth with a cupped palm, "if nothing else, this whole experience is going to be a real hoot to bore the grandkids with. "

Stumbling a bit after sliding over a particularly slick coating of gravel, *Alabama* quickly righted himself and jumped ahead several yards, the back of his *crimson and white* tee soaked through between the shoulder blades. I noted with much amusement at the man's severely bow-legged gait, and was hardly able to refrain from hooting aloud at the mere sight.

"Right with ya, sister...got two little ankle-gnawers back home cheerin' on their old grand-pappy as we speak. Well, bein' that the oldest just turned two, maybe *slobberin' on* is a more apt term.

Anyhow, I'll catch you kids on the flipside…gonna burn some rubber and catch up with *Tennessee*. Me and that boy got some verbalizin' of our own to do. "

"*Tennessee*? Say it ain't so," *Arizona* said with mock astonishment, those hazel beauties pulled as wide as saucer cups, "you got trouble brewing with the kinfolk?"

This time I was unable to contain a guffaw at the lady's woefully executed southern drawl, to which *Alabama* briefly groaned while covering both ears.

"Oh, now that's pathetic…and you had the nerve to squawk at my proper English? Lord, I do believe my ears are commencin' to bleed. Anyhow, my beef with *Mr. Volunteer* is more about dissin' than pissin' off. Stuffy bird hasn't uttered word one since our intro two days back. I'm gonna do my dead-level best to tug a syllable or two outta his ornery hide. Later, gators . . . "

Despite serious reservations in even mulling over such potentially harmful thoughts, I'd quickly come to the conclusion that 'Bama was indeed one of the good guys. Problem being, did there exist a bad guy to root against or provide proper motivation? Perhaps *Arizona, Alabama* and *North Dakota* had been the exception and the majority of the pack would prove to be less amiable and downright unlikable.

Within minutes, 'Bama had put fifty yards between us, vanishing over an approaching hill in bleary segments, as if he'd set foot in a pool of quicksand.

"Seems like a good sort," I half-whispered, reaching up to wipe a build-up of salty moisture from underneath my left eyelid.

"Don't let the *Bubba Buffoon* act fool you. That's one tough cookie. Former prison warden, I understand. No doubt he's as crafty and conniving as anyone in the pack. "

I turned to her, somewhat startled by the grimness of the remark, only to find her visage equally chilling. The good-natured grin had been replaced by a warped frown that instantly aged her a decade.

"We're *all* sharks. Different species or subspecies perhaps, but similar in their predatory ways. Some of us are just too damned polite to get past the amenities. In the end, we've all got the capability to step on the throats of those in our way. We proved as much in the application and interview phases. Otherwise, this computer generated torture chamber would be housing a different crowd altogether. "

"Guess you're right," I conceded after a moment of stilted silence.

"Of course I am, *Kentucky*. We all endured the same tests, right? You do recall the *realm of blackness*, I presume?"

"Oh yeah, most definitely. How could one forget such a joyous experience?" I replied, openly wincing at the mere memory.

The rather depressing banter was briefly interrupted as a lanky African-American female wearing the blue and gold tee colors of *Pennsylvania* sauntered quietly by to our left.

41

"Yep, that was the one," she concluded with a stern nod, "that so effectively weaned out all the wanna-be's. "

"No argument. What a spook-house. "

"Definition *perfecto*," she replied, lifting her right elbow to administer a gentle nudge to my left bicep.

"Believe I'm going to kick it a gear higher, *Kentucky*. "

"Leaving me in the dust as well?" I chided with a return nudge, equally enchanted and repulsed by an inexplicable sense of déjà vu in the woman's presence, "I'm starting to sense a trend here. Honestly, is it my deodorant or perhaps woeful lack thereof?"

She briefly refrained from response as a large black male, easily the biggest in stature of the competitors I'd noticed, dashed by in a semi-jog. Shooting us a passing glance that appeared less polite greeting than dismissive sneer, it came as little surprise upon identification via the back of his sweat-soaked tee that the state flag he so sourly flew was that of *New York*.

"BO is not an issue here, champ," she eventually said, "just a twinge of paranoia. As in, I feel the need to put some distance behind me before they amp up this damn humidity to late afternoon settings. "

"Good point. I'd gauge right now as a typical late June or early July at just before noon. The real heat kicks in around 2 p. m. or so. "

"Heat I can take, Amigo, at least of the dry variety. This is like…," she paused, lifting her arms

42

and twisting until the palms of each hand faced upward into the faux rays of whatever equally false sun beamed down, "...an outdoor hothouse. Where I hail from, ninety degrees doesn't feel half bad as long as the skies are clear.

Besides, I'm just hoping for a decent showing in the first three sectors --- won't be treading familiar ground for this girl until we set foot inside D, as in *desert terrain.* "

I momentarily grew silent at a rather unsettling thought.

"What's wrong?" she inquired, squinting up towards me wearing a deep frown that, mercifully, altered her facial features just enough to appear completely unfamiliar.

"Just pondering . . . if your theory holds true, kind of a 'sector home field advantage' type scenario, I'm the one who should be scurrying forward at the speed of light. "

"How so?"

"Well, southern climes . . . " I replied, first gesturing into the surrounding space and then back at myself while feeling a cool chill trail my sweat-coated spine, ". . . southern *man.* This is my backyard, isn't it?"

"Yeah, supposedly. "

"Then I should be eating up ground *now,* as what's to come is libel to be one serious kick in the behind, in terms of weather. "

"Kind of shoots my theory, then doesn't it?" she huffed, her shoulders instantly slumping, "guess there's a reason the powers that be kept each sector's climate a mystery 'til they handed out gear at the starting point. Head games piled atop head games.

Guess *I* can take it easy and conserve after all. Better take off then, rebel son. This is your time, not mine. "

Lunging clumsily forward with a loud crack from each overextended knee, I afforded *Arizona* a gentlemanly tip of the cap.

"Appreciate the heads-up, Sagebrush, however accidental. Maybe I can return the favor on down the line. "

"Not a problem, Blue Grass. Just leave your canteen 'bout halfway up the trail and we'll call it even. "

I laughed aloud despite a sudden tightness of the gut, silently cursing myself for such blatant lackadaisicalness. Fighting off a building cramp in my left thigh, I continued to gain speed until a comfortable pace was found and subsequently set, all the while pondering why I'd been unable to lock onto to such a logical theory myself.

A series of winding curves and rolling hills ensued, during which time I passed a half-dozen competitors, to include *North Dakota*, who had obviously slowed his own pace and shot me an animated 'thumbs-up' on my way by.

Within a half-hour, while keeping my speed rock steady despite a continuously uneven landscape, I passed four more, to include the perpetually scowling giant from *New York* State, who had momentarily attempted to keep pace before dropping back with a resounding groan. I'd drained a third of my canteen while covering a lengthy stretch of flat terrain flanked by treeless, grassy pastureland on either side as a surprisingly cool breeze temporarily chilled the sweat on my face and neck. At the time, I thought nothing significant of the sudden shift in temperatures. Less than fifteen minutes later, it became horrifically apparent that the dome's man-made weather gurus had something definite in mind in terms of an initial challenge. Something, while not totally unexpected to one familiar with the region being tread upon, still came off a bit sinister in execution. Sinister, and, given the aftermath . . . shockingly brutal.

Part Two: *Storm Front*

Time: One hour, seventeen minutes into the Iron-Will Gauntlet
Place: Sector A
Total miles covered: Six and a half

Pausing just long enough to pull on the comically thin, clear plastic poncho, I took a quick peek behind and found the trial void for a twenty to twenty-five yard stretch leading to the steep, rock-infested hill I'd just conquered. Kicking swiftly back into high gear, I felt the first few drops of chilled water bypass the flimsy poncho hood and sting my forehead just above the eyebrows. Five full minutes passed, wherein the trail stayed relatively flat but extremely curvy and similarly competitor-less, and I was beginning to ponder the rather insane notion that I'd somehow managed to stray off-course though the logic in taking a wrong-turn on the only available trail quickly doused any sincere anxiety. Still, it came across as damn strange that I'd been strolling solo for over forty minutes without sighting a single foe. Never had the ancient saying 'be careful what you wish for' held more meaning than what transpired just moments later. A three-pronged assault on the senses soon had me praying for a return to sweet isolation.

First off, the light sprinkle intensified to a full-blown squall, accompanied by gusting, straight-line winds that threatened to shred the paper-thin poncho into so much confetti and transform my cap-cam into a Frisbee. In kind, the skies turned tar-black in a matter of blinks, as if someone had flicked off an overhead light.

Slowed to a virtually crawl, I was forced to retrieve the backpack from my shoulders before it went airborne, and hugged it to my chest as I trudged forward. What seemed like a half-hour or more of stumbling through a combination wind-tunnel/car wash was probably more like three to four minutes maximum, but it wasn't until I walked smack dab into what felt like a brick wall that the trance was so rudely broken. This is when the second calamity arose, and easily the worst of the trio in terms of the overall big picture. While the other two could be somewhat easily cast aside as temporary irritants, this particular pain in the posterior would turn out to be of the chronic variety. Hailing from the state of *Colorado*—from which I knew little save its capital city, thin mountain air and a tendency to host heavy winter snows—was the competitor later referred to by all simply as the *Ice-Man*. The origin of said nickname held little mystery once you'd been unfortunate enough to cross paths, easily explaining why it was normally accompanied by a slew of profanities. At the very least, my initial run-in with the man assisted greatly in mentally preparing for later duels. At the time, however, that first clash was the equivalent of a hard left hook to the jaw, albeit with an ending that was quite humorous in a freakish sort of way.

"Shit, pal...you *born* this clumsy or was such skill developed over a lifetime of oaf-ness?" the growling voice boomed, though the overall effect was surely muffled by both the screeching winds and my startled state, not to mention a slightly mashed nose.

Stumbling wildly to the left, I almost fumbled the backpack away as both arms instinctively shot out for balance.

"Sorry...M-my bad...did...didn't see you..." I rambled, jittering about like a drunken break dancer as a new series of gusts pounded from seemingly all directions simultaneously.

"Fuck the apologies, cracker. Just stay off my back and outta my tracks. Beats the hell out of me how any of you left-footed imbeciles made the final cut. Pickings must've been *mighty* slim in Hooterville. "

It wasn't until moments later, when both the winds and wetness seemed to pause in a perfectly synchronized time-out, as if taking a much-deserved sabbatical before their next vicious assault, that I was allowed a semi-clear look at my verbal abuser.

In hearing his second volley, I'd instantly envisioned an enormous, muscle-bound lunatic with bugged-out eyes and oversized teeth sharpened at the edges like some hybrid human-piranha. It's strange how a man in his late forties can still imagine scenarios more befitting a spooked teen prepping for a playground beating by the neighborhood bully.

With the hood of the badly twisted poncho effectively cloaking the left side of his face, he sneered at me through a single, rapidly-blinking eye.

"Something to say, shit-kicker? Do I need to

speak slooo-wer so your country-fried ass can fully com-pre-hend?"

Unable to verbalize a suitable response in light of such a monumental misjudgment, I could only chuckle aloud. At first in a low, guttural giggle that quickly manifested into a full-blown belly laugh that threatened to tip me over yet again.

Instead of the hulking menace I'd so vividly created from the mere sound of a threatening voice, cold hard reality painted a portrait so comically opposite that I was forced to execute a similarly outrageous double-take just to ensure its authenticity.

The man was rail-thin to the point of appearing emaciated, with appendages so spindly and a torso so frail-looking I seriously wondered how he hadn't taken flight from Mother Nature's brutal assault. In addition, he stood no more than perhaps five-five or six, though a pronounced bow to his back might've added to the illusion of slightness. From what little I could make of his semi-cloaked facial features, he possessed a slightly crooked, beak-shaped nose and beady, rat-like eyes so dark one might well describe them as blackish pits. All in all, to put it as politely as possible, and to borrow a term from my dear, departed grandmother, the man was as plain as homemade soap. For those less inclined to kindness, the more apt term was 'butt-ugly'. Either way, his looks were a perfect match for his disposition; that of a starving, snarling animal in search of prey—considering his rather miniscule stature, perhaps a rabid *ferret*.

"Redneck *retards*, the whole inbred, ignorant

lot of you," he finally groaned with a disgusted roll of the eyes, or at the least the one I was privy to visualize beyond the mangled poncho.

"Eat shit and die, mister, and good luck in seeing anything of me from this point 'cept for my foot prints. "

He practically sprinted away as the heavy rain returned in spades, pounding down in straight sheets, though mercifully sans the punishing winds. I was left standing at the center of the trail, submerged almost to the ankles in a fast-rising mud-puddle with my ribs throbbing from a hysterical laughing fit that refused to completely abate for another half-minute in the aftermath of his 'eat shit' comment.

The sound of nearby thunder and a series of overhead lightning flashes snapped me too for good, and I managed to immediately kick back into overdrive, using a soaked forearm to wipe a deluge of warm mucus from both nostrils. My vision was badly blurred from both the continuing onslaught from above and a fresh build-up of tears, but I managed to remain on the trail for the most part. Through several twisting curves and an abundance of shoulder-high shrubbery lining both sides of the trail, I lost sight of *Mister Warmth*, a detail that didn't exactly serve to depress. Eventually the storm passed, though how much time had expired or ground covered was impossible to gauge. I'd mostly kept my head down, staring at both feet as they'd sloshed through the surging stream the trail had become, and hadn't dared look up until the pattering sound of raindrops against the poncho had ceased, and a sudden brightness shone off the standing water in bright, gleaming rays.

The sun, or whatever served as such within the dome's bizarre smoke and mirrors universe, beat down with renewed vitality, raising the humidity level ten-fold in a matter of minutes. I quickly stripped away the poncho, sections of which were either badly torn or missing altogether, and carefully draped it over a thick patch of honeysuckle that had extended its girth into the pathway. Amazing how lifelike the scent of said plants, so realistic as to momentarily take me back to childhood memories of my uncle's farm just outside Louisville, where similar intoxicating scents filled my nostrils each spring.

After repositioning the backpack, which was completely saturated despite my best efforts, I plugged in my earphones and reset the I-Pod, obviously waterproof, to the sometimes soulful, sometimes rockin', habitually toe-tapping sounds of Phil Collins and Genesis. Stepping in tune with the lengthy instrumental 'Home by the Sea', I could feel a faint twinge at my bladder, the first such activity in the two-plus hours since entering the sector. We'd been briefed that individual Porto-potties would be scattered randomly throughout each sector, though I had yet to see a single unit on either side of the trail. Perhaps the powers that be figured that even the weakest of constitutions could hold out to at least the ten mile mark, which was rapidly approaching.

Carefully descending a steep, rain-slick hill, I was forced to walk on my heels to prevent a potential slide. Upon reaching the bottom of what the heavy rains had transformed from flat trail to deeply-grooved gully, I was able to gaze over an adjoining peak to see a trio of competitors lining a lengthy stretch of flat ground approximately fifty yards ahead. Of the three, two I instantly recognized. The first, bringing up the rear but obviously at a swifter pace than the two pacesetters, was Sir *Sour-grapes* himself. The second, and leading said trio by no more than five or six yards at best, was *North Dakota*.

I didn't recognize the third of the bunch, a heavy-set man with curly, gray locks hanging from underneath the back of his cap-cam, nor could I identify his state of origin due to the distance between us. Slowing my pace in order to retrieve the canteen for a quick sip, I then sucked in a lungful of man-made humidity and took off in a light jog, suddenly determined to make up some serious ground, the main motivation of which was no doubt fueled by the mere sight of that foul-mouthed reptile passing the field.

I watched with considerable curiosity as *Mister Warmth* split between the two and passed them by while flashing a series of obscene gestures. Though actual wording was impossible to make out due to the distance, I heard a verbal folly erupt between the three, followed by the shaking of a raised fist by *North Dakota* and a double-barreled 'bird flipping' by the stranger with the graying curls.

Wisely easing off the gas in the face of what was beginning to feel like late afternoon summer heat, it still took less than five minutes to catch up to the two men as they walked side by side at the trail's fast-drying center. I had started to speak up as I grew to within ten yards or so, but instead remained silent in order to eavesdrop on their rather animated conversation.

"Jackass is probably a government plant whose sole mission is to royally piss off the rest of us," gray-curls spat, the soaked black and yellow tee announcing him as the representative from *Utah* sticking to the flesh of his back like a second skin, "every good drama has to have a suitable villain, and that little prick is an A-lister for sure. "

"Aw, forget about him. Damn troll won't last two sectors with a build like that. Makes me look downright blubbersome by comparison," *North Dakota* replied gruffly, playfully waiving off the other man with one hand while reaching up to adjust his cap-cam with the other.

"Yeah, guess you're right. I've used fatter toothpicks. "

I waited an additional moment or two just to ensure no further dialogue was forthcoming before announcing my presence.

"Hi-yo there, fellow travelers. Mind if I join you?"

Both whirled about in unison, their eyes pulled comically wide.

"Whoops, my bad…didn't intend to startle. "

"Well, hey there, *Kentucky!*" *North Dakota* exclaimed with a toothy grin, his walrus-style mustache dripping sweat from its bushy edges, "damn, but you're a sneaky one. Either that or those tired old ears are going deafer by the mile. "

"Could be all the rain clogging them up," *Utah* blurted, wiping away a sizeable coating of fop sweat with a bare forearm before turning back around to face forward. I quickly drew even and adjusted my speed to match their own.

"Don't mind the grumpy Mormon to my right, 'Tuck. Glad to see you. Decided to pick up the pace, I see. "

"Yeah, well, being that this is my home field and all," I replied with a grin of my own.

"Better take advantage, right?" he beamed as a virtual torrent of sweat dribbled forth from that sponge-like growth on his upper lip, "I don't know how you southern folks put up with it, 'Tuck. Jesus, it's like taking a stroll inside a broiler oven. "

"Amen to that, brother," *Utah* huffed, his broad shoulders so badly slumped they appeared partially dislocated, "I can suddenly sympathize with every microwave burrito I've ever scarfed. "

The man's ample gut gyrated first up and down and then side to side with each lumbering step. His complexion was fish-belly white; his moistened face the definition of haggard. Obviously not stating so aloud, I couldn't help but secretly predict his departure from the competition as being fairly imminent.

North Dakota spoke while staring into a cloudless blue sky that, at least from our perspective, looked to be the real deal.

"The strategy seems simple enough; burn us, drown us, or freeze us, in no particular order. "

"At the moment," *Utah* injected with a raised forefinger, "I vote for the latter. At least frigid cold is state I can understand. "

Peering ahead, I could just make out Mister Happy rounding a sharp curve and subsequently vanishing behind a line of vegetation.

"Scary thing is, gents, I get the feeling they are just warming up, if you'll pardon the expression. "

"Wish you'd got here a few minutes earlier," *North Dakota* said after a moment's pause, wherein we walked shoulder to shoulder up a slight incline that appeared to be the demarcation line to a completely dry track, as if the storm hadn't gone any further up the trail.

"Oh yeah? I miss something notable?" I replied, trying hard to sound at least slightly indifferent.

"Biggest dick-weed in the tournament, I'd venture to say. "

"Oh, you mean the rep from the Big Apple state?" I inquired, playing dumb though not really sure why, "Yeah, big guy did seem to be quite the grumpy a-hole, but then again, you know New Yorkers and their reputations for act-…"

"Nope, wrong a-hole, 'Tuck," *Dakota* cut in, shaking his head from side to side and accidentally splashing everything within range with flying sweat.

"This puny jackass hailed from *Colorado*. Mouthy punk with a boulder-sized chip on his scrawny little shoulder. "

I laughed aloud at the pun, though peering over at *Dakota*'s confused mug made it apparent such clever wordplay had been purely accidental.

"So, um, what was his problem?" I asked as the three of us marched in stride while descending a slight incline. *Utah* merely scowled in response, while *Dakota* grew increasingly animated as he commenced, his already beet-red complexion growing rosier still.

"Hell if we know. Bony little peckerwood came up from behind us and started ranting and raving. Thought at first he'd already cracked and was babbling solely to himself. That is, 'til he addressed us by name. "

"No kidding. What was his beef?"

"First off, he spewed out something like 'outta my way, lover-boys' or some such homo-related malarkey," *Dakota* continued, waving his arms about wildly. I could hear *Utah* grunt occasionally, as if in complete agreement.

"I think I said something like, 'you talking to us?" Sounds bone-headed in retrospect…I mean, we ain't exactly on a crowded street here, but I guess the surprise of it all got the best of me, logically speaking. "

"That's not even the kicker," *Utah* finally chimed in, sounding frighteningly bushed considering the leisurely pace we'd fallen into.

"Tell 'im the kicker. "

"Pint-sized blowhard flipped us off just as casual as you'd please. Reminded me for all the world of when I was doing long-haul trucking back in the day and some smart ass driving one of those cigar sized sports cars would cut me off and then flash the middle finger out the driver's side window while zooming out of range. Torqued me off no end. "

"Tell 'im what he called himself," *Utah* huffed,

his puffy cheeks alternating color from glowing pink to ashen grey.

With that, *Dakota* snickered, snapping both fingers in sudden recollection.

"Get this...told us to get used to seeing the 'Ice-Man's' backside. The *Ice-Man*, no less...can you believe the gall? Hell, if anyone trolling this trail had the right to claim such a cornball name, it'd most likely be yours truly. "

Thinking back on my own less-than-jovial run in with the man, it hit me how obvious the strategy he'd mapped out.

"Probably just this guy's warped plan on getting under your skins while simultaneously testing the thickness of same. You know the type. Best buck-up, guys, because it's a safe bet he won't be the only one. "

"No wager, 'Tuck," *Dakota* conceded with a combination wink/nod, "but that particular nugget doesn't change the fact I'd like to curl my mitts around his neck and do a bit of squeezing. "

"Ditto," *Utah* growled while displaying a spark of renewed energy by raising his hands and shaping them into claws.

From there we fell into a comfortable silence that lasted until keeping their rather laid-back pace became more of a strain than a relief. Upon cresting the last in a trio of fairly steep upgrades and noting *Utah*'s increasingly worrisome grunts and groans, I was mentally prepping to push into a higher gear when the Porto-potties swam into sight. Having temporarily shoved aside the slight pressure at my bladder, the mere thought of impending relief caused an almost instantaneous spasm that cried out for imminent release.

Like many men nearing the big five-oh, I'd had recently experienced some battles with frequent urination and prostate issues, the latter of which had recently graduated to twice-a-year checks in lieu of my family history, which included both a grandfather and three uncles dying from related cancers.

"Well, thank the good lord above . . . " I heard *Dakota* exclaim with unbridled joy, while *Utah* echoed the sentiment with a loud clapping of hands.

"Gents, allow me to make the feeling unanimous. Now, before I spring a premature leak. . . " I blurted before taking off in a mad sprint.

Drawing to within ten yards of the first of four separate units, all hard plastic and roughly the shape and size of squared telephone booths from another era, I watched a door sling open on the nearest and *New York*'s large frame emerge. Before dashing off in a light jog, the man appeared to break character with a brief smile and accompanying nod, as if somehow reading our collective thoughts. I pondered only briefly how the man had gotten back *ahead* of me before matters of a more dire nature took precedent.

I passed up the first unit, from which *New York* had exited, and chose instead the second, not even thinking about knocking first. Luckily there'd been no one on the stoop, as I'd had my shorts pulled midway down even before the rather flimsy plastic door had shut behind me.

Though I'd drained less than half the canteen

with its allotted twenty-six ounces of spring water, the full minute I'd spent draining my bladder hinted otherwise. I departed the unit with a renewed spring in my step, the resurgent burst of energy probably due to more than sixty-seconds of inactivity while ridding myself of bodily fluids.

Having decided that another period of self-induced isolation was in order, I practically sprinted back onto the trail in order to put some distance between myself and the field, particularly my most recent traveling mates. As I neared yet another steep incline, this one littered in jagged, oversized gravel, I thought I heard either *Dakota* or *Utah* exit their respective Johns, but refrained from turning about in acknowledgement. For some reason, I felt it might come off as mocking, and coming so soon after the shared experience of the '*Ice-Man*', I surely didn't want to be viewed in such a negative light. Strange thinking, really, since the notion of establishing relationships was so logically frowned upon by all involved. I shouldn't have cared one way or another, but was quickly learning that human nature dictates the majority of all we are, no matter the conscious effort to alter one's inbred tendencies. Once I'd topped the hill, thankful I hadn't fractured an ankle on the dangerously uneven, constantly sliding terrain, the solitude I'd sought swam so clearly into focus I was temporarily convinced it was nothing more than a cruel, heat-induced mirage. The trail ahead, for as far as my slightly bleary eyes could see, looked as flat as a freshly heated hotcake, though on the negative side was sans even the tiniest of shade as the surrounding vegetation was sparse at best; nothing but gnarled shrubs and ankle-high sea-grass. Still, after the barrage of curving, rolling mounds that had dominated the landscape for the majority of the sector, it was a sweet sight indeed. Better yet, over the approximate half-mile the flat grounds appeared to cover, not a single competitor emerged. If I played my cards right and maintained a steady speed, I figured to finish out the sector in utter isolation, lost in my own thoughts and without a single outside distraction other than whatever sadistic weather pattern might lay ahead.

Treading cautiously downward, I practically hopped, skipped and jumped from rock infested grounds onto the smooth, soothing clay. From there, I checked my cap-cam for correct positioning and reset my I-Pod for a bone jarring set of late twentieth century heavy-metal tunes.

The next hour or more, was spent in a rather pleasant daze, wherein the heat and humidity steadily increased but the effects minimized by the admittedly cautious, pedestrian pace I'd set and the wonderful distraction of steel-rim guitars, thundering bass and pounding drums. Along the way, I'd purposely slowed a degree upon visualizing a half-dozen competitors fast-walking perhaps a hundred yards in the distance, only one of which I was able to identify. With his emaciated frame and wobbly gait, the Ice-Man pulled ahead of the pack and thus was the first to vanish from sight around a sharp left-hand turn. Momentarily struck by a wave of anger just at the thought of that foul-mouthed blow-hard leading the competition and thus being the first to exit my home field, I took off in a sprint only to quickly wilt in the immense heat and return to a less strenuous pace. Of course, I could only approximate the heat and humidity levels, but figured the former to be hovering near the ninety mark with the latter treading similarly dangerous heights. These were conditions I could easily identify with a late July or early August afternoon, usually on the eve of a particularly nasty storm. The mercifully sparse ensemble we'd been afforded was literally pasted to my person like soggy netting, and my eyes stung with the constant flow of fresh sweat pooling within.

Another fifteen minutes, wherein I'd forgone the I-Pod for the soothing hum of my own semi-labored breathing, and I somewhat reluctantly caught up to the five bodies whom Ice-Man had so effortlessly passed. I split between the first two, both of which appeared to be under considerable strain merely to remain upright, though understandable considering their home states. *New Hampshire*, a chubby black woman with humongous breasts, was huffing like a runaway freight, her drooping eyes and sagging shoulders a testament to what southern heat can do to those unaccustomed to its cruel, merciless ways. Meanwhile, *Delaware*'s chosen rep fared little better, despite the man's slim, taunt frame and athletic looks. His mouth hung open like a lowered draw bridge, a low wheezing sound pouring from his throat as both arms hung limp. As I passed, I could hear his heels dragging on the burnt clay with each cumbersome step; a sure sign of building fatigue.

"Well, look who's gracing us with his blue-blooded presence," I heard Nevada blurt as I'd drawn even.

"Greetings, card-shark," I responded with a tip of the cap-cam, "so how's this south of the border disorder weather treating an old desert rat like yourself?"

Peering upward into a sudden build-up of grayish, rather ominous looking clouds, Vegas covered his eyes with the palm of one hand and scowled.

"As torturous as this blessed heat and humidity are, I'm thinking they're serving as nothing more than a sneak preview of the nastiness to come. "

I also gave the rapidly darkening skies a quick glance and was hapless to do anything save echo the man's remarks.

"Afraid you might have something there. Those cumulonimbus monsters look like they're about to give birth. Might make that last squall look like an April shower. "

To that, the gambler grunted without further elaboration.

"Well, hiya Blue Grass," Ole Miss said with a grin, having whirled about apparently upon recognizing my voice. Walking backwards, she practically ran up the back of *North Carolina*, who groaned his disapproval. A large-framed man with a pointy gray beard and a slight hunch to his upper back, he had managed to avoid collusion only with a graceful side-step maneuver that made me wonder if he had listed formal dance training as part of his resume.

"Whoa, careful there," I said, unable to refrain from a light chuckle at her clumsily executed break-dance, "don't need any avoidable pile-ups on the interstate."

"You see all these lily-livered yanks wiltin' like rose petals in a campfire?" she winked while nodding in the general direction of *Delaware* and *New Hampshire*, who had each fallen a good two-dozen yards behind.

"I understand the strategy, if not the illogic of said plan."

"Say again, Professor Thesaurus," she said with a comically confused scowl. Walking forward yet again, she fell back a few steps until we were stood shoulder to shoulder.

"They figured they could mount a good start amid unfamiliar conditions. All the better with their own home field pending. Thing is, you'd best be able to recover from one sector's punishment to the other. Otherwise, your dead meat walking regardless of conditions or the terrain."

"Dead-mea-. . . damn, boy. . . feed my paranoia, why don't you?" she said with a gentle elbow tap to my left bicep in what seemed a perfectly sincere expression of affection that I found strangely annoying. As cold logic surely dictated, this was not the arena to make new friends nor influence people, though the number of folks that seemed oblivious to these particulars was growing by the hour.

"You know what I mean," I said curtly, moving away a half step.

"Ain't my deodyrant is it?" she replied jokingly with a quick sniff directed at her left armpit.

Try as I might, to not respond might well have tossed me into the same rancid category of Jackass as the Ice-Man, a title I was as of yet unwilling to accept.

"At this point, my lady, I doubt any occupying the pathway can claim to be anything less than paint-peeling polecats. "

Ole Miss laughed long and hard, eventually leaning forward as if to topple face-first into the dusty clay. Such a condition practically forced her to slow the pace, giving me a clear-cut opportunity to break away, which I took advantage of without hesitation though not without a twinge of regret. Much like with Sagebrush or *North Dakota*, I could easily envision her and I establishing an effortless, easy-going rapport. More the reason to escape before the temptation to do so grew stouter than the capacity to flee.

"Take care, Miss *Mississippi*. This *Kentucky* racehorse is gonna make some serious tracks. "

"Y-you go f-for it, B-Blue grass," I heard her reply between strained giggles, "catch y-ya on the flipside. "

I flashed her a final wave without turning and set my sites on *North Carolina* a dozen or so steps ahead. Following his speedy separation from Ole Miss climbing his spine, the man had obviously slowed down a degree and was breathing from his nostrils as a low whistle was heard with each lengthy exhale.

Almost the same exact moment I caught up to

and passed him by switching gears from fast-walk to light jog, I heard *Nevada* chime in with a delayed, but not at all surprising, combination warning/challenge.

"Better build that lead, KFC," he bellowed from between what sounded like cupped hands.

"Come those western U. S. *desert climes*, you sure as hell are going to need it!"

Meaning of course, his home-field of choice, no doubt the one he'd trained hardest to claim, if for no other reason than local pride. To each his own, certainly, though personally I'd set my sites on the two sectors most likely to *hinder* a man of southern U. S. upbringing, that being Northern and mid-western, respectively. For the former, I'd spent many an hour jogging in place and shadow-boxing inside a walk-in freezer with temps set as low as five degrees below zero and box fans positioned from virtually every possible angle. More than once I'd departed said units with ice-coated eyebrows and freezer-burned cheeks of both the facial and posterior kind.

Prepping for the latter sector was much trickier, and consisted mostly of either planning lengthy jogs and/or walks whenever a hard, lingering rainfall was predicted, or similar treks when the forecast was just the opposite, meaning lots of sun and little or no humidity. No easy task that, considering the location of said training. In truth, there was only so much one could do in terms of physical prep, as Mother Nature rarely saw fit to grant such wants. Besides, as with all such marathons, it was truly more about mental toughness than who had the stronger set of legs or lungs. In the end, it was just as Kay the advisor had so eloquently put it during our final counseling session the day before I hopped aboard a plane bound for the dome.

"You can't just out-think or outrun, jump or walk them," she'd said while peeking over the top edge of her bifocals, "you're going to have to out-determine them. You're going to have to transcend what all humans *think* they know about pain and anguish.

The winner of this gauntlet," she'd concluded with a tight-lipped smile, "will be, bar none, the ultimate middle-aged survivor and will surely be crowned as such for the rest of their days and beyond, for no matter how many more such gauntlets are held, they will have been the first. They would have set the bar for all that followed. "

Unfortunately, there were numerous scenarios set in place that were absolutely prep-proof; scenarios that, until faced, made gauging one's response an impossibility. The hard rain and gusting winds had, in retrospect, been nothing more than a rather bland appetizer in comparison to the scorching impact of the main course to come.

Part Three: Path of Destruction

Time: Two hours, forty-five minutes into the Iron-Will Gauntlet
Place: Sector A
Total miles covered: Thirteen and three-quarter

It began with a few harmless sprinkles,hardly enough to moisten the flesh, unlike the previous deluge. As for winds . . . almost non-existent; only the occasional light breeze as a reminder of our presence within the great outdoors, however simulated. For an individual born and raised North or far West of the Mason-Dixon, these two elements meant little in terms of an impending threat from above. Similarly, such an individual might shrug off the woefully out of place yet undeniably soothing coolness of said breeze, happy just for a brief respite from the hellish humidity. However, there are those who view all the above as individual warning signs for potential carnage in the making. Those, say, born below said invisible demarcation line. Those a bit wiser to such sudden drastic alterations in climate, who perhaps had spent many a night hunkered down in a storm shelter hoping to emerge with the nearby homestead still intact. Scanning a darkening cloud build-up that seemed to dip lower by the second, I soon found myself ogling the trail ahead for a suitable ditch.

"Damn, but you're a hard man to run down," I heard a familiar voice boom out, sounding much closer than it actually was due to the over-abundance of dead air.

Turning about and walking slowly backwards, I felt a wave of unabashed relief to see Sagebrush jogging my way at a fairly brisk pace.

"Must be that race-horse pedigree thing rearing its ugly snout. "

Slowing to a virtual crawl once she'd closed to within a few dozen feet, she reached up with both hands to adjust the cap-cam, which sagged from wetness and thus appeared comically droopy.

"Cactus Jane, I presume . . . you sure made up some time," I said rather dourly, fighting hard to play down just how pleased I truly was to be back in her company. Resemblance to that *other* woman aside, I couldn't deny the instant kinship I'd sensed upon our first meeting. I felt at ease in her charming, likeable presence, and despite the usual reservations, was no longer in the mood to fight the feeling.

"Not bad for a skinny chick born, bred and trained for dry-heat. "

"Hey, I can take the raised thermometer with the best of 'em, Buddy-Boy. You're looking at a semi-regular on the marathon circuit back in desert country. Fact is, I finished eighteenth in the Tucson Iron-Woman several years back. Even this southern-fried flesh-cooker can't hold a candle to a forty-five mile trek in ninety-degree heat. "

Pumping out her chest in mock pride, I detected just a tint of defensiveness in her tone.

"Forty-fi-?" I practically shouted, widening my eyes to dramatic effect while placing a hand over my heart, "ah-hah! So exclaims the *ringer*. Safe bet you ran through that last squall without a hitch. "

Reaching back, she gave her backpack a gentle tap.

"Never even unpacked the plastic, dude. If I'd been in possession of soap in bar form, this girl would surely be smelling ivory-clean about now. "

"I have no doubts. Feel that wind?" I asked, spreading both arms up and out as the light sprinkle picked up a bit of steam, as did the aforementioned breeze.

"Yep. . . not good, I surmise. "

"You surmise correctly, my sweet desert flower. As my Uncle Jarvis used to say, and he was definitely the quotable one in the family, '*we in for some serious pandemonium.* "

I couldn't help but find her expression, a warped, comical hybrid of utter confusion and apparent disbelief, equal parts hilarious and strangely seductive.

"And you say this Uncle Harvey was the quotable one? Lord, must've been a regular knee-slappin' hoot-nanny at the annual family reunion. "

"*Jarvis.* . . and you ain't just whistling dixie," I managed to reply as my chest and abdomen shook and shimmied from a barely refrained belly-laugh.

As the showers dissipated yet again, we fell into a comfortable silence while approaching possibly the steepest hill thus far, a pumpkin-shaped mound that appeared to incline rapidly, unlike so many before it that possessed a gradual upswing to allow at least for partial adaptation.

"Break out the climbing gear," I said with a

heavy dose of sincere dread, acutely aware of the faint throbbing at my ankles, knees and thighs.

In response, Sagebrush played the role of optimist, though the sincerity of her tone was far less so.

"Ah, buck up, dude. Just think of the easy ride on the way down. "

Sucking in a deep lung-full as we began the ascension, my only response was a weak shrug.

"Hey, at least they cut off the water-works," she continued unabashed, skipping playfully ahead a few steps.

"Gotta stare down that mythical glass as half-full at this juncture in the game. I mean, if we take the negative approach this early, we'll surely be on suicide watch by Sector C, am I right?"

"Whatever you say, *Mary Poppins*," I grumbled, and upon receiving the expected turn-about and facial frown, shot her a wink. Unable to mask her grin, she whipped her head back around and faced front, and I couldn't help but focus the brunt of my attention on her well-toned buttocks.

"Mary Poppins? Dude, you show all the classic symptoms of being hopelessly submerged in a twentieth century time-warp. "

I shrugged yet again as we grew to within a dozen agonizing steps of cresting the massive hill. Though the clay track was sufficiently dry and grooved just enough to prevent any form of slippage, I felt it more than a mild struggle to maintain a steady pace.

"I consider that a compliment, my lady. That is, having spent my childhood in said century, and a mighty happy childhood at that. Can't honestly state the same in regard to the one that followed. "

Falling back until we were side by side yet again, she tilted her head towards me and placed a clenched fist beneath her chin, studying me intensely.

"Talk to me, dude. This shoulder may be small and a bit rounded, but it's been known to endure bucket-loads of shed tears. "

"Believe me, Doctor Sagebrush m'am," I quipped just as the other side of the mountainous mound began to swim into view, "there ain't a couch wide or waterproof enough to sustain the tidal wave that would ensue. Why, we'd both require life-jackets and perhaps a canoe to be ab-. . . "

The reminder of what was intended to be a witty, charming rant hung at the base of my throat, as if I'd swallowed a mouthful of chalk. Staring straight ahead through widening eyes that no longer held the power to blink, I instinctively dug my heels into the hard clay and felt both knees scream their disapproval. Sagebrush had continued forward several strides, and I can only speculate her own clumsily-executed halt was solely due to my bug-eyed, pale-as-a-ghost expression, as she had yet to visualize the approaching horror awaiting us over that hill.

The cloud buildup to our backs that I'd found so threatening was a fluffy white snow-bank compared to the swirling, tar-black masses ahead, but even that wasn't the most immediate concern. It's what said masses had birthed that caused every nerve ending I possessed to go numb and institute a rash of uncontrollable spasms in and around my lower extremities. The twister rode the trail perhaps a hundred yards ahead, centered so perfectly it was as if it were literally placed there to ride forth on transparent rails like some ghostly runaway freight car. The upper portion, still linked to its parent cloud like a squirming child awaiting separation from the umbilical cord, appeared a mile wide, slimming down to a spear-like tip that dug into the hard clay like a levitating jack-hammer, drilling deep and spewing forth large chunks of mangled earth.

Even worse than nature's fearsome beast itself, it was what I'd seen tossed about within the mighty twister's spinning maw that caused me to temporarily doubt my own sanity. I'd seen legs and arms. . . several sets or perhaps just one...spun around like pureed veggies within the whirling, slashing blades of some colossal blender. At the time, I had to figure what I'd saw, or *thought* I'd saw, was nothing more than a stress-related hallucination; a horrific mirage created solely from the darkest passages of a mind frayed by the starkest fear it had ever encountered. Lord, to be proven wrong on such a logical assumption wasn't the least bit reassuring.

"Wh-what's wrong? Y-you. . . are you alright? Is it your heart?" I think I heard the woman to my left bellow; a woman that I didn't know from Adam but suddenly felt wholly responsible for protecting. Backing slowly away, I reached for her just as she finally turned to face forward.

"Oh . . . sh-hitttt . . . "she mumbled, though by then I was forced to read the words from her trembling lips as the surrounding air had been saturated by a thunderous roar I can only compare to that of standing on a tarmac as a dozen jet airliners simultaneously zoomed overhead.

Pulling her by the crock of the elbow, I found her immensely stout despite her petite frame. She had gone stiff, frozen by fear, her mouth opening and closing in spastic rhythm, like that of a stage puppet whose master was testing its strings. Her eyes were saucers, pulled so impossibly wide I was briefly terrified that they might well pop from their sockets and roll down the adjoining hill like tossed marbles.

"Come on. . . we have to find a low spot!" I shrieked, or at least something similar. It's impossible to know for sure in the midst of such deafening havoc.

I stumbled back and almost fell, the act of hanging onto her arm possibly saving me from a nasty tumble. Finally, mercifully, she snapped too and joined me in backtracking down the hill we'd conquered just seconds before. I looked back only once, using my free hand to secure the cap-cam, and saw a form whiz overhead in a shadowy blur. Perhaps, I pray so at least, it had merely been a section of tree, its attached limbs so closely resembling flailing human appendages due solely to the frayed wiring of an overtaxed imagination. In retrospect, I knew better. At the time, I had to create a plausible excuse or simply go stark, ranting mad; maybe even to the point of simply lying down, closing my eyes and letting the funnel take me for a final, fateful ride.

The deep ditch I'd so casually searched out since first sensing the impending storm was non-existent, but there had been a few select low spots just off the trail that appeared sufficiently concave, slight dips that looked, perhaps not coincidentally, to have been designed especially to house a prone human body.

The thunderous, ear-splitting roar intensified as I'd practically forced Sagebrush into the only slightly depressed spot of earth; in truth it was far less concave than say, your average bathtub, and then dove on top of her. I could only deduce, as the building pressure threatened to pop my eardrums, that the base of the massive funnel had crested the hill and was making a B-line directly our way. Being that the semi-ditch was located no more than a dozen feet or so from the trail, I could only hope and pray the twister would either go airborne before entering our space or, even better, veer off the path completely and perhaps ravage the faux foliage which lined the opposite side. All prayer and good wishes aside, the bottom line was programming; as in, the thing was going to do precisely what it was preset to do by whatever team of sick, demented eggheads had deemed it so.

Though the duration of the event probably lasted no more than forty seconds to a minute, it seemed I lay atop Sagebrush's struggling, squirming frame for at least five times that length. At one terrifying point, I actually felt my feet and legs pulled airborne, along with the backpack, levitating for several horrible moments as if being pulled by the suctioning blades of a powerful industrial fan. Eventually, the trio descended, though not before sustaining a potentially serious casualty as my left tennis shoe had dislodged and apparently sailed into parts unknown. As with the winds themselves, the roar subsided, though its blaring echoes would remain between my ears until Sector A had been duly exited.

"Y-you ca-can get o-off now," I heard Sagebrush announce weakly, a condition easily explainable considering how my dead weight was no doubt constricting her lungs. I rolled away to my left, pulling the back pack forward and digging inside its limited space for my canteen. Feeling a sudden sting at the tip of my right elbow, I peered down to see I'd somehow sustained a nasty gash perhaps two inches wide that had yet to bleed despite appearing significantly deep to do so.

"S-sorry. Just wanted to . . . make sure, you know?"

She arose onto all fours, stretching her neck from side to side to loosen the kinks. Outright bizarre as it might sound, I found her choice of positioning powerfully seductive despite the circumstances.

"N-no complaints, dude. J-just happy to be here is a-all. "

As we stood with an almost comically harmonized groan, I couldn't help but notice how remarkably attractive she remained despite an overall look of dishevelment which included a fresh coating of clay marking the front of her shirt in a wide, maroon stripe. As for myself, I was relatively dust and dirt free except for the healthy portion coating my tongue and teeth, to which I spat several times into a nearby shrub to properly evacuate with the aid of a mouthful of canteen water. Turning back to Sagebrush, who'd been facing the hill as I stood with my back to it, I was temporarily oblivious to her wild-eyed expression as a fresh rant ensued, complete with waiving arms and rolling eyes.

"Can you believe *that*? For a second, once we topped that hill, my mind wasn't able to . . . figure . . . compute exactly what it was I was seeing. It was like . . . nope, that can't be what I think it is . . . not now . . . not *here*. It just didn't seem possi- . . . "

She nodded silently, lifting a shaking hand to point directly over my left shoulder. At that point, though a bit perturbed at the interruption, I turned casually about, no longer on alert since the winds had dissipated to a mild breeze and the skies had lightened a degree.

The steep, melon-shaped hill we'd previously ascended in victory before descending in terror had been reshaped in rather dramatic fashion, looking as if several feet had been shaved off its peak, leaving behind a jagged crater. A crater whose starting point was yet unseen on the other side, though the exact *ending* spot was easily visualized roughly fifteen to twenty feet from where we had lain. Miraculously, or better yet clearly by design, the twister had lifted off before growing close enough to suck us inside its spinning maw. Obviously if in panic we'd chosen a flatter ground for cover six or seven yards further up that hill, the outcome wouldn't have been nearly as positive.

"Saw my share of twister damage over the years," I said hoarsely, refitting my cap-cam, which had been sitting askew, hip-hop style, since the event, "that looks like a meteor the size of your basic semi-tracker played jackhammer . . . repeatedly. Jesus, whatever warped egghead came up with that monstrosity has to be dancing a psychopathic jig about now. "

"Did you, I mean, was it . . . did you see, when we were at the top of the hill and first spotted the funnel . . . " she stammered, and that was when I first realized how truly shaken the woman was. Her hands were trembling so badly she was forced to fold them across her chest, and her eyes gleamed with fresh tears. I started to step forward to comfort her, but stopped just short in the realization of yet another powerful flashback to the person she so reminded me of. A person I was utterly incapable of assisting in any way, shape or form, at least from a conscious standpoint.

"Before you pulled me . . . away, I thought I . . . there were . . . *things* being whipped around inside . . . trapped th-there. Not just branches, but . . . but . . . Did you s-see . . . " she pleaded with an intense stare and slight tilt of the head.

"I saw 'em. Or . . . thought I did. Who's to say it just . . . resembled what we're . . . what we *thought* we saw. In my own case, I wasn't exactly thinking straight, and it's been proven that stress does strange things to the old noodle," I said, tapping a forefinger against my left temple for added emphasis and sounding a shade more defensive than I'd intended.

"How many were in front of us, you think?" she asked as we trudged forward onto the ravaged trail, each of us inexplicably stepping so gingerly one might've thought a live minefield lurked beneath our sneakers, or in my case, sneaker. The humidity was rapidly returning, and what little breeze was present was of the sickeningly warm variety.

"I'd guess twenty, maybe more. Maybe even half the field. "

What she was digging at was no mystery, though I could feign ignorance with the best of them. After all, she might've resembled that *certain* person who'd made reading my thoughts an hourly ritual, but certainly held no such similar power.

"You figuring odds already? Little early, don't you thin- . . . "

"I wonder how many were . . . just up ahead. Just over the hill when that abomination decided to dip down and play road-plow. "

"Dunno," I said, kicking away large chunks of clay with my one remaining shoe to avoid twisting an ankle on their misshapen ranks. Unlike its completely intact predecessor, the center of the hill had been so dramatically gutted we had reached its crest in roughly half the time, "I'd venture to say none in the general area. We were pretty spread out from what I've seen in the last hour. Most of the gun-sprinters were determined to build that initial lead, no matter the future cost, as in a probable cardiovascular meltdown. "

Booting away her own share of toothed debris, she feel silent as we neared the jagged gully that had been the top of the hill, and it wasn't until I heard her gasp that I realized she'd left my side.

"What is it?" I asked, though struck with a sudden bolt of primal fear in the certainty I really didn't want to know. She had fallen to one knee and was staring down into the mangled earth, pawing away at her discovery.

"You tell me. "

Stepping over with a heavy dose of apprehensive dread, I took up position directly behind her kneeling frame and peeked over her left shoulder.

"Kinda makes you wonder what lies beneath, ay?" she quipped with a wry grin, peering up towards me through squinted eyes.

It appeared to be some kind of metallic screen or filter; as black as the ace of spades and littered with dime-sized holes obviously utilized for drainage. Sweeping still more dirt and clay from the ravaged path revealed its presence as anything but localized. Simply put, it served as a, perhaps even *the,* bottom layer of the false nature trail, placed approximately three to four full feet from the equally artificial topsoil.

Placing a socked foot atop the surprisingly solid vent, I gave it a cautious but stout push and felt no signs of give.

"Probably a steel frame of sorts to properly solidify the whole shebang. Or who knows? Could be regulation terra firma holding her up. After all, the *real* stuff has to be down there somewhere, right?"

"Guess I have to concur, Blue Grass," she said, pausing to groan as she arose with a loud popping of knees, "although it wouldn't shock me in the least to find out this whole tragic drama isn't being played out at a higher altitude than we could ever imagine. "

"Meaning what exactly?" I replied with purposeful skepticism as we briefly stood practically nose to nose, though she did so with her face tilted slightly upward.

"Up in the strats, my man—outer space. "

"Say w-what?" I managed following a sincere belly-laugh that felt damn good despite the instant draining effect.

"Just saying. Might be nothing but open space 'neath our sneakers...dead space at that. Hey, what better place to jettison those unfortunate souls unable to complete the gauntlet? *And they were never heard from again,*" she concluded with a combination wink/nod as we whirled about to continue the trek forward. A few hundred feet to our rear we saw several blurred bodies swim into view around a sharp curve, though neither of us seemed interested in identifying any within the lot.

"Interesting theory, if not a bit radical or even, pardon me for blunt honesty, a tad on the loony-tunes side. "

"Really, Mister Smarty-pants? Seriously, they could've shipped us to the dark side of Uranus and we'd be none the wiser. "

"Can't buy it," I smirked, waiving her off, "the stink would surely give it away. "

"Call me a conspiracy nut, but I wouldn't put nothing pa-. . . " she prattled, pausing momentarily before regarding me with a stern stare that was about as authentic as the crumbled clay beneath our feet.

"Oh, you're hilarious, dude . . . nothing like a little anal-wart humor in the aftermath of a near death experience. "

We began our descent on equally savaged grounds, each of us sidestepping the majority of the way to avoid the aforementioned potential for ankle or knee injury.

Upon reaching flatter, though equally mangled terrain, we simultaneously picked up the pace without announcing plans to do so. The next fifteen minutes passed in comfortable silence, the lone moments save our rapidly pumping appendages that of the occasional wiping away of built-up fop sweat from the forehead or face.

"So how much farther to the end of this damn smelting pot?" she asked, possibly trying to sound feisty but falling woefully short as we were being gradually enveloped on both sides of the trail by a gathering of tall pines, several of which had seen major damage from the twister, showcasing either badly twisted or completely severed limbs. A few had even been dislodged from the ground altogether, their upturned trunks sprouting roots that, at least from a distance, appeared painstakingly genuine.

"We're nearing the three hour mark, so I'd venture to guess another forty-five minutes to an hour, tops. "

"Gotta say, dude, it can't come too soon for this girl. I'm in desperate need of a fresh canteen and change of undies, not necessarily in that order. "

"I'm with you, woman, on both counts," I replied in the realization that my crinkled, rain and sweat soaked briefs had long since melted into the flesh of my groin and rear end, "not to mention a shoe to match both feet. "

I'd been the first to spot the body, hanging from a badly drooping pine limb some thirty feet above the trail. Apparently playing off the initial sighting as a mere trick of the eyes, I'd executed a whiplash-inducing double-take that did not go unnoticed by Sagebrush, whose throaty gasp soon followed as we'd both skidded to a stop directly beneath the source.

In terms of the horrors on display, there was both good and bad news; the good being that the suspended casualty's face had been facing upward and thus what was most likely a rather ghastly expression was hidden from our view. The bad, however, seemed to make up for that particular favor, as the body itself was obviously laying face-*down*, hanging appendages and all, within the elbow of the v-shaped limb, meaning said noggin had been twisted completely around in order to avoid all visual intrusion from below. Worse yet, while the left leg, and accompanying sneaker-less foot, swung down freely and even shifted slightly with each passing gust of wind, the bare heel of the right tickled its host's upper left shoulder, the grisly meaning of such astonishing agility not lost on either of us. Sagebrush spoke first, reaching over to gently massage the underside of my left forearm with badly shaking fingers.

"Oh, g-god . . . could he . . . be . . . still be . . . alive?"

"Not a chance," I responded in a voice so strangely alien it was as if my hearing had numbed in time with the rest of my frame, "if that funnel sucked him in, he probably died instantly. That is, if the poor bastard had any luck at all. "

"C-can you tell what...state?" she whimpered, now gripping my wrist in a gradually tightening vice.

"Looks like . . . orange maybe?"

"*Tennessee?*"

"Could be, but I'm not exactly up on my state colors. Didn't *Alabama* talk about catching up with that certain rep?"

"I do believe so, yeah, now that you mention it. "

"Good-sized fella with a head-full of solid gray hair, though that might be the result of what he saw coming at him in those final seconds. Damned if I didn't age a decade myself when we topped that hi . . ."

I heard her wail, under her breath at first like a strained whisper as her nails dug into the crock of my elbow, before cranking the volume several notches to a final climax that was just short of a full-blown scream. At first ignorant to the origin to this latest bout of hysteria, I finally locked on the source once she'd practically shoved me into its line of sight.

This one was obviously female, the majority of

her reddish-brown shirt having been ripped from her torso, leaving only an inch or so beneath the collar. Her long, strawberry-blonde locks, sans the missing cap-cam, swayed and flowed like drifting seaweed within calm ocean waters. Unlike the human tree ornament from moments previous, this one had been placed face down, though similarly had not quite been allowed to reach solid ground. Impaled through the abdomen on the spear-like tip of a decapitated pine, she dangled like a speared fish, appearing to reach down with each outstretched limb for precious mother earth. Her eyes were pulled wide and seemed horribly aware; her blood-drenched mouth fully agape and frozen in a silent scream of eternal anguish. With that, my throat filled with warm bile and I practically shoved Sagebrush to one side in order to turn and step away to avoid a potential projectile emission. Despite obvious distractions, I was able to capture the gist of my traveling companions impending rant while falling to one knee and securing the back of my left hand against pursed lips.

"Dear lord . . . I never dreamed they would . . . allow something like this to actually happen. Is that what we are to them after all? Just f-fodder to be toyed with? And for what. . . ratings? When they babbled about potential dangers, I figured along the lines of heat stroke or severe frostbite at worst. Not . . . not mangled corpses littering the g-goddamn trees!"

"Maybe . . . it was a mistake," I mumbled, still fighting periodic waves of nausea, "maybe their... pet monster ju-just got out of their control. "

Turning on me like a startled cat with its claws drawn and prepped to strike, I was suddenly taken back yet again by a strong sense of déjà vu.

"Is that an ill-timed attempt at humor, man? Tell me you're not *nearly* that dense. You hearing any emergency sirens blaring our way? Seems to me they'd be a plan in place in case of such tragedy, yes?"

Peering up into her contorted, snarling mug, the illusion was surely complete. I'd witnessed a similar expression more times than I'd ever care to recall in an earlier incarnation; one I had spent months attempting, in agonizing vain, to permanently jettison from my subconscious. Suddenly, the urge to sprint away from her at full bore was overwhelming. Instead, I scanned the limited landscape in both directions with the flat of one hand lodged over both eyes to block the light.

"Point taken. Nary a fire-truck or EMS ambulance in sight. "

Rising onto legs so weak and rubbery I was forced to clamp a hand atop each knee for support, I strategically kept my back to the speared corpse. Meantime, my companion began pacing the trail in front of me with her hands folded at her back and her head slightly bowed.

"No such contingency, Blue Grass. They knew . . . know exactly what they're doing. No doubt whatsoever. The viewing public . . . make that *paying* public, loves nothing better than a good, old-fashioned splatter-fest, right? The more gruesome the better. Producers knew they needed to reel 'em in and hook 'em for the long haul with an early completion killing or two. Wasn't about to let us tip-toe outta Sector A without at least a few casualties. Can't have the masses growing bored, no sir, give 'em what they crave. "

Slightly hunch-backed and walking on the tips of her sneakers, she covered the same five to seven yard distance as the rave continued. I couldn't help but think, though with little in terms of actual humor, that she was inadvertently doing a rather impressive Groucho Marx impersonation.

"Not exactly a novel notion, but it surely fits the country's overall mood, for certain. Actually, I'm surprised the last gauntlet was so tame. Nothing more than a foot race, really. You have to admit, Blue Grass, that death and dismemberment beats the living hell outta blood blisters and heat stroke. "

"True," I conceded with a sigh as the trio of competitors we'd spotted earlier emerged yet again from a faraway bend in the trail, "though you have to admit . . . there were hints during in-processing of a possible body count. "

"Yeah, well . . . " she brayed, jerking the cap-cam free and pointing the bill directly towards the dangling deceased, ". . . can't say you were bluffing, now can we? Boy howdy, talk about walking the walk and talking the talk, you boys definitely mean business!"

Still without turning completely about, I gestured with a raised hand towards the oncoming trio headed our way, two of which I now recognized as *North Dakota* and *Utah*. I couldn't help but think of their collective reaction upon viewing the carnage we were about to leave behind. We were all, it seemed, in for one colossal wake-up call—a three-alarm, klaxon-blaring full-bore type call that would certainly go a long way in eliminating all the previous petty bitching and moaning.

"We . . . we need to move on. Company's coming, and I don't much feel like entertaining."

Pulling her headgear back into place, she considered me with a blank, expressionless stare before taking note of the approaching triad.

"Yeah, I concur. Let's make tracks to the finish line. But I'll tell you this much, dude . . . this girl's eyes have been pulled wide-ass open for the remainder of this particular shooting match."

"How so?" I asked, taking up position on her left as to allow a cushion between myself and the carnage. The relief I'd felt at covering fresh ground, sprouting blisters on my socked foot and all, and putting those twin horrors in the proverbial rearview mirror was equally palpable as the humidity which drained our collective sweat glands.

"Just this; all bets are now officially off. The men in the slick suits, leather shoes and tailor-made slacks have removed the kid's gloves for all to take note of. Don't know about you, but despite such unsavory circumstances, there is a definite positive here."

"A positive?"

"Two down, Blue Grass," she grinned; baring her teeth to appear shockingly predatory while lifting two fingers airborne and waiving them in the general direction of the lifeless husks at our backs, "Two down . . . only forty nine remain to beat to the finish line."

"Nice," I replied, unable to form even the tiniest of smiles despite a herculean effort, "warm and fuzzy you ain't, lady."

"*Screw* warm and fuzzy," she hissed, hopping ahead several steps, "it's no longer just survival of the fittest, dude; its survival of the most *fortunate*, and this girl plans on making my peace with dear old Lady Luck. If you're half as smart as I think, you'll do the same."

Though I had not the slightest idea what she was rambling about—a spiritual theme I could only assume—I figured it best to humor her.

"I'm with you, Tumbleweed. Whatever it takes."

The remaining sixty minute jaunt through Sector A went virtually dialogue-free, with the two of us keeping a steady five to ten yard distance between us. The combination of grisly death, blazing sunlight and stifling humidity had drained the urge to verbalize, apparently, a development I had no problem accepting whole heartedly. It was equally relieving, upon visualizing the sector's gated exit, to see *Alabama* blazing the trail perhaps fifty yards ahead. I couldn't help but wonder, watching the severely bow-legged gent approach the great portal that served as an exit from one zone and entrance to another, if he'd ever had that little 'chat' with *Tennessee*, now hanging from a faux pine tree limb with his head sitting atop a grotesquely twisted neck. Needless to say, I wasn't about to inquire. Meanwhile, Sagebrush picked up the pace quite briskly upon viewing the high, brick wall of the portal, bringing to mind perhaps a weary, thirst-ravaged traveler stumbling across a pool of clear, blue water smack dab in the middle of an arid desert.

"Last one to the exit is a rotten egg," I swear I heard her mumble as the distance between us grew to fifteen, then twenty yards. My response, meant as levity, emerged with a faint edge of pent up frustration I hadn't at all intended.

"More like a hard-*boiled* one. "

Sector A was about to be placed securely into the history books. Four hours plus change, and nineteen or more miles soaked in sweat, the initial round consisted mostly of non-events sprinkled with just a pinch of potentially fatal peril that served to liven up the proceedings quite horrifically.

One down, three to go. On the positive side, my personal pains were few and relatively trivial, to include a trio of blisters adorning a certain exposed heel. Mentally, I was still surprisingly sharp and focused, though with the expected, periodic drifts in terms of attention span. Physically, the months of roadwork and grueling two-a-day training sessions were paying off, big time. I'd never been in similar shape, no matter the age.

As for the negative, I couldn't help but think the handful of acquaintances I'd made among my fellow competitors, however artificial in quality, had been a mistake to encourage. One relationship in particular, perhaps not so artificial, had the potential to cause serious conflict if it proceeded further. This would have to be dealt with, and soon. It was one thing to watch strangers mortally wounded or even killed, but an altogether different beast if it involved one considered a budding friend.

The biggest setback, by far, was in the chilling realization that many, perhaps a *majority*, of those competing in the Iron-Will Gauntlet weren't meant to merely walk away humiliated in defeat, but instead, meant not to walk away at all. We weren't just expendable, but as Sagebrush had so correctly stated it, mere 'fodder' to those palming the keys to the magical kingdom. They'd preached the dangers to us, certainly, but only to a guarded degree. There was no reason to think the three remaining sectors would grow easier in succession. Fact was, the safe money spoke to the logic that if anything, the trail ahead would be fraught with fresh danger at every possible turn; a veritable minefield of potential mortality.

As my seemingly wise, if not borderline *schizophrenic* traveling companion had also said, it was going to be as much about timing and luck as skill and perseverance, and this old boy planned on riding a heavy dose of *all* concerned straight to that mystical finish line.

Sector B: Deep Freeze

Part One: Extreme(s): a Pre-Brief

Time: Four hours, sixteen minutes into the Iron Will Gauntlet
Location: Debrief area between Sectors A and B (*Northeastern/Midwestern Winter Climes*)
Total miles covered: Nineteen and one-half

As we neared what I had begun to think of as the '*Great Wall of Change*', the trail narrowed from that of perhaps a four-lane highway to a two and finally to the equivalent of a one-way street. It was like trekking along inside one of those ancient Dr. Seuss 'pop-up' books that had always freaked me out as a kid. Maintaining a ten yard lead, Sagebrush turned back briefly and shrugged without speaking, holding both palms up as if to say, 'what now?'— my sentiments exactly. The Great Wall was a dark shade of brown, as opposed to the ivory shaded metal door at its center. The wall, or at least its outer layer, appeared constructed of marble, and had a slick, moistened look about it. At perhaps twenty feet high and at least twice that in length, it served as the ultimate dead end, an impassable blockade that instantly brought to mind every rat-maze I'd ever seen.

Sagebrush paused at the entrance door, bending with both hands rested atop her knees. She turned in greeting as I approached, sweeping an arm around to indicate the whole of the wall itself.

"I could be wrong, but I'm thinking your home-field advantage just ended. "

"Looks like," I replied, stretching my neck from side to side and hearing several muffled pops in the effort, "either that or we've walked smack-dab into the pages of a Grimm Fairy Tale. "

"There you go with the retro-speak again," she mumbled, rising and turning to the door as if sizing it up for a round of sparring.

"Well, let's not keep 'em waiting. "

"After you, my dear Tumbleweed. "

With that, she reached for the shiny metal handle and pulled it ajar, stepping inside with reckless abandon. I followed several steps behind, and almost gasped aloud as an initial wave of cool, refreshing air slapped my sweat coated flesh. Of course, there was the matter of cruel irony to consider, but at that moment, I couldn't have imagined a more satisfying sensation. From ninety-degree heat, ninety percent humidity doled out beneath blazing rays of sunlight, their legitimacy be damned, to a relatively darkened room cooled with jets of heavenly A/C, it was a temptation to seek out the nearest hiding place and crawl into a permanent fetal position. Alas, those running the show had other, far less tranquil plans.

Once secured inside the stony interior, we found ourselves herded down a narrow hall by two armed, uniformed sentries, each of which gestured in lieu of speaking. They lead us to separate changing rooms which were no bigger than your average truck-stop john. Talk about cutting costs,

I'd guess the Gauntlet's colossal budget had nary a penny to spare for a decent changing area. Handed a blessedly chilled bottle of water, which I struggled not to chug in a single upturned moment of thirst-driven madness, I was then allowed a rather bland-tasting power bar to gnaw on. From there, I was instructed in a comically mechanical tone by my company-assigned assistant to strip down and await clothing and supply issue. Less than two minutes later, I was handed a rather eclectic collection of items, to include an insulated backpack containing the following:

> Refilled canteen (insulated) containing sixteen ounces of water
> Bullet-shaped thermos containing twenty-six ounces of green herbal tea
> Bowl-shaped thermos containing twenty-six ounces of chicken broth soup
> Eight (8) protein bars of unspecified flavors and ingredients
> Lip balm (3 ounce)

In addition, the mute, Vulcan-esque sentry provided a pair of clear eye-goggles, a set of thick, heavily insulated long johns, a thick wool pullover and matching green sweats, one pair of equally bulky socks, and a Hyvent waterproof parka complete with adjustable hood seal. A pair of fur lined mukluks, size eleven and a half, completed the ensemble. I had noted, with a grim smile, the word *Kentucky* stenciled across the parka's upper back region, and couldn't help but dwell on the two or more such coats that would remain ownerless headed into Sector B.

As that little girl from Kansas had been so apt to say just after being whisked off to the magical Land of Oz, I had a feeling the home state, as well as its torrid temperatures and stifling humidity, were set firmly in the rear-view mirror from that point onward.

Minutes later I was decked out in true Nanook-of-the-North fashion, sweating bullets despite the cool interior air, while being led from the changing room down yet another narrow hall and into a sizeable conference room.

A single individual awaited me there, standing with his back turned and his hands folded at the small of his back at the far end of a lengthy oak conference table.

"You're relieved, officer," the man said wearily, hoisting his left arm towards his face to apparently check a shiny timepiece strapped to his wrist, "I'll begin the in-brief upon Miss *Arizona*'s arrival."

"Yes, sir," the robotic sentry replied with all the emotion of a footstool before stiff-legging away with spit-shined boot-heels thumping. Though I didn't recognize the uniform or their weapons of choice, a state of the art Taser of some kind, as being military per say, there was a definite vibe of institutional control with such Gestapo-like individuals roaming about like mechanized Storm-Troopers. Strange, but I couldn't recall laying eyes on a single uniformed type at in-processing. It was all about perception, no doubt, aimed at both the media and competitors alike. Then again, a little security had to be expected surrounding such an event, considering all the vocal opposition to said competition—opposition that included everything from religious sects, anti-government militia and several well established terrorist groups. It was plenty tough enough surviving the internal dangers the Gauntlet provided, much less have to worry about being blown to shreds by outside forces.

"This won't take long," the man said calmly, turning about with all the dramatic flair of a Shakespearian actor; slight tilt of the head and cocked brow intact. Tall and trim, I would've guessed his age as perhaps in the mid-forties to early fifties range despite some obvious facial enhancements and hair so blatantly color-treated it practically glowed orange in lieu of dark brown. Regardless, the man held an undisputable air of authority, be it justifiable or merely a grand illusion. I was reminded of a character actor from the twentieth century I'd admired in my youth-*Fritz Weaver* I believe had been the chap's name. Such men could speak volumes through expression. The expertly tailored suit he adorned was shaded in Mediterranean blue, sans a gleaming, gold-plated tie clip at chest level, and the tips of his dark brown dress shoes appeared as meticulously buffed as the sentries under his command.

"By the way, since you two exited Sector A as one, you will enter Sector B in a similar fashion once the required time has passed inside the pre-adaptation chamber. "

"Excuse me," I replied, tugging on the parka's

fur-lined neck to allow a bit of cool air to leak in, "*adaptation* chamber?"

Placing his hands atop the hips of his shimmering gray dress pants, he appeared the stereotypical annoyed professor on the verge of scolding a rather bothersome student.

"All in due time, *Kentucky*. I'd rather like to avoid a repeat performance or worse yet, have to start anew once your traveling companion does see fit to grace us with her presence. "

"Oh, yeah . . . got'cha. "

Now tugging at the wrists of my gloves for similar relief from the building warmth, I found holding the man's intrusive stare a chore not nearly worth the effort. Instead, I began pacing the spacious room from one end of the lengthy table to the next in an attempt to free at least a level of stiffness from the mukluks, which were binding my ankles like constrictive bands.

Moments later, Sagebrush waltzed into the room with an assigned sentry fast on her shuffling heels. Despite a building discomfort from the overabundance of winter-wear, from which a plethora of flesh-crawling itchiness had been birthed, I couldn't help but guffaw aloud at the comical bagginess of her clothing.

"What're you giggling at, buster?" she retaliated with a huff, blowing away a strand of the hood's fur-lining from pursed lips, "peeked into a mirror lately? You've hardly got room to chastise, *Admiral Bird.* "

Feigning shock, I leaned back with wide eyes and both arms raised.

"Admiral-? Jesus . . . and here I thought I'd been elected the history reference nut. "

She grinned slyly, readying a verbal volley that was never to be in light of a purposely interruptive clearing of the throat from the head of the conference table.

"Pardon me for the intrusion, folks, but we are on a timetable of sorts here," Fritz Weaver's twenty-first century clone interjected with a stern nod.

"You're dismissed, Officer Graves. "

With that, Robo-troop number two sauntered stiffly away, leaving Fritz to lay down whatever competition legality he'd been assigned to explain. Since the room held not a single chair, I twisted around and lifted the bulky rear portion of the parka in hopes of propping my rear end on the edge of the conference table.

"I really, really don't suggest that, good sir," he said dourly, pointing at the spot I'd earmarked to provide temporary relief for legs that screamed for a moment's respite.

"Not being cruel, mind you, but even a few short minutes in said position is going to make resuming the competition that much more difficult. "

Glancing over at Sagebrush, she nodded weakly as if seeing the man's logic, and I somewhat reluctantly resumed my original pose.

"Let's get down to it then, you two. I must say I'm not accustomed to group briefings. The majority are, for good reason, of the one-on-one variety. I presume you are growing quite uncomfortable in those newly issued ensembles, so let us begin . . . "

While speaking in a flat, utterly emotionless tone, much like that associated with computerized phone recordings from a bygone era, the Fritz clone paced the length of the conference table with his hands tucked at the pit of his back and his head slightly lowered. I could only imagine the bone-weary monotony of such an assignment, no doubt repeated verbatim and with nary a single variation, and secretly pondered the possibility that Fritz might well be there to greet us at the entry to the remaining sectors. He was, then, the ultimate talking head, in lieu of say, watching an instructional film. Fritz was a walking, talking Iron-Will operating instruction. Just pull his gold-plated tie clip and away he went, and no doubt for quite the pretty penny.

"First, your delay upon entry is set at fifteen minutes, forty-one seconds. This is timed from the point the last competitor departed our little rest stop, thus said racer is allowed to resume his lead.

Second, I must state, though it is not my duty to do so, that while your arriving together at the entry-point isn't all *that* unusual, this . . . rather unhealthy banter you appear to share is. I know you were counseled on matters of such . . . unwise camaraderie. It must seem trivial and consequently a non-issue so early in the competition, but I'd be derelict without mentioning the budding conflict sure to arise as the marathon progresses. "

I was so tempted to roll my eyes like an unruly teen; I instead focused my gaze on the man's exposed forehead just below his hairline, where I'd taken note of a small splotch of discoloration that, at least from my angle of view, resembled a tiny, brown scorpion set to strike.

"It's simple really, all the misguided friendships you make now might seem harmless, a useful distraction from the pain and fatigue and long, harsh hours on the trail. In the end, however, push will come to shove and the time will come that friends and acquaintances must become enemies. Thus, the following advice isn't likely to shock either of you: Break it off now while it's still relatively painless. To foolishly continue to feed the relationship will only serve to make the inevitable turning more difficult to endure. End of counseling, part one."

Sagebrush and I exchanged a tepid glance as Clone of Fritz halted his incessant pacing, taking up position at the head of the table yet again with his arms crossed and his face contorted in a pained scowl I couldn't help but associate with lingering constipation.

"The choice, of course, is yours. We are, obviously, dealing with a stable of mature adults who really shouldn't require such a dressing down. Now, before escorting you to the pre-adaptation room, allow me to quench a building thirst, curiosity-wise. . . ."

He then fell silent and began to stare me down with a single eyebrow cocked as if awaiting my response. Despite such a brief duration within his company, the man's android-like demeanor and arrogant tone had already grown damned tiresome.

"Well, fire away then, chief . . . " I finally blurted, unable to completely mask my annoyance, "as you stated, the clocks tickin' . . . "

As if to respond to my curt tone, Fritz the Clone then raised his right hand and flashed an ancient, ritualistic salute I vaguely recalled from my childhood.

"Scouts honor, this is strictly off the record and it is something I have and will continue to quiz each competitor who passes through these halls between sectors. "

"Go, man, go . . . " I cajoled, the itching at my neck, shoulders and groin fueling my impatience.

"I know of your backgrounds, of course. Fascinating . . . simply fascinating the scope of each individual case. With that in mind, the question I ask is blunt and to the point. Why?"

"Why? Why what, Slick?" Sagebrush replied after a moment of stilted silence, and I didn't have to actually visualize the sour smirk she'd donned to know for damn sure it was set firmly in place.

"Why put yourself through this? Were your lives that . . . unfulfilling? Was it simply a matter of achieving fame, notoriety, a measure of infamy perhaps? I totally understand if you'd rather not divulge, especially within earshot of one another, but I have to confess to being utterly fascinated at the notion of otherwise intelligent people such as yourselves so casually tossing away all common sense and risking if not your very lives, at least a large portion of your sanity in such a . . . primitive venture. "

In retrospect, considering the man's borderline

100

condescending attitude in basically asking us why we'd been imbecilic enough to compete in the Iron-Will Gauntlet and thus justify *his* paycheck, I believe my reaction was fairly controlled, especially considering the alternative I'd briefly considered—lunging forward to choke the smug superiority right out of him.

"Fair enough question, I guess. Before answering, allow me a similar query. . . "

He nodded weakly, the very gesture a testimony to the man's natural cockiness. He truly considered us lesser beings.

"As you stated, Mister *Kentucky*, fire away. "

"How have some of the others answered?"

"The others," he nodded knowingly, reaching up to stroke his square, clean-shaven chin, "ah, I see. "

"Oh, very impressive," Sagebrush beamed, reaching over to lightly slap my heavily-padded shoulder, "I was kinda wondering about the competition myself. "

For a brief moment, a mere blur in time, I thought I saw Fritz the Clone's eyes narrow to fine slits; slits from which laser beams of searing heat might well shoot out to douse my traveling companion, transforming her into a pile of smoldering black ash. That was one moment. In the next, he was his old stoic, cool-as-a-freshly-picked-garden-veggie self.

"Well, I'm hardly recorded anything for official record, you understand. This is just a personal poll, you might say; a way to gauge the overall mindset. "

Hardly giving the man an opening to continue, Sagebrush fired away yet again with an even healthier dose of sarcasm intact.

"Understood, Slick. So what's the consensus in this little straw poll? What exactly are we saying about one another when no one's around to take offense? Is it truly about the pride, glory and financial well-being of our designated people or are we all just egomaniacal nut-bags with a suicide complex?"

Apparently unfazed by my partner's venom-soaked inquiry, Fritz the Clone stepped back to lean against a far wall, the dull green backdrop of which only emphasizing the gleaming shine of his perfectly fitted suit.

"In truth, Miss *Arizona*, it depends on who I've asked."

"We're not asking you to drop names . . . just their opinions," I injected, pulling the glove off my left hand and tucking it beneath my arm pit so I could engage the maddening itch at the back of my neck with the jagged edges of well-chewed nails.

"Fine. While several did indeed state patriotism and regional loyalty as their sole motivations, a select few others did manage to surprise with less, shall we say, conservative replies."

He paused to brush away a piece of lint from his left sleeve, and I heard Sagebrush's irritated grunt lead off her next verbal volley.

"Such as? Shit, Slick, for a man on such a tight schedule you sure know how to drag out a conversation."

"My apologies—all right, a few select

102

anecdotes and it's off to the prep room, I promise. One rather vocal individual who shall of course remain conspicuously unnamed referred to the lot of you, that being his or her fellow competitors of the Gauntlet, as . . . now, how did he so eloquently put it? Ah yes, a collection of *'self-invested, past their prime, rock-headed limp-dicks and pea-brained, freeze-dried cunts'* with nothing to lose and everything to gain. "

"Ah, a kind, heart-warming rant I could so easily envision pouring from between the gritted teeth of a certain resident of the Mile High city," I blurted with a forefinger raised to the sky, the itch at my upper back so intense I felt a sudden urge to find the nearest curved wall and begin to scratch bear-style.

Meanwhile, Fritz the Clone continued unabated, though checking his watch every thirty seconds or so.

"Um, no comment, *Kentucky*. Opposite such mean-spirited bile came the most patriotic of said reasons, as one of your fellow racers answered thusly with tears brimming from both eyes. She or he said they were doing it for all the starving, under-clothed, and under-educated children of their region. Yes, it sounded like so much syrupy tripe at first I must admit, but as this individual spoke, I saw their hands begin to tremor and shake even as their legs and back stood limber and tall as if called to attention. There was sincere conviction there, people. I truly believe they meant every single word. As for the last competitor through these halls before your arrival . . . well, let's just say they preferred to take the fifth, unless you count threatening to 'choke me silent with my own tie' and then 'hanging my limp ass' from the nearest ceiling fan as an appropriate answer. Quite the surly one, yes indeed, and whose lone facial expression appeared that of someone with a red-hot fire poker shoved deep into their rectum. "

With that, Sagebrush and I each spewed forth a perfectly synchronized guffaw, the effect only enhanced by Fritz's girlish, wide-eyed reaction.

"*New York* I presume?" I asked, tilting my head her way.

"From what I've heard of the big-apple sourpuss, I'd say safe wager," came her smirking reply as Fritz cleared his throat loudly in the background.

"Enough then, what say you two? *Kentucky*?"
I answered as honestly as I knew how. It wasn't as if I had to dwell on it. There was nothing remotely deep to be found. Never patriotic nor self-serving, it was what it was.

"I signed up to prove something to myself... period, end of story. "

Shaking his head back and fro, Fritz then rolled his eyes in apparent dismay. Until that very moment, I didn't think him capable of such emotional flashes.

"That's it? Prove something to . . . *my god*, man, at least feign originality, if only for my sake. "

"Sorry to disappoint, but I rarely lie and only then to friends or close-knit family. As fond as I am for my home state and its people, and the good lord knows the extra funds would work wonders for

104

most of 'em, the Gauntlet was all about pushing your's truly to whatever physical and mental limitations exist. "

With slumped shoulders, Fritz then motioned weakly towards *Arizona*, who stepped past me with a look of stubborn defiance that once again looked oh-so-vaguely familiar, and hardly in a positive way.

"Fine then, be that way. Miss *Arizona*, the stage is yours. "

"Sorry, bud, but what I've got to say isn't liable to perk you up. "

"How utterly shocking to hear . . . " Fritz mocked, followed by a weary sigh.

"Well, it's along same general lines as my esteemed southern comrade here, but with a slight twist. "

"Do tell . . . "

"Sure I'm here to prove something to myself, but also to one other that shall remain, as you're so fond of spouting, conspicuously unnamed. This particular jackass . . . I'll just call 'im *James Doe*, never figured I could wipe my rear end, at least *correctly*, without his help. Years of constant belittlement and brow-beating took its toll, 'til he pretty well had me believing the same thing. I view this gauntlet as the ultimate proving ground. He howled when I signed up, pouted when I made the final one hundred, and practically coughed up a lung when I was finally chosen as State Rep. You see, chief . . . " she continued, her voice shrill; her movements increasingly animated, ". . . the combustible element that stokes this girl's eternal fire is in the belief that James Doe will not get the last laugh. I know the envious prick is rooting for me to fail miserably, even texted me as much just days before I flew out here to compete. It may define the word selfish, but I'm here to see to it that one certain person eats their words, and hopefully chokes on 'em. "

"Well, all right then!" Fritz barked with a loud clap of the hands, a gesture so out of pocket with his normally stoic demeanor I openly winced and hopped back a step.

"That's two votes, *unofficial* votes I might add, for the determined to prove one's self category. Thus far, the runaway winner by far . . . "

"*Unofficially*, of course," I injected with a nod towards Sagebrush, who was still eyeing our MC rather angrily.

"Affirmative, good sir. No records keeping here," Fritz concluded, checking his watch a final time before gesturing for us to follow him from the conference room and back into the dimly lit hallway, "let's be on our way, then. "

"One more quick quiz, Slick, if you don't mind, or *hell*, even if you do. . . " Sagebrush asked, cross-armed and as defiant as ever.

"Of course, but please make it snappy. "

"Two people, at least that we know of, got bagged and tagged out there by your little Wizard of Oz amusement park ride. Was this all part of the script or just a Major-League sized miscalculation?"

The frigid cold I would soon be forced to endure within the glacial realm of Sector B couldn't hold a candle to the chill that arose upon viewing

Fritz the Clone's expression before he responded; so void of basic human emotion it might well have been on display at the nearest morgue laying atop a stone slab.

"No mistake, my dear. Fact is, there are no . . . *accidents* within the dimensions of the Gauntlet, no so called miscalculations. You are *all* part of the plot. The burning question remains, and it is the lone question you should concern yourself with . . . who will survive to the inevitable conclusion?"

With that, I found no dialogue for reply forthcoming. My tongue went numb; as paralyzed as my thought process. The cold hard truth had reared back and slapped the living hell out of all preconceived notions. Belted those mothers right outta the park, you might say. Why, even Sagebrush fell uncharacteristically silent.

Led through a series of winding curves, the surrounding walls as bland and indistinguishable as the slick tile flooring at our feet, I kept a six to eight foot distance between myself and Fritz, while Sagebrush brought up the rear. Within the halls cramped confines, the vapor trail created by the man's cologne of choice was borderline suffocating.

"Since I'm timing your departure into Sector B at just over eleven minutes from now, and the adaptation chamber calls for only five, I believe we have ample time for a brief tour of the com center. You two game?"

"Shit, we have a choice?" I heard Sagebrush growl.

"Sounds like a hoot, as long as we can peel off these parkas," I added, using the fingers of both hands to pry away the jacket's collar away from my skin and allow an influx of cool air.

"Feel free, by all means. "

Departing the hall, we made a sharp right and were soon face to wall with what appeared to be a small freight elevator.

As Fritz busied himself pushing keys on a nearby keypad lock, Sagebrush and I gleefully removed the parkas, folded and tucked them beneath the arm of choice.

The elevator door swung open, and Fritz gestured for us to enter with a combination bow and waive that was positively stately.

"Oh no, you first, Slick," Sagebrush said, pointing into the brightly lit interior, "it's not that I don't trust you specifically . . . just your kind in general. "

Fritz shot me a hurt look, to which I shrugged weakly.

"Sorry, I'm with her. "

With that, he stepped inside and turned towards us, all good humor having quickly departed both his tone and demeanor.

"Really, there is no need for such baseless suspicion," he mumbled as we scooted by and took up position behind him, "I merely wanted to allow a sneak peek into an aspect of the Gauntlet which the participants rarely see or even hear about. "

We descended in silence, though in much less discomfort with the parkas removed from the equation.

When the door reopened, we found ourselves greeted by a pair of uniformed sentinels who appeared cut from the same cloned cloth as the previously sentries; stiff, expressionless drones whose main form of communication was either through telekinesis or a series of curt nods.

Once Fritz flashed a badge of some sort, the twin golems backed away and allowed us passage to a set of dark, green, metal double-doors which were, like seemingly every other room in the place, conspicuously unmarked.

"I do apologize for what appears an overabundance of security, but in these trying times I'm afraid it is necessary. "

"Got'cha Slick," Sagebrush countered as Fritz had turned to face us after punching in yet another passcode, "there's that old *trust* factor rearing its ugly mug, as it is soooo apt to do. "

Choosing wisely to ignore the comment, Fritz reached back to grip a door knob in each hand.

"Good people, I give you . . . the brain center of the Iron-Will Gauntlet. "

The doors shoved inward as Fritz slowly backed away to allow a full view, and I was instantly taken back to every Sci-Fi TV show or flick I'd ever seen showcasing futuristic communications or command centers.

At least two dozen large-screen monitors graced the surrounding walls, spaced approximately two feet apart. A circular table centered the room, where it appeared each of the aforementioned monitors had been assigned their very own controller. Dressed in uniforms identical to the earlier guards, sans the weaponry, each man or woman wore headgear and appeared to be babbling a mile a minute into the wired mike hovering near their respective chins. I briefly pondered who exactly they could be reporting to, that is until being utterly hypnotized by the varied and fascinating scenes being played out on said monitors. Though it took several moments for the frenzied images to swim into proper focus, the origin of these scenes were fairly obvious from the get-go.

"It's the cap-cams," I heard Sagebrush whisper to my immediate right, my only response a silent nod as I stared wide-eyed and perhaps even slack-jawed at the plethora of imagery bombarding us from virtually all angles.

Fritz spoke up, practically shouting in order to drown out the collective hum of the watchers.

"Yes indeed it is, my dear. As you can plainly see, the live feeds appear to show a fairly even split from those still occupying the southern heat of Sector A to those now treading upon the frozen tundra of the destination you two will soon call home. "

True enough, about half the images showcased a clear trail bathed in bright sunlight, while just as many brought home a brutal winter landscape riddled with falling snow and ice-coated terrain. In several cases of the latter, a consistent vapor trail of icy breath could clearly be seen rising up from the cap-cam's wearer. As for the former, most appeared to be suffering from a group outbreak of weariness-fueled tunnel vision, as the majority of cap-cam's seemed focused solely on the trail just ahead of their shambling feet. It was the insufferable heat and humidity, no doubt, having taken a nasty toll on those least equipped to handle the cumulative effect of nineteen or more miles in its slow-roasting grip.

"Boy howdy. Makes me dread the impending cold front a bit less, if nothing else," I muttered, looking over to see Sagebrush nod in apparent agreement.

Stepping forward until he fronted us both in a wide, all-encompassing stance, Fritz raised each arm and flashed upturned palms, and it hit me without humor that in striking such a pose he resembled every sham sales-pitch adman I'd ever seen.

"These fine technicians also have the responsibility of monitoring world events as the Gauntlet transpires. There is the matter of a rather…sensitive political landscape and its possible fallout. These folks are, after all, *soldiers* first. "

Tumbleweed and I exchanged a silent nod in the affirmation that we were indeed under the thumb of some sort of mercenary squad.

"Oh, almost forgot…you'll both be happy to know your own cam-caps have been rebooted and reequipped with special cold-weather protection. A little over six minutes from now, and you'll be right up there representing your home constituency. Doesn't the mere thought provide a much-needed surge of adrenalin?"

Such a tempting opening, thoroughly cornball and seemingly rehearsed, wasn't about to be ignored by my ever-sarcastic, increasingly pessimistic traveling companion.

"Oh yeah, Slick . . . I'm simply *gushing* from below as we speak . . . multiple times, if you get my overly-moistened grip. "

Once again, Fritz ignored the comment and motioned towards the entrance.

"Just over six minutes and counting, folks—on to the adaptation room, then. "

Following a final, lingering look, Sagebrush and I turned as one and exited.

Less than a full minute later, we stood outside a handleless, sliding metal door painted pitch-black, its outer edges coated in whitish frost that naturally stood out amid the tar-colored perimeter. A warning sign, painted in bright red: '*AUTHORIZED PERSONNEL ONLY – Enter at own risk*'. Not exactly comforting, as if we were about to enter a live shooting range. Posed stiffly with his back to the door, Fritz appeared positively downtrodden, even to the point of bowing his head and dropping his gaze to the tile floor as he spoke. If the gist of his act hadn't been so shamefully bogus in its overall execution, it might've rated as at least minimally touching. As it was, the 'caring executive' routine was akin to your basic political speech, the lone mystery being why he even bothered at all. I could only deduce he'd perhaps lain down a series of pre-competition bets on either myself or Sagebrush and hoped for his wallet's sake one or both of us finished well within the top twenty. I'd heard it estimated that Vegas alone had taken in an estimated sixty-eight million in pre-race wagers, the majority of the cash slapped down not in picking a single winner, but a much more popular betting field; that being who would finish in the top twenty. True, the biggest winners would be those talented and/or lucky enough to choose the first place finisher, but most felt it safer, not to mention more favorable odds-wise, to earmark a top twenty and hope for the highest number of correct picks from their chosen group.

"You'll have five minutes before the outer door leading into the Sector is opened. The process might seem overly harsh, but you'll fully understand the method behind the madness soon enough. May I say safe traveling, and good luck. "

"Not to worry, Slick, I'll give it my best shot, and I appreciate both you and your future portfolio's confidence in me," Sagebrush cracked sardonically, reading my mind.

"Or if it's him you're running with," she continued, gesturing towards me with an extended thumb, "you're just another chauvinistic prick I'm out to prove wrong.

Either way, I find it equally motivational. "

Deciding to remain silent in the fear that allowing my lips to part even partially might well produce a maniacal cackle, I instead glanced over to Fritz the Clone and nodded with as much stoic indifference as I could muster. I figured it was only fair in light of his rather lame performance.

"Fair warning, people," he concluded, reverting back to the purely instructional tone of earlier as Sagebrush and I re-donned our parkas and gloves, "keep the dialogue to a minimum in there. Trust me: your throats will thank you for it later. Oh, one final word to the wise; now is not the time to imitate your favorite work of art. In other words, standing as still as the proverbial statue will only serve to enhance the chill. Move about . . . break out in dance if you must, anything to keep moving. Well, that about covers it, then. Best of luck, Mister *Kentucky*," he said, reaching to take my gloved hand and shaking it firmly, "Miss *Arizona* . . . " he continued, whirling about with an outstretched mitt only to find my traveling companion far less accommodating as she stared unblinkingly at the icy door's pitch-black center. Stone-faced, Fritz dropped his hand, seemingly unfazed at the non-gesture.

Stepping between and past us, I saw him reach into a pants pocket and bring out what appeared to be a tiny remote and gently compress his right thumb. With that, the metal door parted smoothly at the center, opening just enough for both of us to enter side-by-side if so desired. Instead, I paused to allow Sagebrush initial entry, admittedly due as much to fear of the unknown as 'woman and children first' politeness, and turned to give Fritz a final glance. As the door was already sliding closed, I was allowed only a moment's view, though long enough to clearly visualize the man's squinty-eyed smirk. It was, simply put, an expression of purely demonic measure; the kind reserved for Nazi concentration camp commanders or similarly heartless dictators whose talents lie primarily in the fine art of eradication. Truly, the only element missing was a set of sharp-tipped horns protruding from the man's temples and perhaps a quick flash of a forked tongue slithering from between pointed teeth.

Needless to say, in light of such a shocking revelation, the parting wave I'd planned for Fritz the

Clone never materialized. Moments later, there was good news and bad that superseded all need to dwell on such trivial doggerel. The good? A sudden burst of scalp-tingling excitement, perhaps adrenalin fueled, at the realization that Sector A was permanently lodged in the rearview mirror. The bad? Within thirty seconds of entering the adaptation room, the exposed flesh of my face had gone completely numb and I had reason to believe my eyes might actually freeze solid in their sockets.

Part Two: White Squall

Time: Four hours, thirty one minutes into the Iron Will Gauntlet

Location: Adaptation room just outside Sector B entryway (*Northeastern/Midwestern Winter Climes*)

Total miles covered: Nineteen and one-half

"Oh . . . god . . . " I heard Sagebrush whimper, sounding as if she were standing out of view, perhaps from the pit of a deep, dark cave when we were, in fact, practically rubbing shoulders. It seemed my hearing, despite both ears being more than adequately covered by the parka's fur-lined hood, had begun to abandon ship just as my vision had upon initial entry.

"Try n-not to . . . talk, like the m-man s-said," I responded, though in truth I had no inkling if I'd actually spoken aloud. The room was an empty box and far from spacious; perhaps twelve by fourteen at most, the four walls perfectly squared and equally indistinguishable. Layered in black ice, they were weirdly vent-less, as was the similarly coated ceiling, making the mystery of the interior conditions all the more intriguing. Though impossible to accurately gauge, I would've estimated the interior temperature at anywhere from twenty-five to fifty below, though the latter might even have been conservative. Regardless of actual readings, all I knew is that despite long johns, a layer of thick clothing and a parka manufactured for

Arctic conditions, a half-minute of standing still inside that stone igloo was basically akin to ice-fishing in my birthday suit. Tucking my gloved hands snugly between each armpit, I began to pace within the pitifully limited space. Meanwhile, my companion in pain continued to whine, though admittedly I was beyond caring while experiencing a level of bone-chilling frigidity I never knew possible.

"Sh-shit . . . I . . . I'm t-tingling...g-going n-numb..."

Standing pigeon-toed and as motionless as a cement bird feeder, she continued to bitch and moan until I was unable to refrain from attempting a little tough love. First off, I slid over and gently nudged her with a shoulder. Once my lips parted in speech, it was literally as if my exposed teeth and tongue had been splashed with a heaping helping of ice-shavings.

"Don't just . . . stand there, woman, mo-move around. Keep the circulation rolling otherwise it's a human-popsicle type scenari—"

Her borderline hysterical reaction was as shocking as it was eerily familiar. Shoving me aside with a double stiff-arm, her wide, bloodshot eyes glowed with rage. Her lips, having already faded to a pale, purplish shade that matched the room's inner walls almost perfectly, quivered like worms on a freshly set hook. I'd seen a similar look countless times, the origin of which was no mystery whatsoever, nor were the sour memories tied to said demeanor.

"K-keep y-your toilet-gr-grabbers off me,

Prick," she spat before executing a textbook about-face while I cringed back as if back-handed, which in retrospect wasn't that far off the beam.

The next three to three and a half minutes passed like ten times that, the two of us pacing to and fro but keeping as much space as possible as to avoid further interaction. We kept our heads low and tucked as deeply into the parka's lined hood as physically possible, like land turtles on a walking trip across the icy plains of Antarctica.

I'd always heard that when faced with such extremes in temperature, it was wise to attempt a mental diversion, as in your basic mind over matter strategy. As it was, try as I might, brief slideshow images filled with sunny beaches, poolside tanning or summer-league softball games did little to elevate the anguish. One would have thought a recent departure from the broiler oven that had been Sector A might've at least served as some relief, but the sad, depressing truth was that the brittle human psyche can only seem to compute such torture in the present tense, having essentially deleted all past ills until a later date, when they could be individually drudged up as situations dictated. I can, of course, speak only for myself, but from what I saw and heard of Sagebrush during this shared segment of inhuman angst, it was a common malady.

Instead of being able to dwell on coziness and warmth to offset the gradual shutdown of my being as a whole, I instead found myself lingering on a specific childhood memory best forgotten; one that had much in common with the present, and hardly in a 'think positive' way.

I'd been seven or eight. It was the Christmas holiday, and my father had driven us, that being my mother, younger sister and myself, to his older brother's home in Billings, Montana. Before such time, I'm fairly positive I'd never traveled outside the borders of my home state, and I recall thinking we'd driven the length and width of the entire planet to reach Big Sky Country. I can only remember the portions of Montana I witnessed, at least the winter version of said state, as a flat, lifeless place with gnarled, hideous shrubbery and a lifeless, continuously gray sky from which the sun's rays never dare emerged.

A few days into our visit—my father's brother had no children so it was mostly a joyless affair from a child's perspective—I had managed to get myself accidentally locked out of the home while dressed only in my stocking feet and a woefully thin pair of pajamas. Though a hearty scream and firm pounding of the back door had allowed for a fairly quick reentry via my relieved but less-than-understanding mother, the duration of said exposure had been lengthy enough to effectively paralyze every appendage I'd owned, not to mention kick off the beginnings of a rather nasty cold. Later, as we'd all sat around the furnace with steaming cups of cocoa in hand, I recall my uncle blurted something along the lines of 'lucky it didn't happen last week when we dipped to the twenty-below mark. The boy's testicles might've popped off like a pair of aggies. ' The laugher at said quip had been universal, all save my mother that is, and the image of my prepubescent jewels rolling down an icy

119

sidewalk filled many dream sequences in the months that followed. All that said, the bitter juggernaut of flesh-peeling cold I'd felt as a boy, a blistering pain so vividly recalled a lifetime later, was merely an irritating night-chill by comparison to the ultra-deep freeze provided by the adaptation room.

By the time the outer door slid open to reveal an equally dim landscape complete with blowing flurries and a stony terrain akin to treading atop badly lain asphalt, we nonetheless lurched forward as if entering a tropical, sun-drenched Shangri-La.

Sagebrush took point, keeping a five yard distance between us for the initial hour. I didn't attempt to catch up, figuring it best for the time being. Her adaptation room blow-up aside, as effective a *woman possessed* scene as I'd ever witnessed firsthand, I couldn't help but think my own desire for a span of privacy had just as much to do with Fritz the Clone's scolding concerning our buddy-buddy ways. That said, I didn't want to sever the relationship altogether, however wise such a decision might be, just slow its progression a degree. As for Sagebrush, it seemed the two of us might well have developed a mutual telepathy, as for that first three miles plus that she blazed the trail, not once did she even hint of turning about to check my status.

As for my first impressions of Sector B, it was truly like nothing I'd ever experienced. Though the snowfall was little more than scattered flurries, the gusting winds seemed to be programmed to hammer us head-on for the duration of the trek. Needless to say, the parka hood was subsequently zipped to its northernmost limit, leaving barely a fist-sized tunnel to peak through. Regardless, without the clear goggles we'd so casually accepted as part of our rolling inventory, there would've been no visualizing the trail ahead without experiencing some sort of eyeball related frostbite; perhaps a permanent snow-blindness from the constant bombardment of twenty to thirty mile per hour winds.

As for the aforementioned trail—mostly clay with the occasional gravel coating on the surface it was hardly slick beneath the mukluk's expertly grooved heels, though it was found to be as hard as concrete and utterly without give. Before growing somewhat accustomed to its jagged, uneven surface, I danced several clumsily executed jigs to avoid either fracturing an ankle or toppling straight onto my face. Thank the suppliers for those thickly-grooved, knee-high boots with extra ankle support. At one point, Sagebrush hadn't been quite as fortunate, twisting a knee and lurching hard to her left before rolling off the trail into a nearby gulley. I had started to dash forward to her aid, but she'd wasted little time before hopping back to her feet, brushing off chunks of red ice from her left pants leg and accompanying buttock. To her credit, she had never looked back to me for support, more likely hoping I missed the incident. The limp she carried immediately after was slight and soon vanished altogether.

On the positive side, the trail itself remained relatively flat throughout the first several miles, with only the occasional rise to climb or curve to navigate. As for the negative, the gusting winds rarely abated, and the swarming flurries and specks of blowing ice made clear visibility a constant struggle. In fact, I'd say the majority of those first four or so miles were accomplished while staring straight down at the tips of my mukluks. I'd felt the initial twinges of a cramp infiltrate my left thigh yet again, but it passed soon enough, leaving behind only a dull ache.

It was around the one hour, ten minute mark, perhaps three and a half miles in, that we caught glimpse of a fellow competitor. Counting the conclusion of Sector A, this had been our first contact with anyone other than Fritz and his hired golems for well past three hours.

I slowed to pull one of the silver thermoses from my pack, gulped down a few mouthfuls of soothingly warm tea, then replaced the thermos and braved the blowing precipitation by staring straight ahead. Through the swirl I'd spotted not only Sagebrush's all-too-familiar walking style as she picked 'em up and put 'em down approximately twelve to fifteen yards ahead, but a form not as easy recognizable ambling ahead to her left. The form appeared that of a large-statured male, his gait uneven and wobbly, as if on the verge of tipping over with every staggering step. I watched Sagebrush finally visualize and then acknowledge the other racer's presence with a quick wave, and then watched them close ranks until they stood practically shoulder to shoulder. Fueled by curiosity and powered by the bitter remnants of the green tea still warming a pronounced track from my chest cavity to the pit of my gut, I picked up my own pace until I drew to within perhaps five yards and could hear the two conversing via timed shouts into and through the bluster.

Finally, having adjusted somewhat to the levitating wall of flakes, I was able to read the lettering on the back of the man's parka and was unable to refrain from cracking a smile, a painful, stinging process considering I could practically hear the tearing of my severely chapped lips.

A five-step jog brought me even with them as I stood just to the left of Sagebrush with *Alabama* still weaving on and off the trail to the far right.

"Hiya, Bama! How they hanging?" I blurted, bending down and peering past Sagebrush through the pinched parka lining. From the angle I'd taken, I could only make out the man's bowed head submerged inside the hood, but nary a glimpse of face hidden within. It wasn't until Sagebrush turned my way to reveal a single glaring eyeball through similar camouflage that it hit me we'd all donned similar disguises. As if on telepathic cue yet again, she broke into a light jog and took the point, allowing me to close ground between *Alabama* and myself.

"Hey, you hearing me, old man? *Roooolllll Tide!*" I practically yelled, instantly regretting the effort and forced inhalation of air so frigid it instantly evaporated the soothing tea effect of must moments prior.

He stumbled forward as if startled, and I quickly reached over and down and gripped his right in an effort to help right his stance. We briefly skidded to a complete stop before resuming slowly ahead, and the big man straightened as if taking in a lengthy breath before gradually turning my way.

There are many specific words or phrases I can drudge up concerning the many unforgettable sights I witnessed firsthand while competing in the Iron-Will Gauntlet, most of which might come off sounding either hopelessly clichéd or borderline demented. In terms of how I would've described what I saw reflected in the man from *Alabama*'s eyes in the harrowing moment, the word was *haunted*, plain and simple. Haunted not as in poltergeist, but haunted as in *doomed*. I saw the expression of a man ensnared in the icy grip of reality. It was a grim, uncompromising reality that spelled out his impending demise under far than ideal circumstances. Cut and dry; *Alabama* was a cold, dead man walking, and knew it. That infectious glee had fled his gaze, and what little I could see of his face revealed chalky flesh that appeared positively freeze-dried.

"Ju-just he-head on do-down the road, s-son. Ya. . . ya c-can't . . . he-help me, even if y-ya wanted or w-was supposed t-to, whi-which ya most d-definitely . . . ain't. I'm. . . way. . . beyond that n-now, I'm afraid. "

Undaunted despite the shock of his initial appearance, I reaffirmed my hold on his arm to prevent his lumbering away.

"You drink the tea or t-the soup? It helps, I swear it does. Warms the insides, and it's like turbo fuel. I know, I just swallowed down a hel- . . . "

"T-tried that already, K-Man. B-barfed it u-up s-soon afterwards," he spat, and I then noticed the frozen, yellowish stain covering the lower portion of his parka just below the groin.

"F-fever g-got me. B-bad s-sort. Felt it co-comin' on just outside A Sector. Damn adab. . . adaption room f-finished me o-off. Came close t-to pe-peelin' off the pa-parka a mile b-back . . . sweatin' like a sumo wr-wrestler in a s-sauna. N-now I'm a w-walkin' Fudge-pop a-again. Jesus Lord, b-but it h-hurts. H-hurts in ways I n-ne-never kn-knew it c-could. "

"It'll pass," I lied, jerking him gently back upright after he'd lurched away yet again, "these gusts are bound to ease up soon, maybe around the next bend. " With that, I took a squinting peak through the narrow vertical slash allowed by the parka hood to see no such magical turn even existed; merely more of the same flat, rock-hard, occasionally jagged track we'd been clogging since first stepping into the sector.

Leaning over and down until we practically head-butted, *Alabama*'s hood parted just enough for me to allow a brief but shockingly clear glimpse into his gleaming, tear-filled eyes. Tears that, I noted with no small amount of horror, had frozen solid within the deep creases of the crow's feet so prevalent at each corner.

"I ain't no q-quitter, Ka-K-Man, but th-this is . . . so mu-much *more* than th-this ol' southern b-boy ever b-bargained for. "

"You just hang on, Bama. I'll see you through 'til this breaks, and that's a promise. "

Weird as it sounds, it wasn't just a series of words spewed forth to ease the mind of a dying man. Going against every natural instinct yet again, I wasn't about to just saunter away and allow fate to play its grisly hand. The big man was on the verge of complete collapse yet somehow found just enough inner grit to remain upright, and for the time being I had no problem playing the part of living, breathing crutch. Once survivor mode went south and said collapse became imminent, yet another decision would have to be made. Until then, hang all the unwritten rules and those who competed by them. I'd had a gut feeling about the man from our initial greeting. A good man; a principled man; the kind of man, as the old saying goes, would give the shirt off his back if need be to help others. By all the outward signs, the odds were bleak at best that he'd last another half-mile, especially if conditions remained unchanged. I could hear his strained, hoarse breathing through the whistling gusts, and felt the warmth of his fever through several layers of protective cloth. Then again, conditions could improve, and there was such a thing as second wind, even in regard to men of our generation. If, by some miracle, the man from *Alabama* was to resurrect, I'd worry about the competitive factor at another spot down the road. There was, after all, much highway yet to cover. As it was, such trivial concerns were just that in comparison to a fellow human's survival. If anything, I could guide him through the sector and to medical aid.

"D-don't w-w-waste y-your time, b-boy," he groaned between muted hacks, the last series of which produced a reddish mist that coated and almost instantly froze atop hideously chapped lips, "be-besides, it's a-all a-about winnin', right? G-go cl-claim the p-prize. L-least you c-can do is b-beat o-out that jerk-w-wad fr-from Col-Colo- . . . Colorado. Y-ya kn-know he ac-actually tried t-to trip m-me a f-few cl-clicks b-back? Evil l-little t-troll. . . "

In response, the last thing I wanted was to come off sounding patronizing. In my own defense and given the circumstances, such a lofty goal was found to be damn near impossible.

"I . . . we'll catch up to him soon enough and return the favor, how's that?"

"L-listen to m-me . . . I a-appreciate the g-gesture, K-Man, I-I really do, but y-you and I b-both know it's a w-wasted ef-effort, now d-don't w-we?" Again with the haunting glare, this time forcing me to look away, to focus on the four-legged jig we danced so ungracefully atop that bumpy, frozen clay.

"Stop talking, you old coot," I scolded without meeting said gaze, "save your energy. The notion of giving up and just laying down is doing more to drain you than the conditions. "

For a time, all too brief, he did just that, seemingly taking heed of my admittedly tame but truth-filled scolding and using it to fuel whatever faint ember still smoldered. Once I'd seen his back straighten and felt his stride strengthen, I'd even released my grip on his arm and moved away a step. As to aid our plight, the gusts seemed to die down a notch as well, though on the negative side what had begun as light flurries were fast transforming into a full-blown snow.

"You got it, Bama," I crowed loudly, a one-man cheering squad as his speed had noticeably increased.

"Pick 'em up and put 'em down. Eye on the prize, that's all, eye on the prize."

A walking, talking cliché, I knew, but desperation has no limits, however ludicrous. If copping dialogue from every inspirationally themed sports flick put to film aided in gassing up the old man's motor, never let it be said I was too proud to comply.

"Looking good . . . picking up steam. . . that's it. That's the ticket, you old shit-kickin' warhorse. Rumor has it you played the part of a hard-as-nails prison warden in another life. With that in mind, my money's on you, all the way."

Glancing ahead, I saw no sign of Sagebrush, though with a visible range of no more than fifteen yards at best, gauging the distance between us wasn't possible. It was like staring into a thickening fog bank.

Damn the architects anyway. Sick, sadistic bookworms with a definite bent towards dishing out the pain. It was truly like they'd choreographed the entire scenario, knowing exactly when to stick in the worst possible roadblock.

The hill started out innocently enough, just a slight upgrade; manageable enough. That is, until it abruptly transformed into a downhill snow-skier's wettest dream of a slope. Worse yet, the ground beneath our mukluks grew slicker by the step, and was inundated by jagged ruts so severely frozen they might well have been formed from lava stone.

Reattaching myself to the big man's left arm, I helped tug, pull and heave us to nearly the halfway point. By the time he stumbled from my grip and a loud, sickening crunch ensued, we'd both been blowing and puffing like twin locomotives. Whipping my right arm about in blind desperation, I was awarded with a glove-full of frigid air. 'Bama tumbled down the hill head over heels, sliding face-first the last dozen or so feet. Hunched down on all fours, I'd watched his descent with utter haplessness, the understanding that I'd done all I could've hardly softening the disgust. Scaling back down the slope as the snowfall let up a degree, I was literally forced to crawl in spots for fear of imitating a similar plunge.

Hunching over his prone form, it was a relief to both see and hear his tattered breathing, the former made obvious by the twin vapor trails of frigid air spewing forth from both nostrils. Acquiring a gentle but firm hold on his left shoulder and upper bicep, I started to roll him over and paused at a particularly befuddling detail that I hadn't noticed upon arrival. Though the big man lay on his belly, the toe of his right mukluk pointed straight toward the grayish sky. Initially, I thought the boot had simply been jarred loose in the fall and had landed in said position. It wasn't until I leaned in to visualize splintered bone protruding from just above the ankle that the grisly truth of the circumstances surfaced. The older man hadn't just broken his ankle, but completely mangled it to the point of twisting the foot into its present state-a predicament I'd often heard referred to as 'ass-backwards'. Quickly refocusing to prevent a possible gag reflex, I pulled him onto his side as to avoid a sudden shift of the shattered appendage.

"Bama, hey . . . can you hear me, man?" I asked in lieu of the more burning question, that being something along the lines of "Bama, that ankle and foot resemble twin ends of a steaming turd . . . that just *can't* feel good, am I right?"

The man's cap-cam had torn away, sliding into parts unknown, while his parka hood had dislodged and was tangled around his neck like a furry noose. There was a deep, bleeding gash across his forehead, and the tip of his nose appeared to have been sheared away. Both wounds seeped consistently, the leaking fluids freezing almost instantly onto exposed flesh or the hard ground below.

"Gu-guess t-th-that's of-off-official-ly t-the . . . ol-old b-ball . . . g-game, p-partner," he whimpered through gritted teeth and a single opened right eye, the left lid having apparently been frozen into place by the aforementioned leaks.

"You just...hang in, old man. Ain't no fat lady barking out a tune that I can hear. "

He smiled at that, the corners of his mouth twitching and convulsing in the aftermath. It was a grin of relieved acceptance; of knowing all the pain and suffering would soon be over.

"Y-you're a-a fu-funny one, y-ou a-are. Y-you p-possess an o-old soul for on-one so y-young. J-just tur-tu-turn ab-around a-and k-keep oh on truck .

130

. . truckin', a-a-and d-don't lo-look b-b-back. G-go. . . p-please. "

That single orb, pulled wide and gleaming with a sudden desperation, spoke volumes.

"I d-do a-appre-appreci . . . th-thak thank y-you f-for . . . th-the e-effort. G-go, b-boy . . . wa-wave t-that r-rebel f-fag fl . . . b-banner h-high. "

I started to argue yet again, spewing another series of Rockne-esque pep talks and in doing so completely milk dry the deep well of established clichés. Instead, I silently leaned over and lifted the man's slumping head just enough to untangle the parka hood from his shoulders and neck and pull it over to cloak his graying locks, the majority of which already held a healthy spattering of frost.

Turning back towards the slope, I began to ascend and did not look back. In truth, I wasn't even tempted to do so. Mainly due to the shudder-inducing fear of possibly seeing the man from *Alabama* crawling up that glacier like a mangled roach searching for a proper hole to crawl into and die. On the way up, I forced several small swallows of warm tea, though the urge to regurgitate was briefly overwhelming.

Part Three: Going Hollywood

Time: Six hours, twenty-one minutes into the Iron Will Gauntlet
Location: Sector B (*Northeastern/Midwestern Winter Climes*)
Total miles covered: Twenty-three and a half

With a modest build-up of snow just above the ankle, a light swirl of flakes returned, giving way to a misting sleet as forty-plus minutes had passed since I'd left *Alabama* to his fate. This development, as with most everything within the Gauntlet's mystical realm, brought equal helpings of news both good and bad. The good was a marked improvement in visibility. One could actually see more than a dozen feet past the tips of their boots. The winds had died down from blizzard gusts to a relatively livable breeze; constant but not near the battering monster they had been. As for the bad, it was all in the terrain—literally. Despite heavily treaded bottoms, the mukluks were beginning to slip and skid once the aforementioned sleet began to mix and mingle with the snow build-up already in place. Needless to say, the added stress and strain of having to treat each step taken as if strolling atop a carton of eggs slowed overall progress mightily. No doubt my own level of cautiousness was raised by the mere thought of *Alabama*'s gruesome injury, the image of jagged white bone pointing into the sky like the base of a battlefield surrender flag a damn hard one to shake. Luckily, the trail had remained strictly horizontal for the most part, with very few peaks or valleys to speak of.

Trudging carefully along, it was an additional fifteen minutes or more before I spotted a fellow walker. At first I'd naturally mistaken the relatively small-statured figure belonging to the opposite sex as being Sagebrush, being as she'd vanished into the storm once I'd paused to assist *Alabama* and couldn't have built much of a lead in such a short duration. As I grew closer, perhaps to within six or seven yards, I realized this particular female was a bit taller and, despite the multi-layers of clothing, substantially curvier, particularly in the buttocks region. The mystery woman with the shapely caboose appeared to have her arms crossed and was leaning forward, her every step a study in intense concentration. The back of her parka, the bottom edge of which was rolled up to her waist, was layered in frozen precipitation though with just enough clearance between the shoulder blades for the letters 'C' and 'A' to break through. With such slow progress, it was only a matter of minutes before I pulled even.

"Well ahoy there, fellow tundra-wanderer," I barked a bit too loudly, no doubt still influenced by howling winds that had recently faded to a fairly harmless draft. My throat was stinging with rawness, though soothed by the sporadic sip of still warm tea.

Surprisingly, considering the access volume I'd utilized, the woman didn't even flinch, just continued lumbering forward at a snail's pace with her parka-engulfed head slightly bowed.

"And here I considered myself the ultimate fish out of water. Bet you never quite experienced a beachhead like this, am I right?"

Still, there was no response. Not the slightest hint that Miss Tanned Bods and Sandy Beaches U. S. A had the foggiest clue I existed. Briefly scanning the trail ahead, which remained as flat and lifeless as the past mile or so, I considered she might've donned headphones and hadn't heard either greeting. Personally, I hadn't considered a musical diversion since departing Sector A. I had always been one to require a certain degree of peace of mind to enjoy my tunes, and thus far the Great White North known as B Sector had provided little if any. Still, she might've been my polar opposite in such matters and be able to utilize the I-Pod for the ultimate distraction. Lucky pup . . . or so I thought.

"Miss? Hey. . . " I babbled, reaching over and down to gently tug at the epaulet atop her right shoulder.

"Don't mean to interrupt, just wanted to say he..."

Though I'm not at all positive, I'm fairly sure I'd ended the sentence not with the intended 'hey' but with a long, drawn-out 'help' delivered in true *female-in-distress* fashion—a screeching wail that was the equivalent of a spooked grade-schooler of the feminine persuasion.

The reason I'd come dangerously near soiling my frozen undies? Two-fold, really. First off, at almost the exact moment my gloved hand had made contact with the aforementioned epaulet, her right arm had uncoiled like a cobra to smack it roughly away. Secondly, and twice as unexpected, the little woman had practically bull-rushed me, landing a solid, surprisingly painful head-butt to the center of my chest that even several layers of thick clothing hardly minimized.

Next thing I knew, I was lying flat on my back at trail's center with her knees propped atop each very effectively pinned shoulder.

"Je-Jesus, la-lady," I babbled, staring up at her through the lone uncloaked eye I still possessed as the parka hood had been pulled askew in the assault, "I was j-just trying to say hi."

"Oh, um, ye-yeah," she answered, leaning down as to study her quarry before pushing away with a double-handed shove that did little to soothe my suddenly aching chest cavity, "my...my bad, fella. Pure instinct, that's all. No control, I'm afraid. Been that way since my first mugging."

Once she'd hopped away, landing on both feet in graceful, break-dance style, I pulled myself up and temporarily remained on all fours in order to re-catch my breath.

"W-wow. You pack quite the wallop for such a tiny stick of dynamite." Sad as it sounds, this was me at my most charming. Truly spoken like a man decades removed from the 'dating' process.

"My last ex learned the hard way about sneaking up. Tried waking me up for a quickie one morning and got a broken nose for his efforts."

She started forward as if to assist, instantly providing all the motivation I needed to practically leap upward. A man has his pride, after all, even one so easily dispatched by a female whom he probably outweighed by fifty or more pounds.

"I'm not about to doubt it. Didn't you hear me address you?"

"Afraid I was zoning out. *Kentucky* is it?"

Having pulled her parka hood apart a few inches, I was finally allowed at least a decent photo of the face concealed within. Miss *California* it was, or as Sagebrush had mentioned she referred to be called, 'Hollywood'. Her gleaming, dark brown eyes appeared huge and seductively inviting, and a tuft of lighter brown hair split the brows and curled slightly at the ends. Her lips were the overly plump type normally associated with regular chemical injections. All in all, the stereotypical west coast gal who, having grown a shade long in the tooth, had long ago deduced that the mythical fountain of youth resided at either the sharp edge of a surgeon's scalpel or the sticking point of a loaded syringe. Regardless, the woman was a knockout, multiple implants and all.

"At your service, Madam. As for intros, next time, how about we just shake on it?"

"If such an occasion presents itself," came her chilly, pardon the choice of words, response, delivered with a sour smirk just before she'd turned to resume the trek, "which isn't likely. Adios, amigo . . ."

Forced to fast-walk forward, no easy task considering the obvious dangers of treading atop a trail growing slicker by the second, I felt the heat of a building anger warm my flesh despite the conditions.

"Whoa, whoa, I understand competitive spirit

and all that, but I wasn't bucking for a dinner and a movie, lady. Just wanted to ask a simple question. "

"Fine. One per customer then. So quiz me already, old ye of the deep drawl and naturally slow thought process," she blurted indifferently, having re-tucked her arms and assumed the same 'leaning tower of Pisa' pose. It wasn't until later, when rewinding the scene with a clearer head, that the 'slow thought process' remark took hold, perhaps proving her point to some degree.

"You happen to see Sag-um, Miss *Arizona* pass you by within the last half hour?"

Not really sure why I needed to hear a reply with only one logical answer, especially if it meant querying such an overbearing source, but at the time it seemed important. Perhaps it was simply a matter of craving human companionship of the still alive and kicking variety after baring witness to *Alabama*'s ghastly demise. On the other hand, I might've just felt a sudden surge of animalistic horniness at the mere sight of Hollywood's meticulously chiseled rear end. Extremes in weather sometimes caused such primal urges to double, even triple in strength, I'd once read.

"Skinny chick, slightly bow-legged and wearing a perpetual frown?"

"Sounds about right. "

"Nope . . . neither hide nor tightly-tucked hair, but don't fret so, Gator-boy. You're sure to find true love again back down on the farm, perhaps even with a cousin or other family member. "

She delivered the last sentence in a horribly mangled southern accent, triggering my inner thermometer to spring skyward yet again.

"Ga-that's *Kentucky*. You know, as in mint juleps and thoroughbreds..." I groaned, rearing my head back to stare into a buildup of once light gray-colored cloud cover that suddenly appeared a foreboding shade of red behind the slightly blurred lens of my goggles, ". . . say, by any chance have you been hanging out with that butthole from *Colorado*?"

"Sorry," she exclaimed with a gloved hand raised palms up as to cut me off from further dialogue, "one question per, remember? Well, see you in the funny papers, Georgia Peach. This girl's got things to do and people to by-pass. "

"That's *Kentucky,* damn it," I practically shouted, struggling for just the right counter-insult as she took off in a comically staggered dash, the bottom edge of her parka tumbling down in full cloak mode as the heels of her boots kicked up large clumps of precipitation.

As it was, said comeback, despite a game effort, was beyond pathetic. I'd never been much on doling out insults, even to that one certain person in my life that had made such a perfect target, at least at the end, during the *bad* times.

"West coast *bubble-head.* Hope those boob implants freeze up and chip off. "

I had no idea if she'd even heard the words, pumping her legs and arms in full-on sprint mode, setting a pace that, logically, would only serve to severely drain the energy reserves desperately needed to survive the remaining sector.

As the distance between grew wider, I forced

138

myself to refocus on my stride. I could see the trail angling off to the left approximately twenty-five yards ahead, a curve Hollywood soon entered and cleared, vanishing from sight as she appeared to be maintaining the same level of velocity. A dull ache was consuming my left knee and ankle, as if I'd recently suffered a minor trauma, while my right hip felt on the verge of locking up altogether. All things considered, I was still moving along at a fairly brisk clip, conscious of the break in severe weather and the probable short window of relief in order to gain valuable ground.

As cruel and unforgiving as the terrain beneath my boots, the surrounding landscape was hardly an improvement. It was as if the designer and/or architects had found inspiration from the harshest winter locale on the planet; a Christmas Eve snapshot of Greenland or maybe balmy Siberia in mid-February. There was no foliage to speak of, only the occasional shrub, bent and mangled to resemble a gnarled appendage protruding from the frost-bitten earth. The grounds bookending the trail were hilly but barren, the two to three inches of piled snow doing little to camouflage the fact there was likely nothing of substance beneath. Unlike Sector A with its forest surroundings, this section possessed literally no buffer between the elements, gusting winds specifically, and the human targets lining its walking path. Safe to say this was no accident. Just another in a long line of torture techniques in what I had begun to think of as the 'Iron-Will Inquisition'.

Sticking to the far right of the trail, there was

literally no shoulder to speak of, I had just entered the curve as a stout breeze penetrated the slim space of my parka hood and caused a temporary closing of the eyes. Upon reopening, I yelped aloud while being forced to hop to one side to avoid a head-on collision.

"Beep beep! Watch yourself there, ya clumsy Cajun!" the voice shrieked as its host skidded by, firmly bumping my left shoulder despite my best efforts to avoid all contact.

Whirling about, I dug with my heels and skated to a stop, reaching up with the fingers of both hands to peel the parka lining apart for a wider view. If nothing else, the diversion made me forget my growing list of aches and pains, the most bothersome of which had been my right hip. Best yet, the mere act of twisting so abruptly seemed to have alleviated an impending cramp.

"Hey lady, you lose something or just decide the lush scenery back there deserved a second look?"

As usual, she ignored me completely, skipping down the trail with both legs and pumping in comically exaggerated style, though in truth the high knee raises had been more or less mandatory in order for her boots to clear the snowy surface. I could hear her humming as she bounded on, a vaguely familiar pop tune from eons gone by, though by the time I was able to get a proper fix on the beat, she'd halted in mid-hum and instead began talking aloud. The distance between us only allowed for every third or fourth word, thus the overall message was impossible to decipher. It wasn't until she did an abrupt about-face, twirling about on one booted foot with a level of grace and agility I never wouldn't thought possible considering the copious amount of clothing and gear involved, that it became all too apparent the conversation being had was of the one-way variety.

"Desperate times call for desperate measures . . . or is it desperate measures call for desperate acts? Ahh, doesn't matter for shit now, Missy. Either way, a pickle is a pickle," she spewed, having pushed the hood from her head, her hair popping up like quills that looked to have frozen solid mere seconds following the sudden exposure.

"And this is quite the spicy dill, for certain. "

Headed back my way, she'd slowed her pace considerably, practicing dragging her boots through the snow in lieu of lifting them over the drifts.

"Benny the prick, Benny the limp-noodled *weenie*. Nine years my agent and *this* is the best advice he could pull from beneath that pathetic hair weave? *Fuck me raw*, why did I listen? I had a few auditions lined up. The well wasn't completely bone dry. There was potential there. Who's to say I wouldn't have landed a nice, juicy gig before the foreclosure police came-a-knockin' to show me the street? Stranger things have happened in Tinsel Town, girly, mucho bizarro things, and it isn't as if you don't have the talent and considerable charms to pull it off, even at the ripe old age of ...*now shut your mouth*!"

Weaving from side to side, she waved her arms about as if addressing a live audience of seated on-lookers, each hand gesturing wildly.

"God, when I think back on all the missed opportunities, a few of which I was a cat's whisker from nabbing. It was always one tiny step forward, two lunging leaps back. Nail down a decent commercial gig, then turn right around and lose a plumb syndicated sitcom role to some fish-lipped floozy who'd likely blown the producer for the part. You'd have thought just by the law of averages that in twenty-plus years of pounding the stone that one, *just one*, mind you, turn of the cards might've went my way. May we then officially index this here monologue a rant of self-pity? Damn straight, sister, and few are more justified to do so!"

As she neared to within approximately fifteen to twenty yards of my still position, she slowed almost to a complete stop and began unzipping the parka from top to bottom, though doing so hardly slowed the constant jabbering.

"Then there was the whole Vidco fiasco, the repercussions from which pretty well drove home the final nails in the ol' career coffin. Wasn't hard enough turning forty and being relegated to auditioning for middle-aged mom roles, but having the job title of 'adult film star' hanging around one's neck like a spiked noose did little but raise eyebrows, and not nearly in a positive light. Might as well have tattooed the words 'over-the-hill porn slut' across my forehead, and all over a fifteen second cameo where I was not only fully dressed, but so honored to blurt out the Grand Teton total of seven fucking words of dialogue. Who would've ever thought such a cheese-filled sentence as *'How's it going, Lance? Need a refill?'* could serve to shovel the last clump of dirt atop the aforementioned corpse-box of an already shaky career? Thanks again, Benny Butt-munch. Best flesh-peddler in the biz is right. Pot-bellied boozer without a clue or decent client to speak of. But then, I was dumb enough to listen. Ah well, desperation is as desperation does, right old lady? An aging hag has to do what an aging hag must in the land of broken dreams and misspent youth . . . "

She'd punctuated that final segment with a heavy sigh and lumbered forward peering directly towards me with a dazed stare that screamed unfamiliarity. Shocking as it was upon confirmation a few seconds later, it made perfect sense in retrospect. From her severely creased brow and dull, listless gaze, it was pretty obvious the woman had no earthly idea who I was.

"You got a sec, Mac?" she asked with a cocked brow, having halting just inches away until the tips of our mukluks practically kissed. Her Vulcan-styled eyebrows were as frost-bitten as her spiked coif, and an inch long icicle hung from the tip of her left earlobe, no doubt formed from sweat build-up earlier in the day.

"I really need to get something off my chest, if you can dig it. Can't really see your mug, but I'm thinking you possess a flexible-type ear. Hope so, anyhow, because I really, like, *truly* need to perform some serious bending about now. "

"Um, look, well. . . I, um," I sputtered and spat, balanced on my heels while leaning back from the sudden intrusion. Strange how the almost complete cloaking of one's face can provide both a sense of anonymity and security, for at the time I was mighty grateful to be peering at the woman through a two-inch space of fur lining. As loopy as she was acting, borderline schizophrenia instantly swam to mind, a plethora of violent acts were possible, to include eye-gouging and groin-kicking. With the latter in mind, I strategically placed both hands in front of said area in case a potential block was needed.

"Shit, Sam, it's not a test. A simple yes or no will suffice. "

Even her eyelashes were frosted; tiny ice-shards snapping off onto her cheeks with each blink.

"Sure, of course. Why don't we . . . um, you talk while we walk this way?" I muttered, pointing forward to grounds yet uncovered since it appeared she didn't know or care about such technical matters.

"Yeah, whatever. I'd rather find a comfy couch somewhere, doc, or better yet a well-cushioned bar stool, but there doesn't seem to be a choice. "

"You, um, might want to pull that hood back on. Little nippy out here," I said cautiously as we'd turned eastbound, the loose flapping of her unzipped parka lightly slapping my right arm.

"Ah, it's not so bad, doc, toughen up. Be a man. What're you, afraid of a little sunburn?"

"Well, um, no, but that's hardly an issue he-," I started, happy to be cut off from a sentence I had nary a clue how to conclude.

"Nice, warm, sandy dune is just around the next corner, I'm sure. Not to worry, doc, I'll let ya borrow some of my flesh-protector. I never leave the house without at least a half-full tube. "

"I'm good for now, thanks. Now, you said something about bending ears. Honestly, it sounds kinda painful. "

The hard slap she administered to the center of my back was sorely unexpected, but not nearly as cringe-inducing as the maniacal cackling that accompanied it.

There was little doubt at this point I was dealing with an individual who had misplaced the majority of their face cards. The only question, and a rather vital one at that, was whether Miss *California* was on the verge of snapping or had already done so. In case of the former, I could continue in my amateur psychoanalysis and hope for a breakthrough. If the latter were true, all such efforts to continue patronizing were completely wasted. I might as well help her strip down until she literally froze in her tracks. For the time being, I had no choice, morally speaking, but continue to keep up the act. It was a verbal minefield that was equally draining as the conditions themselves.

Part Four: Role Play

Time: Six hours, fifty-seven minutes into the Iron Will Gauntlet

Location: Sector B (*Northeastern/Midwestern Winter Climes*)

Total miles covered: Just over twenty-four

"You're a real card, doc! You keep that up I just might let ya cop a feel further up the trail. "

She'd reached up and cupped both breasts during the 'cop a feel' segment of said statement, winking playfully as still more chipped ice flew forth from the connected lashes. In turn, I'd felt my cheeks flush within the hood's fuzzy lining.

"Uh, yeah, sure. Now, what was it you wanted to get off you-, um, what was it you wanted to discuss?"

"Well," she commenced, having unbuttoned the top two or three snaps on the wool shirt she'd donned beneath the parka. Her gait was stiff, mechanical and altogether quite different from the hop, skip and jump technique from just minutes earlier, "it's a lengthy tale, doc. Lengthy, sad and probably a smidgeon familiar, but I'll do my dead-level best to cut it down to the basics to avoid boredom or casual indifference on your part. "

She paused, staring over and up at me as to, I surmise, gauge the initial reaction.

"O…kay…Shoot," I replied with a nod. The wind was picking back up and I noticed a swarm of sizeable sleet-spears sail past my very limited line of sight.

"It appears time is not an issue. "

"What a doll," she exclaimed with a wide, toothy smile, and I took sad note of the fact that her two front teeth were each brown-stained and horribly chipped at the edges, as if she'd recently chowed down on a strip of stainless steel, "You know, doc, if I didn't already have three ex-husbands to feed, I might be tempted to add you to the stable. "

In lieu of this, I simply nodded yet again, content to keep her talking as long as our collective pace didn't slow. As far as I was concerned, she could ramble and rant all the way to the entrance to Sector C, where the powers that be could provide a suitable straitjacket.

"Ya see, I hopped a Grayhound outta Seattle when I was barely nineteen with every intention of making it as an actress *slash* model. Yeah, I know, not exactly novel in terms of originality, but you had to know how confident I was in those days. Dumb as dog-shit, true, but cocky as the devil and willing to face multiple rejections head on. Welllll, flash-forward some twenty-five odd years and here we stand, doc—you and me, the fudge-pop twins, freezing our middle-aged asses off inside some artificial hell for the viewing masses to ogle over and wager on. Sure, we beat out some harsh competition in order to rep our home stomping grounds, but I gotta say, as things and events have progressed, that warm and fuzzy feeling I felt upon learning I'd beat out some thirty-some-odd-thousand potential walkers for this so-called *honor* has worn as thin as a strip of used dental floss. Truth is, I'm feeling more and more like a gullible chump. Can't speak for you or anyone else trapped inside this combination Weather Channel-Sci-Fi network purgatory, but I don't recall signing no dotted line that read 'win or die', did you? I mean, *shit*, I knew, we all knew there'd be risks, but . . . did you see those two unfortunate Shmucks back in A? Artificial twister snapped 'em in two like brittle kindling. You can't convince this girl that whole scenario wasn't laid out there for all to see, as in 'we're just warming up, boys and girls, 'you ain't seen nothing yet' kind of bravado. I've been on many a movie set, doc. Met my share of dictatorial type directors with an unquenchable thirst for power—those who just live and breathe to hoard it over all others—we're in deep doo-doo with whoever's running this particular documentary, that much this over-the-hill, west-coast *bubblehead* knows for darn sure, you dig?"

For a moment, I was unable to respond in light of the *bubblehead* comment, and briefly wondered if whether or not at least a portion of what I was seeing was a carefully choreographed act.

"I understood there would be risks," I finally managed, tap dancing like mad to create the safest, least argumentative response possible, "but like you, I never considered the death-race this thing is fast becoming. "

"Bingo, doc, a death-race. I like that—*perfecto description-oh*. That's exactly what I'm talking about. I mean, deep down I didn't expect to win this thing. You see that brute from *New York*? No way this gnarly old LA woman is gonna outpace that monster. And that sewer-mouthed little weasel from Montana, or maybe it was one of the Dakotas, one of those states where the nips remain perpetually hard . . . "

"Colorado, I think it is, if we're talking about the same sewer-mouthed weasel. "

"Yeah, maybe, anyway, that's precisely the kind of heartless, soulless, cut-throat vermin cut out to win this thing, agreed?"

I thought of simply nodding in agreement, but she seemed to have regained at least a small sense of logic, so, tempting fate, I spoke my mind instead.

"Could be. If that *vermin* classification carries any weight on this trail, he's definitely a favorite. Conversely, he might also be the next one to fall. Just being an asshole doesn't make one invincible. Leastways, I sure hope it doesn't. "

"Ya know, doc, at another stage in my life I might've taken a real fancy to you and that sunshiny outlook, but let's face the reality of the here and now; folks like us are just fodder-lambs to the eco slaughterhouse they've built as our own personal tomb. "

Testing the waters of her mental stability yet again, I posted a mild but undeniable objection.

"Glass half full or not, I'd say we have a good a chance as anybody in the field. Fact is, we're a damn site better off than the twenty or so walkers bringing up the rear from the south. "

From the corner of my left eye, barely within sight from the hood's narrow opening, I saw her turn to me, staring upward with a deep frown and slight tilt of the head. The trail curved sharply and then descended just as a line of lifeless, hideously gnarled trees swam into view as bookmarks on either side. Stripped bare and shaded in gray, they each possessed spiny, curved branches and equally warped trunks, and stood barely shoulder high, making me reconsider the species as perhaps that of winter-ravaged shrubbery. Upon closing the gap between myself and the mystery vegetation, I noted the strangely foreboding presence of countless sharp-tipped icicles hanging from said branches like the jagged, uneven teeth of some alien predator.

"Ya think, doc? You *really* think so?"

"Sure, why not you? Why not me? After all, physicality is only one factor of many. The way I see it, the Gauntlet is more about what's up *here*," I replied, reaching up and sticking a forefinger against my left temple and instantly regretting both my choice of words and gestures.

"Hey, I think the temperature might actually be on the rise," I continued, eager to change to subject. I could see she had yet to break her intrusive stare, and secretly wondered if her eyelids might actually be frozen agape, "if this heat wave continues, we might even see it creep up to an even zero degrees Fahrenheit."

"You might have a chance at that, doc," I heard her say in a hoarse, fatigue-laced whisper while backing gradually out of my line of sight, "if I were the betting type, I just might lay all the chips on your block, yep-per."

I moved ahead another half-dozen steps before halting, my deuced curiosity getting the best of me.

If afforded the luxury of seeing into the future, I would've certainly taken off in a mad sprint without ever turning around. My battered psyche would have certainly appreciated it.

She stood perhaps twenty yards back at the center of the trail. Her head was bowed, her shoulders slumped, her legs wobbly as if her knees were on the verge of buckling. She was naked from the waist up, having left the parka, heavy wool shirt, and long-john top splayed across the frozen terrain in her wake. The exposed areolas had, in a matter of seconds, turned frighteningly pale, the stiffened nipples standing like out like pink shaded quills. I didn't find the strength to act until she'd reached down to remove the mukluks.

"Jesus, h-hold it!" I screamed, having removed my own hood while jogging forward, "stop th- ...hold on . . . don't...just hold it!"

As if to punctuate the building terror, a light sprinkling of sleet began to fall, as I felt its initial bombardment on my exposed forehead and cheeks.

"Don't waste your time, doc. I know I'm quite finished wasting mine," she blurted, kicking the first mukluk free and starting on the second.

"You'll...damn it, leave those. . . leave the boots on! For God's sake, woman. . . "

"Sadly mistaken there, padre," she stated in a tone so casual and matter-of-fact it was as if, for one horrifying moment, she was indeed the sanest individual currently conversing, while my arm-waving mumblings seemed only to further justify her point.

"God, much like Elvis in eras past, has most

certainly *left the building*. Honestly, I doubt he ever had the brass-coated nuts to ever step foot inside to begin with. "

With that, she took off in a bare-footed sprint, her arms pumping wildly and at easily twice the speed of her legs. As for her naked breasts, from which my eyes were momentarily glued, it was hard to fathom whether the lack of movement was from past surgical enhancements or the harsh elements perhaps freezing them firmly into place. As it was, the fresh spattering of falling sleet was fast turning her face and upper body into a spectral vision come to life. She was as pale and freeze-dried in appearance as any ghost I'd ever seen portrayed on the page or on film. I knew nothing of such things, but could only deduce the timeline for her overall survival was five minutes at best. Her exposed areas were likely mere seconds away from a state of permanent damage.

I side-stepped over in an admittedly feeble attempt to block her path, though initially I'd felt it my mission to retrieve her lost boots and at least the parka, there was simply no way save cloning I could hope to accomplish both.

"Hollywood, listen! L-listen to reason, please. You—we've got to cover you or . . . in just a matter of moments the frostbite will se—"

Juking to the left with all the skill of a seasoned half-back, she saw me lean that way before cutting right and dashing past.

"S-sorry, doc. A-appreciate the effort, if not the n-n-umbskull logic behind it, but a girl's gotta do what a g-girl's gotta do. "

With the secondary mission a wash, I turned my attention back to her lost coverings and ran over to where her parka lay, scooping it with one hand while plucking one of the discarded mukluks with the other. Four lengthy strides found me nabbing the second boot, but only after bypassing the wool shirt and long john top, each of which lay curled in separate balls on the trail's western shoulder. I figured the parka could provide adequate body cover for the time being, while the boots were essential if the woman's feet were to be salvaged.

"Now, if you'd just listen to rea . . . " I started, having already executed a surprisingly graceful about-face before lurching forward to give chase. My pursuit halted in mid-lunge as I slid to a stop and threw both arms airborne. Tossing both the parka and mukluks to the ground as my arms had raised, I unclenched my fingers and showed her the palms of both gloved hands.

"Jesus, H-hollywood, w-what? D-don't . . . "

They protruded from her pierced flesh like icy feelers, the thick, blunt ends approximately the size of a quarter. There was no blood visible from the circular entry wounds, and it was of course impossible to gauge how deep each icicle had penetrated her lower abdomen, since I had not actually witnessed the self-mutilation except in its grisly aftermath.

"H-hey, don't s-sweat it, doc . . . " she announced bravely through chattering teeth, her left arm held high, fisting the rounded end of yet another frozen spear and parking its pointy, pencil-thin end mere inches from the corner of her right eye.

". . . I j-just can't do it, you d-dig? I can't endure f-for the sake of s-suffering. I may have played a c-catholic on TV once but that don't m-make the beliefs kosher. I have no such inner guilt to a-allow this . . . torture to continue. Never b-been much of a quitter . . . m-more like the complete opposite for the m-majority of my run, s-so I really don't think the m-man upstairs will hold this against me, d-do you?"

Walking slowly ahead with the positioning of my raised hands unchanged, I never felt such haplessness. The fifty foot distance between us might as well have been a country mile.

"Don't. Don't let *them* win. Don't you see?" I pleaded, reaching back with both hands to remove my parka hood then purposely twisting the cap-cam backwards as to eliminate any possibility what was about to transpire would be nationally broadcast.

"If you do this . . . they win. Every time one of us gives in and gives up, they win. Those who produced it with hopes we'd all give up in such a way, win. Those who shelled out the green to see us give in and give up in such a way, win. Think about it, Hollywood. The only way to beat them—beat them all—is *never* to give in and *never* to give up. Don't...let...the...bastards...win. . . "

"Great s-s-speech, doc, but I got n-news for ya," she replied dourly through one of the saddest smiles I've ever witnessed, her cocked arm visibly tensing.

"The m-minute we entered this domed loony bin, the b-bastards *already* w-won. "

154

She drove the icicle into her right eye with such force I'm fairly certain I heard a distinct series of crunches as the orbit bone shattered, though in retrospect at least a part of that sickening concerto might well have been the snow and ice grinding beneath my own fidgeting boots.

Her entire frame shuddered and fell back, and I stumbled forward, catching the tip of my left boot in a jagged rut and tumbling onto all fours. By the time I dragged myself up and got to her body, all movements had ceased save a final, horrible tremor that caused her bare left foot to kick out spastically. I heard her gasp, the left side of her face painted maroon as blood gushed out from around the circular wound and appeared to freeze almost instantly, creating makeshift waves on her jowl and chin that soon took the shape of budding flower petals. *Rose pedals*, I thought crazily just before leaning past her still form and vomiting a soupy mix onto the hardening tundra.

Following several pained but unproductive dry heaves, I leaned up with the semi-frozen remnants hanging from my chin in brownish clumps. Removing the glove from my right hand, I felt an almost instantaneous tingle at the tip of each finger. Reaching down with an open palm to her bare right shoulder, I found touching the deceased woman's frost-coated flesh comparable to every pack of frozen meat I'd ever scooped up at my local grocer. That thought alone threatened to initiate yet another bout of cookie-tossing, and wasn't helped in the least by the realization that with conditions being what they were and possibly growing worse, her corpse would be butcher-shop ready within a half-hour if not sooner.

Standing on wobbly legs, I refit my glove, turned away and tucked my mouth into the crock of my left elbow, thereby hoping to block any possible eruption. Fortunately there came an immediate diversion in the form of a dime-sized chunk of hale that managed to home in on the bridge of my nose and connect with enough force to temporarily make me forget all other ills.

Staggering past her and completely off the trail, I stood on the narrow shoulder with my nose cupped in both hands before removing them to see a slight reddish hue gleaming in both palms. Though I cannot be certain what triggered the maniacal giggling fit that ensued, or even how long the duration, I do recall that said outburst concluded with hot tears flowing from both orbs as I screamed and blubbered directly into the cap-cam with a voice so raspy it was beyond proper identification even by its originator. Though unable to recall a single word of said rant, I'm sure I'd screamed of the injustice of it all. Similarly, I'd be surprised if I hadn't doled out a threat or two and perhaps also proclaimed myself the underdog to watch—an underdog fueled by thoughts of retribution upon crossing whatever mystical finish line awaited within the mysterious confines of Section D. Eventually, I'd simply ran out of fuel, reset the cap-cam, tucked my overly chilled noggin within the furry confines of the parka hood, and hopped back atop the waiting trail as the sporadic wave of sleet and hale pelted my person. My reasons for not looking back at the dead woman were a shade different than similar behavior displayed with the man from *Alabama*. With him, the fear had been that such a glance would result in seeing a man I'd left alive keeled over and expired. With Hollywood, it was just the opposite. The mere thought of whirling about in curiosity only to discover her trailing me, zombie-like, using the bloody spear protruding from her eye like some makeshift compass, was plenty motivation enough to refrain altogether.

Part Five: Nature's Call

Time: Seven hours, forty-six minutes into the Iron Will Gauntlet
Location: Sector B (*Northeastern/Midwestern Winter Climes*)
Total miles covered: twenty-five and a quarter

Unlike the mostly flat, curve-free trail that had come before, the half-mile that followed was akin to navigating the Hollywood hills, or so I'd been told, as in legendary for its never-ending array of swerving highways that seemed to curl forever upward. Actually, I'd instantly regretted the inclusion of the word *Hollywood*, for obvious reasons, and pushed it away just as hurriedly as it had come.

Light bands of sleet had given way to a spastic mix of large, billowy snowflakes intertwined with the occasional deluge of marble-sized hail, either of which made navigation of the gradually inclining track a slow, deliberate affair. My left thigh was acting up yet again, along with what felt like considerable swelling of both ankles. What had been only an occasional pit-stop for rest or nourishment became commonplace. Not surprisingly, I'd lost my taste for soup and raided the tea canteen instead. Though on the bitter side, it still contained enough warmth to soothe my frigid innards, and the caffeine kick it soon provided was equally welcome.

I'd just put the canteen away and proceeded

through still another winding curve when the first of a series of mild to moderate cramps racked my lower extremities. Understanding the impending need but obviously unable to comply at the moment, I had just cleared the bend as a heavy flurry of large flakes temporarily reduced visibility to practically nil. As it was, I almost walked directly into the side of the first of a trio of porta potties For a brief moment, ever so transitory, elation reigned supreme. The timing couldn't have been better, as I'd already envisioned being forced to drop trousers and do my business without the benefit of enclosed walls to block the cursed winds. As for the aforementioned rush of joy, it came to an abrupt and rather painful end once I'd reached for the handle only to have the door shoved violently outward before my fingers ever found the prize. The impact of said door was a mystery, as my next semi-clear recollection was peering upward into the light gray sky as fresh flakes toppled into and began to fill the crevice of my parka hood.

"You're really beginning to worry me, Slim," I heard a deep, foreboding voice spew forth from what sounded like a great distance.

Leaning up onto my elbows, I huffed and puffed, albeit with limited lung power, and cleared the snow path blocking my view through the fur liner. The large man wore a perpetual scowl, and said expression was plainly seen as his own parka hood curled around an impossibly thick neck. He shot me a double thumbs-up before slowly twisting his hands about to display the opposite gesture.

"You some kinda potty perv, boy?" the Big

Apple's burly, surly rep continued without a hint of humor, "we gotta stop meeting this way. "

Struggling to my feet as separate shooting pains racked both my upper chest and right wrist, each obviously having taken the brunt of the potty door's outward thrust, myinability to respond to Big Apple's rude gestures was two-fold in particulars. Number one: a woeful lack of useable oxygen which would have limited said reply to a hoarse whisper at best. Number two, and easily the main issue: it's damn difficult to respond to remarks so strangely off-the-cuff, and from a total stranger no less.

"Down the road then, redneck," he concluded with a mock salute before whirling about with the athleticism of a prize thoroughbred and jogging away at an amazingly brisk pace considering the elements.

"Sc-screw you too, Yankee-Doodle *Dick-weed*," I managed once he was so far out of earshot it mattered little. Walking shakily with a hand pressed to my throbbing breastbone, I hobbled to the second unit, choosing to bypass the one *New York* had just departed in fear of a potentially fowl-smelling booby-trap. I should've realized, considering how downright shitty such instinctual choices had been of late, that there were much worse things than inhaling a vapor or two of semi-frozen feces. Take Porto-potty number two, for example, which contained a much nastier surprise by far.

Upon pulling the door ajar, no easy task considering the recent sleet had practically welded it shut, I'd barely stepped a boot-tip inside its cramped interior before backing out in a clumsy jig with both arms pin-wheeling to avoid yet another topple onto the petrified terrain.

With her mouth hanging agape and a thick tuft of frost-coated blonde hair cloaking the majority of her face above the nose, I was forced to move in for a closer inspection in order to satisfy the gut feeling that we'd met before.

Though I was able to obtain a proper ID, in truth there was very little recognizable in the stiffened corpse propped atop the potty with the bubbly blonde vixen I'd so briefly conversed with on media night in the hotel lobby. In reaching out with a shaky hand and brushing away a strand of sleet-stiffened hair, I discovered her left eye partially opened, the pupil having literally marbleized from the elements. Her arms dangled at her sides, gloves still intact on tightly clenched fists that death had apparently locked permanently into place. Leaning back on the closed toilet lid, her legs splayed out in a V-shape, I noted the placement of her right foot, which was twisted so grotesquely to the inside it appeared to have suffered a horrific break. For a moment, I pondered the possibility of a potential homicide, that is until the haphazardly written message she'd scribbled onto the inside of the Porto-Potty door swam into view upon my backing out.

Far from preachy, it spoke volumes with so very few words, almost eloquent in its sad simplicity. I stood back and read it several times, perhaps even aloud without being conscious of doing so.

Lord I pray the next life brings eternal warmth had been carved out from a quarter-inch of ice build-up, the inside door's dark brown shading in stark contrast to the whitish hue surrounding it.

As to procure evidence that Miss *Texas* had been the author of said suicide memorandum, I leaned inside one final time and lifted her right glove, figuring the odds that she'd been a southpaw were few and far between. With no small amount of relief, I found the glove's index finger showcased an obvious buildup of frosty slivers leftover from her efforts.

Although I'd considered removing her from the porcelain tomb she'd chosen as a personal burial ground and perhaps propping her next to or even behind it, I merely closed the door and did some writing of my own on the outer door.

I walked away whistling what little I knew of the ancient ditty '*Yellow Rose of Texas*'. Call it corny, but I simply couldn't think of a more proper tribute on such short notice. As for the message I'd left behind, it was simplicity in itself: *Out of Order.* In my opinion, the recently deceased hardly deserved being ogled like so much frozen lunch meat by every passerby with a need to pass bodily fluids.

The third of the mobile johns was, mercifully, void of either vengeful muggers or slumping corpses. The act itself went off smoothly enough, though I'd never before experienced the displeasure and discomfort of toilet paper so hardened by the elements it actually *crunched* when folded.

Part Six: (Frozen) Peas in a Pod

Time: Eight hours, thirty-six minutes into the Iron Will Gauntlet
Location: Sector B (*Northeastern/Midwestern Winter Climes*)
Total miles covered: twenty-six and a quarter

By my own approximation, purely speculative as it might be, the torturous terrain centering Sector B was being covered in roughly double the time as its predecessor, and one hardly had to be above average IQ to ascertain the reasons why. For all its hellish humidity, unbearably high temps and the occasional rainstorm or funnel cloud, Sector A's summertime theme couldn't hold a candle in terms of overall discomfort or level of difficulty. This, of course, coming from a man much more accustomed to the aforementioned conditions than the Antarctic nightmare so expertly laid out in round two. Then again, I'd wager even those born and raised in the upper Northeast and Midwest would be inclined to agree. As for my brethren from the south and southwest, it was becoming sadly obvious we were getting our warm-blooded behinds handed to us, big-time. For proof, one had to look no further than the three casualties whose untimely ends I'd been unfortunate enough to witness thus far; *Alabama* and his feverish collapse, *California's* ghoulish meltdown, and finally Miss *Texas* choosing to expire inside a hard-plastic crapper in lieu of enduring additional punishment from the elements. I

163

thought it no coincidence whatsoever that not a single citizen of either the Midwest or Northeast had been found in similar shape. At least, that is, not to that point. It would be interesting, if indeed the god of mercy chose fit to allow my future participation, to see what effect Sector C would have on said cold-weather mavens. Perhaps purely for inner motivation, I'd made a stern promise to myself upon returning to the trail following the discovery of that last stiffened corpse: I would survive Sector B's bone-chilling inquisition if only to feel sunlight, however manufactured, warm my bare flesh one last time.

As the trail had flattened somewhat a few hundred feet past the porta potties, a thick fog drifted up, essentially blanketing the icy terrain and thus making it a virtual impossibility to preview one's steps. Not at all a good thing, especially when I thought back to *Alabama*'s grisly ankle fracture. As for the skies? They'd spat out an ever-changing menu of assorted flakes, sleet and freezing rain, though none in great enough quality to hinder visibility above the ankles. In terms of surroundings, the walking tracks sparse shoulders had been bookended by jagged dirt and rock formations one might expect on a mountainous trail from some ancient TV western. Speaking of which, I had no doubt from what I'd witnessed of the faux landscape that at least a few of the scientific masterminds behind the Gauntlet's design were big into TV and film nostalgia. I half expected, though hardly pined, to soon be chased down the path by robotic polar bears.

I'd been trudging along at a snail's pace, cautiously feeling out every blind step as the whirling fog continued its soupy dominance, when a familiar voice cut through the chill from just up ahead. A fairly sharp curve loomed, and it sounded as though they had bellowed from just beyond my sights.

"Walking on eggshells, are we? What's the matter, Bluegrass, you scared of throwing a shoe?"

The word 'scared' had been pronounced 'scart' in a hilariously butchered southern accent, its originator unmistakable despite the severe hoarseness of their voice.

The grin that spread across my face beneath the tightly-secured parka hood was wholly involuntary; otherwise I would've surely refrained from the stinging pain it brought forth due to flesh surely on the verge of frostbite.

"Hey, prize thoroughbreds such as yours truly have to protect the gams, lady. Snap an ankle or twist a knee and this old warhorse is liable to be staring down the end of a loaded shotgun. "

"Whew! You going all negative on me now, dude? Seems Mr. Eternal Optimism has flown the coup. . . "

I half-stepped through the curve with all the speed of a crippled sloth on downers. As the swirling fog reached my upper calves, I saw her standing at the center of the trail with her hands atop her hips. Though her parka hood was pulled as taunt as my own, I could just make out a warped sneer beyond the fuzzy liner.

"Nah, he's just been replaced by a distant

cousin . . . *Mr. Reality is a bitch*. You got a problem with that, Missy?"

Thick plumes of water vapor spewed forth from the narrow liner opening, her familiar chackling a welcome sound despite the noted hoarseness.

"None whatsoever. 'Bout time you came over to the dark side. "

She stepped forward until we stood facing one another, and I briefly fought the very tangible urge to reach out and apply a bear hug of considerable force. After her blow-up in the Adaptation room and our subsequent breakup thereafter, I wasn't sure we'd cross paths again, or at least not willingly.

"Figured you for Sector C by now, what with the way you took off like someone had attached rocket-boosters to the heels of your boots. "

Squatting down, she peered up at me with a single, dark brown eye visible through the liner's slender opening, her lower legs and rear end essentially swallowed up by the soupy mist.

"Not a chance. I was setting a pretty good pace until the ground went all NHL on me. As god is my witness, Bluegrass, upon departing this domed deep freeze, I'll make it my life's mission to avoid any and everything chilled. "

Backing away a step, I lifted my boots one at a time, as if expecting to see the fog had transformed my feet to jagged stubs.

"Uh-huh, I hear you. Easy to say *now*. Talk to me once we make the waltz into Sector D. You'll be offering up the keys to the kingdom for a popsicle. "

She said nothing for several moments, and I secretly feared she'd taken the comment as belittlement.

"Yeah, you have me there. Had any company in my absence?"

"A few, but none that could match your winsome charm," I said, relieved, concluding with a slight bow that triggered a hoarse chuckle yet again, "and you? I take it our acquaintances were the same, being that you'd have had to pass them up before I ever had the pleasure of their company. "

She stood with both arms outstretched, a fresh plume of vapor spewing forth as she yawned loudly.

"May I say you are one sharp middle-aged male specimen?"

"Indeed, my lady, and may *I* say your powers of observation are simply magnificent. "

"You see the big, bad brute from NY?"

"Oh yeah," I replied, suddenly reminded of the stinging sensation at my breastbone, "we, um, shared a moment, you might say. Anyone else?"

"That crazy chick from *Cal-i-for-ni-ay* was be-bopping along, having a fine conversation with herself. I practically dashed by her just to avoid prolonged contact in case it was catching, you know?"

"We spoke. She was, well, having some problems. "

"Nutty as a three-layered fruitcake, in my unprofessional opinion. "

Though unsure as to why, I struggled mightily whether or not to come clean concerning Hollywood's fate. In the end, once we turned as one and commenced walking, I decided that sharing my most recent misery was best, at least from the standpoint of unburdening a frazzled mind.

"She . . . expired. "

For a moment, I didn't think she'd heard me and started to repeat the refrain with increased volume. Overhead, the skies were shaded a foreboding orange and gray hybrid that had yet, mercifully, to hatch anything substantial save a few stray flakes. As for the layer of fog dominating ground level, there seemed to be no relief in the lengthy flat stretch that lay ahead.

"Hollywood, you mean?"

"Yeah, she . . . wigged out back there and, well, there was no going back, apparently. "

Sagebrush glanced up at me briefly with that single dark eye, stumbling at bit in the process before righting herself.

"Wigged? What'd she do, exactly?"

Pausing, I was straining to string together the proper response and felt quite relieved in wake of her follow-up.

"I mean, that is if you . . . feel like discussing it. Hey, I'd sure understand if you told me to put a cork in it and just move on. "

"No, it's just that, I want to avoid being too graphic. "

"God, *that* bad?"

I nodded without looking her way.

"Let's just say she lost all sense of the brutality of these conditions. I tried to stop her, talk her out of it, but she was too far...gone I guess. At the end, there was nothing more I could do. "

I heard Sagebrush sigh heavily, and even release a faint sob.

"Ah *shit*, and there I was getting my jollies ridiculing the poor woman for talking to herself. If there's a nugget of truth in that old saying *what comes around goes around*, this girl is definitely treading crap-ola creek without the required paddling gear. "

Leaning over and down, I gently nudged her shoulder.

"Don't beat yourself up, Tumbleweed. We need and crave distraction from the reality of what we signed up for, right? Anything to pass the time and help us forget what the evil weather gods are apt to dish out next. "

She hopped over and ahead several steps, as if skipping across a series of aligned stones.

"I hear what you're saying, dude, but my conscience is spewing forth a different take, behavioral excuse-wise. It's called being a mean-spirited old hussy, and it's about time I policed up such antics. If nothing else, I'd sure think better of myself in the end. "

We lumbered on in relative silence for several minutes, my right thigh and calf throbbing with equal intensity, the reemergence of said ills no doubt brought on by the continuing need to hobble along on transparent eggshells courtesy of the fog-line that refused to dissipate. To add insult to numerous injuries, I'd developed quite the stiff neck since the Porto-potty incident, to the point where the simple act of turning my head caused a tangible wave of dizziness. Once dialogue did return, it was I who initiated, feeling the need yet again to share my misery.

"*California* wasn't the only casualty I ran across. "

As before, I figured she hadn't heard due to an immediate lack of response, but soon enough she whirled about and began to backtrack cautiously. Using both hands to spread the parka liner, I couldn't help but be amused by her bug-eyed, slack-jawed expression.

"You mean *another* suicide-walker? Man, should I start to worry about sharing the same length of track with you?"

I chose to ignore the second query, though there was no denying a twinge of deep-seeded concern at such a wild notion. Then again, what if she had a point?

"This one was . . . different. "

She waited until I caught up before facing forward yet again.

"So says the Reaper. How so?"

"This one was already deceased upon my . . . the discovery. "

"I'm intrigued...not to mention sufficiently creeped-out. Who and where?"

"Miss *Texas*. Found her in a Porto-potty, frozen as stiff as you please. "

"Damn. How'd she, uh, well, do the deed?"

With that, a sliver of sleet infiltrated my hood's liner and pierced the bridge of my nose. I peered up through the slender gap to witness similar spears descending downward at a sharp leftward angle due to the fairly stout breeze blowing at our backs.

"Couldn't really tell, but she left a note scribbled into the frost on the interior door. From what she'd written, I'd ascertain it was the conditions themselves that got her. She just couldn't take it anymore and just huddled inside and passed out. Hypothermia, more than likely. Wouldn't take long to expire in this mess if you've lost the will to go on. "

The pronounced sigh surfaced once again, as did a thick cloud of vapor that temporarily floated past like some colossal smoke-ring.

"True enough. *Brutal.* Well, seems as though my fellow gal competitors are falling like flies. "

A sharp curve lay ahead perhaps thirty yards in the distance, leading past a jutting hillside that hung over the shoulder like the giant dislodged tooth of some recently unearthed dinosaur. With great disdain I noted the fog seemed to have drifted upward another inch or so, nearly reaching the top-half of my mukluks, while having already swallowed Sagebrush's legs past the top of the knee.

"What's with this cursed soup? Wouldn't know it if we were stepping off a cliff, for Christ's sake," I moaned, though with limited ire despite a healthy dose of sincere concern.

Sagebrush shrugged, hugging herself tightly across the chest. I thought of chugging down the remainder of my tea before reconsidering once my midsection grew instantly sour at the mere suggestion.

"You got me. Can't be due to any radical change in temps, right? My bet is the old heat gauge hasn't wriggled its way past the negative range since the word go, and that's not counting these damn winds. "

She paused before nudging me with an upturned shoulder.

"Share a secret if you promise not to tell. "

"My lips are sealed," I replied light-heartedly, the dialogue almost drowned out by a sharp crunching sound beneath our collective boots. Gravel, more than likely, or perhaps shattered ice from a frozen puddle; though it was impossible to verify without lying flat to catch a peak beneath the fog line.

"Purse the lips too tightly and that might well happen," she giggled, the strained croak of her voice more evident than ever. When next she spoke, it was an equally gruff whisper barked forth through cupped hands.

"Anyhow, word is that a certain female walker from the Grand Canyon state can no longer feel her tootsies. "

I instantly slowed a step, a maneuver she had apparently expected while matching my sudden pause.

"Numbness? You mean the toes, or the whole foot?"

"The whole feet and nothin' but the feet, dude. "

We resumed our previous pace, though the deep ache in my leg and neck seemed to kick into overdrive immediately following this rather grave announcement.

"How long?"

"Shit, fifteen minutes after the adaptation room, tops. Fact is, this girl just isn't cut out for glacier hikes. "

As if on cue, the third deep sigh since our reunion then filled the surrounding air with a thick, frosty cloud, and I found myself temporarily unable to form a suitable reply.

"Bottom line is pretty clear," she continued instead, hugging herself tight and leaning forward as if walking on tip-toes, "gotta vamoose from this particular sector as soon as humanly feasible or I'm apt to be a damn site shorter when all is said and done, if you catch my rather grisly drift. "

"Hey, numbness doesn't automatically mean, well, you know," I babbled, turning towards her as a sharp stinging sensation raced from the nape of my neck down the length of my spine, briefly blurring my already shaky vision.

"Can't say my own little piggies are exactly warm and toasty at this point, despite the boots and triple-layer of thermal wrap. Besides, we should be nearing the finish line pretty quick. Feels like we've spent twice the time in here as we did in A sector. "

"Indeed it does, and covered roughly half the ground, I'd wager," she replied morosely as we sauntered past the jutting stone tooth and entered a c-shaped bend.

"I don't think they're going by distance," I countered weakly, hoping and praying said assumption wasn't merely a highly desperate case of wishful thinking.

"To them, I think it's all about time and obstacles, and I'd say we've done our share of dodging potential danger thus far, wouldn't you agree?"

When she didn't immediately reply, I peered over, wincing with the effort, and saw she was reaching out with both arms and pointing straight ahead, resembling a shell-shocked sleepwalker on a midnight jaunt.

"Hey, check it out . . . " she said with renewed spark as my gaze followed her gesture in order to lock on target, ". . . pace-setters I presume?"

In clearing the curve, the distance ahead swam gradually into view; a long stretch of flat terrain occupied by four closely huddled competitors and one front-runner spaced perhaps ten to fifteen yards ahead.

"Looks like. I recognize at least two of 'em. " Unfortunate but true, *New York*'s burly rep was easily spotted, tucked between two medium-sized walkers whom he dwarfed by nearly a foot in height *and* considerable bulk. As for the leader of said pack, there was a sickening familiarity in both the wobbly, uneven gait on display and the frenzied pace behind it.

"Good guys or bad?" she asked with such indifference I considered lying just to conserve energy.

"Well, the two I've ID'ed definitely don the dark hats, especially that *Black Bart* jackass riding point. Not sure about the remaining trio. Besides, when push comes to shove, they-. . "

"I know, I know. . . they're *all* the enemy," she finished as we simultaneously sped up a degree despite the unknown context of the mystery terrain below.

"Why, ain't you proud, though?" I teased as we

built speed to a light jog.

"Proud of what exactly?" she huffed in response, though I deduced through at least a small smile.

"Why, how you've slowly turned this otherwise innocent southern boy to the dark side?"

"Surely my greatest accomplishment," she said, the short giggle that followed serving to briefly warm my severely chilled innards despite it all. Taboo as it was, there was flat-out no denying how good it felt to have my regular traveling companion back in tow. Better yet, she seemed relatively sane despite the confession concerning potential frostbite. One tragedy at a time, I recall thinking at the time. Talk about prophetic, the latest loomed just moments away.

Part Seven: *Hail on Earth*

Time: Nine hours, eleven minutes into the Iron Will Gauntlet

Location: Sector B (*Northeastern/Midwestern Winter Climes*)

Total miles covered: Just over twenty-seven miles

It began innocently enough, as so many of its ilk so often do. A light sprinkling of sleet so insignificant we brushed it off without a second thought. After all, we'd been slogging through similar variations on and off for the past two hours. Why, even as tiny spears began to transform into pea-sized pellets, bounding off our parkas like BB's, we blundered forward with the single-minded goal of catching up to and passing those blazing the trail ahead. At that point, the thought of recent history should've sounded off like a blaring klaxon; light bulbs with super-nova intensity should've lit up above our heads like lighthouse beacons to indicate that something bad had been planned—a sinister plot conceived, expertly weaved and soon to be set in motion. At this juncture in the game, we should've been wiser, more perceptive. The hints were there; the clues in place. We should've known the *boys in the lab* were hardly finished dolling out misery. As it turned out, they were just warming up, pardon the misnomer.

Gaining ground with each lunging step, we soon drew near enough to make out the dark, lettered initials gracing the parkas of the aforementioned trio I was unable to ID from a distance.

Spaced apart by perhaps three to five yards, all three were similarly hunched over as sporadic specs of ice soon became marble-like missiles. Closest to us on the left was *Rhode Island*, a tall, lanky gentleman with bird-thin legs who turned to shoot us a casual glance as we ambled briskly by. Being as all three had their hood liners pulled as tightly as our own, actual facial recognition was an impossibility, and in *Rhode Island*'s case, I'd briefly spotted a single blue eye size us up through the liner's narrow gap.

Second in line was *Idaho,* a thickly-built man bent so far over he appeared positively hunchbacked. Peering down into the swirling fog as if scoping the grounds for a lost contact lens, he never bothered to acknowledge our presence as we passed him by. *Point of order*: as far as red flags go, foreboding-wise, I'd witnessed and quickly dismissed the initial down-pouring of larger hailstones bouncing off the man's neck and upper back. Whether or not my traveling companion took note of this, I have no clue, though neither of us reacted to its presence at the time, verbally or otherwise. In truth, even if we had, there would've been little time to create, much less successfully initiate a plan of action. We were, as usual, playing the role of sitting duck in a shooting gallery.

We had just pulled even with *Illinois*, a roly-poly individual whose sex I was unable to determine merely from body type, when the bottom truly fell out from above. Literally within the blink of an eye, moderate hail transmogrifiedf into a full-blown meteor shower. I heard Illinois grunt in pain as a circular stone that perfectly mimicked a cue-ball in both size and shape, bounced off the left side of his parka hood, followed by a flurry of similarly bulky nuggets. If nothing else, the distinctly feminine whine had answered the earlier question concerning gender.

Our pace immediately slowed, Sagebrush and I exchanged a worrisome glance just before the worst of the barrage ensued. The details of what transpired in that chaotic few minutes is mostly a blurred tapestry of frenzied movements layered in grunts, groans, and anguished cries. In terms of mass, the aforementioned marbles soon begat baseballs, and baseballs begat softballs. Hopping about clumsily as if performing some ritualistic dance to perhaps ward off the onslaught, I watched several of the latter ricochet off Sagebrush's shoulders and upper back as she crumbled to the ground with a weak moan. At one point, I must've reverted to mythical movie-hero mode, having leaned over her fallen form in true 'human shield' fashion. For initiating such a gesture purely on instinct alone, I do confess to hoarding a sense of pride. As for maintaining said posture, it lasted only long enough for the first boulder of ice to hammer a gash into the top of my noggin. Having surely blacked out, I awoke flat on my stomach directly next to Sagebrush as the assault continued full-bore. I heard screams nearby, some muffled but others banshee-like in their intensity, no doubt originating from at least two but perhaps all the recently engaged trio singing out in true barbershop quartet fashion.

I'll cut to the chase, as the majority of the battering in question mercifully slips my mind due to both its brief duration and the mild concussion I most assuredly suffered in its wake, only two of the original five who bore witness to said calamity would survive to press on and persevere. The method to said survival was less ingenious than luck; driven by panic and desperation. I cannot, in truth, take an ounce of credit for its inception, much less its effectiveness, though I might well have been responsible for both. Blame the aforementioned skull-thumping for such a woeful lack of clarity. When asked, Sagebrush drew an equally blank slate, stating she could recall little after the initial bludgeoning. Regardless, each of us awoke buried beneath the lifeless, pummeled husks of those we'd seemingly used for cover as the worst of the storm had progressed. It had taken me several frantic moments to shove the representative from *Idaho* from atop my numbed frame, catching my breath only after I'd rolled completely free of his mangled corpse, from which I'd actually heard the sharp snapping of bone and subsequent gnashing together of multiple fractures from along the area of his ribcage and upper chest. He'd rolled over onto his back, his parka hood pulled back to reveal a bloody, mangled pulp hardly recognizable as a human face. Crawling onto my left side, I used both arms to brush away the massive build-up of hail that had seemingly attempted to bury us alive in an avalanche of ivory ball-bearings.

Pulling myself up on all fours, I watched Sagebrush crawl from beneath Miss *Illinois*, who'd apparently been lying face-up during the worst of the storm and had, predictably, paid a horrendous price. Perhaps a dozen feet to my right lay *Rhode Island*, whose ravaged carcass was so grotesquely misshaped it appeared he'd been flattened by a runaway Zamboni. As desperate as I was to rush to her side as she struggled to free herself from the woman's ample dead weight, physically I simply wasn't up to the task. My entire frame, from the balls of the feet to the tip of the scalp, tingled and itched from an extreme case of mass numbness, and I recall the stark fear in realizing such symptoms might mean I'd suffered a significant stroke. Pulling the already warped parka hood completely free, I sucked in a deep, labored breath and was instantly rewarded with a sensation akin to swallowing down a large cube of ice.

"H-hey, y-you o-o-alright over th-there?" I heard Sagebrush whimper, having finally pulled herself completely free. She lay on her back with legs and arms spread as if preparing to create a snow-angel, only in this case a hail-angel would have to suffice.

"No, can't really say I am . . . and you?"

"Dunno y-yet. Feel l-like I just p-popped out of a b-biscuit can. "

Resetting the hood, I attempted to stand and made it stick on the fourth try. The mighty hailstorm had withered down to a light mix of sleet and flakes, though the wind gusts seemed stouter and more frequent in the aftermath. If there was a positive to be had from such a hellish event, the storm had at least served to whisk away the lingering ground fog that had been such an annoyance, though in retrospect it was hardly a fair tradeoff.

Stepping cautiously atop the icy buildup, I was briefly reminded of the kiddie ball-pits once so common in fast-food joints. Leaning down over her, our eyes locked briefly, and I saw a twinge of madness in the reflection that was as unnerving as it was strangely exhilarating. I had little doubt she'd noted a similar trait within the mirrors to her own soul. We were survivors, her and I, perhaps fated to be so but hopelessly lost within whatever grand scheme had branded us as such. For whatever reason, we'd dodged numerous bullets when others had not. If one was to believe in such things as kismet, she and I had much to be positive about indeed. If not, one had to wonder when exactly such blind luck would run out. Gripping her gently behind the left shoulder while cupping her elbow, I helped her sit up.

"Anything busted or broken that you can tell?" I asked, keeping my arm propped at her back for support.

She lurched forward as if to vomit, then righted herself and sighed heavily.

"Well, I've g-got the Mount Rushmore of all headaches and. . . my right eye feels like it took a direct hit, but the remainder of the inventory seems. . . stable enough. Then again, I could have multiple fractures of both feet and probably wouldn't know it. "

"Still completely numb then?"

"Yep . . . all the way up to the ankle. "

"We need to get going," I countered, digging deep to play the role of fearless, stalwart male, "you up to traveling?"

Bowing her head a final time, she paused a moment before peering up at me with a wry grin that, despite the condition of its bone-weary originator, appeared refreshingly sincere.

"Is there an alternative?"

"I'm with you, lady. Let us shag ass for greener pastures. "

Taking an extra moment to straighten the cap-cam, which had surely taken a battering of its own, I thought of turning back to the misshapen bodies of our former competitors for future rant material, but quickly discovered I had neither the strength nor stomach for such antics.

We departed with little of the fervor to back up such bravado, limping along like the broken-down, fatigue-ridden road-warriors we'd most assuredly transformed into over the previous twenty or so miles. Neither of us bothered to glance back to the horror we were leaving behind. Death had become a constant companion as the seemingly infinite trail stretched on. The novelty had long since worn off. Besides, there would surely be more to come, so why bother fretting over past horrors? The trio of torn, broken, disfigured corpses at our backs desired no company; no wailing mourners to clasp their cold, dead fingers in tribute. In truth, my biggest fear wasn't joining their ranks per say, but the timeframe involved in doing so. In some ways, I deduced depressingly, they had gotten off somewhat easy, as surely a worse fate befell those destined to continue down the long, arduous path to a more torturous demise. I said a silent prayer, the first of many to come, that if my destiny did *not* include departing the Gauntlet with a beating pulse, for the reaper's blade to descend swiftly and with limited pain.

As my loyal traveling companion and I trekked on, approaching still another sharp bend in the path, we leaned together for added support. Surely the light at the end of the hellish igloo that was B Sector grew near, I hoped and prayed yet again. As it was, the powers that be had scheduled one last hurdle to complete their sadistic jollies. It was to laugh, really, once said hurdle swam into sight as we'd cleared the aforementioned curve. Then again, such spontaneous gaiety, if given its head while in a state of almost total delirium, might soon transform into a shriek of anger and utter hopelessness that would surely spell the doom for its originator. Thus, I managed to remain the calm, stoic warrior despite an overwhelming urge to reach up and tear out my own eyes.

Part Eight: The Ivory Sea

Time: Nine hours, forty-three minutes into the Iron Will Gauntlet

Location: Sector B (*Northeastern/Midwestern Winter Climes*)

Total miles covered: Just under twenty-eight miles

"You see what I see?" Sagebrush croaked weakly, the ravages of laryngitis haven taken a mighty hold.

"Well," I countered as whimsically as humanly possible considering a sudden twisting pain at my gut, like steel bands being slowly tightened, "if you're referring to the door to salvation across the way, I most certainly can confirm it is not a hallucination.

On the other hand, there is the little matter of what lies between us and it. "

"Doesn't matter," she replied in a hoarse mumble that was only made audible by a total lack of wind, "whatever blockade they tossed up . . . this girl's gonna crawl, dig or fly her way past it. Gotta find some sun. Gotta...find some heat...any heat s-short of setting fire to my own underwear. "

Having peeled away her hood, she appeared a full decade older than the bubbly, hyper-energetic woman I'd first encountered in Sector A. Her hair, frost-filled and limp, clung to her scalp like barnacles to a rusty hull. Her dark brown eyes, once gleaming with enthusiasm, held an ancient, haunting glare, and appeared to have sunk impossibly deep into their respective sockets. Her lips had narrowed into purplish slugs, the flesh of her face a dull, ashen color that screamed terminal disease.

Looking back over my left shoulder, the trail was predictably deserted with no evidence, visual or verbal, that company was forthcoming.

"Sure wouldn't mind some assistance, like maybe a team of snowplows," I quipped sourly. I watched her kneel down, almost falling forward in the process, and massage her shins just above the boot line. She then whimpered softly, no doubt in response to the total numbness discovered there.

"Alright then, just follow my lead," I replied nonchalantly in perhaps my best acting job thus far, "we just have to be patient. You know, take it one step at time and all that jazz. You with me, woman?"

Before pulling the hood back up and over her haggard features, she glanced over and managed a weak, pathetic smile.

"Blaze away, Nanook. Lead me to the promised land. "

With that, I took a deep breath and took a lunging goose step forward, only to see my right leg subsequently vanish up to the thigh. My left leg, throbbing like a rotted tooth, soon followed, and was similarly swallowed whole, the overall effect serving to re-chill my entire frame much in the same way the adaptation room had—a bone-numbing full-body shiver that rode the length of my spine like a slowly ascending ice-cube.

Though it was impossible to accurately gauge, there appeared to be perhaps seventy-five to one-hundred yards to the sector's exit point, only the top portion of the structure's dark red doorway still visible above the drift-line.

As the mission progressed, an old classic rock tune soon stuck in my head—a tune whose righteous guitar riffs and thundering bass steadfastly refused to fade until the arduous deed at hand neared completion. I recall vividly pondering said tune's significance, not at all satisfied with the obvious clue contained in its title. In retrospect, it made perfect sense, as would have a most recognizable TV theme song from my father's day—'*Mission Impossible*'. As for the tune in question, I was somehow able to turn the negativity of Cheap Trick's '*Surrender*' into a positive.

Logically, at least from a meteorological standpoint, the surrealistic scene before us made no sense whatsoever, and on so many varied levels. Adjusting my hold on Sagebrush's left wrist, I was able to organize a mental checklist of said nonsensical details while using both legs and my free arm to dig out a workable pathway.

Illogical fact number one: How exactly does a four foot snowfall, complete with five to six foot drifts, blanket only a specific stretch of the walking trail, that of course being the last three to four-hundred feet leading to the sector's exit? In studying the outer perimeter of exactly where the heavy snow had started, the edge of the initial drift was impossibly slick and squared off, as if the bulk had not fallen but literally been dumped there by the truckload. The shoulders on either side had been similarly packed, and peering up into the faux backgrounds, there wasn't a patch left untouched by the monstrous downpour. Trees, though likely CGI creations one and all, had been buried to the hilt with only their gnarled tops popping through.

Of course, over the years I'd heard stories of both rain and snowstorms effecting only select portions of space, i. e. , people standing at the center of a room with windows on either side and seeing hard precipitation on one side and bone-dry conditions on the other. Such bizarre cloudbursts weren't that uncommon if one considered the simple fact that precipitation simply had to start at one point and end at another. Still, this particular 'beginning' looked to have been measured off and manicured in true ice-sculpture fashion.

Illogical fact number two: Being that both that snarling, brooding hulk from *New York* and that scrawny weasel from *Colorado* had built only a forty to fifty yard lead from the rest of the pack about the time those frozen cannonballs began to fall, how exactly did they avoid wading through the aftermath of a snowfall that had to have taken hours to accumulate? I mean, short of my *dumping truckloads* theory, such a massive buildup doesn't just happen in the blink of an eye, Super-cell blizzard *or* scientific trickery be damned. We'd arrived at the edge of those puffy snow-dunes with nary a hint anyone or thing had so much as poked a pinky finger into the upper layer. Unless those two bastards were buried beneath the drifts or could somehow levitate over 'em, there should've been a dug out trail already awaiting us.

Illogical fact number three: For temperatures most likely dipping just below zero, the snow in question was remarkably soft and sticky. It was, in fact, the perfect texture for building snowmen. Again, this was hardly reasonable considering the conditions, which should've dictated a tundra-like substance one could easily trek atop of with minimal give. As it was, playing the part of human snow-shovel was the only option in moving forward. I have to believe this was hardly an accident. Clever devils, those *inquisitors.*

Finally, though this was more along the lines of a 'I'm not paranoid, but everyone *is* out to get me' type thought; it truly seemed, if taken at face value, that the final hurdle in escaping B sector had been created exclusively for the two of us. I mean, hadn't I mentally pondered the possibility of a final barrier existing? A barrier manufactured as punishment for those who somehow managed to survive the hailstorm from hell? As far as sadism goes, it all fit well enough with the patterns already in place. *The inquisitors* of the Iron-Will Gauntlet were a proud group of forked-tongue sadists, no doubt, and we had been the two lab rats clever enough to endure their greatest, most dangerous trap. To allow safe passage to C Sector would've been to admit defeat, and I cannot help but deduce that humility is a trait unknown to such entities.

All told, I approximate it took over forty minutes to navigate that final brutal stretch, and another fifteen to dig out a passage wide enough to pull open the door. I'd been forced to not only clear away the massive buildup literally one square foot at a time, but also pull Sagebrush along like a conjoined twin. She toppled over several times, constantly halting our forward progress as I'd been forced to pull her from the quagmire. Finally, upon reaching the mostly buried doorway, I'd constructed an impromptu throne from the dug-out masses and propped her limp form atop it. Since the door pulled outward, it was quite the chore clearing out the required space, especially considering the effort already expended.

Once I'd cleared enough room to pull it ajar by perhaps a foot and a half, I shimmied over and hoisted Sagebrush over my left shoulder. Backing into the opening, it took several clumsy moments to work us through the opening, but not without banging an already stinging shoulder against the door's solid steel frame to prevent dropping my flaccid, barely coherent rider. Almost immediately upon clearing the space, I felt a pair of stout hands jerk Sagebrush from my grip.

"We've got her now, sir," the robotic voice barked stoically as I was whirled forcefully about by the upper arms, the room so dimly lit in comparison to the brightness we'd just departed that I could make out only a slew of jumpy, darting shadows.

"Follow me, sir," another chimed in, equally mechanical, "infirmary is just up ahead. "

I cannot be sure how many steps I actually completed before finding myself lying face down on the carpet, or who exactly hauled me back upright and carried me forward. Though specific recollections are foggy at best, mere snippets really, clarity returned somewhat with the aroma of antiseptic as I was being propped upon a narrow cot and my outerwear subsequently removed.

While being unceremoniously stripped to my undies, I caught only blurred images of those around me, the room itself only slightly better lit than the murky hallway beyond. Whatever dialogue was being spewed was mostly unintelligible, fractured medical jargon and mumbled orders to whomever was reliving me of my clothing.

At the time, I must confess little curiosity as to what was transpiring. Whatever the scenario, no matter how ghoulish or grave, there was no apprehension or fear to be had. *Aliens* prepping me for dissection? No problem. Carve away and feel free to Handi-wrap those samples! Ravenous *cannibals* readying my emaciated carcass for a boiling vat? Hey, toss in some carrots and fresh celery and the feast was on me! All that mattered at that time—the only thing that meant squat—was the warmth, or better yet, the delightful, *praise-the-lord and pass the refried beans* lack of frigid cold. As far as I knew, interior temps might've been hovering near the freezing mark, but compared to the previous five hours, I might as well have been sitting atop a sand dune in the tropics with my naked toes buried in warm, soothing sand with searing sunlight blistering every inch of exposed flesh. I recall a needle, perhaps even two, being jabbed into the interior of my left elbow, and even being made to sip thick, glutinous liquid from a clear plastic cup.

Blacking in and out, it's impossible to distinguish reality from dream sequence, though two very distinct visions do stick out from all others, the first involving the quickly passing image of *New York's* surly rep, who fast-walked by flashing a toothy grin that showcased several gold choppers in what was once famously referred to as a 'grille'. He'd also raised his right hand and exhibited a peace sign that was conspicuously absent the ring and pinky fingers, both of which appeared to have been sheared off at the knuckle. Though I only had a brief moment for evaluation in wake of his hasty departure, I could only deduce he'd fallen victim to a nasty case of frostbite. With that in mind, I'm fairly sure I performed a half-hearted self-inventory of my own hands and feet to ensure all previous digits were indeed present and accounted for.

The second vision would, unfortunately, prove to be as real as the small hairs it had aroused to erection upon viewing Sagebrush, who was occupying the cot across from my own. A trio of lab-coat wearing individuals had been kneeling over her, and it wasn't until they all backed away as one that I caught a glimpse of her feet. Sans the mukluks and thick socks that had been peeled away and discarded nearby, what was revealed beneath went a long way in snapping me out of the comfortable daze I'd been so happily occupying. Honestly, it wasn't merely the visual, but the horrid stench that occupied it—a scent so rancid and overwhelming I'm fairly sure I heard at least one of the lab-coats wrenching in the background. The aforementioned antiseptic was, in the face of such a reeking onslaught, helpless to do anything but dissipate as if whisked away by a fearsome gust.

Instantly, in wake of such a shocking revelation, I thought of her complaints of pain and numbness. In retrospect, it's truly hard to comprehend the level of misery she'd endured, or how she'd managed to persevere through it. In studying her pale, gaunt features, showcased so dramatically minus the thick parka and equally copious wool shirt, my heart sank and warm tears blurred my vision. Then again, I could only contemplate my own haggard appearance as perhaps being equally gruesome and felt fortunate no mirrors or similar reflective devices sat nearby to confirm this as fact. By the time I'd been helped from the cot by a pair of stoutly built uniform types whose bland, expressionless faces I could never recall under oath, near full consciousness had returned. Perhaps it had been the combination of mystery juice and whatever tonic they'd plunged into my veins, or perhaps it had been the revulsion of Sagebrush's blackened, grotesquely swollen feet, the big toes of which had plumped to the size of a Florida orange. Regardless, I sincerely wish the daze could've continued for an additional few moments, at least long enough to dull the memory of one Lieutenant Gil Masters, *asshole in charge* of Sector C in-processing.

Sector C: *The Bog*

Part One: Ass-Chewing(s): a Pre-Brief

Time: Ten hours, twenty-two minutes into the Iron Will Gauntlet

Location: De-brief area between Sector's B and C (Hybrid climes: Upper northwest/southern U. S. coastline)

Total miles covered: Just over twenty-eight miles

"May I ask you a question of you, *Kentucky*?"

"Y-yeah, sure. "

"Are you truly the best that particular state had to offer?"

"Pa-excuse me?"

"Surely to the great lord above choosing someone as stone-cold dumbass as yourself had to be a colossal error in judgment. You southerners have never impressed me with being the sharpest tools in the belt, but *shit on a Caeser Salad*, tell me this is all just some bone-headed practical joke gone too fucking far. . ."

"I'm not follow-w-who are you again?"

Having barely received the required gear for Sector C, that being a backpack containing raingear (to include knee-high rubbers so comically oversized I couldn't help but think in circus-clown terms), various water bottles (forty eight total ounces of 'vitamin enriched' H2O), a small spray can I'd been told 'would definitely come in handy when the time was right' and a dozen or so energy bars (I prayed these didn't hold the same card-board flavor as Sector B's collection), I had been led to an empty room roughly the size of a shower stall and instructed to await the impending pre-brief. After pulling on the rubber boots and pacing a bit for breaking in purposes, I strapped on the backpack and leaned against a far wall, my thoughts instantly turning to Sagebrush and the horrific replay of her bloated, blackened feet.

I'd had time to remove and study the adjusted cap-cam, this time buried within the bill of a light blue ball-cap, when the sound of hard-heel boots thumping the adjoining hallway's stone flooring redirected my attention. Staring straight ahead, the source of the clamor skidded to a robotic stop at the room's entryway, performed a textbook right-face maneuver then paused before leaning into the empty space head-first wearing an angry snarl. He looked me up and down through tightly squinted eyes and huffed before taking a cautious step inside. With his pale complexion, clean-shaven head, stout torso and freakishly puffed biceps, all contained within a relatively short frame, he appeared every bit the stereotypical SS Skinhead come to frightening life. As if pasted on for effect, an 'L' shaped scar ran the length of his right cheek from just beneath the temple to the lower portion of the jaw line. Not surprisingly, his voice was well-deep; a gravelly tenor complete with turbo boosters and side-pipes. Despite an initial wave of apprehension at the man's obvious attempt at intimidation, a small part of me instantly labeled him a walking cliché; more actor than actual instructor *slash* pre-briefer. Much like Fritz the Clone from Sector B, I just couldn't completely buy into the act without serious reservations.

"Lieutenant Gil Masters, Gauntlet Security OIC, like that means beans to the likes of you. "

"Um, is there a problem, Lieutenant? Pardon me for saying, but you seemed a mite peeved. "

"Oh, this isn't ticked, mister," he sneered, standing less than three feet away and forced to tilt his head slightly upward in light of my four to five inch height advantage, "this is only slightly perturbed. Believe me, those of your ilk aren't even capable of bringin' out the true bear in me. It takes failed expectations to do so, wasted potential, all characteristics you seem woefully void of possessing. "

Swear to god, the man smelled of talcum powder and Wrigley's chewing gum, too ancient scents it took me several frustrated moments to pinpoint.

"I, um, see. Then, might I ask why the pert—"

He cut me off with the tilt of the head and a hand raised palm out, his jaw muscles wound so tightly I thought I might soon hear the crunching of molars.

"One question, mister, that's all I need answered before I proceed with the contractual crap. I've got just under six minutes to try and straighten you out before you're booked to the adaptation room. "

I paused, unsure whether to respond verbally. Once he replied with a dramatically cocked brow, I then proceeded.

"Ohhh-kay. That one question being?"

"You enter this competition to win or play nursemaid?"

"Say what? I don't underst—"

"You that hard up for trim, mister? I mean, you got a handful of *Ultra-Viagra* burnin' a hole in your pocket?"

For that, I found no response other than a wild, high-pitched giggle.

"Just wonderin', since you practically carried that broken-down hussy from the desert the last several miles of track, diggin' through a mountain of packed snow before piggy-back riding her crippled caboose to the Promised Land. What gives, bub? Chick promise you a knob-slob at the end of the race or can we chalk up such Jack-wagon behavior on Cupid shooting an arrow straight up your gullible ass?"

Not knowing whether to guffaw aloud or take a punch at the square-jawed prick, I instead decided on treading a higher ground and plead the fifth.

"Left-tenant, that's at least *five* questions, none of which I feel obligated to answer."

"Fine," he replied sourly, crossing buffed arms across an equally muscular chest, the two-sizes too small uniform he'd donned enhancing the effect several fold, "stupid is as stupid is, I take it. As long as you do understand the ultimate goal of competing in the Iron-Will Gauntlet, which is to cross that mythical finish line all by your lonesome, are we at least clear on that point or did one of those hail-spears nail you between the eyes and permanently warp the perception?"

Taking the time to readjust the backpack's straps, I felt a sudden surge of anger in being brow-beaten for displaying basic human compassion.

"I understand the concept, yes. In the meantime, I've got a few questions of my own, Lt. Just to…clarify what you and *your* ilk define as a warped perspective. We, that being the competitors . . . do still qualify as human beings, correct? Or is that a concept the organizers of this freak-show long since lost touch with?"

"Bleedin' hearts are destined to halt beating in this particular universe, bub," he whispered, leaning up on his tiptoes until we were practically eye-to-eye. In response, I fought off the strongest of urges to refer to him as 'Shorty'.

"Hurting the ratings with my Boy Scout ways, am I, Left-tenant? Guess the viewing masses prefer hefty portions of blood 'n guts over acts of kindness. "

With that, he actually shrunk back a step, resting that boxy chin against an upturned fist.

"Just hurts the boys in the booth to see ya piss away a great shot 'cause your heart is overshooting your brain. "

"Come again?"

"Three times, bub. Count 'em. Three times in B Sector you stopped to render aid to the enemy, and that's not even taking into account playing ER nurse to Miss Arizona. I mean, come on! There's a whopper of a difference between showin' kindness or *showcasin'* blatant stupidity. Deep down, you have to be questioning such lunk-headed antics, but so far there isn't a shred of evidence ya have a blessed clue. "

Feeling the heat of anger gradually depart my flushed cheeks, I sucked in a lung-full and gave myself an additional moment to further cool down. The man was obviously a company puppet, nothing more, sent to plant the seed for his faceless, soulless superiors. The message he'd been instructed to hammer home was about as subtle as its perpetually squinting, teeth-gnashing messenger. Cut the Sainthood crap and get on with the walking, preferably around or over as many competitors as possible.

"Don't misunderstand," I finally retorted calmly, "I know what must be done when the time comes. "

Shaking his head slowly from side to side, the Left-tenant's tone and mannerisms were again of the 'wise adult scolds ignorant child' mode. Staged act or no, it was growing particularly tiresome considering I spotted him at least a decade in age.

"The time is now, buddy-boy. You may not be aware, but you've created quite an unexpected stir within the global betting circles. "

"So Vegas sees me as a real threat, do they?"

A tiny smile, barely noticeable, creased the corners of his mouth.

"Threat my squared-away butt-cheeks, bub. As of your exit from B Sector, you were sitting at exactly three-to-one on the big board. "

"Really? Three-to-one? Might I guess the

identities of the two I so boldly chase?"

"Whoa," he chided, wide-eyed, "you some kinda fancy-pants playwright or something?"

Unsure as to why exactly, perhaps it was just the mood, I decided to extend the dialogue just to see how far the company stooge would go. As for my sudden bout of boldness, I had to give some credit to whatever mystery-juice they'd shot into my veins. I recall a wave of energy coursing through me; as if the previous twenty hours of physical and mental torture was being slowly, methodically, flushed out of my system. Be it steroid, HGH, or a liquid mix of Flintstone's chewables, I was soon feeling my oats as I hadn't done since the starting line.

"Why, you surprise me, Left-tenant. I figured it a requirement you know everything about me before garnering this here counseling position, right down to underwear size and what flavor toothpaste I prefer."

"Not me, bub. Recruiting services handle all that garbage. I'm just a salaried man with specific duties to carry out, security being the main, counseling when required being secondary."

"So basically what they're telling you is to instruct me to stop being so damn considerate and start looking out squarely for number one."

He nodded stiffly, purposely breaking eye contact for the first time while backing up a step to scan the hallway in both directions.

"You got it, Ace. People just love a longshot. Can't get enough of that 'underdog goes for the gold' crap."

"I'll do my best, then, to uphold said creed. "

His brow creased dramatically, and I could barely refrain from laughing aloud.

"Is that a yes, bub?"

"Left-tenant, I give you and the board my solemn promise that from here on out, I will be the biggest prick northeast of the Mississippi. "

"Third-biggest, pal," he said, grinning, "do your devil-worshipping worst and you still ain't apt to hold a lit candle to that stone-faced muscle-head from *New York* or that *sour-grape sucking ass-crack* from *Colorado.* "

"Ah-ha!" I exclaimed with a forefinger raised high in the air, evoking a slight cringe from Mister Square-jaw, a reaction I couldn't help but savor, "I take it you speak of the betting man's favorites. "

"Nope, not quite. That Rocky Mountain Hick presently stands at two-to-one to the Big Apple's finest. Word is the former is being referred to as *Ice-Man*, what with the way he scampered through the tundra of B Sector practically untouched. As for the muscles from Yonkers, they're calling him the *Ebony Exterminator*, supposedly for all the pale bodies he's leaving in his wake. Charming, huh?"

"Well, he's a specimen, no doubt," I agreed with a solemn nod, "but personally I don't view anyone as invincible. He can be had. No sure thing exists in this mobile madhouse. "

Having fallen back into android-mode, his reaction was predictably jaded.

"Bingo, bub, and good luck with that. Dude moves with a purpose, and is built like an all-pro linebacker.

Still," he continued, leaning in and dropping his voice a level or two, "if it's any consolation, there's a shit-load of folks rooting for you to smoke both of those grouchy butt-wipes. "

"And why might that be, Left-Tenant sir?" I replied with a smirk, matching his lean until my chin practically brushed his forehead.

"Let's just say you're viewed as a more…well, media-friendly choice. "

"Media friendly?"

"From a PR standpoint, you'd make a better rep. "

"How so?"

"Well, number one, you come off as less of a prick than either of those two jack-offs. "

"And?"

"Your background provides a better backstory in terms of overall PR. "

"Thought you didn't know my backstory, Chief," I said, winking playfully.

He didn't seem to get the humor, purposely biting or no.

"I don't, bub. Just passin' on what I've been told. "

"Got'cha. Well, you can pass on to your superiors that I'll surely do my down-home best to provide them with the most marketable angle possible. "

"Then, you agree to forego any further incidents such as the conclusion of Sector B?" he asked, utterly oblivious to the sarcasm I'd so openly spewed.

"You got it, Chief," I said, clicking the heels of

my rubber boots before executing the stiffest salute possible, "no more Mister Nice Guy."

"Good to hear it," he said with a resounding sigh and subsequent wipe across the forehead with a bare forearm.

"Besides, Miss Chick-a-Dee from the desert ain't likely to be a factor in terms of heart-strin pulling from this point forward."

"Meaning what?"

"Well," he concluded through a warped grin that, in retrospect, I wish I'd at least attempted to wipe clean with a balled fist.

"Unless that broad finds a way to limp down the trail minus her landing gear, I'd have to conclude she's packed it away for the duration."

"Woman's got a lotta heart, Left-tenant. Thing like that can overcome many an obstacle."

"You're not comprehendin' the full gist, bub. From what I saw while strolling through the infirmary, chick was a hot needle and electric hacksaw away from earnin' the permanent nickname 'Nubs.'"

"Lieutenant, you sir are a grade-A horse's ass," I spewed red-faced, hardly conscious of the fact that I'd clenched both fists until I followed his eyes to them.

"Now that's the spirit, bub," he beamed, flashing a set of teeth as square as his jaw, "now put that anger to work on the trail, and we're in business. I say that because, well, truth be told . . ." he continued, leaning in with a cocked brow and speaking from the left side of his mouth as if to minimize the volume, ". . . nobody but *nobody* in upper management wants either of those other two pricks to be last man standin' once the smoke clears. Both of 'em come off like they just took a big ol' healthy bite out of a cow-turd sandwich. Now, why the bosses don't really mind such unfriendly, un-PC types setting the pace, that don't mean they prefer to see their sour mugs at the finish line, you understand. That leaves you, Mister. Think about it. You could become the biggest celebrity to come out of your home state since Lincoln split his first log. You can't tell me being privy to such info doesn't serve to feed the inner fire. "

For some reason, perhaps it was merely *smarminess* overload, but this irked me to the extreme. If trapped within the confines of an old Looney-Tunes cartoon, I'm fairly sure this would've been the point that plumes of smoke spewed from each ear and veins the size of cable cords lined my forehead.

"Afraid you assume too much, Amigo," I retorted sternly while having to consciously avoid grinding my teeth, "fact is, I'd lay down a sizeable bet that you've had similar, separate conversations with those two pace-setting pricks. "

The man's upper body, so freakishly chiseled and cut, instantly tensed; his wry grin having transformed into a pained grimace.

"Of course, you're welcome to correct me if I'm wrong," I concluded with a playful wink, "but even then, I'd most likely have to label you somewhat of a fibber. Actually, the label this old log-splitter would prefer is *lyin' som-bitch*. "

For a split-second I thought he was actually

going to spring forward and throttle me. His cheeks pulsed red; his fists clinched and released numerous times as he took a single step forward to cut the space between us to no more than two feet. In the end, he simply sighed, bowed his head and stepped back with the fingers of both hands splayed out and flexing. When the verbal response did occur, it was relayed with a voice virtually void of emotion; a mechanical playback so woefully insincere I actually felt a twinge of embarrassment for the man. It was obvious that he'd long since been castrated by his superiors; more than likely a once universally respected, tough-as-nails officer of the guard reduced to playing corporate stooge *slash* conman. Whatever sense of authority the man had carried in previous incarnations meant absolutely beans in this present-day incarnation. Hired to steer through intimidation, he was a wolf without teeth; a declawed predator that was truly all growl and no bite.

"Proceed down the hallway to the adaptation room," he'd said tight-lipped, having already broken eye contact to back out into said vestibule.

"You'll have approximately five minutes inside before continuing to the entranceway to Sector C. Good luck. "

He then backed stiffly down the opposite end of the corridor to allow clearance, and as I stepped gingerly by, I could've sworn I heard the lieutenant release the faintest of groans. Kicking into a swifter gear in order to put distance between us, I half-expected to be tackled from behind and subsequently bludgeoned. In retrospect, the odds of such an occurrence had truly been slim and none. Company men are rarely so willing to toss away what must've been a sizeable paycheck.

The adaptation room held little in the way of shock or awe. A squared, miniscule room containing a single, high-backed wooden chair and four vents—two walled and two floored—it was designed for a single purpose; to lower the body temperature in a similar vein of a gymnasium sauna. Already everglades humid upon my initial entry, the open vents soon spewed forth air so thick with heat it I could practically hear the sweat bubble forth from my pores. Decked out in full raingear and forced to drag the backpack along in true ball-and-chain fashion, it was only a matter of moments before my entire frame effectively stewed in its own juices.

Much like the prep room for Sector B, five minutes passed more like a half-hour. Upon departing with wobbly knees and a decidedly parched throat, I was handed a tall glass of semi-chilled water and injected with yet another syringe filled with liquid of unknown origin. I could only surmise perhaps a B-12 boost or something similar, though by that time I knew better than to inquire when the odds of receiving an answer were absolute nil.

Withall the emotion of a houseplant, the stone-faced sentry who'd provided both the liquid and needle refreshment instructed me with a pointed finger to continue down the hall.

Roughly fifty yards later and following several inexplicably ominous curves, I came to a set of slick, metal double-doors and the uniformed sentinel assigned to front said space. Standing behind a wooden podium, he regarded me with little more than a half-nod as I removed my backpack for a final inventory. Tall and lanky and sporting the obligatory buzz-cut that seemed mandatory for all such drones, he had his head tilted slightly to the left and was constantly reaching up to adjust the left earpiece of his headset. Securing the backpack, I stood with arms crossed as the guard's blank, unblinking stare alternated between myself and the circular timepiece attached to his left wrist.

"Thirty seconds to entry, sir," he said robotically, stepping from behind the podium to face the doors while gripping what appeared to be a tiny remote in his right hand. I heard a nearby radio transmission from somewhere near, the voices garbled and their words equally inaudible.

In those final moments before the doors parted and yet another alien landscape beckoned, my thoughts turned to the lady from *Arizona* and her tragic plight. I found no embarrassment in confessing that her companionship would be sorely missed. If nothing else, she'd served as the ultimate in distraction. Within the first few steps atop the newest Sector's slushy, soggy grounds, my focus turned entirely upon the task at hand; to search out that decidedly odd couple which Left-tenant had been so gleeful to brow-beat in the name of his superiors. As unlikely and downright patronizing as his '*rah-rah, you the man*' spiel had been, there was a chance, however remote, that it contained the tiniest nugget of truth. After all, when compared to

New York or *Colorado*, I was indeed Golden Boy material. Then again, in regard to that pair the same might be argued for *Jack the Ripper*.

Regardless, I could hardly deny the surge of adrenalin I felt at the mere thought of being universally rooted for, however fictitious the notion. I'd decided to ride the accompanying wave of emotion for the duration. Too bad it broke all too soon.

Part Two: Snake-Eyes

Time: Ten hours, fifty-seven minutes into the Iron Will Gauntlet
Location: Sector C (Hybrid climes: Upper northwest/southern U. S. coastline)
Total miles covered: Just over thirty

The initial half-hour indoctrination into Sector C was fairly uneventful; almost tranquil, in fact, though an underlying wariness seemed to float overhead like a drifting specter.

Yes, it was predictably humid, though not unbearably so; and yes, the occasional flare-up of misting rain made a sporadic appearance, though not nearly intense enough to make me think twice about removing the raingear and wrapping it snugly around my waist. The grounds were soggy but passable, making me long for a pair of sufficiently padded, ankle-high tennis shoes over the cumbersome rubber boots I'd been issued. The trail itself was littered with ankle-high weeds but little in the way of jagged rock or gravel, and held firm for the most part despite the perpetual wetness serving as its constant host. The accompanying shoulders and CGI matte background were an eccentric mix of cypress trees protruding from the murky swamp water like furry traffic cones, and an overgrowth of 'sea-grass', the everglades version of kudzu. Bouncing along at a fairly brisk pace, especially in comparison to the slow-motion death-march the final stretch of Sector B had been, I thought I'd even spotted several shadowy outlines of reptilian origin slithering along beneath the puddled muck on either side of the trail. Computer generated or not, I wasn't about to quench any faint curiosity concerning the authenticity of said beasts, be they snake, eel, or floating stick.

As for the whereabouts of any fellow competitors, the constant barrage of sharp, bending curves that riddled the track made it difficult to gauge. Despite Left-tenant Square-Jaw's insistence that I had ranked third in terms of the wagering masses entering the sector, I had a difficult time buying it, mainly in recollecting how few competitors I'd passed since the opening gun. Still, there was always room for speculation, and considering I'd been forced to wait upwards of thirteen minutes to allow the front-runners their timed lead, I wasn't about to slow my pace in the outside chance he hadn't just been blowing corporate smoke rings up my wazoo.

A light, chilly rain began to fall around the hour mark, or at least approximately, and I soon found myself re-donning the rain gear while standing in an ankle-deep puddle that had quickly become the trail's trademark. It wasn't long after that a series of cramps began to strike my inner left thigh and calf, faintly at first but with increasing fervor as the trail transformed from merely mushy to full-blown soaked. Predictably, the vigorous pace I'd been so determined to set for the foreseeable future slowed considerably as I'd alternated hands to massage both trouble spots. Once, perhaps two-hundred yards were covered in true 'one-legged man' fashion, as I'd limped and stiff-walked until eventually wobbling to a complete stop. While the twisting, burning sensation had subsided somewhat in my calf, my thigh felt as if it were being wound increasingly tighter with barbed-wire serving as the constriction device of choice. I cannot be certain how long I remained stationary, balanced on my right leg with the left splayed out as if to trip up whoever roamed into its stiffened, constantly flexing path. I would guess the duration as short as eight or nine minutes or as long as fifteen. It was beyond my means to even care about the passing of time as eager fingers dug into spasmodic flesh and the hardened muscle beneath with a single-minded mission of relief.

By the time the cramp had eased almost to normality, I'd already heard faint voices in the background; voices that grew increasingly louder as I'd stood erect and began pacing back and forth to test the throbbing appendage's workability.

Peering back on grounds already covered, I watched as the enigmatic pair swam into view from beyond the bulk of a protruding shrub just as I'd been on the verge of hopping back into the muck and rejoining the race. Both struck similar poses while trekking forward at a fairly decent clip, their arms swinging high as their legs pumped piston-like in the popular 'fast-walking' style.

Whirling about to face front, I felt a sudden wave of dread tighten my gut at the mere thought of making contact. Perhaps the Left-tenant's harsh words concerning my bent for playing the role of human ambassador to one and all had left a psychological mark after all. Though I'd never had reason to ponder the true worth of such a well-worn cliché, the possibility that *nice guys* truly did *finish last* was gaining credibility in light of what I'd experienced thus far.

Alas, despite my best efforts to reset the pace of old, the left leg was far too weak to comply just yet, and soon I could hear the sharp splashing sounds of multiple boot-steps drawing near.

"Well, I'll be a chimpanzee's uncle! Is that KY I see limping about in my crosshairs?" a vaguely familiar voice chimed from my left as twin shadows were cast on either side.

"Embarrassing as it is to confess, but that big *K* on the back of your slicker wasn't ringing a single bell in this cob-web infested noggin of mine. "

Twisting my head about and removing the hood to get a clearer view of my mystery addressee, it took me a moment of intense study to drudge forth even a semi-positive ID. The plump-faced, pot-bellied man I'd briefly met and spoken within the first few miles of the race had seemingly been replaced by this gaunt, pale-fleshed clone.

"Hiya there, Gambler," I finally warbled, surprisingly out of breath despite my recent forced siesta, "you're looking no worse for wear, I have to say. This weather agreeing with you?"

"Hey, I'm just happy to have *Iceland* planted firmly in the rear view mirror, my man. Turn your head and say hey to Poncho. . . "

"Albuquerque, New Mexico," the gentlemen introduced himself politely with an outstretched hand. I closed the deal with a firm shake and matching smile. Short but slender, all save a pooching gut so round it looked to have a regulation basketball stashed inside the raingear, the man appeared to be in his early to mid-fifties and was of obvious Hispanic descent.

"Lexington, Kentucky. Good to know you. "

Almost instantly, we fell into a steady, comfortable pace, strolling down the sodden trail as if joined at the hips. Not surprisingly, my earlier trepidation had faded almost as soon as intros had commenced.

"Poncho and myself have been going steady since about the halfway point of B Sector," Nevada beamed as the rain pelted us a bit harder, "he's a top-notch companion. Only speaks when spoken to, right Ponch?"

"Right as rain," New Mexico replied, peering up into the murky grayness while replacing his hood.

"See what I mean, KY? That's one wise old owl. Would've made one hell of a poker player with that ready-made face of stone. Ol' rock-mug, that's him. He and I have already shared some sights, by god, a few of which I wish we hadn't. Fact is, we had been a traveling threesome 'til about halfway through B Sector. Lost *Puerto Rico* Rick to one helluva bad case of frostbite. Poor dude's entire face was peeling off like a rotted banana peel. I tell ya, those brutal winter climes play hell with these South-of-the-Border types. I figured Poncho for a goner right off, but he toughed it out like a real storm-trooper. How about you, KY? Don't tell me you've been soloing the whole time. "

"Not at all. Spoken to countless, mostly in passing. Little lady from *Arizona* was my main squeeze, at least until we dug ourselves out of the North Pole. "

"*Arizona*, huh?" he queried between huffs, the skin pulled so tightly across the man's face he appeared positively skeletal.

"So where is she now?"

"Haven't seen her since we clawed our way into the transition station. She, um, had a slight frostbite problem. I'm hoping they were able to patch her up, but it . . . didn't look good. "

"Hmm. Damn shame. Good company is hard to find, right Poncho?"

"Damn right," Poncho exclaimed blandly, his arms flailing uselessly by his sides and not at all keeping rhythm with his stride.

"The man's a jewel . . . a real jewel," Nevada replied with a giggle, what little hair he possessed atop his shrunken noggin plastered down in snow white, pencil-thin strands.

"Poncho and I are gonna open up our own combination taco stand and craps casino once we're sufficiently healed up from this shit. Gonna call it *The Gambler's Delight*. All the south-of-the border grub you can scarf down for a nominal fee, that is as long as you're actively laying your money down on whatever game of chance you prefer. Already got the spot picked out too. Just a hop, skip and jump from the main strip. Gonna be swimming in greenbacks, am I right, Poncho?"

"Damn right," Poncho echoed, though if possible even less enthusiastically. I noted yet again the dead-weight swing of his arms, the fingers of each hand dancing a spastic jig, as if he were limbering up for an impending piano recital.

"Most agreeable son of a bitch I've ever run across. I could've swapped greenbacks for *wetbacks* and ol' Poncho would just nod, grin, and keep on truckin'. "

"Um, did you guys happen to notice if anyone else was entering the sector behind you?" I broke in, our collective pace having slowed substantially since the falling rain's increased intensity.

"So, KY, think we're nearing the halfway point yet? These damn knee-high rubber boats are starting to feel like someone filled 'em to the rim with cement mix. "

I'd hoped to get a specific update on Sagebrush, or at the very least some vague idea of exactly who was trailing close behind and their overall condition. Instead, the man had either completely ignored the question or was oblivious I'd even spoken. Either way, I'd felt a sudden chill race the length of my spine that had little or nothing to do with cool rainfall. Unsure of exactly how to respond, I decided to inject a bit of humor and prayed I was on the right track.

"Oh sure. Finish line is probably right around that next bend, give or take twelve more miles. Hey, if the water gets deep enough, we could always tie our slickers together and make a raft. "

"Fucking snow 'bout did me in, KY," he blurted, his voice suddenly hoarse and cracking with emotion, "should've done me in, by all logic. Thought it *had* done me in.

Poncho there saved my bacon. Pulled me out of a drift that had swallowed me whole. I'd tossed in the towel already. Didn't care anymore. Just wanted out of the cold by whatever means was the easiest. Laying down and giving up won by a landslide. Just...wasn't meant to be. Poncho came along and saw to that. Fucking Beaner might be small, but he's stout as a bull. Carried me on his back the last mile or so. Even dug out a trench to get us to the exit. All by his lonesome, no less. Strong as a Brahma bull, that little burrito-scarfer. "

He looked past me then—actually, *through* me might be a better description—staring towards *New Mexico* with tightly squinted eyes that glowed red with a lethal mix of disenchantment and rage. Sadly, the man's sanity was no longer debatable. I'd seen the same wild, edge of madness gleam in Hollywood's eyes just before her grisly meltdown. The Gambler was, in layman's terms, currently paddling the boat with a single oar.

"Do me a favor, KY, will you?"

"Um, sure, if I can," I replied hesitantly as the three of us simultaneously slowed to a grinding shuffle.

"Ask the sadistic son of a bitch why he bothered?"

"Bothered?"

"To pull me out of that drift. Ask him what I ever did to him to justify such blatant . . . fucking . . . *cruelty* towards his fellow man?"

He leaned forward and continued to peer angrily past me towards the other man, who had yet to display even the faintest clue of the conversation

215

pointed his way.

"I told 'im . . . I'm sure I did. I told 'im to leave me be and let me die already. Stubborn SOB would . . . not . . . listen. Pulled me outta that snow bank like he was saving his mama, for god's sake! I was done, KY, done! I'd made my peace. Now look at me . . . take a good, long, hard stare. I'm a goddamned husk . . . a walking, talking cadaver. The barely living . . . barely breathing . . . fucking undead," he practically pleaded, tilting his head back and briefly returning his focus to me. The stark fear reflected so vividly in the man's horribly bloodshot eyes proved so shocking, so weirdly entrancing, that I hadn't even noticed we'd halted in our tracks and stood completely stationary, our collective boots buried to the ankles in brownish muck.

"He . . . felt an obligation, that's all. An obligation to his fellow man; a sense of decency to do so," I countered, thinking of my own recent sacrifice for Sagebrush, for whatever good it seemed to have done either of us.

Shuffling forward, Nevada almost tipped over several times before taking up position directly in front of *New Mexico*, who stood at parade-rest with his shoulders pulled back. I was unable to visualize any part of the man's face, as unlike *Nevada* and myself, he'd kept the raingear hood pulled firmly in place, his cap-cam positioned awkwardly to one side until he resembled a completely bonkers, middle-aged citizen rapper.

"Not his call, KY, not his call!" the Gambler bellowed, leaning in until he and the other man

216

were practically smooching. I reached in with my left arm to provide a blockade of sorts just to see it roughly slapped away.

"Who is he to make such a decision? I didn't ask for his help. I wanted the pain. . . the torture to stop. It was a relief, don't you get it?" he ranted, foamy froth flying from the corners of his lips. The man truly resembled a fading specter in some ancient black and white horror film. Though only his skeletal facial features were exposed, I could easily imagine the absolute paleness of his entire frame—like that of a naked corpse lying atop a cold slab.

"Now it feels like . . . I'm s-stuck here . . . like the suffering is infinite…. eternal; like this fucking trail has no finish line. Has no end. Don't you feel it? Don't you feel the hopelessness? Don't lie! Not to yourself! We're never getting off this beaten path…not 'til we're all lying face down like…l-like vulture meat!"

As with *Hollywood* in what felt like a lifetime ago, I could find no words, no response to effectively counter the man's lunatic ravings without coming off sounding utterly patronizing. Besides, in all honestly I most assuredly would've been lying. I had indeed felt waves of hopelessness, of being merely one of fifty-one such pawns set up for the ultimate fall. Guinea pigs, one and all, having willingly signed away our very souls for a faint glimmer of fame. We'd all willingly shaken hands with Beelzebub from the moment we'd first applied to compete, and the Prince of Darkness had slowly, gradually began to make good on collecting our souls. I'd lost count of the individual carnage by that time, only 'Bama, Hollywood and Miss *Texas*, respectively, sticking out in my mind as particularly tragic ends. What had initially served to jolt the senses was now nothing more than a bothersome trend.

Apparently sensing no answer forthcoming, *Nevada* collapsed to one knee, staring up into the mist as if praying for salvation. From afar, one might've thought he was bowing to *New Mexico* as one would some revered, holy shrine.

In retrospect, the fire-and-brimstone sermon that ensued, though quite impressive in a hokey, over-the-top sort of way, might've been unconsciously misdirected. Thinking back, I can't honestly say who exactly I was trying to convince. Though the intended target was obvious, I could just as easily been staring *myself* down in the nearest pool of reflective swamp water.

"*Nevada* . . . Gambler, listen, you've got to keep moving. . . we all do. If not, what in god's name did all this mean? Think back to the selection process . . . the mountains of red tape you cleared to be picked over thousands of other applicants. The countless interviews and tests, being poked and probed like a lab rat, the media both local and nationwide—how they pried into every aspect of your previous life as if challenging *why* you'd been chosen at all. Then, after all that, the struggle and strain to survive those first two hellish sectors; an accomplishment so many others are no longer around to claim. Remember the Gauntlet Creed we were force-fed since day one? Sacrifice *all* or don't bother sacrificing at all, right? Ring a bell? You hearing me, mister?"

Having previously lowered his head as if to pray, he slowly peered up and over until we locked eyes. Much like with *Alabama* a full sector ago, I was allowed yet another horrifying peek into the face of imminent death. The inner fire, the life-source necessary to sustain, had ebbed away to a dim, fast-fading ember.

"G-great speech, KY," he blubbered through trembling lips so cracked and pale I thought they might soon peel away like ivory flakes, "I'll give you that—belongs in a h-high school locker room or maybe on the p-political tr-trail. Wasted on m-me, I'm afraid. Day late and a buck-fifty sh-short. "

"One step at a time, *Nevada*," I countered, reaching down to gently cup into his left arm pit, "it's all about getting that second wind. We'll pin you between us if we have to, right NM?"

"It's his decision," his much-maligned traveling companion replied, the majority of his face sufficiently cloaked.

"I won't force the issue this time. I . . . don't have the energy, or . . . the will. Not this time. "

Mildly shocked, I turned back to *Nevada*, the wide, toothy grin on display a hideous mask of unbridled relief.

"Music to my ears, P-Poncho-a symphony for what little r-remains of my s-senses. "

With that, I turned my frustrations on *New Mexico*, stepping past *Nevada* until we stood eye-to-eye with less than a foot separation.

Reaching back with a single hand to remove his

hood, the man stared past me; through me. His eyes were slits; his nostrils flaring wildly. I instantly decided to refrain from releasing the angry torrent of disgust initially aimed at his nonchalant response to *Nevada's* plight. Instead, I reverted back to what had inadvertently become my trademark of late; pleading mode.

"So we just leave him here? Is that it? That's acceptable to you?"

Despite my best efforts to maintain an even keel, the man's stiff pose and seemingly compassionless non-reaction soon saw me waiving my arms and pacing like a lunatic.

"I don't get it. I just don't get it. Explain why you'd go out of your way, as I gathered taking some extraordinary measures, to save a man's life only to cast him away like a sack of soggy garbage just hours later?"

"Can you not see?" he finally retorted curtly, though I swear I never saw his tightly pursed lips part even a hair. Perhaps because he had spoken so little since our introduction, I hadn't noticed even a tint of an accent until that time. It was faint, hardly noticeable, and possibly only surfaced in times of great duress.

"The man's spirit is completely broken. The first time, that . . . first time, there had still been a spark. Otherwise, I would not have sacrificed so. Now, there is no hint of such. Let it go, as he has let it go. There is no room for personal guilt. He has every right to choose how to end it, as we all do. "

Stepping back to collect my jumbled thoughts, I saw that *Nevada* had collapsed onto his back at the center of the trail, happily immersing himself within a shallow stream of rainwater collected there.

I'd parted my lips to renew the argument when I saw *New Mexico*'s eyes stretch comically wide, his lower jaw unhinging as he raised an arm to point over my left shoulder. Before turning towards the source of his apparent astonishment, I became acutely aware of a grinding buzz invading my head like a swarm of angry bees. Whirling about, I'm fairly sure I laughed aloud at the irony. In that fateful moment of unrestrained jocularity, however unintentional, I felt yet another vital strand of sanity snap free like a guide-wire beneath a machete's razor-sharp blade.

What transpired in those next few adrenaline fueled moments would prove equally damaging to a psyche already tittering dangerously close to permanent meltdown.

Part Three: Things with Wings

Time: Twelve hours, six minutes into the Iron Will Gauntlet

Location: Sector C (Hybrid climes: Upper northwest/southern U. S. coastline)

Total miles covered: Thirty-two and three quarters

"Wha-what the hell is that?"

New Mexico had posed a reasonable enough question, I thought at the time, considering that upon first glimpse there simply was no definite answer to be had. My initial guess, of the knee-jerk variety, would've been to label our mystery guest a low-drifting cloud of some sort. Ludicrous I know, considering it appeared to be hovering less than seven or eight feet from the ground, but it certainly held the shape and drifting movement of a rogue cloud formation. As it grew closer, perhaps to within thirty or forty yards from our position, it appeared to pulsate at the core of its being, not unlike a power surge of sorts. Following this, its brownish mass seemed to pick up speed while cutting a rapid path directly our way, the buzzing noise that accompanied it increasing twofold.

"Oh dear god . . . bloodsuckers!" I heard *New Mexico* screech just as the first wave engulfed us from all sides. I felt the first series of bites at the back of my neck, and reached to pull my own hood into place as the second stung the backs of both hands. Slapping the back of the left with the palm of the right, I drew back to a spattering of blackish fluid smeared atop my knuckles. Within seconds, they looped, swayed and buzzed around my eyes in search of a suitable landing pad with which to commence feeding. Having grown up in what any entomologist worth his salt would confidently deem 'mosquito alley', I'd seen my share of the insect world's version of *Nosferatu*. That said, this particular species appeared not only considerably larger in size, but nastier in terms of inflicting pain with their syringe-like snouts. *Mutated* was the word I'd drudge up later when reluctantly reliving the whole nightmarish episode.

I began to duck and weave wildly while pulling the sides of the hood snugly together. All the while, I could hear *New Mexico* whimpering in the background, the occasional English curse word mingled with its Spanish counterpart.

As the nucleus of the colossal cloud of parasites had yet to reach us, I quickly hopped over to where *Nevada* lay staring up into the sky and straddled his chest, reaching down to obtain a firm grip on either side of his slicker.

"You're coming with us, man."

Still wearing the same warped grin birthed at the moment of *New Mexico*'s rejection, he was either unwilling or incapable of computing my request. That is, until I jerked him upright into a sitting position, his neck whiplashing back violently. Upon straightening, the sickly, emaciated target of my panic-fueled aggression flashed an altogether different expression; a pained frown pared with the crystal clear exposure of gnashed teeth that appeared fang-like when coupled with the low growl that spewed forth like a slow leak from a punctured tire.

"This pony's blew a shoe, KY . . . so let me die already," he fumed, jerking viciously from side to side.

My first mistake was to temporarily loosen my grip from the shoulders of his raingear, as this allowed him to back up a full step. My second was the wide stance I'd struck in the aftermath. Harmless enough under normal circumstances, such a pose provided the perfect target for an upturned knee. The searing pain at my groin soon transcended to my lower abdomen, as such well-placed blows are wont to do. Tumbling onto my left side, I watched haplessly as *Nevada* sprinted directly into the path of the approaching horde, calmly stripping away his raingear as he went.

In attempting to rise to one knee, I managed to topple in the opposite direction and landed face-first in soupy mix that reeked of stagnation. Blowing mud-pies from both nostrils, I'd hardly had time to roll onto my back before being hauled up by the armpits. *New Mexico*'s words were whispered hoarsely into my right ear as he practically toted me back onto the trail's slightly elevated center, which was predictably soppy but much less so that the track's outer edges.

"He's . . . given us a window. We have to go now. "

Nevada had been tugging at his tee-shirt as we chugged by-spouting wholly unintelligible dialogue I could only deduce was a parting prayer of sorts.

Still reeling from the intense pain at my gut and legs that were practically paralyzed as a result, I recall looking back only briefly through vision partially blocked by a flurry of flying parasites. The man from Vegas, as if fated to play the part of sacrificial lamb, had stripped down to a pair of blue Jockey shorts and brown-shaded athletic socks. He was reaching to the sky with splayed fingers and a toothy grin, screaming incoherently just as the massive swarm swooped down and swallowed him whole. For an instant, a mere blink in time, I watched in stunned amazement as his entire frame was engulfed from head to toe. It was as if he'd dipped himself in honey and rang the dinner bell.

Not sure how long or far *New Mexico* carried me before we collapsed as one into a shallow puddle on the left shoulder of the main path, a puddle what was, thankfully, mostly muck and mud free. The man continued to huff and puff for several minutes while posed on all fours. As for myself, I sat upright and stared directly inward into a partially blue sky, though still consciously wary of any mysterious dark cloud formations that might appear without warning.

My self-imposed daze was snapped at the stark realization that *New Mexico*'s harsh breathing wasn't letting up with the passing of time but intensifying.

"You all right?" I blurted foolishly, as it was pretty damned obvious he most assuredly was not.

He had his back to me, bowed over with the palms of each hand propped atop a matching knee. Every few seconds he seemed to pause for breath and lurch forward, as if attempting to vomit.

"Pon- . . . NM, you can cool the jets now. Seems you hauled us out of range, at least for now. "

Once he toppled over onto his left side, releasing a squawking moan that droned on far too long to be a positive sign, I finally realized something was horribly wrong.

Limping over on legs that still felt strangely alien; I kneeled down in front of the man and placed a hand atop his left shoulder, which instantly shuddered beneath my touch. His head was still bowed, and I could hear a harsh wheezing noise whistling forth from either his mouth or nostrils, or perhaps both. Overhead, a cloud as dark as tar floated in from the West, parking itself directly overhead as if specifically marking us as suitable targets.

"Hey, you gonna make it?"

His head, utterly cloaked by the raingear's sagging hood, arose an inch or two before descending yet again, as if he didn't possess the required energy to complete the task.

"What say I piggy-back you for a spell? You certainly earned the privilege, my man. "

His only response was a muffled grunt that sounded as if it originated from deep within a severely congested chest. Believing I'd seen something pass overhead, I glanced upward only to ogle a single brown leaf sail by. Within that single split-second of distraction, *New Mexico* had managed to turn his face upward sans the hood, which he'd apparently found strength enough to remove.

There are actions, however instinctual, that in retrospect one wishes they could reverse. Such was the case once my gaze had set upon the man's exposed features and I'd not only flung my hand away from his shoulder as if from the searing redness of a fully-heated oven eye, but also cringed back with both arms and legs pumping in reverse. In that terrible moment, I saw a dreadful sadness reflected in the downtrodden eyes of a man who, just moments earlier, had carried me to safety with little regard of what hellish bill might ultimately come due in the aftermath. His mouth had been relegated to permanent ajar status, with both lips so grotesquely bloated and curled inward as to resemble a pair of metamorphosed slugs. His jowls were similarly swollen, the left so shockingly puffed it hung past the edge of his chin like a pulsating polyp turned inside out. Even the lobes of each ear appeared freakishly inflated, the right having grown so heavy its rounded bottom half hung almost to the tip of his shoulder.

Worse yet were the man's eyes, or to be specific, the lids and under-lining of said orbs. Pitch-black and pus-filled, each attempt at blinking on the man's part resulting in a sickening discharge of yellowish fluids bubbling forth in glutinous waves before trailing down his pock-marked cheeks like volcanic lava. As for said pock-marks, there didn't appear to be a single square inch unoccupied from just beneath his hairline to the base of his neck; pellet-sized welts with fluid-filled centers drenched in dark maroon.

"J-Jesus, m-man. I-you just sit b-back and I'll... um, just let me see if I can f-find someth-something to . . . h-help with th-that," I babbled red-faced, suddenly acutely aware of even the faintest itch. As my ravaged savior leaned up on bent elbows, his breath growing raspier with each passing second, I removed my backpack and began to rummage within as if expecting to uncover some miraculous cure for being eaten alive by hordes of mutated mosquitos. Mosquitos no doubt created in some government lab exclusively for the Gauntlet and with the sole purpose of turning human flesh into the bloated, bubbling horror my personal messiah had become.

Pawing past handfuls of energy bars and assorted water bottles, I then came upon the unmarked spray-can and palmed it for several moments before casually turning it upside down and checking its rounded, concaved bottom. I recall reading the single word imprinted there several times, perhaps even aloud, even going to the extreme of pulling the can so close to my unblinking, unbelieving eyes that the outer edges actually tickled the accompanying brows. At some point, I commenced to giggle. This soon transformed into a full-blown, gut-wrenching, tear-spewing howl, at which point I could hardly maintain a grip on the eight-ounce can. Curling into myself like a cheap tent in a typhoon, I soon struck a fetal pose, hugging the can to my chest like an infant's bottle and temporarily dismissing the individual slowly dying a few feet away. Though I'm fairly certain no actual sound was escaping my lips at that point, I continued to mouth the word nonetheless, over and over until warm snot coated my lips and tongue to force the inevitable snap-to from that particular realm of madness.

Repellant, it had read. Repellant, as in bug-spray. Lord love a waddling duck. *Repellant*. Yes, they had supplied it freely enough, but left when and how to use it exclusively up to us. Piss on a penguin. *Repellant.*

By the time I'd refocused enough to sit upright and crawl to his side, *New Mexico*, that brave, caring soul *Nevada* had so lovingly referred to as Poncho, had quit breathing. Though I'd taken my share of CPR classes through the years, my frantic attempts to revive proved futile. There were several reasons for said failure, the two most glaring being that, *one:* the air flow to his lungs seemed hopelessly blocked, and *two:* with each and every chest compression I'd administered came a fresh glut of fluids spewing forth from not only his mouth and nostrils, but the blackened edges of each eye as well. Astonishing as it seemed, it had taken roughly fifteen minutes for whatever poison those lab monstrosities had injected into his veins to transform a perfectly healthy, middle-aged man into a quivering pus-balloon. Looking over the dozens upon dozens of reddish bumps littering my own hands, wrists and upper arms, I was left to ponder why I'd been spared a similar meltdown. If some sort of chemical allergy to the swarm's bites was the culprit, how was I able to walk away with merely a spattering of itchy but otherwise harmless lesions while the poor bastard I only knew as Poncho looked as though he'd been dipped repeatedly in a vat of sulfuric acid? Why exactly had I yet again been spared such a ghastly, agonizing end? I kneeled at my savior's side for several additional moments, mulling over the strange mystery of my continued survival, rising to depart only when it became increasingly apparent that no clear-cut answers were forthcoming. Before officially rejoining the competition, I used the man's own rain gear as a shroud to cloak his atrophied remains. My booted feet splashed back onto the slushy trail just as a cool, hard rain began to fall.

Repeatedly scanning the skies, I trekked along at a mighty clip that initial half-hour, ignoring the plethora of aches and pains that teamed to incessantly warn of a potential breakdown. Throbbing left thigh or not, I was *motoring*. Stiff neck or no, I was *motoring*. Possibly separated right shoulder be damned, I was *motoring*. Right calf on the constant verge of cramping, so be it . . . this boy was *motoring*. In some vague way, perhaps such an aggressive stance was tied to the myth of outrunning death. Regardless of specific motivations, it was all about distance. As in, putting significant distance between myself and the reaper's wondering blade, a blade that, for the time being, had struck down so many who'd dared to share my company while only managing to graze yours truly.

For the record, I saw nary a single insect, flying or otherwise, the remainder of my time wondering the Gauntlet's harrowing path. For that at least, I was infinitely thankful.

Part Four: A Shift in Scenery

Time: Thirteen hours, sixteen minutes into the Iron Will Gauntlet
Location: Sector C (Hybrid climes: Upper northwest/southern U. S. coastline)
Total miles covered: Just over thirty-five

Around two or two and a half miles past the spot where I'd mumbled a final prayer for New Mexico's valiant warrior, there was a dramatic shift in not only the climate, but the surrounding landscape as well. This had been no subtle change either, but more a complete realm-shift engineered within a radius of no more than a quarter-mile. Where once Cypress, Blackgum and Wax Myrtles littered the faux terrain, now stood Ash, Cottonwood, Douglas fir and Hemlock, showcasing brilliantly vibrant leaves in mid-spring form. Gone were the rivers of muck that had lined C sector's trail since the inception, replaced by narrow, hollowed-out trails of running water so clear they appeared to have originated from a nearby well-spring. The constant rainfall had at last slowed to no more than a steady trickle, even allowing for the occasional flash of sunlight which, however manufactured, still managed to naturally lift my downtrodden spirits by its mere presence.

As for the trail itself, while predictably hilly and curve-filled, it had a fairly firm base for travel, replacing the pudding-like substance from earlier. The one negative was the noticeable change in temperature. Though hardly rating as anything more than uncomfortable, the twenty to thirty degree drop coupled with the sudden lack of humidity that had been so garish just an hour earlier, there was the matter of adaptation, especially considering the lack of gear issued for such a drastic shift. A cotton tee, jeans and a thin layer of raingear might've been spot-on perfect for swamp trekking, but was hardly adequate for the cool, lush forests of Oregon or Washington State, from which the latest backdrop had obviously been modeled.

As the next forty-five minutes to an hour passed, during which time I'd reset my IPOD to the admittedly corporate slick but undeniably catchy classic pop/rock sounds of Phil Collins and *Genesis* (Peter Gabriel's earlier incarnation of the band far too eccentric and cerebral for my simple tastes), my thoughts were frenzied and unfocused.

I pondered (as Phil crooned about the pros and cons of being an '*Illegal Alien*') the fate of Sagebrush, whose sassy attitude and saucy dialogue I secretly credited with helping me navigate, endure and mentally overcome the most trying of waters in both sector's A and B.

I recalled with bemusement (as Phil, Mike and Tony jammed so meticulously on '*Home by the Sea*') a pre-competition nugget of wisdom passed on by Kay, my personal advisor, who'd nonchalantly stated 'the biggest challenge you're libel to face is tedium'. Tedium? As in *boredom*? Talk about venturing waaaaayyyyy off base, that single line had to qualify as one of the more colossal swing's and misses of recent times. As far as I could recall, there hadn't been a single moment in thirteen -some-odd hours to justify any variation of said word.

I recollected with much sadness (to the strangely apt lyrics of '*Land of Confusion*') the many faces, both valiant (*Alabama, New Mexico*) and broken (*California, Texas, Nevada*) fated to breath their last in such a harsh, fictional realm, and hardly in a dignified manner. Strangely, out of that lot it was *Texas* that seemed the most troubling. Strange in that I'd barely made the woman's acquaintance while she still possessed a working pulse. Finding her sitting atop that Porto-Potty toilet like some masterless puppet, slack-jawed and eyes frozen ajar, was easily the hardest image to shake amongst admittedly stiff competition. *New Mexico* would, of course, rate a close second, if for no other reason than his selfless act involving yours truly. In the 'felt like I lost a close relative I hardly knew' department, *Alabama* won in a landslide. A jovial, kind-hearted soul, so many would surely say at the news of his demise.

Finally, I went a bit retro, at least Pre-Gauntlet, and harkened back (as, in top form, Phil belted out '*Throwing it all away*') to that one particular individual that had fueled my competitive fire since day one; minute one; second one. The one responsible for my filing out the initial application and persevering through the plethora of interviews, testing, and mountains of red tape that followed. She would be watching—of this I had no doubt. She would seek out and glue herself to the nearest monitor, be it low-grade plasma or ultra-HD 3D, searching out and hoping for a glance, a glimpse, however brief, of the man she'd unconsciously driven to self-destruction. Or perhaps *self-discovery* was a better term; a more positive twist. And Lord knew I needed all the positive vibes I could drudge up, however insincere and self-serving they might've been.

It wasn't long after I'd allowed myself a much-needed nutrition break, to include not one, not two, but three energy bars washed down with nearly a full bottle of vitamin water, that what had been a light shower intensified to a steady rain. Descending one of the countless knolls littering the trail, a trio of porta potties appeared in just the nick of time, as it seemed the aforementioned power bars had literally ran right through me. Not surprisingly, with Miss *Texas* so prominently etched in the subconscious, I'd felt a twinge of fear upon entering that boxy outhouse. Luckily for my already shredded psyche, I'd found it's cramped, sour-smelling interior mercifully corpse-free. I'd also found a sense of peace while doing my business, the sound of hard rain pounding the hard plastic exterior almost drowning out the thundering drum beat at the conclusion of '*Mama*', my personal favorite within the Genesis canon, perhaps due to the creepy, quasi-horror elements.

Mother Nature having been duly satisfied, I allowed myself a moment or two to linger in the blissful act of non-movement before resetting my ensemble to depart. The backpack had grown much lighter since initial issue, what with only one of three water bottles still present. Still, I had felt a definite increase in the discomfort building in and around both knees. This, coupled with the continuing throbbing of my left thigh and right calf; not to mention a stiff shoulder and similarly rigid neck, turned the simple act of standing upright a wretched symphony of pops, cracks, and snaps. It wasn't until I'd been back on the trail for at least ten minutes that the muscles and joints warmed enough to allow a reestablishment of my earlier pace. As for the terrain, it was quickly taking on standing water in light of the harder rain. Though much firmer than its everglades cousin, it appeared more susceptible to flash flooding. Pulling my face as far into the hood's draping flaps as possible without splitting seams, I focused on the tips of each rubber boot as they alternated kicking up what appeared to be increasingly thicker waves.

Soon, the rain was falling with unrelenting force, pounding my scalp and shoulders with force akin to an ensemble of battering fists. Such a ferocious siege had already rendered my IPOD useless, effectively drowning out all attempts to rock 'n roll it into submission.

As the ground swell of flowing current reached my ankles, I had to step more cautiously to avoid losing balance. Mere minutes later, or at least it seemed that brief, I was forced to raise each leg knee-high in order to maintain the needed traction to move forward.

Allowing myself a brief glance forward through the straight-line torrent, my heart instantly sank. It wasn't merely the sight of the massive incline that loomed, easily the steepest I'd encountered in any previous sector. It was the increasingly aggressive waters descending from its rounded peak. Halting in mid-stride, I sucked the deepest breath possible before bracing my entire frame as if to prepare for impact with a massive Tsunami.

Fearing my thundering heartbeat might well beat my lungs in a frenzied race to implode, I'd actually managed to navigate well over half the rise before having my left knee battered to the point of nearly bending backward. Though it's fairly reasonable to assume my ensuing shrieks fell on deaf ears, I was hapless to control their release, nonetheless. I'd only seen the thick, jagged tree limb that had administered the damage in passing; as thick as a Louisville Slugger and almost as slick, perhaps already having had its bark stripped away by the building current. Miraculously, I'd somehow been able to stay upright despite feeling as though my leg had been bent completely backward on impact. If there was a positive to such an unexpected bludgeoning, it was that all my other assorted ills were temporarily placed on the backburner.

I must've stood there for several minutes, bent over grasping the source of my misery with both hands and wailing like a wounded infant, at least until a significantly more prominent distraction arose. Looking back and shoving all overly dramatic clichés aside, I would honestly have to chalk it up to fate, kismet incarnate, that I'd spotted him at all. If not for the absolute cracker-jack timing involved, that being the very moment I'd chosen to forego the rubber-boot gazing for a sneak preview of what lay ahead, I'd have never been allowed the bleary, faint image that caught the corner of my left eye just a few feet off the trail's sloped shoulder. I'm sure I executed a double-take of sorts, perhaps more than one, once my eyes had fixed on the glare of pale flesh lying atop that squared bank. Bending down for additional balance as I'd side-stepped over, I felt a sudden, full-body shiver as each boot simultaneously began to take on the icy cool waters, which had risen just past the kneecaps.

Posed cautiously over the prone form, which was positioned on its left side and thus unidentifiable, I was at a complete loss at my next move. The act of playing EMS techie *slash* Mother Teresa had hardly proved successful thus far, and of course there was that whole logic factor to deal with-as in, *why* continue to provide aid and comfort to the enemy at this late stage of the game? Despite my best efforts to shove away such vile, black-hearted thoughts, the immortal, not to mention *immoral* words of Lieutenant Gil Masters, he of the buzz-cut noggin, steely glare and rock-jaw: 'You enter this competition to win or play nursemaid?'

As for the source of my latest humanitarian dilemma, there were no signs of life to speak of; not the slightest leg or digit twitch nor hint of active breathing. The rain gear had been stripped away from the upper torso and had knotted around their waist and groin to bind their upper thighs. Incredibly, the hood had remained securely in place, having been severed from the majority of its host-wear like a displaced pop-top. The cotton shirt underneath was in tatters, ripped from the collar to the lower spine, exposing a roadmap of scratches and minor cuts. A single rubber boot remained intact, though it too appeared on the verge of desertion, what with the heel digging into the calf portion. The other foot was bare, and I could see a deep gash on the sole that was weirdly bloodless. There was no backpack present, nor any signs of its contents scattered about.

I continued to ponder my next move when the building rapids decided to interrupt with a sudden surge of current, causing my left boot to slide forward. Forced to execute a clumsy break dance, I barely avoiding tumbling back, the frenzied wind-milling of both arms eventually aiding to reset my balance. Leaning forward onto the bank with the fingers of both hands digging deep into the hard soil, I took in several labored breaths before peering upward at the exact moment the beached person of mystery decided to come too and roll over.

To say I was shocked at the reveal would be a stone-cold lie, as I'd suspected as much from minute one. Suspected, and hoped, in fact, that said suspicion would pan out. That said, the re-introduction which followed was as astonishing as it was downright terrifying.

Part Five: Floater(s)

Time: Fourteen hours, twenty-two minutes into the Iron Will Gauntlet

Location: Sector C (Hybrid climes: Upper northwest/southern U. S. coastline)

Total miles covered: Thirty-eight and one quarter

During my impromptu ten to fifteen second dance recital, the body in question had not only managed to turn over onto its back, but began to hack and cough, leaning to one side to in order to spit forth thick streams of a water and mucus mix from its mouth and nostrils.

"Well well, it lives and breathes after all," I mumbled aloud, though not nearly loud enough to be heard over the raging waters.

Following a final violent gurgle, from which it appeared to cough up and casually discard a trio of broken, jagged teeth fragments that might've been crowns, it leaned up onto its elbows and appeared to take notice of my presence for the first time.

"Morning Sunshine," I blurted, holding out my right hand palms up as to assist.

Its eyes pulled wide, it leaned forward as if to confirm I wasn't some sort of concussion-related mirage.

"Ah sheeeeeiiit. This c-can't be good. "

"Now, is that any way to greet the Calvary?"

"Shove off, redneck. They'll ho-hold the winter Olympics in h-hell before I ever require he-help from the . . . likes of y-you or a-any other w-whose grave I plan on d-dancin' on. "

Yes indeed, being battered to a pulp and tossed onto the shoulder-bank like a dying mackerel hadn't depleted the man from Denver's natural charm and charisma a single iota. His beak-like nose was leaning hard to the left, most likely broken, and there were a trio of several squared, inch-long gashes adorning his pasty forehead, as if someone had used a sharp-edge to initiate an unfinished game of tic-tac-toe.

"Nice. Well, suit yourself," I exclaimed, retracting the extended arm with a shrug before gesturing to his bare foot, "better dig up that missing boot though, unless the nickname 'peg-leg' blows your skirt, because you're libel to lose a toe or two to the river floor otherwise. "

"I'll m-manage, dirt-bag. Adios . . . "

"Sure, of that I have no doubt," I shot back with what I'd hoped to be my first and last returned volley directed towards Mr. Happy, "you sure did one hell of a job beaching yourself on that bank. "

I'd already turned away from his perpetually frowning mug, having found a suitably firm stone from which to balance and pivot beneath the churning waters, which by that time had begun to soak my upper thigh.

"Smart-ass shit-kicker!" I heard him croak, the realization that I'd penetrated that reptilian skin serving to birth a wide, pleasure-fueled grin the likes of which I'd long since given up on ever flashing again.

"Wait 'til you're slapped in the face by a ten

240

foot tidal wave and dragged a few hundred yards! They'll be fishin' your spare parts outta the drink for weeks to c-. . . "

Being that the final word of his shrieking rant had been cut off so abruptly, I glanced back around to see his scrawny frame bent over and clawing frantically into the bank, his bootless foot sliding haplessly as it pumped and flapped against the slick terrain. It was obvious he was trying desperately to cover some ground in the opposite direction, but the source of such panic wasn't clear until I became aware of a thunderous roar originating from just beyond the impending hilltop's rounded peak.

I stood frozen with wide-set legs, pulling the backpack around to hug it tightly to my chest with both arms. *Colorado* continued to whimper and moan in the background, though I'd quickly lost interest in his feverish attempts to flee whatever horror neared from just beyond the horizon as thoughts rapidly turned to saving my own hide.

Once the source of our shared anxiety crested the hilltop in all its fearsome glory, descending downward like some massive, magically levitating wall, it became all too apparent that *Colorado*'s off-the-cuff remark about potentially fatal tidal waves was apt to become tragically prophetic. Simply stated, the levee had collapsed . . . the dam had broke . . . that strategically placed finger had pulled free from the dyke. In terms of role-play, I was the *S. S. Poseidon*, just seconds away from being flipped from keel to bridge by a colossal wall of water.

Even as the monster wave barreled closer,

drawing to within twenty yards or less of my stiff-legged position, I wasn't completely convinced what I was seeing, however horrifying at face value, was an authentic threat. There was a part of me that couldn't shake the vibe, however preposterous, that it was no more than a yet another particularly well-constructed computer effect. This lingering doubt, this faint surge of hope, despite rapidly rushing waters ascending my lower torso and threatening to bury me alive.

The hypnotic effect might've loitered to fatality if not for the floaters snapping me too. There were severed tree limbs of varied shapes and thicknesses; gnarled wads of sea-grass and *evergreen huckleberry* that darted and swirled like leafy jellyfish; even assorted patches of fully-bloomed *Hardy Lilac* levitating both within and atop the monstrous churn as if magically affixed into position. Much worse, I could've sworn I'd spotted several appendages of the *human* variety float to the surface, to include a clenched fist so bleached it gleamed like exposed bone, an equally ivory-shaded torso that surfaced so briefly I was unable to distinguish whether it had been a front or back, and a bare foot and attached ankle that had bobbed up and down several times before a final submersion. Now, whether or not these gruesome images had been more than fear-induced hallucinations remains a mystery wrapped firmly within an enigma. If I were a man inclined to wager, I'd have leaned heavily towards *seeing was indeed believing*, though such a choice is undoubtedly bias considering the alternative being a severely cracked mind.

Speaking of choices; mine had been woefully few considering the circumstances and limited timeframe with which to act. Chances of survival, no matter the strategy, appeared slim at best. If I'd been foolhardy enough to stand my ground, drowning only after being crushed like a clamshell beneath a descending sledgehammer was the probable outcome. On the other hand, attempting to swim with the impending current would've most likely saw me imitate a sand pebble tossed rather viciously against a granite mountainside, but not before being dragged along the trail's jagged bottom like a ricocheting pinball. That left alternative number three, which consisted of climbing the nearby bank in search of a possible high ground; or at the very least something semi-solid to latch onto. Needless to say, I chose number three merely by default.

As fate would have it, the first tree I attempted to grasp hold of, while resembling an elm, turned out to be of the CGI variety. Having immersed myself in red clay from elbows to knees while scaling the slickened bank, I'd leapt up with both hands to grip a low-lying limb and watched in horror as my fingers passed directly through, briefly blurring the image, before slamming into an equally faux wall of shoulder-high shrubbery. Figuring only seconds remained before being splattered and subsequently swept away, I ignored the battering my lungs had sustained and hopped up from the muck in a desperate attempt to latch onto the nearest tree limb of authentic variety.

Less than a dozen feet away from where my latest scramble began stood a slightly leaning Sycamore, it's palm-shaped, pointy-tipped leaves in full spring bloom. With literally no time to spare as a fine, cool mist splattered the hood and upper back of my raingear, I lunged forward and, following two lengthy strides, vaulted upwards with arms extended and fingers splayed. Despite the deafening roar at my back, I could still just make out *Colorado*'s distant screeching.

Half-expecting to slam into yet another illusionary blockade, I'd tensed, flinched and winced in perfect synchronization just as both palms wrapped firmly around a lower limb. Slim but stout, the limb held as I'd concluded my swaying follow-through, swinging both legs up and out to wrap around a thicker appendage. Pulling myself up, my hood was torn askew by a thicket of leaves, though the cap-cam somehow managed to remain intact. I'd just managed to reach up and snag yet another branch, this one bent permanently upward and stouter still, when the deadly wave in question came ashore. The experience itself is impossible to describe, more so than anything I'd ever witnessed first-hand. Thirty, perhaps forty seconds in length, it was many things; *terrifying* certainly, but also undeniably *exhilarating* as well. There was a rush of adrenaline unmatched in my forty-plus years, coupled with the birth of a primal, survivalist instinct I'd never before knew existed within the soul of such a natural coward.

Under normal circumstances, I couldn't have possibly held any grip, double-handed or not, nearly as long. In rodeo terms, it was akin to an eight second ride on the most ferocious of raging bulls. The wave's initial impact had, not surprisingly, spun me like a human top, my legs and torso flung into adjoining limbs that were systematically snapped or sawed off upon contact. Through it all, I somehow managed to retain my grip, that is until my supportive branch gave up the fight with a resounding snap, sending me sailing off in what felt like permanent spin cycle. Before plunging into the waiting drink head-first, I heard a sharp, echoing crunch as the mighty Sycamore's trunk also gave up the ghost.

How long I was under before resurfacing with a strained gasp is anyone's guess, though I'd never been very adept at holding my breath, even as a child splashing about the shallow end of the kiddie pool. Still, much in the same vein as the initial leap of faith and Olympian limb-grip, I had suddenly acquired quite the penchant for survival. The wave had long since passed, the damage done in its wake floating all about me in the form of assorted debris, only a portion of which remained recognizable. Fact was, I myself was a substantial part of said debris, paddling weakly towards the nearest land mass like a semi-drowned rat.

The portion of dry bank I crawled upon was laughably miniscule, no wider than a pitcher's mound, though at the time it appeared positively huge when compared to the swaying, foamy lake of natural disaster dominating the landscape.

I lay on my back several minutes, perhaps as long as five, staring into a party-cloudy sky no more real than the elm tree I'd first attempted to cling too or the massive, arena-sized wave that had initiated all the drama. My backpack was of course, long gone, as was the back-half of my raingear, leaving only the hood, shoulders and sleeves intact. The cap-cam survived, as always, it seemed, though my specially programmed IPOD had fallen into the casualty category.

"W-wake the fuck up, Cracker," I heard a voice croak so faintly I wasn't immediately convinced of its legitimacy.

"Better yet, ya might as well keep your seat. I'm s-sure you got some serious cryin' and self-pity to tend to, like m-most pussies do after such a traumatizin' event. "

Despite universal fatigue, I found the strength to roll my eyes.

"My god, *it lives* part two. You know, I'm beginning to believe you've got some roach DNA mixed in with all that meanness. "

Despite the intended vileness of my response, I had to admit to admiring the scrawny man's spunk. As I struggled to lean onto my elbows, I could hear him closing ground as faint splashing noises grew increasingly clearer.

"Keep yakkin', p-plowboy," I heard him reply, a strange wetness to his tone, as if he were gargling a mouthful of the same floodwaters being treaded, "we'll s-see which b-bug takes a s-stompin' he-here shortly. "

Curling my knees to my chest, I hugged them to me and clamped the fingers of both hands for support while fighting off a series of dizzy spells that momentarily kept my vision semi-blurred.

"So tell me, how did you manage to dodge being squashed anyhow? The tree I attached myself to wound up playing toothpick about halfway through impact, and I gulped down what felt like half the Mississippi in the aftermath. You dive into the base of that wave or what?"

Reaching up with a shaky hand, I attempted to rub the blur from my eyes with fingers that had yet to regain full circulation, during which time *Colorado* hadn't bothered to respond to my query save a series of soggy, rattling coughs. I was about to crack wise about the possibility of his *swallowing* the wave to save his own hide, but that was precisely the same time my vision cleared and all thoughts of sarcastic humor skittered away like flies from a bonfire.

Flinching back from a spastic wave of primal shock, the support hand I'd still had in place slid on the muddy terrain, causing an involuntary shift of position. Yet again, I can only deduce that Father Fate or Lady Luck interloped on my behalf, as the alternative was far too grisly to contemplate.

Part Six: Fleshy Driftwood

Time: Fourteen hours, thirty-six minutes into the Iron Will Gauntlet

Location: Sector C (Hybrid climes: Upper northwest/southern U. S. coastline)

Total miles covered: Thirty eight and one-quarter (no significant ground gained)

The serrated shard of wood he'd no doubt aimed for the center of my torso had instead only grazed my left shin just above the ankle, though forcefully enough to rip away sizeable sections of, in order of mutilation, my rubber boot, the pants beneath, and finally several layers of skin.

Rolling over and back until I waded into chest-high waters, I knew instant terror in the realization that I'd apparently stepped directly into a soft-mud sinkhole. As my boots sank deeper into the trail's variation of quicksand, I reached back and gripped the bank's curved edge and heard my pursuer growl in apparent frustration at missing out on such a ripe opportunity. Peering back over my right shoulder, I watched him crawl from the rapidly descending waters like some recently unearthed corpse rising from a watery grave. Patches of hair, what little hadn't been torn from his mutilated scalp, clung to the side of his face like blood-soaked seaweed. Slinking across the sparse mound on his bare, bony chest, he held the spear-like shard high in his left hand while his right served as a rudder of sorts. It wasn't until he'd completely emerged from the fast-shrinking lake that yet another horrid wound swam into view, though it still ranked a distant second in terms of overall shock value. Dragging himself forward with his belly digging a narrow trench into the moistened terrain, the arch of his left foot nonetheless faced upward towards the sky, a sliver of jagged white bone protruding from each side of the shattered ankle like skeletal antenna.

Unable to free either boot from its spongy prison, I curled the toes of each foot in an attempt to free my bare feet. Wading forward, I released my grip on the bank just as the pointed edge of the wooden shank tore away a chuck of clay in the exact spot my fingers had previously occupied.

"G-give it u-up, ass-lick. I've already a-ack-accepted th-the fact I ain't w-winnin' this bad boy a-after all," I heard him garble gleefully, pausing briefly for a series of hacking, water-logged coughs.

"Makin' my newest and l-last mission to ma-make dah-damn sure a c-chicken-pluckin', p-pig p-porkin' c-cracker like y-yourself t-takes a s-similar d-dive."

Unable to turn and face my attacker, pure instinct alone inspired me to swing my right arm back in a blocking pose, and though the descending shank did manage to slice away the tip of my pinky finger, it was effectively deflected from its original target, most likely the back of my neck.

Hoping to prevent a follow-up blow, I clamped onto his wrist and jerked forward with all the energy and leverage my meager bodyweight would allow. Still, even as utterly drained as I'd been, *Colorado* was a slight load at best, and I was able to sling him over my shoulder judo-style. Sailing into the drink head first, I saw his badly broken foot submerge last, flopping about like a loose sandal. The whiplash effect of the shoulder-toss forced me to collapse back from the effort, though my trapped legs served to eventually spring me back upright like a human Jack in the Box. Holding up my wounded hand, I'd hardly had time to survey the damage before falling under siege yet again. A bony, stick-like arm was the first to resurface, sans the jagged shard but pumping a clenched fist, nonetheless. Once his mostly hairless skull followed, accompanied by a combination gasp and rebel yell that caused me to involuntary join the concerto with an embarrassingly feminine yelp of my own, I must confess the internal coward meter had pretty much pegged out. Of course, being that no avenue of escape existed, weaseling out of the situation via means of 'flight' over 'fight' was a non-issue, leaving only the single option of, primitive and clichéd as it sounded, *kill or be killed*. Up to that point, I'd merely defended myself. As the crazed madman from the Rocky Mountain State reared back for yet another attempt to snuff out my very existence, I found it frighteningly easy to transform from prey to predator.

Intercepting what turned out to be a rather feeble swipe, I clasped his right wrist and held it airborne with my left hand while reaching out with my right to grasp the foreign object protruding from his neck like a leafy appendage. Minutes earlier, as I'd leaned up to greet the man from the tiny beachhead, I'd initially thought it to be a fragmented bone, though there was little logic in the existence of a mandible roughly the size of a pool cue and adorned with blood-drenched leaves. Bug-eyed and mouth ajar, I was able to fix on the wound at his neck just before his initial attack. It seemed the flesh had effectively sealed around the protrusive branch, as blood leakage appeared shockingly minimal. If nothing else, the origin of his soggy-sounding vocals was duly explained from such internal wreckage. As for how he'd sustained such a grisly injury, I doubt if even he knew the answer. No doubt the massive tidal wave had played a major role, possibly tossing him onto an upturned limb or shoving said branch into his body with such force the flesh and sinew caught in its path had separated with ease.

Shoving the branch upward, my face was splashed by a glut of warm stickiness that shot from his wound in a blackish torrent. I then plunged it downward with equal force until it snapped off in my hand. That initial twist had, more than likely, ended the man's life. I'm no doctor. No pathologist or similarly trained specialist in such matters, but in terms of sudden blood loss, that had certainly been a doozy, as in *femoral artery giving way* doozy. The second twist had been the closer, as I'd seen the man's eyes roll back and felt his arm fall limp in my grip. There had been no famous last words; no departing wisecrack. He'd merely collapsed like a puppet with cut strings, gliding gently away like human driftwood with nary a parting waive. I was privy, as he'd gradually floated onto his stomach, to viewing what had surely been the branch's entry wound; a stubby limb hanging from just beneath his rib cage, leaving a narrow, dark-maroon trail atop the suddenly calm surface. Peering down, I could visibly see the water growing shallower, and found great relief in the knowledge that soon I might be afforded freedom from the sinkhole that had so effectively consumed my boots. As the level dropped from upper abdomen to groin, groin to lower thighs, lower thighs to barely ankle deep, I watched *Colorado*'s lifeless husk fade from view around a far curve. Strange, but I'd felt little emotion at the sight, be it elation, depression or guilt. Not exactly warm and cuddly when stable, at the end the man had been mad as the proverbial hatter, going to the extreme of all extremes in psychotic behavior, that of a sadistic, conscienceless murderer. It was fact that I hadn't known the man at all other than to endure his baseless insults, but there was something about a person attempting to end your very existence that put a damper on any potential feelings of remorse.

Pulling my boots free from the glutinous muck with a series of wet, sucking sounds, I turned towards the beckoning trail and trudged painstakingly forward, halting only long enough to rip away select portions of my cotton undershirt to use as gauze on my pinky finger and shin, respectively.

By the time I'd crested the top of the great hill, the floodwaters had receded to a mere inch or so of standing wetness.

Warm rays of sunshine soon bathed the landscape, and I felt myself fall into a uniquely tranquil daze. The temperatures had warmed considerably—definitely a good thing considering the majority of protective clothing had been torn away, and what little remained was soaked through. Waves of dizziness mingled with bouts of severe drowsiness soon followed, though somehow I continued to lumber forward, zombie-like, until finally the bright sunlit sky and all it surveyed faded to black. A forced powernap, one might say. Voluntarily or not, it turned out to be a blessing in disguise.

Part Seven: Relations Redox

Time: Fifteen hours, eleven minutes into the Iron Will Gauntlet
Location: Sector C (Hybrid climes: Upper northwest/southern U. S. coastline)
Total miles covered: Thirty-nine and three-quarters

I had to be dreaming. Drifting half-in, half-out, my entire being racked with a countless array of aches and pains and my eye-lids hanging so heavy as if weighted down. A soothing, though simultaneously troubling dream, I pondered weakly. It was the only logical conclusion to surmise, though in truth to think logically while wandering the bizarre, mirage-filled realms of the Iron-Will Gauntlet was beyond merely foolish, but an utter waste of brain cells.

She leaned over my splayed form, cradling my head with the palm of one hand while gently caressing my bare forehead with the other. The small smile she wore was from the *good times*, chock full of sincere concern. Her gleaming, dark brown eyes shone with a level of deep, infinite caring. She smelled of my favorite perfume, the brand name escaping me as always, and her touch was nothing short of magical, as it had always been during the *good times*. Her lips, naturally ruby red and full, parted ever so slightly, and I caught the faint whiff of *Classic Juicy Fruit*, always her gum of choice during the *good times*. She began to speak then, though whatever message she'd attempted to convene remained a mystery. I'd either gone stone deaf, or some egghead techie at Gauntlet HQ had accidentally pressed the 'mute' button. She continued to mouth the words and stroke my head until all went dark yet again.

We were making love, the missionary position; not my personal favorite though I did enjoy watching her facial expressions alternate from lip-pouting tease to wild, passionate frown. Soon I would initiate doggy-style, the position of choice during the *good times*, and if all were right with the world, as it was so often during the good years, we would climax as one. I pulled out of her and, taking my cue, she instantly rolled over onto all fours. With unbound lust, I moved forward in great anticipation.

"Hey, Blue Grass...you planning on taking up permanent residence in the great northwest or what? Come to, now...come to. "

Forced into a rapid blinking session in order to clear away the cobwebs cloaking my vision, I was eventually able to obtain a semi-clear view of my addresser.

"Well, hello there. You really seeing me this time or are we still wandering about our own personal la-la land?"

"I-I'm...um, g-give m-me a s-sec..." I babbled with a tongue as heavy as lead and with the texture of sandpaper. Though the waking process felt real enough, body aches and assorted scrapes painfully intact, as well as continuous throbs of a more serious nature near my left shin and right pinky

255

finger, I wasn't quite convinced reality had yet taken a full hold on my consciousness.

"By all means, ye of the battered body and wilted mind. Just don't take too many seconds or we'll find ourselves being overrun by infidels. "

She assisted in leaning me forward until I was able to sit upright in a semi-lotus pose, and I soon found myself reaching over to give her bare right forearm a gentle pinch. Her strawberry blonde locks were matted flat to her skull and neck as if glued into place, and her badly bloodshot eyes had protracted deep into their sockets, but otherwise she appeared no worse for the wear considering I'd resigned her to either death or at the very least a lifelong handicap a full sector back.

"Ari-Sagebrush, i-is that re-really . . . ? B-but how did . . . I mean, y-your feet. . . "

"Guess you figured to be calling me nubs by now, is that it?"

From her wry expression, my ghost-like complexion must've briefly flashed a shade of red.

"Well, m-maybe not to that ex-extreme, but they were . . . looking pretty . . . um, well . . . "

"Ripe for the bone-saw? Yeah, I'd have to agree. I was lying on that cold metal slab praying harder than I've had reason to in decades, just in the hopes I might keep a toe or two. I watched 'em bum rush you off, by the way. I, uh, appreciate the concern, and well, all you did to get me to that point. "

Fighting off a massive dizzy spell, I pulled my head in as close to my knees as possible and slowly lowered my chin.

"But h-how are you able to . . . well, compete?"

"Can't say for sure," I heard her reply, though barely over a sharp ringing in both ears, "all I do know is a team of 'em scampered into the room, all wearing lab coats and armed with loaded syringes. Not that I had a choice, mind you, but at that point I was more than willing and able to play pincushion. After that they hooked me up to so many different IV's I was surely looking more squid than human. Twenty or so minutes later, they wrapped my feet in what one of them called an ultra-healing pack and away I went. Might sound nutso, but the first mile or two of this particular sector was like a tiptoe through the tulips for this girl. I have never in my life felt more energized. Starting to wear down a bit now, and I'm sure all that water collecting in my boots wasn't exactly conducive to healing, but hey . . . I'm just damn happy to be here at all. "

"G-great . . . really f-fantastic," I blurted just before being forced to lean over and spat out a mouthful of warm bile.

"Pardon me for saying so, dude, but you don't look so hot. I take it you caught the brunt of the floodwaters a mile or so back?"

Straining to catch my breath, I had excavated the last spattering of phlegm before attempting a suitable reply and hoped the pathetic grin I'd flashed wasn't as hideous in appearance as it had felt to administer.

"No sw-sweat whatsoever. Ju-just your everyday, r-routine forty, f-fifty foot tidal wave. Saddled t-that filly u-up and broke her but g-good. "

"Uh-huh. I hear you, Aquaman," she cracked,

standing stiffly and scanning the trail on both ends. She backed up several steps, and I noted for the first time just how shrunken and brittle she appeared in comparison to our initial introduction in Sector A. I could only imagine my own gruesomeness. If the old adage held true and I looked as bad as I felt, *Arizona* had truly been holding court with the living dead. Amazing what a few short hours in egghead hell hath wrought.

"Waltzed through the aftermath a few miles back. Wasn't a tree left standing or a blade of grass left unbent. Looked like one of those old A-bomb test sites they used to show us in school. You know, those grainy black and white jobs about the Axis of evil?"

I nodded in fond remembrance.

"Y-yeah, I re-remember. Scared the Raisinettes o-out of me w-when I was a kid. "

Forced to lower my head from yet another impending dizzy spell, I could nonetheless visualize the abrupt change in her tone from light to grim.

"I saw a . . . body floating in the debris. At first all I saw was a single arm sticking out from a pile of branches. Looked like..." she paused to giggle—a horrible, choked hybrid of hysterical laugh and pained sob, "it was . . . waiving at me. Asking for help, you know? Well, silly me moved closer and surely got an eyeful," again with the wild cackle. It was at this point I was actually afraid to look up in fear she might be on the verge of gouging out her own eyes, "goes without saying it was no SOS. More like a claw frozen in anguish at the time of death. It . . . the body . . . what remained of it, was impaled by branches. Dozens of 'em, sticking out like quills, for Christ's sake. I think the . . . head was missing. Needless to say, I decided to forego any intensive search. "

"Probably *Colorado*," I blurted, still unable or maybe unwilling to raise my head. If nothing else, I was beginning to feel both my lung capacity and circulation normalize a tad.

"You . . . saw . . . but how can you be sure?"

"Ran into him along the trail just before the dam broke. Beat all to hell and back but mouthy as ever. Wave . . . took 'im, along with every pre-planted tree, shrub, and spec of gravel. "

She paused for a moment, sucking in a heavy dose of air through flaring nostrils as if somewhat hesitant to broach the next line of questioning.

"So Aqua-dude, How'd you manage to avoid Davey Jones' locker?"

Finally forcing my pounding noggin upward, I answered while staring at her booted feet, the attached legs comically stick-thin, as if the knee-high rubbers she donned had been stolen from the doorstep of some mythical giant.

"What can I say? Somebody up there either adores me to keep saving my hide or hates my guts enough to prolong the torture. "

"So you dodged the wave or . . . "

Strange, but I recall being slightly irritated at her continuing fascination with the details of my most recent bout of miraculous survival.

"Grabbed hold of the nearest limb and hung on for all I was worth, however meager sum that might be. Limb broke . . . tree shattered like a toothpick . .

. and I found myself in the rinse cycle at full bore. Woke up beached like a sand crab with nary an inkling of how I got there. "

"Bluegrass old salt, I hope you don't mind sharing a little of that magical aura from here on out, 'cause this girl is planning on shadowing your rear end for when the next natural disaster rears its ugly head. "

"Well, it's not as though there weren't a few casualties. "

At this point, I paused to raise a hand to showcase a certain severed digit, followed by a jagged rip in my upper boot and the reddish smear outlining it.

"Nasty yes," she nodded with a deep frown while focusing on the blood-drenched wrap atop my mutilated finger, "but from what I saw of the landscape and . . . *Colorado*'s remains, you got off practically unscathed, buddy-boy. Can't say I'm sad I missed that particular display of Mother Nature's bitchier side. Deepest I waded through was ankle-high. Guess timing *is* everything. "

Rising to a crouch and pleasantly surprised at being able to maintain the stance without immediately toppling over, I managed to execute the weakest of smiles before shooting her a similarly feeble wink.

"Yeah, well, in my case maybe its fate, chickee-baby . . . kismet . . . karma of the highest order. Maybe I'm the King Egghead's pet of choice in this little *track meet of lost souls*. From what I've gathered, albeit from a highly shaky source within the Gauntlet's chain of command, you're sharing space with the number two bullet in the betting chamber. "

She regarded me with obvious bewilderment, as if I'd just sprouted turnips from both ears.

"Betting chamber? What are you talk . . . you sure you don't need another minute or two of R and R, champ?"

"*New York*'s the public favorite, Sagebrush. *Colorado* was number two. Obviously his stock has fallen dramatically in the last half-hour. Sooo…guess who's moved up a notch into his sadistic shoes?"

Her head titled, her eyes widened. I had the distinct feeling those turnips had morphed into a full blown spring garden.

"And you were told this by whom?"

"Can't recall the blokes name just now," I answered honestly enough, though the man's comically squared chin and buzz-cut did carve quite the clear image despite my still foggy thought process, "but I don't think he was yanking my chain. For some reason, I bought into the spiel. After all, what possible motivation would he have to lie?"

"You got me, champ," she finally responded with a frown, whirling about to check both ends of the trail for at least the fifth time since my awakening.

"So, you gonna be able to stand the pressure of hanging with a crowd favorite?" I chided good-naturedly, though secretly pondering what the future might bring if the two of us did decide to continue as *traveling companions*.

261

Without meeting my gaze, she turned her eyes into the sun-drenched sky with a strategically placed hand propped over her brow.

"I'll suck it up and take my chances. You up to taking off?"

"Yeah, I'm starting to feel my oats. Just another few ticks. "

With that, she pulled her backpack free from between painfully thin shoulder blades and removed a canteen, taking a quick swig before offering it to me.

"You're too kind, my lady, but I wouldn't think of it. "

"Bubby-boy, this isn't the time for pride. Take it . . . "

Pushing myself upward on legs so wobbly I briefly thought both knees were going to permanently lock, I politely waived her off.

"No, really Sagebrush, I appreciate the gesture, but it wouldn't be rig-..."

"I've got another, hero. Besides, if you could see yourself right now, you'd be bowling me over just to lick the cap. "

Involuntarily licking my lips and possibly only seconds from salivating at the thought of liquid refreshment of even the semi-warm variety, I relented with only a slight twinge of actual guilt.

"I'm sure that's a valid point, 'cause if I look only half as bad as I feel, there's one foot planted firmly in the grave and the other is slowly slipping over the edge. "

Indeed, the vitamin water was lukewarm at best. It even held a tint of sourness, as if bottled for far too long at its present state. Said cons aside, I've never tasted sweeter. How ironic that so recently I'd been literally engulfed by similarly wet stuff, my very existence threatened by its menacing, overwhelming presence. All a matter of incarnations—and timing, of course—always it's about timing and circumstances in this life.

"Gadzooks but that hit the spot. We can go now," I announced, handing the bottle back over with my chin dripping freely what my mouth had somehow managed to misplace.

"Did you just say *Gadzooks*?" she replied with a raised brow, both her hands propped sassily atop her bony hips.

"Dude, your vocabulary needs a serious tune-up."

Stumbling forward like a toddler newly acclimated with the power of walking upright, I couldn't help but smile.

"Seems someone else I used to know reminded of said verbal weakness on a daily basis."

"Is that right?"

"Yep. Motivated me to ad lib and at times purposely butcher the language whenever I felt especially mischievous. Drove that poor woman nuts…I'm happy to say."

Leaning hard to the left, I barely avoided tripping over my own feet, the usually lightweight boots suddenly as cumbersome as lead. Quickly righting myself, I'd heard the pattering of her boots as she'd rushed to my side, and even thought I'd felt a hand brush my upper back as if prepping to grab a hold.

"I believe it. Say, you . . . um . . . need a prop, Champ? Just for a while, I mean?Don't want to see you take a header into the nearest ditch. "

"Don't fret, my dear. Just working out the kinks," I replied, stretching my neck from side to side and reveling in the faint, strangely pleasurable soreness which resulted. Maybe it was the vitamin water, or perhaps just a matter of receiving the mythical 'second wind' that supposedly exists somewhere between severe fatigue and utter collapse, but I'd felt a palpable surge of renewed energy with each passing step.

"You're the doctor. "

A cool, soothing breeze struck my face and neck, and I reached up with my non-injured hand to run splayed fingers through my tangled, rapidly thinning coif, a large majority of bangs having long since deserted ship.

"How long you think they'll let the calm prevail?"

A few lengthy strides and she'd drawn even, obviously no longer feeling obligated to monitor my progress from the rear.

"Who's to say? Every time I think they've run out of nasty tricks and even consider letting my guard down, here comes yet another nightmare scenario straight from the files of the *Weather Channel*'s all-time shit-storms. "

I peered over at her and feigned shock, complete with bugged-out eyes and comical jaw-drop.

"Such language, woman! What if your dear, sweet old nana is listening at home?"

With that, she reached over and twisted my cap-cam towards the back of my noggin.

"Problem solved," she grinned while flipping her own headgear to a similar pose, "Besides, dear sweet Nana, when she was still above ground, was always a bit of a potty mouth. "

"Whew. Love to be a fly on the wall at your family reunions. "

We trudged forward for a bit, perfectly content to be treading a mostly flat, sun-baked trail temporarily hazard-free. Rounding the second in a trio of sudden sharp curves, a third competitor joined us quite unexpectedly. A competitor whose very presence, be they unwilling catalyst or no, seemed to kick off yet another round of grave peril.

Part Eight: Shake, Rattle and Dive

Time: Fifteen hours, forty-two minutes into the Iron Will Gauntlet
Location: Sector C (Hybrid climes: Upper northwest/southern U. S. coastline)
Total miles covered: Forty and a quarter

"Holy steaming hamster-crap on a saltine cracker! You 'bout made me make squirrel nuggets in my shorts. "

These were the exact introductory words from the state of *Oklahoma*'s lone representative, a bandy-legged fifty-something gentleman with comically bushy eyebrows the color of freshly laid tar but whose precious few locks of snow-white noggin hair stood out in stark contrast. Stripped down to a white cotton tee (the narrow back adorned with the word '*Okie*' sewn in dark blue), he'd obviously discarded the raingear somewhere along the trail or perhaps had it stripped away like yours truly. Strangely, he had a rubber boot tucked beneath each spindly arm while treading the gravel-infested trail in bare feet. Being that, like myself, he'd somehow become backpack-less, there was the distinct chance he'd had his own run in with the recent flood.

"Apologize for sneaking up on you. Wasn't really expecting company," I replied, feeling a tangible wave of disappointment at the man's mere presence at that particular juncture in the competition, as I'd already convinced myself that

New York had been the lone soul remaining left to surpass.

"I can surely second that motion . . . *shit!*" I heard Sagebrush whimper, holding a palm tightly to her chest as to ward off a sudden coronary.

"Yeah, I'll bet. Weren't many choosing this bird for front-runner status. I mean, hell, just look at me! I got life-long slacker written all over my scrawny carcass. But you see . . . um, I'm not much with colors...what state you hail from, son?" he paused his shrill monologue, a forefinger raised and frozen in midair as to soon continue his point.

Halting all forward motion, I performed an admittedly gawky about-face in order to showcase the rear portion of my own shirt before twisting back around with a bit more grace. Gesturing with an extended thumb, I never got around to formally introducing Sagebrush.

"Oh, yeah, I see. Well, *Kentucky*, like I was saying . . ." he interceded in the same booming voice, and I began to wonder if the man wasn't suffering from a serious bout of hearing loss.

". . . it's the old 'can't judge a book by its worn-out, scraggly-looking cover. Took 'em all by surprise, right out of the gate there at Sector A. Tore off the starting line like I had fire ants building a sizeable hill smack dab in the crack of my ass!Heard a few cat-calls, most notably from a few of the younger set . . . you know, upstart, wet-behind-the ears forty-something's like yourself. . . ha! One of 'em, might've been New Jersey or Washington state, started whistling and called me *Captain Burnout*. Well, lemme tell you, all that snickering and giggling and talk about me not lasting the sector without croaking out was nothing but extra motivation for a stringy, bow-legged geezer like myself! Weren't no stopping me after that, rheumatoid arthritis be dogged! Captain Burnout my pasty-fleshed buttocks! I've outlasted 'em all!"

As the man's raucous rant continued, seemingly without the need for the occasional inhale, I would occasionally glance over to my right to gauge Sagebrush's reaction, and soon found myself fighting an unrelenting urge to laugh aloud, an itch better left unscratched lest I find myself lying at the center of the trail in the midst of an unstoppable giggling fit. With that in mind, I purposely avoided viewing her skilled assortment of warped facial expressions, the majority of which were so comically exaggerated I could hardly recognize the perpetrator. At least, if nothing else, the sudden barrage of unexpected distractions did serve to temporarily ease the severity of my many physical ailments.

". . . not to say it's been all smooth sailing. I mean, there have been a few substantial bumps in the road, none more inconvenient than trekking the better part of two miles in chest-deep rapids. Damn good thing I spent half my adult life teaching PE, to include competitive swimming. Even then, there were a few iffy moments there when the undertow almost sucked me to the floor. Rough as playing human pontoon boat was, I'd take it in a minute over all that damn snow and ice. Pardon my butchered French, but that shit just plain hurt . . .

268

right to the bone marrow it smarted. Another few hours of staggering, sliding and sledding over that rut-infested hockey rink and I just might have cashed it in for sure, and I'm not usually apt to giving up regardless of the circumstances, you understand. As far as what's to come, well, let's just say I'm..."

It was around the point that *Oklahoma* began to predict his eventual victory march through Sector D that I found the inner mute button to effectively tune him out. As far as I can recollect through the foggy mist of a severely impaired memory, the man's blaring rant continued unabated for the next fifteen or twenty minutes, at least till the ultimate in scene or mood changers reared its anger-filled head to cut him off in mid-riff.

At first I paid little attention, as it began in so subtle a fashion—practically unnoticeable. The initial hint of something being amiss was a mild tingling at the bottom of my feet. Hardly fair warning, as I'd instantly shrugged off the sensation as a circulation issue. Seemed logical enough considering the total mileage covered and woeful lack of padding provided by the flat-soled rubbers. In glancing briefly over at Sagebrush, I read nary a hint of concern in her stoic, determined expression. The second and easily more tangible hint occurred as my teeth began to chatter involuntarily, as if triggered by a sudden, frigid chill. From my left, I heard Oklahoma mutter *'what the hell'* in triplicate, with each refrain growing increasingly shrill. The third and final hint before the big reveal came when the mere act of keeping balanced atop a fairly level trail became damn near impossible.

Forced to strike a painfully wide-stance with my feet set at least two feet apart, the landscape began to blur as ground tremors intensified.

"Ohhhhh shiiiiiiiit! Somebody's rattling the cage but goooooood!" Oklahoma moaned, his voice comically shaky, though at the time I could drudge up little in the way of sincere humor.

Sadly, that initial outbreak of tremors, shocking and raucous as they seemed, were the equivalent to a gentle shake of a baby's rattle when compared with the mother lode to come.

In fact, for a single, frozen moment in time, all movement ceased. This pause, pitifully brief as it had been, allowed for little but a rapid self-inventory, during which I noticed my stance had altered from fully upright to a toady squat.

"Whew-weeee baby! What a ride! Those boys in the lab-coats sure know how to lob those curveballs. Felt like disco night at the local dancehall- . . . " I heard *Oklahoma* begin before the trail before us began to split directly at the center, peeling open as if from the razor-sharp blade of some massive, underground table-saw.

It's a hard thing to describe when one's equilibrium is bludgeoned and all connecting systems go completely haywire. At first, there was a sense of weightlessness—of floating in zero gravity. This was soon followed by the exact opposite, when your legs and feet are molded in cast iron and the entirety of your torso and upper body are paralyzed by a surreal mix of shock and awe. Then there was the utter helplessness that ensues—all-encompassing—the mind is left in a state of suspended animation in the face of total chaos. Being that one is left without options and relegated purely to pawn status, there is a stout sense of unreality present, not unlike a dreamscape.

The narrow chasm spread dramatically as it grew closer to our position, resembling a gradually expanding spider's web. Forced to my knees while being shaken viciously from side to side, I attempted to check Sagebrush's status to my right but was unable to focus. I could hear *Oklahoma* cursing to my immediate left, a few select profanities slipping through the thunderous roar. From the corner of my left eye I caught a faint glimpse of his shadow, which appeared to shift, buck and tilt dramatically to one side and then the other several times before eventually being jolted upright yet again.

Stumbling from side to side like a punch-drunk pugilist, I was trying to back down the trail as the spreading chasms grew near but was unable to acquire a suitable foothold. It wasn't until the terrain directly beneath my feet began to swell and pulsate, finally bursting forth as if giving birth, that I was heaved airborne, and landed awkwardly at least a dozen feet back on the trail's grassy shoulder with my upper back taking the brunt.

It was there, lying flat and being shaken to my very core, that I saw *Oklahoma* tip over into the chasm, which by that time had widened to the length of a semi-trailer. Oh, he'd given it his best effort to avoid said dive, wind-milling and flapping his arms as if attempting to take flight and dancing a wild, reverse step jig that in the end only served to make matters worse. At the end, I watched him nosedive headfirst with the rubber boots he'd continued to hoard still clamped tightly in each clenched fist. *Captain Burnout goes down with his boots on*, I'd thought crazily as he'd vanished from sight.

Fearing the worst, I'd managed to roll over while scanning every possible direction for a glimpse of Sagebrush. Finally, just before being flipped over like a flapjack on a griddle, I saw her crawling southbound on all fours with the backpack trailing close behind as it appeared to be strapped onto her belt. Somehow, perhaps by staying close to the ground, she'd already put a fair distance between herself and the rapidly splitting terrain. I won't lie…there was elation *and* jealousy in equal measure upon witnessing her escape. I might well have sold my very soul at that moment to be by her side.

The quake halted as abruptly as it had begun, the sudden, total stillness as eerie a phenomenon as the utter mayhem preceding it. I recall lying perfectly still on my back for perhaps as long as two or three minutes while awaiting aftershocks that never materialized, staring into a criminally blue sky. Snapped to by the sound of Sagebrush's approach, I leaned up groggily and hugged my knees to my chest.

"Hey, champ . . . you . . . are you o-okay?" she asked timidly, rushing over to kneel down directly in front of me.

"Y-yeah, as good as can be expected, I guess.

Back and neck took a thumping, but it'll pass. You?"

"Twisted both ankles, but can't complain otherwise. So where's the blowhard?"

In lieu of a verbal response, I pointed northward instead.

I heard a low gasp before watching her limp slowly towards the tip of the newly formed crater splitting the trail.

She stood at the edge of the abyss, which from a distance did indeed bear a striking resemblance to a spider's intricately spun web.

"Do you see him?" I inquired without a semblance of actual hope.

"I...I think I see a . . . his arm. Almost looks like . . . a tree's root. God, it's like the ground closed up around him, s-sealed him in. I think...I see the tip of one of his boots. "

Lowering my head, I mentally replayed the man's frantic dance of death and instantly felt a twinge of guilt for the woeful lack of empathy involved. True, I hadn't known the man at all, but there was that nagging matter of basic human compassion. Perhaps all the sudden, unexpected death I'd witnessed on the trail had served to harden me somewhat. Perhaps it was simply hitting a wall emotionally—that particular wall constructed of equal parts physical fatigue and mental disillusionment. Or maybe, just *maybe*, I'd come to the conclusion that one less competitor was indeed a good thing, newly christened worm dirt or no. Regardless, I could've done without the instant replay of *Oklahoma* playing cliff-diver into that carnivorous void.

"He . . . he couldn't dodge it. He tried. Tried like hell, but he wasn't able to move back or even from side to side. Damn sink hole just . . . swallowed him up. "

"So how'd you manage?" she asked, still staring down into the crevice as of hypnotized by its very presence.

"How else? Pure unadulterated luck. The ground below my feet commenced to bulge and swell, flinging me out of harm's way like a clay slingshot. "

Without bothering to view her expression, I could literally feel her disbelief.

"I kid you not," I concluded with a shrug, reaching up to adjust my cap-cam.

"As I've stated countless times since first making your acquaintance, please allow me to follow closely in whatever shadow you cast. "

I pushed myself up with a groan, my checklist of assorted pains having increased by two, what with a fresh throbbing between my shoulder blades and at the base of my neck.

"Not sure that shouldn't be the other way around. "

"I don't follow, Champ," she replied, stepping behind me to gently tap away layers of dust and dirt buildup from what remained of my tattered shirt.

"Well, didn't see you depending on random chance. I'd say in terms of agility and speed, you've got my battered old carcass beat hands down at this juncture in the race. "

As to avoid delving further on the subject, one

she'd apparently deemed too dicey for continued discussion, we moved forward in relative silence. In passing the multi-cratered portions of the trail, especially the widest chasm that had served as Oklahoma's personal tomb, I'd purposely averted my eyes. As I was would forever be saddled with the memory of the man's lunge to meet his maker, the last thing I needed at that point was to visualize the end result.

It would be at least fifteen minutes of walking at a fairly steady pace before we cleared the crater's starting point, and approximately another ten or so before a new line of dialogue commenced.

"I didn't want to leave you behind back there. "

She had practically whispered it, as if not intentionally meaning to speak the words aloud.

"I just lost it. I've never...*ever* been so . . . freaked out, you know? Twisters are one thing. Scary as hell but whoosh and they're gone. Snow and ice . . . well, fortunately I don't recall a major chunk of that specific sector. I missed out on the severest of the floodwaters. But, that . . . back there. I just . . . I dunno . . . lost it. "

"Sagebrush . . . "

"It's like it wasn't even me scampering away like a . . . like some roach from a kitchen light. Talk about your out-of-body experiences. . . . "

"Hey, it's alright. "

"I didn't mean to . . . you know, leave you there. I, I know it must've appeared as selfish as it gets, but I wasn't. . . didn't mean to leave you behind. "

Her voice cracked with that final refrain, and I

felt compelled to turn towards her, reach out, and take her right hand gently into my own. We stood stationary at the center of the trail, that spunky lady from *Arizona* and myself, our hands and eyes locked.

"Don't sweat it. These are far from normal circumstances. One cannot expect normal behavior. I think no less of you. Just let it lay and let's move on, agreed?"

It was, perhaps, the most honest words I'd blurted since the race's inception. It certainly felt so, anyway.

"Agreed," she blubbered as the tiniest of teardrops dribbled forth from the corner of her left eye, "let's shag ass outta this here schizophrenic sector once and for all. "

I gave her hand a final squeeze and we proceeded to do just that, without another mention of the quake, *Oklahoma*'s grisly demise, or the many similar tragedies we'd previously bore witness too at the hands of the Gauntlet.

The trail stayed relatively flat and curve-free for those few miles, though a light rain did begin to fall about halfway and the surrounding shoulders did grow steep and hilly. We were sharing the last of her vitamin water when a low rumble at our backs saw us both execute a panic-fueled double-take. With surprising aplomb, we watched as approximately twenty or thirty yards back the shoulders on both sides of the trail rapidly caved in and met with a wet, sloppy kiss at almost precisely the halfway point. It went without saying that if our pace had been perhaps two minutes slower, that ten-ton mud slide would've reduced the both of us to bottom soil.

"Huh, looks like the boys in the lab-suits were a smidgen slow jerkin' the old trigger," Sagebrush had quipped without a tint of humor in either her ragged tone or stone-faced expression, and although exhaustion prevented a full-blown guffaw on my part, the weak giggle I did manage was unavoidable.

"I get the feeling that's their way of saying put some steam in your step. "

She nodded and we bumped shoulders playfully before proceeding on, albeit at a slightly jazzier pace.

In that final mile, covered in a brisk ten to twelve minute jaunt that harkened back to our A Sector velocity, there were no more floods, quakes or mud slides. It seemed the powers that be had inflicted their quota of natural disasters, the body count significant enough to call off the catastrophe dogs, so to speak.

Sagebrush and I spoke only sporadically, conserving our energy for that final sprint to the exit port. What was being left unsaid was the obvious quandary that lay ahead; a dilemma that would not, *could* not, go unresolved for much longer.

As we turned a final curve in Sector C, clearing the way for our first glimpse at the exit, she and I exchanged a worrisome glance.

Soon, we both realized, the partnership would have to be dissolved.

Soon, all loyalties would be declared, by default, null and void.

Soon, there could only be one.

Sector D: Mere Specs in a Sea of Sand

Part One: Empty Nest

Time: Sixteen hours, twenty-eight minutes into the Iron Will Gauntlet

Location: De-brief area between Sector's C and D (Desert climes)

Total miles covered: Forty-three and two-quarters

"Hello? Hey, who's minding the store already?"

Sagebrush had been repeating virtually the identical refrain since our low-key entry through an entrance door standing partially ajar. Though adequately lit, the place was found to be a virtual tomb. After a bit we'd split up and individually checked every room within the structure, easily the largest of the three ports in terms of square footage, before reteaming in what appeared to be the supply issue area.

"Anything?" she inquired wearily before kneeling down to remove her boots.

"Nada. Now why would they leave the place deserted? Not that I was looking forward to the mandatory lecture on my lack of killer instinct, but this is damned weird. "

"I'll say," she replied, wearing a pained grimace while massaging her feet, "but you know, it

279

would've been a hell of a lot weirder if we'd stumbled across, say a few steaming cups of coffee left unattended or a warm, mussed-up cot without the body responsible, you know?"

"Flying Dutchman," I muttered amidst the faint smell of infection emanating from her bare feet.

"Wow. Impressive, Bluegrass, *very* impressive. You sure you weren't some sort of literary professor in that other life?"

"I refuse to answer in the fear I might incriminate myself. "

Forced to turn away from the rancid scent, I trained my focus on the lengthy, twin conference tables we'd taken position between, one of which held stacked sector packs and the other the prerequisite change of clothing. In taking a quick inventory, I counted exactly fifty of each. In repeating the task, the tally was the same.

"What's the verdict, teach?" Sagebrush asked abruptly, startling me into an involuntary flinch I was proud went unnoticed.

"Oh, um, well . . . according to what's left, it seems as though only one other has come before us. "

"Let me guess-big black dude with muscles of steel and a sneer ugly enough to crack glass. "

"That'd be my guess. Front runner and pre-competition favorite from that big ol' rotted apple. "

"Hey," she practically shouted, briefly ceasing the two-handed massage of her left foot, the flesh of which I noted was shaded in light purple, "what do we do about the mandatory lead delay?"

"Mandatory lea- . . . " I replied, temporarily

perplexed before the meaning sank in, "oh yeah, that's right. Without the robo-guards and their damned stopwatches, I guess it's wide open, huh?"

Her eyes pulled wide with excitement, she practically leaped to her bare feet.

"So what say we clean up, clothe up, pack up and get out?"

"I say it's go time, Tumbleweed," I grinned, turning about as swiftly as my stiffened reflexes would allow and snatching a set of pre-folded clothing from the tabletop, one in specifically labeled 'large' sizes.

"Meet you back here in five minutes or less, dude," she replied, quickly searching out and snagging a 'small' sized equivalent.

"Let's shoot for less than five. "

With that, my parting quip, we jogged away in separate directions towards our respective shower and change areas.

In actuality, it was closer to ten before we met back up at the tables to first choose, then inventory, and finally attach a suitable sector pack. As with the chosen attire; wide-soled flip-flop sandals, loose fitting, cotton parachute pants, light cotton tee and a long-sleeved over-shirt made from material so thin it was practically see-through, the accompanying packs had obviously been designed with desert climes in mind. First off, we'd been provided with additional means of hydration in the form of six separate canteens, each holding approximately sixteen to twenty ounces of either pure filtered water or an unspecified sports drink. Plus we'd each been afforded a pair of Nitro-Pak freeze-dried food packs which could be eaten straight from the container—one clearly labeled diced chicken and the other diced beef. Seeing that I'd probably dropped a good twenty pounds since Sector A, the mere thought of chowing down on anything other than energy bars was a mild thrill indeed. In truth, I had long begun to fantasize about the variety of dishes contending for my initial post-Gauntlet meal, to include assorted pasta (my biggest weakness by far), seafood, and just about anything layered in cheese. As for desert, there was no competition. Three words: German chocolate cake. Heavenly layers, plain and simple.

"You think this is some kind of test?" Sagebrush asked, effectively breaking my daze as we walked shoulder to shoulder down a narrow, sparsely lit hall.

"I don't follow," I replied honestly, feeling a renewed surge of energy simply from having rinsed off the buildup of crud and donning a fresh set of duds. Though the hot water and suds had initially set my assortment of open wounds afire, the cleansing rinse, a supposed mix of liquid antibiotics and hydrogen peroxide, had provided ample soothing. As a precaution, a stout spraying of ultra-absorbing UV protection served as a surprisingly refreshing final coating.

"You don't feel like we're being watched?"

Without raising my head, I allowed my eyes to dart about the surrounding walls and ceiling.

"Don't see any cameras. "

"Oh, they're not gonna be that obvious, Champ. I don't recall seeing any mounted in the other way stations either, but that sure as hell don't mean they weren't there. "

Reaching up, I tugged gently at the bill of my cap-cam.

"Then why bother with these particular eyes-in-the-sky?"

"Window dressing for the TV masses, dude. Don't think for a minute Big Brother isn't going to trust the story strictly to us. "

Tipping the bill yet again, a question suddenly arose.

"Speaking of which, I didn't see any reload cartridges, did you?"

"Nope, though I can't honestly say initiating a search ever crossed my mind. "

She paused as we neared a sharp bend and giggled.

"I really wouldn't fret, Champ. "

"I'll bite. "

Reaching up with both hands, she gave her cap a series of light taps.

"My guess is there never were any cartridges to speak of. Nothing but an empty shell masquerading as a camera. "

"Tumbleweed," I blurted between a few select chuckles of my own, "you are indeed the queen of conspiracy. "

The hall soon grew wider, eventually leading to a guard station not unfamiliar, as we'd viewed similar posts fronting the adaptation rooms inside the previous two sectors. Beyond the deserted podium lay a single steel door void of any visible entrance knob.

"Oh swell, now what? Can't step foot into the sector without passing through there first. "

"Simplicity in itself, my lady. Observe and learn..." I replied, while purposely sticking out my bony, emaciated chest.

Leaning over the podium, I discovered a series of four unmarked buttons on an otherwise blank pad.

The third pressing had been the charm, and the door slid smoothly open with nary a screech.

"How'd you know wh—"

"A keen sense of observation is one of my few strong points. Trick is," I continued, flashing a mischievous wink her way, "I saw 'em trigger those doors in B and C sectors in a similar fashion. "
Taking a half-step back, I bowed slightly and gestured her forward.

"Ladies first. "

"How refreshing," she shot back after the perfunctory roll of the eyes, "chivalry lives. "

She tip-toed cautiously forward, sticking her head inside and performing a brief scan before entering.

"Whoops. Looks like somebody didn't pay the heating bill, Chief. "

I followed close behind and instantly found it unnecessary to question the meaning of said remark. The room itself was undistinguishable from the other adaptation rooms we'd frequented; perhaps ten by twelve in circumference with four walls and nothing in the way of amenities save a trio of vents. The marked difference this particular time was an obvious lack of extremes of the temperature gauge variety. Considering the climate we were about to be exposed to, logic dictated a rather steamy mix of toasty temps and ultra-muggy air. As it was, conditions inside the prep room were almost identical, give or take a degree or two and the faint odor of mildew, to the rest of the facility.

"Something's rotten in Denmark, Champ, and I'm not just referring to the musky reek this air holds," Sagebrush blurted good-naturedly enough, though with just a twinge of barely refrained anxiety, "by rights we ought to be cooking but good about now. "

Reaching up to place a bare palm over the nearest wall vent, I felt not the faintest sign of warmth.

"Room temperature, my lady. Seems the juice has been out quite a spell if this is any indication. "

"Well then," she shrugged, stepping forward to lean her back against the exit door that would serve as our gateway into the fourth and supposed final sector of the Gauntlet, "if that brutish bozo from the Big Apple was allowed a pass, why should we feel any guilt?"

After a moment, wherein I'd adjusted my own pack, I turned back to the adaptation room entranceway and nodded.

"A damned good point, that. Allow me . . . "

Back at the podium, I punched the keypad one last time.

"Open sesame…"

Turning back around, I saw Sagebrush back away from the rust-colored steel door as it began its ever-so-gradual swing inwards.

"Speak the truth, Bluegrass, it's just you and me here. Well, us and *whomever* back at the command center who just might be eavesdropping. Oh, and the *millions upon millions* at home with their ears similarly pricked. You ready for this?" I heard her ask as I moved in behind her and struck a parade-rest pose.

"Hmm, without sounding overly cliché for the aforementioned listening audience," I replied with purposeful curtness, "with sixteen some-odd-hours and fifty or so miles in the can and despite hauling about a most diverse assortment of cuts, bruises and possible hair-line fractures, I'd have to say yes, my lady, I'm positively *stoked*. You?"

She turned to peer over her right shoulder and our eyes locked. I read a lot in that single, ever-so-brief exchange, not the least of which was a mutual admiration.

"Ditto, Champ. Ditto. "

"Powerful come-back, Tumbleweed," I quipped, leaning forward and nudging her with an extended elbow just seconds before a gust of dry, scorching wind slapped us back to reality.

Soon enough, an opposite reality, this one equally cold and just as unforgiving, would have to be dealt with. The reality of what to do about the unofficial traveling partnership that had served us both so well.

Part Two: Boiler-Plate Breakdown(s)

Time: Sixteen hours, fifty-six minutes into the Iron Will Gauntlet
Location: Sector D (Desert climes)
Total miles covered: Forty-four and one quarter

"*Good god*, I know what I was expecting. I mean, if there's *one* thing this girl knows, its heat. June, July and August in Tempe meant daily highs between one-fifteen and one-twenty. So, you might think I'd be sufficiently prepped from a mental standpoint. Honestly, I'd pictured Sector D as my own personal home-field advantage, ya know? Well, I'm here to officially state, Bluegrass, that this here is ten-fold worse than anything I imagined. Just my opinion, but I'm thinking they modeled this particular sector on the surface of the blessed sun. "

"Mind over matter, my dear 'weed, mind over matter. Simply hark back to Sector B in all its Antarctica glory. Ahh, instant cooling relief..."

The old saying goes *talk is cheap*. As such, I cannot recall a time in my forty-plus years when I'd spoken more frugally. In the half-hour to forty minutes since stepping onto the sandy terrain of the Iron-Will Gauntlet's concluding sector, I had already transformed from semi-reenergized to woefully wilted. This despite having already guzzled down two full canteens of my allotted rations, one sports drink and the other plain old H2O, within the sparse distance of a quarter-mile. Actually, a large portion of the water bottle of choice had been poured atop my scalp, splashed onto my face and leaked down both the front and back of my unbuttoned shirt. Amazingly, and despite the constant bitching, Sagebrush had yet to even acknowledge her backpack. Yes, there was a twinge of jealousy felt on my part, but also a larger jolt of continued appreciation at the woman's rawhide toughness. Whatever the ungodly temperature, which I would've conservatively estimated at between one-hundred ten to one-hundred twenty flesh-baking degrees, it was more the blistering sand beneath our sandals causing the majority of the discomfort— literally akin to treading atop lit coals.

"You're a bad liar, Champ," she replied, reaching up to adjust her outer shirt, which she had wrapped loosely around the cap-cam in a homemade turban of sorts, "Not your forte at all, from what I've seen. Mr. Honesty through-and-through, that's you. "

"Don't be so sure, woman. I can be as purposely obtuse as the next slowly frying mammal. "

"My sweat-soaked ass-crack, Champ. I know a boy scout when I hang with one. You've probably been the badge-collecting type since grade-school. "

Caught off guard by both the unexpected crudeness of her dialogue and animosity-laden tone in which it was delivered, I turned towards her and cocked a brow.

"Say, aren't you about due to crack one of those canteens open? A cool sip might do wonders for your present temperament."

Alas, there it was. I had, for the first time in our brief relationship, openly berated my traveling companion. As was the case whenever I stooped to such low-class tactics, an instant twinge of guilt soon followed, from which I immediately acted upon via renewing our dialogue .

"I mean, this damnable heat might make the Pope curse in tongue. This is no time to begrudge yourself much-needed nourish-..."

Her reaction, so wildly exaggerated to appear almost comical, albeit in a tragic fashion, nonetheless caused me to flinch back as if physically slapped.

"Oh for god's sake, would you stop patronizing me, Jackass!" she'd bellowed, turning on me like a cat and poking the forefinger of his right hand just inches from the tip of my sweat-coated nose.

"Have the balls, for *once* in your miserable, by-the-book life, to stand by your own words. I'm not your mama...I'm not your mistress...I'm your fucking *competition*. I step out of line . . . I touch a nerve. . . I stomp a delicate toe ... you've got every right to call me on it. Jesus wept, Mister PERFECT, sprout a backbone already!"

"Tumble-...I, um, didn't mean..." I babbled, my arms spread wide with the palms of each hand exposed in true 'surrender' mode. Despite of or perhaps because of the utter ludicrousness of the situation, I was on the very edge of a giggling fit of hysterical proportions.

"And I'll take a drink when I damn well feel like it, understand? Not before! Surely not when a fellow competitor urges me to! I look that stupid to you? Do I have *M O R O N* stamped on this forehead?" she barked, spewing frothy spittle onto my chin and upper chest while continuously stabbing her forehead with the tip of a finger.

"Listen, I was tryi-..."

From there, she took off in a huff, kicking up ruffs of sand with each heel and swinging both arms like mini windmills.

"Sage- I didn't mean . . . you know I didn't mean it to come off . . . "

I stood there for a full minute, perhaps even two, my outstretched arms unmoved. Truly pleading. I watched her blaze a virgin trail through the center of the massive dune that had become our pathway through what I'd jokingly referred to as 'Death Valley Daze' upon our first stepping onto the beachhead. If anything, her pace picked up as moments passed, her bony arms pumping like skeletal pistons as handfuls of sand shot airborne with each take off and subsequent landing of a respective heel.

After a time, it occurred to me that regardless of the origin of her inexplicably rage-fueled outburst, the woman from *Arizona* was putting considerable space between us. For once, in my own mind, our sudden separation wasn't at all about loneliness on the trail...it was all about the competition. A true revelation, as was the sudden surge of panic at watching my traveling companion vanish over a far dune. To define that latter revelation took but five simple words: *I truly wanted to win.*

Sector D was unlike the previous divisions in one specific way; there was no defined trail to follow. It appeared, in its entirety, as a wide, wavy sea of sand. There existed the occasional shrub or desert flower; even a budding cacti plant or twelve. A desert dandelion here, a devil's claw there—mere window dressing pulled from images of dozens of such landscapes worldwide. Similarly, it mattered little the majority of both the aforementioned flora and the perimeters on either side were, of course, computer generated. To scan from both side to side and backwards and forwards and be bombarded by nothing save the color of sand was, pardon the phrasing, nothing short of *chilling*. If created with the sole purpose of sending the already battered psyches of the remaining competitors spiraling into some final, fatal phase of insanity, it was undoubtedly a masterpiece.

As for conditions, Sagebrush had nailed the description quite effectively with her *surface of the sun* comparison. This wasn't merely hot…this was scorching. This was crispy bacon and fried eggs cooked to perfection on either shoulder sizzling. This was barbecue a three-inch sirloin on top of either shoe blistering. Of course it went without saying the sand beneath my sandals felt positively pre-heated to broil, and the sun's blistering rays beat down with invisible flames that, within a matter of minutes, had penetrated my cap-cam and began to slow-cook my scalp.

Meanwhile, the air was deadly still. This, of

course, might've been good or bad, depending on the outlook. On the one hand, a breeze, any breeze, might serve to cool by default. Oppositely, said wind might've simply served to heap misery atop misery by speeding up the baking process. Regardless, I hadn't felt even the faintest *poof* of air since inception. Small wonder Sagebrush had blown a fuse at what she'd mistakenly translated as mean-spirited ragging on my part. There I was giving serious consideration to pulling and chugging yet another canteen when she'd yet to crack open her first.

Fighting off said urge, I kicked it into a higher gear. Pools of fresh, salty sweat had invaded the open wound on my shin and my severed finger throbbed like a rotted tooth, the stoutest of a variety of pains being magnified by the stifling heat. No longer armed with a preloaded IPod, a much missed distraction device perfect for such a setting, I instead decided to sing aloud as a substitute, or at least hum aloud to the inner-CD spinning about my semi-broiled brain-plate.

Funny the tunes that swim forth from the subconscious during times of extreme duress or trauma. Obscure in terms of being listed as an all-time favorite, not even a top fifty really, though familiar enough to ensure the lyrics contained within are permanently locked in and ready to vocally butcher whenever needed. Strange though, considering the circumstances, how perfectly fitting said ditty. Had to be a subliminal thing. No way to chalk it up as simple coincidence. Far too pat...too tidy an explanation. Regardless, the words came easy…without effort—no memory strain whatsoever.

"…It's two a. m. , the fear has gone
I'm sittin' here waitin', the gun still warm…"

Removing my outer shirt, I aped Sagebrush's earlier act by wrapping it turban-like around my chin and skull, though there was a specific method to such madness.

"…maybe my connection is tired of takin' chances
Yeah there's a storm on the loose, sirens in my head
I'm wrapped up in silence, all circuits are dead
I cannot decode, my whole life spins into a frenzy…"

Wrapping the shirt in such a way to provide the narrowest of 'tunnel-visions', thereby eliminating the hypnotic pull of the outer perimeters, I was able to create a center trail of sorts.

"…help I'm steppin' into the twilight zone
The place is a madhouse, feels like being cloned
My beacon's been moved under moon and star
Where am I to go, now that I've gone too far…"

Illusion though it might have been, I felt a tangible swelling of pride at matching the master magicians of computer-generated effects at their own mind-bending game.

"…Soon you will come to know,
When the bullet hits the bone
Soon you will come to know, when the bullet hits the bone…"

It was around my sixth, maybe seventh rendition of the *Golden Earring* classic when I'd crested a particularly mountainous dune and spotted

Sagebrush posed yogi-style at the center of the trail. Her chin rested atop her chest, rising like a creaking drawbridge as I grew nearer. To state the painfully obvious, I hadn't a clue what to expect. I could only guess the reasons for such a weirdly timed sabbatical; either she'd halted in midstride to purposely allow me to catch up or, and I truly feared this to be the case, she'd run out of fuel soon-after the temperament meltdown. As it turned out, I was only half-right on one count, and the truth was much worse than anything I'd imaged.

Part Three: Resignations

Time: Eighteen hours, nine minutes into the Iron Will Gauntlet

Location: Sector D (Desert climes)

Total miles covered: Forty-six and three-quarters

"Weird place for a powernap, Tumbleweed, if that's what you've got in mind," I said once I got to within a dozen feet or so.

She regarded me with a cold, unemotional glare; a Vulcan gaze of pure iciness.

"Still in an ostracizing mood, are we?"

Backing away a half-step, I prepped for the worst.

"Just asking...no offense meant. "

The grotesquely wide smile she flashed was, to put it kindly, hideous. Her sunken eyes, gaunt cheeks and ashen flesh were at once haunting and gut-wrenchingly sad to observe. Yet again, such slanted thinking forced me into pondering my own appearance, no doubt equally ghastly. It was truly as if we'd been wandering the Gauntlet's perilous plains for seventeen *days* in lieu of hours.

"I'm pulling your chain, Champ. Misplaced that infamous southern sense of humor, have we?"

"Well," I shrugged, reaching over and down to offer a helping hand, "once burned, twice shy, pardon the rather cruel pun. Still, I do despise being misunderstood. "

With that, she reached up and snagged my left wrist and hauled herself up with a yawn. I was instantly struck at how feather-light she'd felt—like a hollowed shell of bare bones.

"Shall we venture farther into yon desert then?"

She nodded, rewrapping her turban.

"Yep, batteries are sufficiently recharged. Lead on then, Lawrence of Arabia. Like the look, by the way. My compliments to your fashion designer. "

"Well then, gotta give credit where credit is due, my lady," I replied with a slight bow and instantly regretted the act as a dizzy spell dotted my eyes upon ascent, "you set this here *par-tic-u-lar* standard in desert-wear. "

She stepped away first, and I noted the book-ended set of empty canteens sitting lopsided in the sand. To this, and barely regretting the cracked lips which ensued, I couldn't help but grin.

The next fifteen to twenty minutes were mercifully uneventful. I followed her lead, two to three strides behind, and following a shaky start, fell in comfortably with the surprisingly stringent pace she'd set. I turned only once to visualize the slightly waving twin trenches we'd created, never questioning why there had been no such pathway previously dug out. All that mattered now was the mission, the agenda of said mission brutally clear, though how realistic the goal a different matter entirely.

The *Sour Apple Roadrunner*, as she'd so cleverly dubbed him, would not be chased down or subsequently surpassed without superhuman effort. Despite the Gauntlet recruiting team's best efforts, the great state of *New York* had somehow managed to slip in a ringer—an ultra-physically fit ringer equipped with a steel-trap determination. An emotionally detached, seemingly soulless ringer who had literally sprinted out of the gate and set the pace from minute one and had, more than likely, yet to relinquish his lead since first separating from the pack. To merely draw even with such a man would take a stroke of biblical proportions. As for successfully *overtaking* such an android-like being, the impossibilities truly boggled a severely scorched mind.

"Hey, what if...what if we're wrong?" I heard her murmur in so muted a tone as to be inaudible save the surrounding dead air.

"Wrong about what?"

"What if...what if ol' Sour Apple is...well, *trailing us?*"

"But how could that be? He's been the frontrunner. I never passed him. "

"Shifting sand, then?"

"How's that?" I asked after a short pause, a sudden tingling at my scalp that had little or nothing to do with the blistering heat.

"No sandal prints, Champ. No clue anyone tramped atop these dunes before us. Am I missing something?"

"Like you said...shifting sands. Eggheads must have the terrain set on auto. Head games, my lady. All part of the plot. Same old same old. "So damn hollow, those words had sounded. She'd planted a bothersome seed, no denials.

We trekked on in grim silence, at some point veering so badly off course as to inadvertently locate the perimeter's false wall via physical contact. Having consistently remained three to four steps behind, I'd keep my eyes focused mainly on the back of her sandals, literally hypnotized by the precision timing of each step and the whiff of sand tossed airborne in the aftermath. With that in mind, I'd hadn't seen her scrape a shoulder against the invisible blockade, and by the time I'd noticed the sudden shift in her stride, from straight ahead to side-to-side, my right elbow had made the same discovery. Hopping away as if from a sudden electrical shock, I heard her croaking giggle just to my left and felt a twinge of anger that quickly melted away.

"Ain't that a pisser, champ? First time I nudged it, I thought you were tugging at my shoulder. "

Leaning forward with open palms leading the way, I stared into the unique falseness of what appeared to be an infinite desert-scape, flinching back once said palms impacted the cloaked obstruction.

"Must've drifted off the beaten track, Tumbleweed," I replied, tilting my head from side to side as if to find even a semblance of falseness within its design, "some navigator you are. "

"My bad. Guess I was dozing on and off; mostly off. Gotta…gonna have…. " she stammered, bowing over with her hands atop her knees, "guess it's ample time for…for a confession. "

I felt my emaciated chest tighten a degree.

"What's up?"

Remaining crouched, she peered up at me through the deep tunnel of her turban. What I saw in those deep-set, bloodshot eyes briefly transformed every bead of steamy sweat coating my pale, pasty frame to tiny shards of ice.

"It's…my legs…the ankles a-and feet…shit, all the way to the kneecaps really. "

"The numbness again?"

"If only," she answered hoarsely, pausing to lower her head yet again, "haven't been able to really feel 'em since that last chemical shower. No, it's…afraid it's a bit more than just a circulation issue. "

"Was…is it the frostbite effect?" I asked timidly, weary of the forthcoming answer.

"Well, j-judge for yourself, Champ, then you tell me. "

Collapsing into the sand with her legs splayed in front of her, she reached down with trembling fingers and began to gradually peel her pants legs upward.

One would've thought my skin would've been significantly thicker by that time. After all, I'd witnessed all manner of grisliness. I'd stared into the face of death numerous times and hardly blinked. In terms of constitution of inner gut; my innards were forged of cast iron.

Or so one would've thought. I doubt, however, that those endowed with such intestinal grit would be forced to lurch away and dry heave, no matter the level of gruesomeness visualized. Then again, perhaps I'm selling myself short. Maybe the reason my knees had turned to jelly and my midsection to mush was due to the personal stake involved. I doubt, then, I'd have had the same woeful reaction if say, a total stranger had revealed their blackened, rotted flesh to me. Gooey, mucus-coated flesh that reeked of fatal decomposition. After all, I considered this woman a friend, a confidant, a partner-in-crime of sorts. Striking up such a union had, obviously, been a mistake, but it was far too late to dismiss its presence. I wasn't *Colorado*, the man without a conscience. I wasn't *New York*, the win-at-all odds android. I had begrudgingly realized, somewhere within Sector B, that without the companionship of the fair representative of *Arizona*, my Kentucky-bred goose would've long been cooked. This, of course, made accepting her horrid condition damn near unbearable.

"Sorry 'bout the stench, Champ. I…this is why I made it my mission to put some space between us a while back. Didn't want…didn't want you to catch the draft. "

I'd turned back to her by this time, having ridded myself of nothing more than a mouthful of stomach acid despite a dozen or so back-warping heaves. Thank god she had taken this time to re-cloak the wounds.

"H-how long you b-been…has it been this bad since we hit the sand?"

"Just about. I…once I blew my fuse, it grew worse by the step. When…once you caught up with me, I'd long-since stopped to…survey the damage. Wasn't planning on getting up, but just seeing you relit the pilot light, at least for a while. "

300

"So...that whole yelling match back there was a put-on?" I whispered, pointing weakly in the opposite direction.

"Oh *hell* no. Make no mistake, dude, I was... royally pissed at you, though I'm fairly certain the build-up of infection and fever...not to mention this damn heat, contributed to the overall rant. Guess the miracle meds they pumped into me had an expiration date. "

I found myself temporarily muted, far too drained to broach the subject that would not be ignored. Instead, I stepped away and scanned the road ahead, which of course held little or no change from grounds already covered. The desert landscape we inhabited, manmade or not, appeared infinite— the *forever* dune. It mattered little, at that terrible, frozen moment in time, that the majority of what we visualized simply did not exist. At that terrible, frozen moment in time, there truly seemed no way out; no viable means of escape save to simply lie down and expire. Weakened as my mental state was at that very moment, as downtrodden and laden with despair as I'd ever been, no such option held serious weight. For that, at least, I'm proud, as it would have been so effortless to hoe that easy road to the ultimate surrender. She spoke as my back was turned to her, and the message her words conveyed were no less painful than a battering ram to my midsection.

"Better make tracks, Champ. Trail isn't getting... any shorter standing here watching... me decompose. "

This time, it was I that turned like a feral cat, hovering over her splayed form like a drooling predator.

"You can stow that kind of talk lady, understand? It's not happening! Not a chance...not a chance in hell!"

My hands trembled so, I was forced to first clench them tight and then tuck them forcefully to my thighs. My vision had blurred from a sudden buildup of desperation -fueled tears.

"You're wasting... precious time, B-Bluegrass."

"No, damn it!" I screeched, pacing stiffly about and no doubt appearing from afar as the raving madman I'd most certainly become.

"I'm not leaving you here! Walked away in too many similar situations already, okay? This boy's guilt meter is sufficiently pegged, thank you very much. Won't...will not...refuse...reject...tilt...you get the picture? Now drop it and get on your feet. We've got a certain *Sour Apple Jackass* to run down. "

Her laugh was equal parts hacking cough, but powerful enough to send her toppling onto her left side in hysterics. Despite my best drill instructor impersonation, in truth I was on the verge of joining her. There were worse ways to go out than to stage a good, old-fashioned set-in and laugh one's self into the grave.

"What the hell's so humorous? Get up, damn it! Let's move!"

"D-did you...did y-you really s-say ti-til-tilt? Wha-what the...ti-tilt...f-for real?"

With that, I was hapless to refrain. For the briefest of moments, the façade fell away and we did indeed share a joyous belly-laugh. It was priceless despite the circumstances. A fine, fond memory hidden within the gallery of horrid images that made up the majority of the Gauntlet.

"Oh, you're a r-real tou-tough guy, Sergeant R-Rock s-sir," she continued, pushing herself up onto shaky feet as I stepped forward to provide an arm to latch onto.

"Go on, get your jollies, Tumbleweed," I replied, using my free hand to wipe the warm wetness from each eye, "but it got your butt moving, didn't it?"

Moments later, following a shared canteen drain, we reentered the competition as the same twosome who had shared three-fourths of the trek as partners, albeit in a dramatically altered fashion.

Again, it was amazing how little she weighed, literally feather-light. Having combined the three remaining canteens into my backpack before tossing hers aside, I had subsequently strapped it to my chest in order to make room for my reluctant passenger.

"You're a c-cracked e-egg, Champ," she'd sighed, resting her chin atop my turban.

"Aw, just pipe down and enjoy the ride," I replied between spitting out specs of sand that had blown between my barely parted lips. The wind, before nonexistent, was suddenly becoming a presence, and hardly a welcome one.

We proceeded on, the gallant yet foolish knight and his mortally wounded cohort, my legs having almost instantly grown numb from the added burden. Being forced to pull my sandals free from the soft sand was becoming increasingly laborious, as the added weight was causing them to sink deeper with each lumbering step.

After a time, perhaps no longer than ten minutes or as lengthy as a half hour, during which time I figured she had nodded off into a semi-peaceful slumber, a soft whisper tickled my outer left ear through the turban's loose folds.

"Somebody has to… win, Champ, and it… ain't gonna be you if… you keep this up. "

"So we'll split the winnings, how's that?" I replied without hesitation, taking the opportunity to hoist her skeletal frame a bit higher with the knowledge of her consciousness.

"Stu-stubborn as…a mule," she croaked, briefly tightening her grip on around my shoulders.

"That's a *Kentucky* mule, lady, and don't you forget it. "

The wind velocity continued to strengthen ever so gradually, though fortunately it was pelting us from the south, thereby providing me with a bit of a push that was sorely needed. Just as fortunately for both my seared lungs and partially paralyzed legs, the desert terrain had remained relatively flat, with only the occasional mound to navigate.

Somewhere along the line, I drifted squarely and securely into a La-La Land of my own creation, no doubt to offset both the mental and physical strain. During this stretch of surrealistic non-existence, I recall nothing—a blissful blank slate wherein pain was declared off-limits and the searing heat had temporarily misplaced its passport. The actual duration of this delightful, self-induced fog is unknown, though there's little mystery in pointing out the exact minute its cloaking veil was so rudely lifted.

"S-sand...s-storm...s-sss-sand-st-storm..."

Seemingly in the blink of a grain-filled eye, it was upon us; a swirling cloud of dust specs that enveloped us whole. Didn't know it at the time, but we were experiencing the first sign of trail's ultimate end.

Part Four: ...*Two*

Time: Eighteen hours, fifty-eight minutes into the Iron Will Gauntlet
Location: Sector D (Desert climes)
Total miles covered: Forty-seven and two-quarters

"H-hang on! I'm gonna p-push on th-through!" I shrieked, my teeth, tongue and throat instantly coated with jagged grit. Her only reply, at least audibly, was a low, drawn out whimper that could've been taken in context as being fueled by either panic or apathy. Non-verbally, her grip initially tightened but grew increasingly weaker as I fought to navigate through the blinding storm. Numerous times I was nearly toppled by hurricane-level gusts that seemed to strike from all angles simultaneously. Strangely enough, the addition of Sagebrush's added weight actually aided in keeping me upright on several such occasions.

Wobbling forward, I'd been forced to bow my head to avoid the bee-like sting of the blowing sand. Sometime in the midst of the incessant battering, my upper body joined my lower in the throngs of total paralysis. Soon after, I came to the horrid realization that the load I'd been hauling had grown substantially lighter, though it wasn't verified until I ran head-on, literally, into the hard-plastic shell of a partially leaning Porto-Potty that Sagebrush had been lost.

Unable to breath and feeling as though my

chest was caught in a slowly tightening vise, I somehow managed to engage the portable john's door handle, jerk it ajar with deadened fingers and pour myself inside. Collapsing onto the toilet scat, I spat grit and sucked greedily of the air locked inside regardless of its foul stench.

Lord knows my initial plan was to depart that sour-smelling box, safe-haven or not, and search out my missing companion as soon as my lungs had sufficiently refilled and my blurred eyesight had been cleared of built-up particles. Why, I'd even cried out her name like a baying wolf for its missing mate, followed by an equally impassioned cursing out of the powers that be and their damnable penchant for instigating natural disasters at precisely the worst time.

As for Sagebrush, my intentions had been of the most honorable sort. The stuff true heroes are made of. Even as I was being rattled and jostled about like a dislodged bb inside that repugnant tin can, forced numerous times to shift my position in order to avoid tumbling over like a bowling pin, I could only think of the living hell she was enduring. The odds of a strong, *uninjured* individual surviving such mayhem were slim at best; toss into the mix her severely weakened state and said odds quickly bottomed out to damn near zero. With that singular thought gnawing unmercifully into my already frayed gray matter, I temporarily ignored having been forced to play human puree inside that hard plastic blender and reached for the door handle. Following several frenzied attempts to shove the door outward, I backed away the single step I was allowed and began to ram alternating shoulders into its upper quadrant. Eventually the door pushed ajar just enough for me to squeeze through and quickly unlock the mystery behind the sudden blockade. In the few minutes that I'd taken shelter, a two to three foot drift of blowing sand had built up around the unit's base.

Having secured my homemade turban before attempting escape, I'd been left a tunnel no larger than the bottom of a soup can to peer through. Belted about like an inflatable ball in a typhoon, I was unable to focus on any specific areas and soon found myself wandering about covering the same exact grounds.

Regardless, and despite the thunderous roar of the storm, I continuously bellowed out for her, hoping for any kind of audible response. Soon enough, I lost my balance and was tossed onto the flat of my back, the turban torn asunder as every exposed orifice instantly filled with sand. Flipping onto my stomach, I crawled about haplessly, digging my fingers into the spongy terrain and pulling myself blindly along, all the while spitting out chunks of moistened soil.

Then, as quickly as it had arrived, the storm abated. Winds subsided as if a switch had been tripped—a very *likely* occurrence actually—dying down to a pleasant breeze as I pushed myself up onto all fours and began the arduous task of clearing my mouth and nasal passages of what felt like pounds of impacted sand. The sudden tranquility was initially as deafening as the storm's ungodly gusts. Coughing up what I'd hoped were the final remnants of glutinous soil from the back of my throat, I then used an inner portion of my tee-shirt to wipe similar gunk from each eye.

Upon standing, I looked over my left shoulder to see the tail-end of the dust storm drift to the south. For one terrible moment, the swirling cloud seemed to hang in suspended animation, and I envisioned it making an abrupt about-face and heading my way yet again. Thank god this turned to be nothing more than an optical illusion witnessed through bleary, sand-coated eyes. Following yet another eye cleansing and several brief coughing fits, I was finally able to settle in and begin my search.

The terrain had, not surprisingly, seen quite the transformation in the storm's aftermath. Mainly, it had been flattened to an almost perfectly horizontal plane, void of all previous mounds or wavy dunes. As far as my still-watering eyes could see, it was pancake-city save the trio of Porto-potties, the ones positioned on either side of my own having toppled over onto their sides. As for my aforementioned search, it lasted only as long as it took to turn about and scan both directions. Since there didn't seem to be a single sand-spec out of place as far as visibility allowed in both directions, it left but one logical conclusion. My traveling companion had been buried beneath the shifting sands, and buried so deeply, so completely, that there had not been even a single hint of her whereabouts. No slightly bowed, grave-like mound, no protruding appendage or splayed, grasping fingers, no evidence of her ever being present when the storm pulled her from my back. Of course, none of this stopped me from stomping around in a wide circle, calling for her as if expecting a muffled reply from below, the mere thought of which actually served to frighten as much as it did exhilarate. In truth, the overwhelming emotion I'd felt during those hectic few moments was frustrated haplessness; a sensation I had become *far* too familiar with of late.

As far as officially giving up the search, I was never given the chance. I had just about twisted a knot in my neck at the initial sound. By the time it became apparent the noises weren't just some cheaply manufactured hoax courtesy a deeply-fried subconscious, I had sprinted over to the source and kneeled down, bending a cautious ear as if not quite convinced of its credibility.

It had begun as a subdued thumping; no more than a mild pecking really, that soon escalated into a sharp knock and then, once I'd squatted nearby, a full-blown hammering that shook and vibrated not only the potty door, but the unit as a whole. Like its twin a dozen feet away, the Porto-unit had tipped over onto its back side, giving the two outer units the look of dust-painted bookends.

Sagebrush! I deduced, my heart skipping several beats as I reached over and down to grasp a slightly warped outer door-handle. *There is simply no keeping that woman down! Tank-tough she is, and twice as ornery!*

As I tugged and pulled, pulled and tugged in frustration, eventually using both hands, I can't say for sure I was buying into my own propaganda. I surely *wanted* to believe, despite insurmountable odds…at the moment, it was enough. Alas, soon the fantasy was shattered two-fold at the very moment the unit's door flew upward with a resounding squeak. Flinching back as its outer edge scraped my bare left forehead with enough force to remove a layer of moistened flesh, I watched the figure emerge in true Jack-in-the-Box fashion, accompanied by a beastly growl that was right in character.

"Awww, shit! I should've known," I blurted in disgust, having tumbled onto my backside in the aftermath of the sudden reveal. The figure leapt from the box in a fiery display of frenetic energy, only to collapse weakly onto all fours a moment later.

I sat unmoved, observing with great curiosity as the slumped figure alternated between sequences of violet hacking, sneezing, and dry-heaving. The display was both alarming, considering the source, and, if I must confess, quite enjoyable to witness from a competitive standpoint.

"You going to make it, big guy?" I said smugly, pushing myself up as a fresh wave of fatigue washed over and temporarily dotted my vision.

Unable to reply between coughs, the man from *New York* did, however, manage to turn and shoot me a cool, reptilian glance.

The idea struck me suddenly, a virtual bolt from the blue. Waddling over as fast as legs of melted rubber would allow, I literally dived atop the door to Porto-potty number one before yanking the door ajar and almost off its flimsy inner hinges.

My thumping heart instantly sank. I had hoped

to be greeted by that wide yet pitiful grin of hers. She'd spout something sassy like 'bout time, Bluegrass…got a roll of t-paper handy?"

Instead, I visualized a shattered toilet and the bluish fluids that had spilled forth from its cracked base.

By the time I turned back around to revisit Mr. Sour Apple, he was practically leaning into me.

"Wha-?" I shrieked, flailing back in a clumsy jig, but not before landing a pretty solid right to the underside of his sand-smeared chin.

Regaining my balance, I posed in the classic pugilist style with clenched, trembling fists raised at ten and two.

His nostrils flaring wildly, he rubbed his chin with the flat palm of his left hand and took a single, non-aggressive step forward and I reacted the only way befitting a natural coward: I stumbled back and fell onto my bony rear-end.

When next I peered upward from a sitting position, I found the rays from a counterfeit sun effectively blinding me. That is, until the space was so amply filled in by his hulking presence.

A hand shot out, and I recoiled yet again. Surprisingly, the expected impact never materialized. Instead, I looked back up to see an outstretched palm hovering overhead.

"You're a persistent man. I'll give you that," he said calmly and without malice. As I reached up rather cautiously to accept his offer of assistance, I was simultaneously relieved and terrified.

Hauled up to a standing position, I was still half-expecting a throttling even as he backed away several steps.

"Never figured you for a top five, correction...make that top *two* contender, no sir," he continued, wiping a bare forearm beneath bloody nostrils. Slapping a fresh build-up of sand from my backside, it suddenly came to me exactly whom the man from NY resembled almost to a fault. Sad, but at that particular moment I don't believe I could've drudged up my late parent's names with a gun barrel shoved against my skull, but the name *Yaphet Kotto*, a former TV and film character actor from the late twentieth century spewed forth from the recesses of my fragmented memory with frightening ease.

"Yeah, well...I don't take it personally. Over time, a person learns to use being underestimated as their personal secret weapon. "

He nodded before peering over with a pained grimace at the Porto-potty he'd recently called home.

"I hear that. What state you hail from again? Can't quite place the accent, region-wise. "

"*Kentucky.* "

He whirled back around with a wide-eyed scowl before looking me up and down several times. I couldn't help but note his strained breathing and slumped posture, both of which appeared weirdly out of place coming from such an immaculately chiseled frame. Depressingly, he seemed not to have lost a layer of muscle despite traipsing through the same three-plus layers of hell on earth that had reduced me to a walking cadaver.

"Ken-...damn, here I was all this time thinking

upper Midwest or even West Coast. Definitely losing my touch. "

"So, if you don't mind my asking, how long were you in there?" I asked, motioning towards the fallen unit with the door hanging askew, a faint layer of sand particles still coating my tongue that no amount of spitting and hacking seemed to eradicate.

"Dunno-ten, fifteen minutes...maybe more. Who knows? I lost the power to track time about...say, halfway through Sector B. "

He leaned forward and spit, and I watched a spattering of crimson kick up tiny puffs of dust near his feet.

"Appreciate the excavation, by the way. You sure as hell had no obligation. Fact is, most logical thing would've been to find some big-ass boulder and park it atop that jammed door. Most in your position would have. "

I couldn't help but laugh, though as dry-roasted as my throat had been, it came out sounding more like a garbled belch.

"Can't lie to you. Well, guess I could, but what would be the point, right? Truth is, if I'd known it was you packed inside the ol' sardine latrine, I might've considered a similarly sinister act. "

His own laugh, more a wet, choking cackle, surpassed even my own in its gruesomeness.

"Wow, such frankness. You continue to surprise. All the good folks from your home-state as *Honest Abe* as yourself?"

I shrugged good-naturedly and made the mistake of bowing my head, the wave of dizziness that followed almost bringing me to my knees.

"What can I say? It's a legacy we all bare. By the way," I paused, reaching up to rub the tip of my chin, "Sorry about the shot. Afraid fright brings out the light-weight boxer in me. "

He waived me off while sucking in yet another labored lung-full of broiled oxygen.

"Forget it. Barely felt it, and not because the punch didn't carry enough zing. Paralysis of the upper extremities, you dig?"

"Oh, yes, how I can *dig*," I answered with complete honesty, "I could stick serving forks in both thighs and never blink a watery eye. "

We nodded in perfect unison, sharing a moment of solemn understanding that only we two could truly comprehend.

"Heard you calling out a name before— sounded like 'Sane-bush' or 'Sad-butt'...what gives? Looks to me like you're all alone out here, Bubba. "

The words were like a sharp punch to the gut. Whatever diversion his surprise appearance had created vanished in that very instant, the reality crashing down on my frayed psyche like the jagged edge of a tossed brick.

"Sagebrush. I called her Sagebrush. *Arizona*'s rep. One fine, classy lady...tough as leather. The storm...she was having...some feet issues and I was carrying her until the storm...swept her away. "

He regarded me with a slightly titled head and a cocked brow, as if sizing me up for a Straight Jacket.

"Carry...so you were...aiding and abetting the

enemy? Why exactly would you do that, Bubba? No trophy for sharing, least that's how I understood the rules. "

I stepped away and began to cover a wide semi-circle, kicking free large chunks of sand as I went. The pulse at my throat and temples throbbed mightily with the effort, and I feared there was a fatal stroke in my future, be it from the heat or a blown valve.

"Damn the rules. She was my friend, mister. If roles had been reversed, she would've done the same for me. "

"Have to take your word on that. Anyhow, it'd take an army of backhoes to find her in this ocean, and even if they did, no way she's still breathing. "

I halted in mid-kick, bending down to catch my breath and also, painful as it was, to resign myself to the man's coldly blunt but undoubtedly wise analogy. I so wanted to shed a tear for my fallen comrade, but a woeful lack of bodily fluids prevented such a tribute. Instead, I nodded solemnly towards the final stretch of terrain we'd covered as a team before turning back towards my lone surviving competitor. Standing there bare-chested with his meticulously defined arms crossed, he was every bit the Goliath to my David. My heart sank at the sight, and not just at being so clearly outgunned in a physical sense, but in the sudden realization that I'd lost my mental edge as well, buried somewhere within a massive lake of sand. Sagebrush had been my buffer to the pain, the anguish, the surreal *ludicrousness* of the reality we'd chosen. She'd left me adrift without a paddle to float and flounder without purpose...without drive...without hope. I can never say what might've happened in that faithful moment when we would've had to make a choice on winning or losing. I'd like to think I'd have done the gentlemanly thing and waived the white flag. In all honestly, however, I cannot say. Maybe, in some sad way, its better such a grim scenario was fated never to materialize. I just wish the circumstances of why could've somehow been different.

"Well, now what?" the big man asked curtly, surveying the trail ahead through tightly-squinted eyes.

"Guess there's no rhyme nor reason in standing still, huh?" I grinned.

His clean-shaven head riddled with tiny puddles of sweat, my erstwhile opponent took a moment to scan the lifeless landscape as if visualizing something other than an infinite sea of granules.

"Nope. You know they're watching...scoping us out like two prized zoo exhibits. Home audience must be going bonkers. Best drama Pay-Per-View can buy. The odds-on favorite faces off with the upstart underdog. "

"Ratings, my friend," I agreed, "through the roof ratings. Give 'em what they want to see, right?"

"Ready if you are, Bubba. Let us march..."

I followed several steps behind in the beginning, comfortable in the role. It only seemed natural, after all. The man was a beast, and would eventually walk me down no matter how heroic my efforts to prevent same. I had been somewhat of a realist in that previous life so long ago, and though the Gauntlet had undoubtedly eliminated a large chunk of my sanity in the past nineteen some-odd hours, not to mention a sizeable portion of body weight, believing in *fairytales* simply wasn't my bag.

It wasn't until I'd tossed the last of my canteens onto the sand, having drained it of every last steaming drop of life-giving elixir, that I noticed the narrow, dark-crimson trail dotting the sand. Casually dropping the canteen a few paces ahead, I had proceeded to administer a playful boot that sent it spinning away like a silver top. Insensitive and downright cruel as it might sound, from that innocent enough act, I re-discovered my edge.

Part Five: *Meltdown*

Time: Twenty hours, seventeen minutes into the Iron Will Gauntlet
Location: Sector D (Desert climes)
Total miles covered: Forty-nine and a quarter

The leakage wasn't slowing in the least. From whatever the origin, it was gaining in severity.

Who's to say how long his predicament? I surely wasn't about to inquire. Still, for a man bleeding like a stuck pig, his pace remained vigorous; unrelenting.

A gash beneath the ribs perhaps? A deep slash on the buttock? Perhaps a wide tear on an inner thigh or the lower abdomen...more than likely inflicted in a previous sector or maybe even as recently as the crash of the Porto-potty. He might've been battling said leak for hours, having attempted numerous times to plug the dike only to have yet another natural disaster reopen the dam wall.

I could only guess his blood loss at a pint or so since we'd began our two-man jaunt to the finish line—a substantial amount under normal circumstances, as in laying back on a soft cot with an intravenous tube running from an inner elbow. Considering the hellish temperatures, lack of liquid nourishment, and most disconcerting, trekking in flimsy sandals atop pliable terrain that was akin to walking on lit coals, it amazed me no end the man was able to stand upright, much less continue to blaze the trail.

Consistently remaining three to four lengthy strides to the rear, I was able to deflect my horrific thirst and the overall feel of being slowly broiled alive by focusing solely on the blackish trail my worthy opponent left in his wake. With that in mind, I was understandably perplexed once said path abruptly vanished from sight, only to lunge back in shocked surprise to find him standing just to my left.

"Got any family back home, Bubba?" he asked as we'd practically bumped shoulders.

Regaining my composure somewhat, though unable to completely control a series of spastic facial tics that caused my left eye to flutter and wink, I swallowed hard before replying, my throat so raw and dry it was as I'd gulped down a mouthful of glass.

"My parents passed away years ago, and I was an only child. Got a few distant kin scattered about near Louis-. . "

"No, no, I mean a wife, kids," he interrupted with a raised hand I couldn't help but notice was moist with freshly lost fluids. I caught a stout whiff of copper but forced myself not to turn away.

"Had a wife...once. Just another divorce stat, sad to say. No offspring, thank the lord. Just would've made it harder. You?"

We were, of course, breaking commandment number one in such competitions, an unwritten but duly understood rule: *though shalt not share details of one another's personal lives.* Obviously we were beyond adhering to such garbage at the time, though I must confess feeling a tad guilty about speaking so freely and openly about such matters when even Sagebrush and I had avoided similar topics like the plague. Chalk it up to exhaustion, impending heatstroke, or perhaps even the beginning stages of fatal hysteria.

"Lavonna, that's the wife…twenty-seven years and going strong. Two little ones, well…not that damn little anymore," he paused to snicker, the overall effect more a choking gargle, "Jevon, my son, he's nineteen now. His sister Loretta just turned sixteen. "

"Lucky man. "

"You think, Bubba? As we stand here melting under a fake sun…locked inside a giant fucking sauna with the gauge cranked up to the max setting…lumbering forward like a couple of half-baked cadavers. Gotta say, fortunate is not the way I'd describe myself right about now…"

"Hey, at least you got something . . *someone* to get back to when the curtain finally falls," I replied, practically shouting despite each word seemingly stripping away yet another layer of flesh from my ravaged throat, "and I'd say we're a hell of a lot better off than all the piled corpses at the opposite end of this trail. "

He paused, sighing deeply, and in the aftermath I heard a wet, grumbling echo from deep within his chest. The man was dying in varied ways, and nobody knew this fact better than him. As if reading my thoughts, he peered over at me and flashed his most menacing scowl. Unlike earlier incarnations, however, this particular attempt at intimidation was more pathetic than frightening.

"I *got* to win, Bubba. I got no choice. Don't expect me to stop, no matter what. My family...I got to get 'em out of those damn projects. It's a fucking graveyard, man. It's draining the life from 'em. Jevon's already gang-banging...already into the dope scene. He won't last a year. Gotta...pull him out. Give him some options. Can't...can't let my little girl go down a similar path. The prize is mine. It's gotta be mine. So, just to let you know...where things stand...ain't no quitting in me. "

I stopped short of reaching over and delivering a solid, heartfelt tap to his bared, taunt shoulder, but just barely.

"Of that I have no doubt, big man. Make no mistake though, I'm gonna make you earn it. "

"Devon Lee Jackson the second," he countered, holding out the same blood-smeared hand while breaking yet another revered commandment. In response, I did not hesitate in completing the age-old ritual between men both friends and foes alike, the stickiness of his palm nary an issue.

"Garrett. Carlton Jerrod Garrett, the one and only. "

Our shared contact was brief but firm, the accompanying eye-contact mirroring a mutual respect that made verbalizing seem wholly unnecessary.

We walked side by side in a comfortable silence, though I did sneak several quick peeks and saw him grimacing in obvious pain. The hand he used as a tool for official introduction clutched his lower abdomen in a vice.

"I'm a hurting pup, Carl. Guess you noticed that already. "

There was no need for dishonesty; regardless, I hadn't the energy for games.

"Yeah, you've lost a lot of blood. Open wound?"

"Worse. Eternal damage...pretty damn nasty from what's seeping out from down below. Can't stop it...can't control it. That's what I was trying to do inside that Porto-John when the storm added insult to injury. Ain't no tourniquet made to tie off a shredded gut. "

I caught yet another stout whiff of copper but managed to refrain from displaying any facial hint.

"How long?"

"Left C sector knowing it was bad. Didn't know how bad 'til I peeled off my duds for their little chemical shower. Ruptured something...vital I do believe. "

Spurned by a nagging curiosity, I selfishly veered off subject.

"You tell the med staff?"

"Wasn't nobody there, bro. Damn place was. . . totally deserted. I.... yelled out...checked every room. You see anybody when you passed through?"

Yet again, I found no viable reason to lie.

"Not a soul. All part of their master plan, I guess. "

"Just my luck, Bubba," he said after a long pause, during which time I noticed his breathing had transformed into a continual, drawn out wheeze.

"What's that?"

"Breezed through the first two sectors without a

single hitch, ignoring any and all assistance from those med squad geeks. First time I actually needed 'em, all of the sudden they made like the dinosaurs and vanished without a trace. "

Watching the big man wince and scowl with each and every step, suddenly straining to keep pace, my sympathetic reply wasn't at all forced.

"A true pisser, my man. Sincerely. Was it the flood?"

He began to huff loudly between words, tempting me to intervene with advice to save his strength.

"Ye-yeah. First b-big wave. Thought I was braced. Plowed me over and pulled me un-under. Thought I'd seen the worse by the t-time I popped to the surface like a human buoy. Sucked in a couple 'a deep breaths, turned around and got nailed right square in the breadbox by the flattened end of a tree trunk. B-big sucker too…like a phone pole. Ne-next thing I knew I was la-laying on a soggy dune fee-feeling like a tractor-trailer had u-used me as a p-pothole. "

I had a sudden image of *Colorado*'s punctured corpse floating away like a leaky balloon.

"Not good. I…had some issues of my own during that stretch, only mine were mostly of the *human* variety. Super-wave was only a warm-up. "

"Let me guess…some Crazy a-asshole from Denver. "

"Bingo. I tried to help him and he returns the favor by attempting to crease my skull with the pointy end of a branch. "

Devon laughed at this, though it could've easily

been misrepresented as a choking sob. Our collective pace had slowed considerably, and he used both hands to cradle his midsection as if holding back a mass spillage. Concerned as I was for his plight, I must confess a certain dullness of sympathy in the face of my own ills. The heat, merely unbearable upon entering the sector, had since intensified by several torturous levels, from light bake to full broil, in a matter of hours. Thus, the sandy surface beneath had no choice but follow suit, gradually turning the soles of my sandals into semi-melted tar. In a nutshell, we were essentially being cooked from all sides, what my dear old grandma might've referred to as an 'even stew'.

"Hey, you a-ain't gotta tell m-me, Bubba. I spent m-most of two sectors trying to sh-shake that little bandy roo-rooster. Dude c-called me everything b-but nigger. "

"So why didn't you shut him up, Muscles?"

"Well, there were numerous times I th-thought about k-killin' 'im, but I really d-didn't want to ta-take it that f-far, ya k-know? Kinda figured c-cold blooded m-murder might disqualify me. "

"Good point that. "

"So...he st-still trailing us, you think?"

The floater image returned in clear, high-definition, though mercifully it faded just as rapidly.

"From the last I saw of him, I highly doubt it. "

"Y'know, Bub...Carl, you s-sure don't talk like the southerners I've m-met or watched on the tube. You s-sure you ain't from Delaware or DC?"

I glanced over and flashed a wide, sarcastic grin, and felt layers of overly cooked flesh peel away from my cheeks like flittering puffs of ash.

"That's 'cause I hail from *Northern* Kentucky, my brother. "

With that, he bent over and howled before collapsing onto his knees in a coughing fit that saw blood spray from between his lips, both nostrils, and God help him, even the corners of each eye.

The dark side of my soul nudged me forward—to abate from even the slightest glance back—and truck on towards that enigmatic finish line to certain victory. *Let him choke on his own fluids*, Lord Vader shrieked, *for once and for all cut out the nursemaid crap and do what you came here to do.... win*! Alas, as had been the case since mile one of Sector A, the dark side rated hardly a blip on the inner radar. Thus, I stumbled back towards Devon Lee Jackson, the media and public's prohibited favorite, with every intention of lending whatever aid necessary to keep it a two-man race. In leaning over the big man mere moments later, it was painfully obvious no manner of aid would suffice, be it an empty-handed Kentuckian on the edge of delirium or a fully staffed medical team with an ER's worth of equipment at the ready. The man from *New York*'s eyes were pulled saucer wide and shone clear as glass, and in those twin mirrors I clearly viewed the emaciated horror I myself had become. Reaching over, my hand froze at a sudden sensation below. I peered downward to see my sandals had been drenched in the man's leakage. Something inside him had given way, opening the floodgates. I felt a sudden pressure at my right wrist and looked back up to see he was holding it in a

326

vise.

"Y-y-you w-w-win, B-Buuub-baaa," he stammered as liquid pools poured from between his trembling lips. So unfair, he must've thought...a physical specimen such as himself, bleeding out at the feet of a man who better resembled a lumbering scarecrow.

"Th-the p-p-prize is y-y-yours..."

It came to me suddenly, a notion of infinite good deed. My pitifully concave chest must've swelled with pride at possessing such inner goodness at that crucial juncture.

"Your family...Devon, what's their names...their address..."

Mere seconds away from expiring, the man's face nonetheless creased with confusion.

"Wh-what d-d-do.... y-you...m-my fam..."

"Quick man, tell me...the address...I'll remember...I swear I'll remember. I'll make sure they're taken care of!"

His left brow cocked dramatically, his right eye having already closed off and permanently sealed.

"...one, t-t-two s-six...e-e-east M-M-Marion A-Aven...nue...H-Har-lem..."

I squeezed his left hand with my right and watched myself nod through his remaining orb.

"One two six, East Marion...got it. It's taken care of, my man. Rest easy, they're gonna be fine. "

His face began to twitch and the curtain fell on his left eye. The smile he flashed was ever-so-brief and unable to remain formed as he drifted away. Regardless, I know what I saw, and it warmed me in a positive way, so unlike the inhuman conditions of that fatal sector.

Before trudging forth, I rolled him out of that bloody circle and onto his stomach. For some reason, I just didn't think it right to let the man-made radioactivity inflict further damage to the man's upturned face. Call it bizarre. Call it the warped thinking of an overheated mind. Call it the first *Iron-Will Gauntlet* burial ritual. Allow me, yet again, to reference the term simple human decency.

Shambling forward, I thought of Devon Lee Jackson's wife and kids, more than likely having just witnessed the grisly, heart-wrenching passing of the family patriarch. I hoped and prayed that whatever secret camera caught such footage also captured the accompanying audio. True, I had garnered evil, selfish thoughts at first becoming aware of the man's injuries. I'd played the heartless villain role to a fault, at least until we began to converse and the humanization effect nudged its way into the fray. Funny how it takes so little time to form a kinship, especially when the people in question are forced together under such cruel, dire circumstances.

I'd hoped and prayed the powers that be, not to mention the mass audience as a whole, had heard the promise I'd made—a promise I had no intentions of breaking. All my many weaknesses and faults aside, CJ Garret was not the type to go back on his word. CJ Garret had always been honest to a fault, one of many personality traits viewed as honorable by all save *one* who had known him. Gaining a measure of wealth and worldwide fame wasn't apt to change that particular characteristic.

That I mind, I had yet another reason to persevere and trek on, despite the fact that the simple act of taking in a breath was becoming damn near impossible.

Part Six: Faces in the sand

Time: Twenty-one hours, twenty-three minutes into the Iron Will Gauntlet
Location: Sector D (Desert climes)
Total miles covered: Just over Fifty

The sand began to flow like gentle river waters beneath my feet, swelling and shifting and forming picturesque ripples with each new step. Occasionally I'd hear the flapping of wings overhead and the occasional chirp, though the few times I'd mustered up enough energy to lift my eyes to the sky, there was nothing to see other than the same bland, infinite stretch of pale blue sky.

Strange is the hallucinatory effect of heat prostration. While the obvious symptoms had all stood up to be recognized; cramps, nausea, and even the beginning signs of edema as my ankles appeared roughly twice their normal size, I'd never before experienced or even heard of such mind-bending mirage possibilities.

The first of several similar '*I know I'm seeing things but damn ain't it realistic*' scenarios to arise involved none other than one of my fonder Gauntlet acquaintances, *Alabama*, who'd suddenly popped up out of nowhere to take up position to my immediate left. He was decked out in full Sector B winter gear, to include a dark red parka and matching mukluks, although the right foot hung crooked and appeared to drag a bit.

"You're lookin' a might piqued, partner.

Where's the fire anyhow? I mean, other than underneath this cursed sand. "

Leaning over, I stared in at his reddened features through the deep tunnel of his parka hood.

"Wha-what you mean, 'B-Bama?"

"I mean, why keep up the charade, K-Man? It ain't like there's anybody left to chase down at this point. "

"I don't f-follow..." I slurred, temporarily hypnotized by the layer of fresh snow coating his shoulders.

"You tryin' to outrun yourself, partner? What's the point? I mean, if it's the guilt fuelin'ya, don't give it a second thought. I mean, I can't honestly say I'd have done the same given the situation, but we'll never know now, will we?"

A bit perturbed at my old pal's line of questioning, I faced front and stammered out the only answer my sunny-side-up cooked brain could manufacture.

"Gotta keep...gotta move forward. Sh-shit man, that...that's what we *do* here...just keep...moving forward. One... one step at...a time. "

Movement to my right caused a minor stumble, and I watched a portion of my left sandal peel off and hid away in the sand.

"Colonel Sander's is right as rain, Doc. Time to hit the brakes and accept the spoils already," Hollywood said through a bloody grin, fresh seepage dribbling into her opened mouth. The icicle protruding from her eye socket bobbed and shimmied with each step, a single glistening drop of water hanging precariously from its pointed tip. A pointy tip I longed to stick my tongue to, at least until I saw that precious, crystal clear drip of life-source abruptly turn a dark shade of maroon.

"C-can't st-stop…if I s-stop, I…if I stop…"

"You'll die?" she interrupted, her naked breasts coated in her own spilt fluids, "well hell, doc, *dead* isn't so bad…I can surely testify. I know I should be pissing and moaning about…well, all that final scene drama we shared, but hey, I can dig your reasoning. Besides, I'll take my *cold* flesh over your baked hide any day of the week. Just slooooow down, boy…you know the suits aren't about to let their new golden boy kick the bucket on the eve of his greatest triumph, not to mention their biggest ratings bonanza!"

Twisting my head back to the left, I discovered *Alabama* had become the Gambler from *Nevada*, whose grotesquely swollen face and neck were riddled with open sores, many of which still held leftovers from the army of mosquitoes responsible, their lifeless husks still attached by the proboscis.

"The one-eyed chick with the nice rack knows of what she speaks, KY. You beat the odds, son—the insurmountable type. Sure, you had to bend the rules a might, even break a major commandment or two, but it's high time to slam on the brakes and stop being so bull-headed. Just…let it go already…. cash in all those chips you've damn well earned. "

As he spoke, several live bloodsuckers sailed free from a large gash beneath his chin, a few of which were so bloated they resembled flying ticks.

"I…I dun…don't know…don't want t-to be…c-called a q-quitter…"

I blinked my eyes, actually allowing them to remain closed for a lingering moment, and upon reopening them was greeted by yet another figment of a surprisingly active imagination—this one easily the most jarring, not to mention heart-wrenching, of all.

"You've proven yourself above and beyond, Champ," she said as a virtual rainfall of sand spewed from between her lips, both nostrils, and even her eyes, "no one's calling you a quitter. Dude, you are just the opposite."

"S-Sagebrush...oh g-god..." I blubbered, shambling forward on deadened limbs as my already failing sight was worsened by a sudden deluge of tears, "...I...I'm s-so s-sorry...I...I l-lost...I cold...couldn't f-find y-you...s-so so so-sorry..."

She stood with open arms, hands out and palms up, her head titled slightly downward as she flashed an expression of angelic forgiveness.

"I don't blame you, Champ. It was just meant to be. You...did what you had to do. I applaud the courage it must've taken...right there in the homestretch. Gotta say...I was as impressed as I was shocked."

Try as I might, I was unable to lift my own arms in order to complete the impending embrace. As I grew to within reaching distance, she slowly began to vanish.

". . Y-you were...s-so im-impart...spe-special to m-me...I...I could...couldn't have...m-made it wi-without...I didn't...it was never person-..."

"Just remember, Champ, it was *me*...not you,"

she cooed, seductively pursing horribly chapped, sand-coated lips, "...you deserved better than me. You *always* did.... "

I tumbled through the exact spot she'd been inhabiting...or *not* been inhabiting, a split-second later, sliding face-first into a fire pit of scalding sand as I'd been unable to use either hand to buffer the fall. Rolling over onto my back, I could easily visualize lying atop a red-hot grill. There was a strong temptation to remain prone and allow the inevitable to transpire. In fact, for several terrifying moments it seemed I might have no choice, as finding the physical strength to rise seemed implausible at best. As for possessing the needed will, I had to think no further than the death-bed, or *sand-bed* if one cares about such details, request of one Devon Lee Jackson, not to mention an inner motivation that hit so much closer to home. It was obvious the mere fear of dying no longer provided the required fuel for survival, not when one's lower body from the waist down suffers almost total paralysis; not when one's throat feels as though it's been peeled from the inside by thirst; certainly not when one's upper appendages hang uselessly at his side like the swaying tentacles of a floating octopi. As any veteran marathon or Iron-Man competitor worth their sweat would say while poking their own temple with a stiffened forefinger, 'in matters of such pain, it's the old noodle that either allows continued participation or shuts you down cold'. In my case, fifty-plus miles of enduring extreme temperatures, a checklist of the worst natural disasters Mother Nature, albeit a computer-birthed version, could cook up, and even a lunatic fellow competitor or two, the body was indeed a thoroughly siphoned shell. The mind, more specifically that portion of the brain in charge of will, clung like gangbusters to the idea of mission completion despite being overtaxed, overburdened and underfed. Indeed, there existed a working chip buried within that crispy-fried gray matter yet. As long as that was the case, there would be no such surrender for all to witness.

There must have been a reason no bells sounded, no spotlight appeared, no applause or similar celebratory act occurred the minute of Devon Jackson's demise. Despite the logical dialogue spat out so wisely by the ghosts of Gauntlet's past, I had to deem such non-action at the moment of my ultimate triumph to be yet another test of sorts, perhaps to see just how long and far I'd shamble with no sustainable motivation. Perhaps, for the paying crowd's sake watching from home, this was considered my 'victory lap'. Regardless, I flat refused to stop until someone of an official nature did the stopping. Honestly, once I'd managed to arise and lurch drunkenly ahead, *Mr. Auto Pilot* took over, and that was one ornery SOB behind the control panel.

Somewhere along the line I lost all concept of being. Call it sleepwalking of a sort; call it acting purely on instinct—as in *dead man walking* syndrome. The thought process had ceased to exist. Visually, there was the endless monotony of seeing my bared feet, the sandals had been sheered away completely by then, digging into and subsequently out of a river of sand. In terms of visual memory, that's the gist. As far as how long this particular death-march might've gone on? Hours or minutes, or any amount in between. I have no earthly clue. Fragmented dream sequences possess more depth, more back story.

What snapped me back into a badly blurred state of semi-reality was not crossing some gaudily marked finish line lined with cheering on-lookers waiving their media credentials, nor was it the sudden melting away of the desert terrains CGI matting. I recall hearing the faint sound of an automotive motor, first so faint it justified no effort in seeking out the source. It grew steadily louder, however, and I recall twisting my head about even as my numbed lower appendages continued to pump steadily forward.

The bulky, squared jeep, a dark green Hummer I believe, pulled past me on the left, and I was quickly swallowed whole by the drifting cloud that followed. By the time I emerged from said dust cloak, the vehicle sat parked sideways at the center of the trail, effectively blocking it.

Unsure if its surreal presence indicated yet another mirage, I had every intention of trekking right through it—that is until the passenger door swung open and banged my left knee.

I don't recall falling, nor landing, just a jumbled set of voices and the segmented words each spewed as their faceless shadows hovered overhead. I tasted water...cool but not cold, refreshing, and surprisingly tart, coat my lips and tongue, then slide down my throat with a burning sensation both painful and pleasurable. I believe I tried to speak. I might've even managed to choke out a word or two. If so, said words were more than likely of the 'out of the way' or 'gotta keep moving' variety, I'd wager. I soon found myself hauled airborne, and that's where all memories of Sector D mercifully ceased.

Upon waking, there would emerge revelations. Revelations so stark, bleak, and shocking they would make all that had come before seem downright mundane by comparison, and actually make me pine, ever-so-briefly mind you, for a return to the hellish pathways of the Gauntlet.

Sector X: The Spoils

Part One: Distant Replay(s)

"Fifty-three and two-tenth miles, Mister Garrett, covered in exactly twenty three hours and eleven minutes. "

"And…I've been ou-out for…for how long?"

"Um, eighty six hours and some odd minutes. "

"Three…over three…th-three and a half days? I…was…have I been conscious at all?"

"Well, yes and no. You…appeared to come out of it briefly. An interview was…attempted but never fully completed. Besides, you needed the downtime if for no other reason than to replenish the cells and allow the meds to begin the healing process. "

Through rapidly blinking eyes, Garrett studied the myriad of tubes littering both arms before following a similar line leading to his nostrils. A trio of I. V. stands was but a reach away to his left, while a rolling serving tray, conspicuously empty, took up position on the immediate right. Moaning softly at a sudden burning sensation at his right shin, he could feel the fog slowly lifting, an assortment of dull aches and stinging wounds discovering a similar awakening. His legs and feet felt strangely heavy beneath the beige blanket that so efficiently cloaked him from the chest cavity down.

"Damn but I h-hurt all over. "

"You're about due for medication. Give me a moment…"

Tugging lightly on the oxygen tube beneath his nose, Carl Garrett heard the intake of air give off a faint squeal.

"Give it to me straight, doc…am I g-going to make it?"

"Remains to be seen, Mr. Garrett, but for now," the man paused, sighing deeply, "I'd say the odds are highly favorable. "

Stretching both arms to the limit the I. V. allowed, Garrett yawned and heard a muffled pop from the right side of his jaw.

"I'll b-bet the media h-hounds can't w-wait to get their m-mitts on me. "

His host stood with his back towards the bed, glaring up at a trio of muted monitors that each blared white static.

"Um, I'd have to concur. Mr. Garrett, do you consider yourself fully awake?"

"Uh, yeah, I'd say close enough for two-way conversation. "

The man Garrett had secretly dubbed *Fritz the Clone* in what seemed like an eternity ago twisted gracefully about on a single heel. Dressed in a lab coat, faded blue jeans and high-top jogging shoes, he barely resembled the same stiff-shirted company man that had once played propaganda-spouting tour guide.

"Fine then, though for now I'd just ask that you listen. "

"Spout away, Frit-…ugh, by all means, it's a deal, that is as long as I'm allowed equal forum afterwards for questions and answers. "

"Agreed. I should provide fair warning: I'm afraid what I have to say might well…um…add to your table of inquiries. "

"Duly noted. "

Reaching to scratch his left knee through the blanket, Garrett winced as if physically struck.

"Jesus…that hurt more than it should've…I g-guess. "

Before collapsing back onto his pillow with a complexion as ghostly as the bed sheet he lay upon, Garrett pointed in the general direction of his feet.

"So wh-what's up down there, doc? Something you need to tell me perhaps? As in, if I sneak a peek beneath the blanket a couple of sawed-off nubs might stare back?"

The man waived him off with his free hand, the other cupping what appeared to be a tiny remote device.

"Not at all. We…there was some stitching necessary on a rather nasty gash on one of your shins. Afraid a bit of infection had taken hold, but the antibiotics should clear that with little difficulty. "

Coughing into a clenched fist, Garrett then peered back at the man with a cocked brow.

"Well, while we're on the subject, is there anything else I should know about?"

"Quickly then, if a checklist reading is required," the man replied somewhat wearily, turning back towards a nearby conference table and retrieving a clipboard from its cluttered top.

"First off, I'd approximate a weight loss

upwards of twenty pounds. Looks like you lost three toenails off the left foot and two from the right. Second degree burns on each foot. The aforementioned shin wound, duly stitched and treated. Your neck and shoulders also suffered second degree burns, most likely courtesy the artificial sun of Sector D. Meanwhile, upon initial treatment the fingers of both hands showed symptoms of frostbite. As you can see, they have responded well to treatment. You are still being administered liquids to offset a severe bout of heat stroke and dehydration. Lastly, we believe you might have also suffered a slightly dislocated right shoulder and from the black and blue markings, a deep bone-bruise of your left thigh. "

Gently replacing the clipboard back atop the assorted overflow of the tabletop, the man then turned back to Garrett and shrugged before joining him at bedside and palming a small hand-held linked to one of the numerous I. V. stands.

"Here's that booster shot I promised. You'll feel a slight kick in a moment or two. As for your present, well, physical condition, that's the gist, Mr. Garrett. I'd say considering the ordeal so recently endured, you're well on the road to recovery. "

Leaning forward with a strained grin, Garrett licked horribly chapped lips that appeared to be, at best, in the middle stages of recovery.

"Appreciate the words of encouragement, doc…um, what is your name anyhow?"

"Oh, my sincere apologies. Kerns. *Conrad Kerns* at your service. Now, shall we proceed to the heart of the matter at hand?"

"You're the doctor, Kerns. Well, so to speak. "

Conrad Kerns turned his back yet again, striding forward and striking a 'parade rest' pose with his hands cupped at his lower back and his feet spread wide apart.

"In your, uh, present state of mind, I'm not quite sure you're ready for what I'm about to divulge. I wish there was an easy way to proceed with such news, but the...way things currently stand, I see no such avenue of dialogue. "

Falling back onto the pillow, Garrett surveyed the entirety of the room for the first time and noticed just how out of place the bed, IV stands and med equipment seemed in what otherwise appeared to be a small communications room of some type.

"Uh-oh, that doesn't sound good," he said somberly, peering up at the semi-hypnotic white static blaring from the monitors and instantly falling into a dazed trance.

"Don't tell me somebody crossed the line before me. If so, there needs to be an immediate investigation, doc, 'cause that's one cheating SOB. "

"No...no, it's...well, it's a bit.... well, complicated. "

Carter swallowed hard, a slight taste of antiseptic coating his tongue.

"Mr. Garrett," Kerns continued, his shoulders stiffening a bit, "please, if you have the strength and the...mental faculties, explain to me what you believe to be your present situation. "

With a loud creak, the room's lone entry door, located approximately a dozen feet to the left from the head of Garrett's bed, flew open as if by a stout wind. The succeeding sound was of heavy boots clopping nosily against the tiled flooring, following by the sudden entry of the wearer of said boots. Whipping his head about and wincing with the effort, Garrett didn't recognize the figure at first, though proper identification of their mystery guest was verified soon enough via the first few spoken words.

"Say hey, CK, how's our comatose guest this fine morn-. . " the man's eyes flew wide upon locking onto Garrett's upright form, the heels of his boots squeaking loudly upon skidding to a sudden halt. Having traded in his Security Cop *slash* Gestapo garb for a dark blue suit, checkered tie and black dress shoes, Gil Masters still managed to retain a stony, hard-edged look reserved for those of career military or law enforcement status.

"Well, I'll be shit. It lives. Top of the morning to ya, bub. You're looking more dead than alive, but at least the bulb relit. A might dim yet, I'm sure, but lit nonetheless. "

"Greetings yourself, *Left*-tenant," Garrett replied with a mock salute, the IV tubes whipping about his forearm and hands like tubular pasta strands, "my but you appear positively ecstatic. Just back from a satisfying session of torturing small animals, I take it?"

"My, I see Mr. Lippy hasn't lost that lovable cockiness, *unlike* most of his body weight. Damn, but the Gauntlet played hell with your looks, son. You look like a fried egg that's been kicked around the kitchen floor," came the mocking, wide-eyed

343

response, "I take you haven't yet broken the news?" he continued, turning towards Conrad Kerns with a scowl.

Keeping his back towards both men, Kerns stared up at the center monitor with his head slightly titled.

"I was just...on the verge. He's appears still quite...perplexed. "

"Still playing dopey to the reality, is he?" Masters replied, his square chin resting atop a clenched fist, "sticking to his guns, so to speak. No shock there, doc. Personally, I'd have been shocked to hear otherwise. "

Kerns bristled, tossing up his arms in apparent frustration.

"What say you leave the analytical questions to those versed in said field, Lieutenant? Just do what you came here to do and let's be done with it. "

As to break up their private, coded dialogue, Garrett blurted out as loudly as his parched throat would allow.

"Must say, you're looking as square-jawed and squared away as ever, Left-tenant. Don't tell me *this* is the award-presentation phase. "

Seemingly ignoring this last remark, Masters walked stiffly over to Conrad Kerns and leaned in as if to share some closely-guarded secret, though his bombastic tone remained unchanged.

"Shall I, doc? I mean, I surely don't mind. Might be easier...a more seamless transition coming from me. That is, if it's not. . . frowned upon from a medical standpoint. Sure don't want to stomp on those *well-versed* toes... "

The other man dipped his head a bit as if to deeply contemplate.

"Go ahead, then. I can tell you're practically chomping at the bit. I'll...standby in case I'm needed."

Masters grinned, peering back at Garrett with unrestrained enthusiasm.

"I would surely appreciate it, doc. Make sure you have a loaded syringe or two at the ready, hear?"

Shrugging his shoulders, Kerns then resumed monitor watching.

"Shouldn't be necessary, that is, depending on the subtlety of the reveal."

"Trust me, doc, I'll try my dogged best to be gentle," Masters replied with a heavy dose of sarcasm before turning to face their bedridden guest, "after all, I'm as proud of a peacock of our...*my* boy's performance."

"Um, hate to sound impatient, but is it too much to ask to be clued in on what exactly is going on?" Garrett injected jadedly, "can't say I'm too big on solving riddles, and this hasn't exactly been the victory celebration I'd envisioned."

Clutching a palm-sized remote to his muscled chest like a treasured artifact, Masters stepped purposely towards Garrett and halted at the edge of the bed. His complexion had gone ruddy as he regarded their bedridden guest with a cocked brow.

"All in good time, bub. First off, I got a question for ya. I'm hoping you got an answer."

Despite great effort to remain cool in the face of such uncertainty, Carl Garrett swallowed nervously before responding.

"Fire away. "

Masters grinned, the color instantly returning to his pockmarked cheeks, before whirling about and pointing the remote towards the center monitor. Meanwhile, Conrad Kerns backed up several steps as to acquire a better view. Just as white static cleared to a bright haze, Masters quickly paused the screen and turned back towards Garrett.

"First off, allow me to set the video feed. I've had this bad boy freeze-framed for the better part of a day. Took the boys in the editing room forty-eight hours plus to assemble this special collection of, well, let's just call 'em *Carl Garrett's greatest hits.* "

"Video footage from the cap-cam's, I take it?" Garrett asked, ignoring the plethora of body aches and various tingling sensations slowly encasing his entire form into a tapestry of throbbing misery.

"The majority of what we're about to see, yeah. Shit's a bit jumpy, but that comes with the territory. There is of course some footage taken from wall and ceiling cams, but the money shots, the close-ups we required, were all of cap-cam origin. Glorious stuff bub, like ticks on a blue-hound. What the wall and ceiling cams had in quantity, the cap-cams made up for in quality. How many wall and ceiling units were there all told, doc, something like five-thousand?"

The other man's reply was comically stoic, borderline robotic.

"More like seventy-five hundred, all channeled into a single server. "

"Yeah, buddy…" Masters added with a wink, "if any of you trekkers scratched his nuts, adjusted his package, or picked his or her nose, bet your bottom dollar we got it on film, one way or another. "

"How…about audio?" Garrett inquired wearily, rapidly losing the initial burst of energy he'd been allowed upon awaking.

"Shaky for the most part, dependin' on the elements at the time. If the weather was clear, we picked up every sniff, fart or belch. If Mother Nature was raising Cain, probably not. "

"We figured as much. "

"Yeah? Well, now that you've broached the subject, it's that 'we' part I'm bound by duty to go over with ya, bub. "

"Meaning what, Left-tenant?" Garrett asked sheepishly, the dark circles beneath his eyes growing more pronounced with each passing tick.

Closing ranks, Masters leaned onto the far edge of the bed and gripped the rail with his free hand.

"Just so I know exactly where we stand, tell me what's going on. "

Garret frowned, following up with a pained grimace as he reached up to massage a badly burnt section of his upper left shoulder and neck.

"S-say what?"

"Simple question, pal. Where are ya?"

"Somewhere in the dome, I'd venture to say," Garrett sighed wearily, "med lab maybe or what serves as the facility clinic. "

Wearing an expression that was equal parts smugness and indifference, Masters droned on as if reading from a pre-memorized checklist.

"Close enough. This next one should be a gimme, then…why are ya here?"

Flashing a knowing smile, Garrett's pale features suddenly gained a level of color.

"Oh, I get it…checking the old noodle for post-combat stress. "

"Yeah, that's it precisely, bub. Just humor me. "

"Well, unless I'm roaming the magical Land of Oz, I'm laying here recouping from walking away with the grand prize. "

"That grand prize being?" Masters inquired with a cocked brow.

"Why, champ-peen survivor of the Iron-Will Gauntlet, that'd be me. Bucked twenty-five to one odds, as I understand it. "

Bowing his head, Garrett fell silent for a full half-minute. Once he regained the power of speech, his voice had lowered dramatically and cracked with a sudden wave of emotion.

"Watched…saw a lot of good people die in there. Good, decent people. People with…families. People with…a purpose. Yeah, I won alright, but it's a…it's a dark victory at best. "

Releasing the rail, Masters whirled about in the opposite direction and peered up at the paused image gracing the center monitor.

"Dark…victory, yes sir, very apt analogy, bub. Wouldn't you agree, Doctor Kerns?"

Regarding the other man with a stern stare, Kerns remained conspicuously silent.

"What's up, doc? Don't feel a bit of…psyche-altering intervention is due about now?"

Ignoring Masters' completely, Kerns looked at and spoke directly to Garrett.

"Those...*good, decent* people you speak of, Carl, I take it, that even in the aftermath of your great victory, you feel a certain degree of...guilt?"

"Of...course...of course I do, damn it. Isn't that...natural under the circumstances? I mean, you people saw it, didn't you? You watched them fall, right? You're still...*human* enough to feel sympathy, right? F-fucking m-monsters.... fucking n-no feeling m-maniacs..." Garrett replied, his hands shaking uncontrollably in his lap, causing the numerous IV tubes to wriggle about like live electrical wires.

With that, Masters and Kerns exchanged a lingering glance as Garrett was left to sob into the splayed fingers cloaking his gaunt, skull-like visage.

"Touchin', ain't it doc? Really tugs on the ol' ticker strings. From openly boasting of his victory to a blubbering cryin' jag concerning the circumstances of same...priceless. "

"You are undoubtedly one cruel, heartless bastard, Masters," Conrad Kerns snarled with a disbelieving nod.

"Hey," the other man shrugged, "comes with the job description, bub. Shall I burst the imaginary bubble now or give 'im another minute or two to revel in the anguish of it all?"

"Are you asking for my *professional* opinion?" Kerns inquired with a hateful stare, "or, in your own crude vernacular, merely *pulling my chain*?"

"Afraid ya got me there, doc. Honestly, this

laughable charade has more than run its course," Masters replied gleefully while rubbing his palms together briskly, "Besides, I'm about to raise a boner in anticipation. "

Turning away in obvious disgust, Conrad Kerns whispered through ghostly-pale, tightly-pursed lips.

"Of that, good sir, I have no doubt. "

Facing their patient once again, Masters continued to address the other man even as he half-stepped towards the bed.

"Don't be that way, doc. It's only natural. After all, that's my boy layin' over there all fucked up and confused. Seems only right I straighten his bony ass out on the truth of it all. "

Standing at the foot of the bed, Masters casually placed his hands in his pants pockets and spoke in a guarded, deliberate tone, as if addressing the mentally challenged.

"Alright then, bub, let's start carvin' at the heart of why we're standing here jawing in this oversized locker room instead of attending your victory parade. "

Peering slowly upward, Garrett used the underside of his palms to rub warms tears from the corner of each eye.

"It's al-alright, Lieutenant. Ri-right now I could care less about such…meaningless tripe. Ma-maybe in a few da-…weeks, but I'm pretty fried, as you can plainly see. "

Master nodded agreeably, peering down at the tips of his shiny dress shoes.

"Just not up to the attention are we?"

"Not…really. Maybe in a few days. "

350

Masters continued to nod understandably.

"Yeah well, as it turns out, bub, that won't be a problem, leastways, not the kind of attention you're figuring on."

Peering up to lock eyes with their bedridden guest, Masters kept his head strategically lowered.

"Afraid the parade's been scratched, bub, as have any associated celebrations."

Obviously taken aback, Garrett's upper body visibly stiffened, his forehead creasing dramatically.

"Oh? Well," he replied, his expression and body language quickly reverting back to slack and lifeless, "t-that's good. I'd make a pretty gruesome guest of honor about now."

Backing up a step, Masters momentarily glanced in Kern's direction, the other man having taken a seat at the nearby conference table. He proceeded to speak only after Kerns, sitting slumped with his hands in his lap, had shrugged weakly.

"Your looks and physical condition have nothing to do with the decision to eliminate the awarding of any victory spoils, Garrett."

Garrett regarded him with a comically puzzled sneer, a fresh coating of perspiration coating his ghostly-pale forehead.

"I don't...unders-..."

Pacing the length of the room like a nervous father-to-be, Masters' hands remained tucked inside his pants pockets even as his overall posture stiffened a bit.

"America, for all her vast troubles; political, moral, and financial, still loves a winner, bub-especially a winner nobody expected. The masses root for the underdog...always have. Nothing sweeter than when said underdog pulls a shocking upset. The media feeds it, the public eats it up—that's the way it's always been. "

"Yeah, I concur," Garrett replied timidly.

"That's where you came in, bud. You do recall our little chat between sectors?"

"Indelibly, yes. "

"One of my better spiels, I must say, though delivered with complete honesty...no hyperbole necessary. Facts were facts. You were the chosen dog remaining in the pack with the odds stacked firmly in the other guys favor. "

Blinking rapidly, Garrett tilted his head a touch to the left.

"For good reason. "

"But you bucked the odds, brother!" Masters exclaimed excitedly, pumping both fists into the air, "smacked those mothers right outta the park! There's gotta be a ground swell of pride tucked away inside that emaciated chest about now, am I right?"

Shrugging his bony shoulders, Garrett couldn't help but flash a rather feeble smile.

"Never been one to...gloat, Left-tenant. Not in light of all the...lives lost and families devastated in the aftermath. Besides, I have to believe fate was simply on my side. "

"Really? How so?"

"Honestly, there was the matter of catching some breaks along the way, especially there...at the conclusion. "

Taking a single step forward, Masters tucked both hands back into his pants pockets.

"Such as?"

"You know. You...*saw.*"

Master's cocked his left brow.

"Again...humor me."

"Well, all the...disaster that seemed to befall those around me I somehow managed to dodge or avoid altogether, not to mention the sudden illnesses or major injuries that...proved fatal to so many others. Luck played a huge role, no denials."

As Garrett fell silent, busying himself by loosening a tangled IV tube that had gotten tucked beneath his left hip, Masters began to slowly pace the floor to his left.

"Sounds like a solid enough theory, bub, though there is another I'd like to toss out there and see if you agree."

"What's that?" Garrett inquired with an exasperating huff, having tugged the line free.

"Just this; sometimes a man does well to create his *own* brand of luck."

Leaning back with a sigh, Garrett reached up to massage both eyes.

"Afraid I'm on the verge of drifting away, Lieutenant. If I'm not...any immediate obligation, media or otherwise, could we possibly cut this short?"

"Not to worry...just getting ready to cut to the chase. Besides, there is a group of folks waiting just down the hall who'll need to jaw at ya before nap time."

Garrett nodded indifferently but didn't speak as

Masters continued to pace while eyeing his interviewee through slightly squinted eyes.

"Damn it, man, let's wrap this up. Think I'm in dire need of a nap of my own," Conrad Kerns suddenly blurted, having arisen from his chair to lean against the squared edge of the conference table.

Ignoring the comment and its openly agitated source, Gil Masters hesitated a moment longer before resuming questioning, as if mentally prepping the ultimate query.

"So how 'bout it, chief?"

Garrett peered up weakly, his left eye lid momentarily sticking closed.

"What...what's that?"

"I'd mentioned a man being wise to engineer his own kind of luck, especially when faced with great odds, such as you yourself were out there on that long, treacherous trail. What say you?"

"I'm...really not following, Left-. . ."

"Think about it, bub," Masters interrupted light-heartedly, tilting his head dramatically to one side, "focus on what I'm diggin' at. See if it don't come to ya. "

Blinking rapidly as if the act alone would somehow assist in drudging up a long-lost memory, Garrett's face, arms and neck glistened with a fresh coating of sweat.

"I'm.... trying to follow, but.... are we still talking about luck?"

His face contorting like a man struck with a sudden, severe intestinal cramp,

Masters whirled about on a single heel towards

where Conrad Kerns stood nodding in apparent disgust.

"He doesn't have a clue, Gil, don't you see that? It isn't an act...he truly does not recall any of it. You're wasting everyone's time with this second-rate interrogation."

"Horseshit on the half-shell. Ain't buying it, doc," Masters shot back, a wide, purple-shaded vein growing more prominent just beneath his hairline.

The two men shared a brief, intense stare, the moment shattered by a barely audible whisper coming from the other side of the room.

"W-what are you...am I being accusing of some sort of ...of malfeasance?"

With that, Masters turned like a cat, baring small, perfectly squared teeth that glowed unnaturally white, like a sudden flash of ivory light.

"Malfe-...why, yes Mr. Prosecutor, as a matter of fact, you most certainly fucking are."

Swallowing hard several times to clear a suddenly parched throat, Garrett then coughed weakly into a cupped palm before response.

"But...what could I have possibly..." he paused, his badly drooping eyes widening with a sudden realization "...oh, I get it. Is this about that whole aiding and abetting the enemy thing again? I explained this before, Lieutenant, remember? The word you seem to struggle with so mightily is *compassion.*"

Masters' smile grew wider, grotesquely so, accompanied by a high-pitched cackle.

"Com-...compassion? You positive you want to stick with *that* one, bub? I won't be allowin'

355

rewinds, so make damn sure. "

Throwing up his pencil-thin arms in frustration, Garrett peered briefly over at Kerns, who in-turn lowered his gaze to the darkly-tinted stone floor.

Retrieving the small remote from his left pants pocket, Masters reached up and out to aim directly at the center monitor.

"Fine and dandy; I'll take that as a yes. Compassion, you say. Let's just see if this here taped footage jives with said definition. We'll have time for a quick question and answer session afterward. Just sit back and relax, *Kentucky*, and enjoy the blessed silence, for this is one silent movie that needs no narration what-so-ever. "

Following a momentary pause, during which time Carl J. Garrett felt an inexplicable fluttering within his frail chest, the monitor blazed to life. The footage which followed ran a mere two minutes and forty-eight seconds, wherein a total of seven individual segments were showcased, and in its deafening, fade-to-black aftermath there was heard but single, anguished cry. A low, whimpering sob that spoke volumes in terms of both shock value and, ultimately, an anguished wave of unbridled guilt.

***

Standing shoulder to shoulder, the two men exhibited comically opposite expressions.

"Why the long face, Kerns? You got something against justice being served?" Masters said through a frozen smirk.

356

"Not justice as a rule, *no*," Kerns replied while wearing a mask of revulsion, "only when its doled out in torturous increments and the subject of said justice appears genuinely clueless. "

Each man watched with undeniable fascination as a trio of uniformed sentries, each decked out in pitch black with maroon and white nametags that read USBH (*United States Bureau of Homicide*), continued to encircle the bed occupied by their soon-to-be exiting patient.

Every few seconds they would envision a break in space between the sentry's shifting bodies and catch a brief glimpse of Garrett's bug-eyed, shell-shocked visage. The man's lips quivered uncontrollably as he was being read his Miranda rights by one agent and shackled at the wrists and ankles by the other two.

"Still buyin' the, now what did you call 'em again, *schizoid blackouts*?" Masters inquired with a contentious nod, leaning back onto the edge of the conference table.

Kerns paused his response as the trio of sentries backed from the bed as one and whispered quietly amongst themselves as their newly bound prisoner regarded them with comic befuddlement.

"As a matter of fact, yes I am. I saw no indication in his reaction to the footage to believe otherwise. "

"Face facts, doc. . . . you of the multiple degrees and walls peppered with diplomas. His estranged ex provided all the motivation he needed to go balls out to win this thing. You heard that teary-eyed confession he spewed forth right there at the end…right before he clammed up like that Fed muscle sewed his lips shut. Brief as it was, the admission was clear as crystal, brother. "

"Perhaps…but it was also a realization…as much a shock to him as it was to us. "

Crossing his arms defiantly, Kerns started to reply but hesitated yet again as one of the sentries broke from the pack and bent over the bed, looming over Garrett like a human cloak.

"It still infuriates me to think the suits knew what was transpiring down there and did nothing to stop it. "

"Who says for sure they did know, doc? That cap-cam footage was iffy at best. Took a dozen techies with all their computer-nerd hocus-pocus to bring out the evidence in all its sick, twisted glory. Ain't no accident the pay-per-view shots are *all* taken from the wall and ceiling cameras. Besides, say the powers that be did know…try provin' it. "

"True enough, Lieutenant," Kerns replied wearily, reaching up to run splayed fingers through his disheveled coif, "and even if it were being broadcast in Hi-Def Ultra-Three D, it isn't as if the blood-thirsty masses that make up the viewing public would've objected, right?"

This time it was Masters who paused with pre-parted lips as the sentry moved away to reveal the strap-on muzzle he'd been tasked to affix across the center of their patient's face, effectively gagging him like a rabid animal.

"Right as a torrential rain, pal. Might've triggered nationwide riotin'and lootin' if they'd pulled the plug. "

"My god, is that really necessary?" Kerns barked, taking a single step towards the sentries but instantly freezing in his tracks upon viewing the guarded, intense stares each fired his way.

Backing to his original position, Kerns openly flinched as Masters leaned over to lightly nudge shoulders.

"Don't sweat it, doc. It ain't just cruelty for cruelty's sake. They just don't want 'im spewin' off to the gatherin' press hordes as they're loadin' him onto the paddy-wagon. "

"Why the hush-hush? The media and public will demand an answer. "

"Yeah, and they'll get it in due time," Masters said, grinning mischievously, "gotta think one up first, and they'd better make it a damn good one. Remember, there's a shitload of fed money on the line, not to mention state pride. The good folks in *Kentucky* are apt to be a tad on the ticked side, no matter the explanation. "

"What do you think they'll do...with the benefits I mean?" Kerns inquired somberly as the sentries prepared to roll Garrett, still wide-eyed and fidgety, from the room.

"Split up the funds fifty-one ways? Hell if I know, doc...not my problem. Gonna be a PR nightmare, no matter what. "

Frowning, Kerns trudged slowly forward, as if planning to escort the sentries as they began to roll the bed towards the opened door.

"Small price to pay, I suspect. They got their precious ratings and the boatload of new revenue that came with it. What's a little after-the-fact tap-dancing? Rest assured they'll find a way to use all the bad press to pump up future broadcasts. "

As Garrett was being wheeled through the entrance into the darkened halls, a sentry posted at each side of the bed and one pushing from the foot, Kerns lunged forward in pursuit until a firm hand clamped atop his left shoulder.

"Whoa, doc, where ya headed?" Masters asked, stepping ahead of the other man and essentially blocking his path.

"I…just feel…an obligation. "

Masters flashed a smile that reeked of insincerity.

"I'm head of security, remember pal? Your job is done here. Me and my boys will back-up the feds 'til he's jettisoned off-site. "

Backing away a step as the other man's grip loosened a notch, Kerns was allowed a final glimpse at Carl Garrett as he was wheeled out of site. Gagged and apparently sedated, their patient was slumped to one side with his chin resting on his upper chest.

"Where…will they take him?"

"Psych eval for sure. Some Top Secret locale as far away from the press and cameras as possible. Eventually I think the man's in for some serious hard time behind federal bars, but then that's just one man's opinion. 'cuse me, doc…. better catch up to the rolling parade. "

Masters whirled around and took two lengthy strides before pausing at the door. He spoke with his back to Kerns, whose slumped pose screamed fatigue.

"Cheer up, doc. You couldn't possibly have seen this comin'. Nobody could've. All their fancy psyche tests and expert-panel interviews didn't mean squat. Then again, it ain't nobody's fault but the man responsible, and he just got wheeled away."

Once Masters had vanished down the same dim hall as his patient, Conrad Kerns stood motionless for several moments before turning around and staring back up at the center monitor. Shuffling towards the conference table, he reached down and scooped up the small remote device Masters had left behind. Lifting it eye level, he alternated glances to the monitor and back to the device several times before lowering it back to the tabletop. He'd began to turn about, fully intending to discard the device altogether, but instead stood his ground and released a soft grunt. The feds had, of course, obtained their copy of the found footage for evidence, and though he figured he and the rest of the free world might soon be bombarded with said images (if it were indeed ever allowed to go public), he was unable to fight off the urge for one final personal screening.

With that, he stood back, pointed the remote at its intended target and pressed play.

***

Snippet One
Duration of footage: One minute, eighteen seconds
Picture Clarity of footage: Marginal
Footage origin: Ceiling cams, cap-cams

Audio: Inaudible
Location: Sector B

Competitor (later identified as representative of *Alabama*) is shown being assisted (aide later identified as representative of *Kentucky*) up a steep, ice-covered hillside, only to suddenly collapse back to roll roughshod back down the same incline. *Footage is briefly jumbled.* Moments later, *Kentucky* kneels down over *Alabama's* crumbled form, and, after a short, mostly inaudible series of whispers, is clearly shown strategically placing a knee over the fallen man's throat and systematically squeezing. Approximately half a minute later, *Kentucky* rises and turns away from the *Alabama's* lifeless body and trudges up the same hill yet again.

Snippet Two
Duration of footage: One minute, thirty-eight seconds
Picture Clarity of footage: Marginal to fair
Footage origin: Wall cams, cap-cams
Audio: Muffled
Location: Sector B

Competitor (later identified as the representative of *California*) stands partially nude at the center of the icy terrain, gripping a sharp-tipped icicle that hovers mere inches from her rapidly blinking eyes. The representative from *Kentucky* moves into the picture (viewed from the rear), moving slowly toward her with his hands raised, palms-out. *Footage is jumpy and jumbled-*

temporarily fades to black. Seconds later, footage reveals California's mutilated visage, the icicle having penetrated her right eye. Her frozen hair is matted to her forehead, her eye lashes and brows coated in ice. Her lips quiver uncontrollably as she speaks (Muffled but audible):

"O-oh g-god…I…it h-h-hurts…p-p-pl-please h-h-help…he-help…m-m-me…"

A gloved hand is clearly shown reaching over and gently grasping the thick, outer edge of the submerged icicle, an accompanying voice (*first few words inaudible but last few clearly heard*): "…afraid you're beyond any help now, little lady. "The icicle is twisted viciously from the left to the right before being plunged deeper into the ravaged socket. *California*'s legs spasm and quake before her entire form grows limp. *Kentucky* squats near her prone form for several moments before rising to depart, shaking a spattering of reddish ice slivers from his right glove.

Snippet Three
Duration of footage: One-minute, nine seconds
Picture Clarity of footage: Marginal to fair
Footage origin: Ceiling cam, cap-cams
Audio: None available
Location: Sector B

Kentucky is viewed from a sky-shot pulling a door ajar on an ice-coated Porto-potty. The next shot (cap-cam) is what appears to be a barely coherent female (identified as Miss *Texas)* sitting atop the toilet with her head lolling wildly from one side to another. She is grasping her chest as if in the throngs of cardiac arrest. Appearing initially to be offering aid, two gloved hands reach towards her gyrating form with splayed fingers. Suddenly awake and aware, her eyes widen dramatically as the hands wrap around her neck and begin to squeeze. Obviously in a weakened state already, her struggles are woefully in vain. The hands that choked the remaining life from her then prop her gently back onto the stool. From the cap-cam that sits crookedly atop the murdered woman's tilted scalp, a brief shot of her killer's face is revealed. *Kentucky*'s nostrils flare wildly; his mouth hanging slightly ajar as whitish specs of drying spittle line the corners of his mouth.

Snippet Four
Duration of footage: One minute, forty-eight seconds
Picture Clarity of footage: Marginal to fair
Footage origin: Wall/ceiling cams, cap-cams
Audio: Muffled but partially audible
Location: Sector C

Standing in waist-deep flood waters, *Kentucky* is viewed standing near a small embankment, the majority of which is also submerged. Another competitor (identified as *Colorado*) is lying atop the sparse land mass as Kentucky addresses him from a close proximity (approximately two feet). As what appears to be a verbal altercation of sorts ensues, only a portion of their dialogue is audible:

Colorado: "…help, cracker. Got plans…run your redneck ass into…ground. "

Kentucky: "…. no letting up…there? You…look fragile…staring to believe…. like a cockroach…nuclear fallout…kind of survivor type. "

Colorado: "Yeah, well…uck off, cow-tipper…you…. eat my Rocky Mountain dust…"

Hopping into the water, *Colorado* clearly raises a fist and shakes it very near *Kentucky*'s face before turning to wade away in the opposite direction. Though his words are garbled and inaudible, *Kentucky* can be seen wording dialogue while wading forward in *Colorado's* path. *Colorado* *turns*, snarling, just as Kentucky's right arm shoots from the rising floodwaters grasping an unidentifiable object. Pin-wheeling back with eyes pulled saucer wide, *Colorado* slides back into the water. Floating backward, he paws at the jagged stick protruding from his neck, finally pulling it free with a massive tug as a jut of crimson spews forth in the aftermath. Stepping forward, *Kentucky* raises his booted left foot and plants it at the center of Colorado's chest, driving the smaller man back into the drink. *Colorado* submerges completely for several seconds before bobbing to the service, his lips and chin coated in dark maroon, before descending for good. Moments later his pale torso can be seen floating downstream like hollowed-out driftwood. Standing statuesque, *Kentucky* peers downward as the waters around him swiftly descend from waist to knee level, then to just above his booted ankles.

Snippet Five
Duration of footage: Fifty-three seconds
Picture Clarity of footage: Poor
Footage origin: Cap-cams
Audio: None
Location: Sector C

Through footage that shakes and tremors, *Oklahoma* is seen standing at the center of the trail as the terrain splits before him as if spliced apart by some giant, unseen carving tool. The man gyrates and dances from side to side as to avoid the approaching, ever-expanding chasm. His balance appears to right itself just as a pair of black wading boots enter the frame, striking him in the lower back and shoving forcefully forward. *Oklahoma* leans forward and spreads his arms as if to take flight, then topples forward into the crater. Following several moments of jumbled, indistinguishable footage, *Kentucky* is shown crawling away from the expanding hole and directly towards a similarly slithering *Arizona*.

Snippet Six (shown in two parts)
Duration of footage: Part one: thirty-eight seconds. Part two: One minute, twenty-three seconds
Picture Clarity of footage: Poor to marginal
Footage origin: Ceiling/Cap-cams
Audio: None
Location: Sector D

Part one: (*Ceiling cam*) Moving across the sandy plain at a snail's pace, *Kentucky*'s sandals dig a deep, zigzag-shaped path as he totes *Arizona* 'piggy-back' style. The sandstorm is upon them in a matter of seconds, barely giving *Kentucky* the opportunity to turn about and visualize its impending fury. The screen quickly transforms into a brownish blur, swallowing their figures whole in a swirling, churning cloak of solid grit until fading to black.

Part two: (*ceiling cam*) frantically pacing the sand in a tight semi-circle, *Kentucky* occasionally pauses to dig up a specific area of sand with his bare feet. Abruptly falling onto all fours, he appears to have made a discovery and uses both hands to excavate. (*Cap cam*) With all but the middle portion of her face completely buried within the pliable terrain, *Arizona*'s nostrils flare wildly, like a beached fish struggling for a single whiff of precious oxygen. Her eyes blink rapidly, pebbles of sand dribbling from the lashes with each new repetition. Though the dialogue is wholly inaudible, her lips quiver and shake as she addresses her would-be savior. Suddenly, the incessant blinking halts as her eyes grow saucer wide. This just a split-second before handful after handful of sand is forced into her open mouth, followed by an additional dozen or so scoops that coat her eyes, pack her nostrils and eventually complete the job of burying her alive. (*Ceiling cam*) *Kentucky* poses over the makeshift grave for perhaps a half-minute before rising with an unsteady gait. Just before turning towards a nearby trio of Porto-potties with a

367

look of total dismay, he raises two fingers to his forehead as if providing the recently created gravesite with a brief salute.

Snippet Seven
Duration of footage: Fifty-eight seconds
Picture Clarity of footage: Marginal to fair
Footage origin: Ceiling/Cap-cams
Audio: Barely audible
Location: Sector D

(*Ceiling cam*) *New York* topples face-first into the sand like a collapsed house of cards as *Kentucky* rushes to his aid. Kneeling, *Kentucky* grips the larger man by his bare, muscular shoulders and slowly rolls him over onto his back, large clumps of grit pasted to the man's chest and belly by a massive hemorrhage. As if administering the late rites, *Kentucky* leans in until the two practically bump foreheads. *(Cap-cam)* Squirming like mad, *New York*'s eyes bulge wildly from their sockets as thick streams of blood spew forth from between gritted teeth and both nostrils. The bony, sun-blistered knee planted at the center of his throat shoves inward with increased force until his spastic movements cease. Moments later, following a final ferocious thrust, the knee is removed. *New York* stares into the blaring sunlight with a single, lifeless orb, the other clamped as tightly as the permanently barred teeth that clamp onto the edge of a blood-smeared tongue. An outstretched forefinger enters the frame and gently pushes the stuck eyelid shut.

(*Ceiling cam*) *Kentucky* tucks his arms beneath

368

the larger man's upper torso and struggles mightily to flip the body. Once accomplished, *Kentucky* stumbles back and appears to bow his head in a brief prayer before whirling around and shuffling out of frame.

***

Having powered down the monitor, Kerns flipped the remote onto the table-top and watched it slide to the far end and into a pile of stacked manila folders. Exhaling nosily, he squatted down with his elbows fixed snugly against the table's slickly waxed surface, thinking back to Carl Garrett's befuddled expression and exasperated response to the same footage.

***

"Th-that's...that didn't happen...none of th-that happened. It's...a...it's more of that CGI crap. Wh-who...why would s-someone do th-that...is this...some kind of j-joke?"

Barreling forward as if to physically throttle the bedridden man, Gil Masters had stopped just short of banging his thighs against the bed rails.

"Bullshit! I ain't buyin' what you're sellin', Garrett," he bellowed, reaching back with an outstretched arm to gesture towards the blank monitor, "that carnage up there is real, and unless you had a teleporting clone roamin' about doin' your dirty work, their ain't no questioning I'm jawing directly to the only... logical... suspect. "

"B-but, I do-don't…I don't re-recall…any…of…th-that," Garrett had replied weakly, flipping both heavily dressed hands palms up, "…it…it just…c-can't…be. "

"Oh, it *be*, pal. It must certainly be. Talk about winnin' at all costs, somebody hand you a maniac's list of rules that included murderin' any and *everybody* that got in your way of securing the prize?"

Looming over the patient with his arms crossed tightly over his chest, Masters had every bit resembled a sleek, hybrid mix of prosecuting attorney and prison warden.

"Bold but bone-headed, bub, I must say. You start thinkin' you were the invisible man or something? The camera don't lie, buddy. Especially that *many* cameras…. it wasn't that hard to dig up the right angles to catch you red-handed, pardon the unintentional grisliness. "

Shaking and twitching as if in the throngs of a major epileptic fit, Garrett commenced to blubber uncontrollably, spewing forth a series of grunts, groans, and sobs that were utterly incomprehensible.

"Aww, cut the *SHIT* already!" Masters screamed, having leaned down to within 'head-bump' distance to Garrett's wildly swiveling noggin.

Almost instantly upon enduring the verbal assault, Garrett's incessant body tremors had ceased. Lowering his head, he laid his suddenly rock-steady hands into his lap, crossing them over as if to meditate.

Moments later, as his chin gradually arose, the mask he donned was that of an entity neither Masters nor Kerns had previously met. The squinting eyes were entirely void of emotion, the purplish lips puffed out in a childish smirk—a dark, frigid expression without a trace of conscience or humanity. An expression birthed by a tar-black, poison-filled heart. An expression fueled by animal savagery. The expression of a cold-blooded assassin.

"I had to show her, don't you see?" the soulless stranger had whispered in a voice as alien and emotionless as his newly displayed visage, "I had to show the *bitch*...make her eat her words. "

"Yeah?" Masters had countered, apparently unfazed by the man's sudden transformation, "And exactly what bitch we referring to, pal?"

"Don't toy with me, Left-tenant," the Garrett-thing had replied with a playful wink, "I'm not gonna sit here and hash over what you already know. "

"I see...ol' ball and chain undersell your worth of late?"

The Garrett-thing nodded its head amiably.

"Always. Practically since day fucking one. "

His entire deportment altered to that of continuing a casual chat, Masters backed from the railing and flashed a knowing smile.

"Irritating, ain't they? Treat ya like a turd on legs...brow-beatin' cunts, one and all. "

Alternating cool glances from Masters to Kerns, Garrett eventually settled back on the former and cocked a brow.

"Obvious patronizing aside, Left-tenant, are you...attempting to pretend to take my side? I take it Doctor Kerns is adequately prepped for the role of *bad cop.*"

Throwing both arms airborne in mock surrender, Kerns' was unable to hide the undercurrent of excitement in his tone.

"Not at all...this is the left...um, this is the lieutenant's show...bystander only."

"Besides," Masters injected with a raised forefinger, "afraid you misinterpret my intention, bub. I wasn't patronizing...I was baiting."

Emitting a sharp clicking sound from the left side of his mouth, the Garrett-thing nodded.

"Got'cha, always need to know where I stand."

Masters began to pace the length of the bed yet again, his hands cupped at his lower back.

"Y'know, Carl...may I call ya Carl?"

"By all means.... *Gil.*"

Unfazed, Masters blared on.

"Well, Carl...it seems around the time you were wading floodwaters and about to let the air out of a certain *Colorado* windbag courtesy a sharp-tipped tree branch, the body of a rather prominent lawyer was bein' fished out of a lake just a few miles outside the city limits of Lexington. Your hometown, right?"

Holding his right hand airborne, Garrett studied the IV lines hanging there with great interest.

"Born and raised."

"Wife still resides there?"

"Ex-wife."

"Oh yeah, that's right. My bad. Signed the

372

divorce papers just a few weeks before the Iron-Will. "

"Separation was months before. Four and a half, to be exact. "

"Infidelity play a role?"

"Prominently, yes. "

"You shackin' up or was she?"

"I think you know the answer to that one, Left-tenant," Garrett replied with a frown.

Masters exhaled deeply, as if prepping for a lengthy stretch of dialogue, his lips just parting to commence when Garrett chimed in flatly.

"Yes, I killed the bastard. Snapped his preppy neck, stuffed 'im in the trunk of my car then drove 'im out to the Westmoreland Bridge and tossed 'im in. "

Before turning his attention back to Garrett, Masters shot Kerns an evocative glance.

"Sorry to steal your thunder, Left-tenant. "

"No problem, Carl," Masters replied with a shrug, no longer pacing but instead striking a parade-rest pose a few feet from the foot of the bed, "you just eliminated a butt-load of purposely obtuse questionin' on my part. "

Following a comically exaggerated nod, Garrett's focus again returned to the IV lines hanging from each bony, ghostly-pale hand.

"Happy to help. No need for any tap-dancing at this stage in the game, right?"

"If you say so, pal. Not exactly one of your best-kept secrets, though. With all the incriminating DNA ya left in that Mitsubishi's trunk, a five-year old with a magnifying glass would've had ya dead to rights. Even found a dislodged tooth tucked beneath the spare tire. "

"Wasn't personal," Garrett countered blandly, "although he really should've known better than to intentionally woo a married woman. "

"W-woo?"

Flashing a broad smile, Masters had to briefly cover his mouth to refrain from giggling aloud.

"Um, yeah. Your wife was employed as his administrative assistant correct?"

Peering past his upturned left hand towards Masters, Garrett's eyes squinted to fine slits.

"I thought all silly questions had been deleted from the checklist. "

"Sorry, bub. But…if it wasn't personal, as you say, why not just off the ex instead? I mean, her porkin' her boss on the sly was the main source of irritation, yeah?"

Resting his gray-stubble coated chin atop a balled fist, Garrett cleared his throat loudly, the words to follow laced with emotion for the first time since the transformation.

"I wanted her around for the Iron-Will. I wanted her to watch me, to squirm as I gradually worked my way to the front of the pack, to feel a sense of panic as the media officially dubbed me a long-shot underdog with a puncher's chance, and finally to fudge her pretty pink panties as the crown was placed atop this boy's head. "

"I gotta ask, pal…I…just *gotta* know…why? Even if there was a way to get away with it, was it worth playin' the Gauntlet assassin just to show up this woman?"

Brandishing an animalistic snarl, Garrett pumped out his frail chest.

"Fucking right it was worth it, *bub*. I'd do it again in a heartbeat...no hesitation whatsoever. Bitch used to call me Captain *Milquetoast*...Major *Meek*. Got that horseshit language from her father...a career jarhead with a chest full of combat medals.

The woman said I had no ambition...no fire...no...competitive spirit. Boy-toy lawyer was on the fast-track to holding a judge's gavel, she said, while I would never do any better than stuffing mailboxes with sales flyers and sorting envelopes in a mailroom. "

Leaning forward with the spindly fingers of both hands grasping the bed rails on either side, his garish grin revealed teeth that practically glowed yellow in comparison to his chalky complexion.

"Questionable methods or no, Left-tenant, you gotta admit..." he paused to wink, "...I proved that cheatin' slut dead-wrong. "

As Garrett collapsed back onto the waiting pillow yet again, apparently drained by the sudden burst of emotion, Gil Masters forced a wry smile before side-stepping away.

"That ya did, bub...if nothin' else, *that* you most certainly did. "

Just moments later, as the trio of feds had entered the room to begin the process of extraction, the previous version of Carl Garrett reemerged, sobbing and wailing and professing his utter befuddlement and disbelief.

Pushing himself away from the conference table with a groan, Kerns arose from his voluntary squat and exited the room with a slightly stiffened gait. It was a short walk down the eerily quiet hallway, wherein the lone audible sound was the clicking of his own boot-heels against slick stone flooring.

Upon reaching his assigned office, Kerns slid behind a wide oak desk and powered up the laptop adorning its center. Leaning back in a high-back, black leather chair, Kerns soon placed his hands behind his head and exhaled noisily as the varied images besieged his bone-weary psyche. Images filled with hordes of media lining the dome's outer entrance like swarming bees to a freshly constructed hive, waiting to pounce on their newest creation so fittingly dubbed '*The Iron-Will Eliminator*'. It seemed that despite the best efforts of the powers that be to cover up the killings, footage had leaked out via a rogue technician who had, no doubt, auctioned off said clippings to the highest bidder. Now what was already destined to be a media-madhouse had become a veritable feeding frenzy of network, newspaper and on-line reporters pounding the grounds for even the briefest glimpse of the newest maniac of the hour.

"Yes sir, Garrett, you certainly showed her who's boss. No if's, and's or but's about it. Managed to make yourself infamous in the process."

Wearing a grim smile, Doctor Conrad Kerns shook

his head in comic bemusement.

"I ascertain only time will tell whether or not you still think it was worth it. "

Outside the metal entrance gates to the Iron-Will Dome, a light snow began to descend upon the gathered masses of media representatives, the threat of an impending blizzard doing little to quell their thirst for carnage.

FOURTEEN AND A HALF YEARS LATER:

"Um, excuse me Miss. "

Peering up into a bright mid-day sun from beneath a floppy flower hat, the woman is unable to make out the vague shape standing on the opposite site of the picket fence.

"Yes? Can I help you?" she asked, having to briefly look away to relieve the array of circular floaters littering her eyes from the sudden bombardment of direct light. She heard the man clear his throat as she stood from her crouch, where she had been tending a row of recently planted tulips.

"I, um...well, I wondered if you might need my...our services. I represent Benson Pest Control and we're out attempting to round up some fresh clients. "

Her vision still a bit spotty, she backed away onto the meticulously trimmed grass next to the flower bed, a silver trowel held loosely in a gloved right hand.

"Oh, no thank you. I tend to my own treatments. "

"I understand, ma'am. I'm sure your husband has it under control. "

Peering up with the flat palm of one hand shielding her eyes just beneath the hat's sagging bill, the woman was finally able to focus on the man, whose voice seemed vaguely familiar despite the presence of an unidentifiable accent that might've been either Irish or Scottish.

Possessing an average build, save a prominent midsection that appeared to be straining the lower buttons of an overly snug light blue uniform shirt, he wore a light brown baseball which proclaimed 'Benson's Bug-Hunters' in dark red. The sunglasses he wore were comically oversized, virtually enveloping the whole of his face save a neatly trimmed, gray-spattered beard and matching mustache.

"No, no...I do it myself. Have been for years and haven't seen a single uninvited critter inside the homestead in as long as I can recall. "

"Mind if I leave some samples with you then?" the man asked, gesturing towards a light blue S-10 pickup parked at the curb, the company logo painted onto the passenger side door, "that is, just in case that initial multi-legged beastie does rear its ugly head. There's a new strain of lava-ant that can do more damage than your average termite. No obligation, of course..."

"Well, I...don't kno..." she began, forcing herself to look away from the wide sweat-stains smeared beneath the arm pits of the man's shirt.

"...I don't think I nee..."

She craned her head forward a touch just as the man turned away to stroll towards the vehicle.

"It's no bother, ma'am. I'll be right back then," he announced cheerily, lifting a forefinger into the air.

Annoyed yet also inexplicably intrigued, she watched him step towards the truck, a slight but noticeable hitch in his gitty-up.

A little aged and gimpy for such a physically demanding line of work, she pondered while giving her tulips a final once-over. *Then again, you're no spring chick yourself, woman.*

Leaning into the driver's door of the vehicle, which faced away from the woman's home and into what appeared to be an infrequently used residential street, the man reached into the glove compartment and retrieved two specific items.

Having cased the neighborhood a half hour earlier, he'd noted not only a lack of parked vehicles on either home bookmarking the woman's residence, but also an overall lack of movement within the general vicinity.

Popping open a box of combination rodent and insect glue boards, he pulled out a handful and stashed the two mystery items inside before gently closing the truck door.

God, do I look so different? I hardly recognized her. Must've packed on thirty, forty pounds. She's so...so droopy looking. She always did have a weakness for the sweets. Guess she finally quit fighting it.

Tucking the box beneath his right arm, he barely refrained from giggling aloud.

Sad to say, brother, she'd surely say the same about your flabby rear end. Doughy hag or not, I damn near peed these undersized khakis at the sound of her. A little raspier, maybe she picked up smoking, but no mistaking the old familiar nagging ring to it.

Strolling slowly past the truck bed, he caught a

glimpse of a bare right foot sticking out from beneath the plastic tarp. After first peeking over the top edge of his sunglasses to ensure the woman's focus was centered elsewhere, he reached casually over and tucked the pasty toes security beneath the crinkled cloak.

Flashing a warm, broad smile, he then strolled purposely back towards the modest brick home, the occupant of which it had taken him a full year to track down.

The woman, having already stepped away from the flower garden, was making her way casually towards a railed, wooden front porch.

Didn't note a twinge of recognition, though for a second there she did appear to freeze up. Facial-fuzz and extra pounds turned the trick, I guess, but I should've worked harder on the accent. Whatever...the goal is definitely in sight, and once I step foot inside that front door, it's a done deal.

Pushing through an unlatched picket-fence entrance, the man stepped gingerly up a flat-rock walkway, all the while whistling the ancient Irish folk ditty *'down goes McGinty'*.

The woman, having removed her floppy hat to release lengthy blonde locks that spilled loosely onto her shoulders, had halted on the porch's top step. Turning to face him as he neared, she held out the palm of her right hand as to accept an impending gift.

"May I ask a favor, Miss?"

"Yes?"

"It seems my company cell has kicked the virtual bucket. Might I inquire to use yours to call the shop? I promise it'll only take a few ticks. "

Her lips quivered briefly, and the man unconsciously tightened his grip on the glue board box.

"Why...yes, certainly. My phone is on the kitchen table. "

She turned, stepping towards the front screen door with outstretched fingers before pausing. In turn, the man's heart skipped several beats.

"Would you like a drink of water? Lemonade, perhaps?" she asked timidly, as if instantly regretting the invite.

"Why yes, I would surely enjoy a cool drink...yes, ma'am. Thank you kindly for asking. "

He followed her inside the chilly, air-conditioned confines of the dimly lit living room, practically skipping inside with the newly charged vigor of a man at least two decades his junior...or perhaps merely a *single* decade. As the woman vanished from the relatively small but elegantly furnished living room into what he presumed was the kitchen, the man stood atop the plush carpeting and dug greedy fingers into the glue-board box. He would wait for her in this exact spot, he decided, as she filled her hands with a cell phone and whatever chilled drink was to be so politely offered.

As for his own hands, Carl Garrett was amply supplied for the task at hand.

In his left was a filled syringe, the stoutest of sedatives dripping from its pointy tip. In the right was grasped a surgical scalpel, from which a dull gleam shone from its razor-sharp edge, having been struck from the light shining through a nearby picture window.

"Come to papa now, darling..." he whispered through a mad, insanity-fueled grin that fourteen-plus years of intense psychological treatment and prescribed medications had done little to eradicate, despite a final, fateful diagnosis that was woefully misguided, ".... your Captain Milquetoast is *finally* home. "

Meanwhile, inside the spacious kitchen, which smelled of cinnamon spice and freshly baked bread, the former Mrs. Carl Garrett poured freshly squeezed lemonade into a pair of tall, ice-filled glasses. The icepick she'd utilized just moments earlier to jab large chunks into smaller ones had already been strategically placed inside the left front pocket of her gardening smock. Tucked within the right was a serrated bone-knife taken from a nearby utensil drawer.

Upon hearing of his release, she'd somehow known this day would come. Changing her name and non-voluntary participation in a government-organized relocation did little to alter such a foreboding premonition. She'd long since dismissed calling authorities.

She'd barely refrained from openly shuddering upon his fatal slip-up, that being the utterance of a simple four-word phrase uttered without benefit of an otherwise flawless accent—a butchered phrase he'd so often used or *misused* on so many occasions during their tumultuous marriage, to include the faithful day she'd confessed to the affair.

"Well, well, well," he'd muttered blandly in the aftermath of her confession, "it appears wedded bliss has kicked the virtual bucket, courtesy a faithless whore who can't keep her legs closed. "

Strange that despite all the rage-fueled, profanity-laced tirades that would soon follow until the eventual separation, the exact wording of that specific sentence had never left her. Perhaps all the times she had ridiculed his inexplicable use of the word virtual over *proverbial.*

Sighing heavily to exorcise all remaining apprehension, she loaded a metal tray with both glasses and a bowl of assorted fruits. Three-plus years of martial arts and weapons training would not be for naught. The only man she'd ever truly loved had been stolen from her by a psychotic wolf in sheep's clothing currently taking up space in her living room.

In the end, she mused with stony resolve, it would simply come down to who wanted it more. *It* in this case referring not only to survival, but also the satisfaction of long-awaited retribution served.

"Heeeere we are," she cackled with mock politeness before taking that initial step onto the impromptu battlefield, her plan being to wait until they stood almost toe-to-toe before heaving the entire tray towards his face. Then, as he reeled from the abruptness of the attack, she'd fill both palms with the pre-chosen instruments and strike with expert precision but without a semblance of mercy.

Bounding cheerily into the living room, she was greeted by a warped, maniacal smile and gleaming yet weirdly soulless eyes that blazed insanity.

Sadly, if the former Mrs. Carl Garrett had

peered into a mirror at that precise moment, her own expression would have provided an eerily similar reflection.

THE END